RED
STRING
THEORY

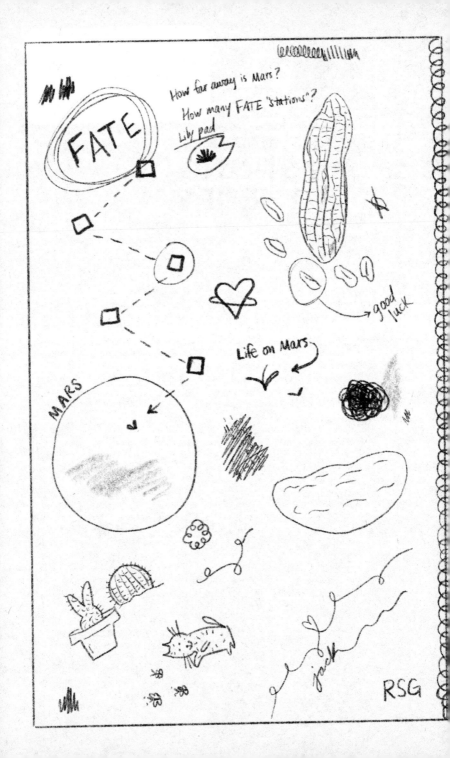

PRAISE FOR LAUREN KUNG JESSEN AND *LUNAR LOVE:*

"Tradition meets modern progress, and it's a delicious combination!"
—Abby Jimenez, *New York Times* bestselling author of *Yours Truly*

"Debut author Kung Jessen does an impeccable job helping two adversarial lovers find common ground in their Chinese American heritage and creating a slow-burn romance with lots of humor, family, and food." —*Library Journal*, starred review

"Jessen's debut rom-com hits all the beats of a tried-and-true rivals-to-lovers narrative." —*Publishers Weekly*

"A refreshing and unexpected take on matchmaking! This will be a perfect match for any reader looking for a heartwarming romance steeped in cultural traditions."
—Jesse Sutanto, national bestselling author of *Dial A for Aunties*

"Rich and tender in the best of ways, *Lunar Love* wraps an enemies-to-lovers story around a tale of family devotion and love."
—AllAboutRomance.com

"Lauren Kung Jessen writes supremely satisfying slow burn and rivals-to-lovers. There's heat, friction, sparks—it's a lit match."
—Sarah Hogle, author of *Just Like Magic*

"*You've Got Mail* meets the Chinese Zodiac in Jessen's delightful ode to food, Los Angeles, family, and finding your perfect match. A delicious treat for fans of Jasmine Guillory and Helen Hoang."
—Georgia Clark, author of *Island Time*

"*Lunar Love* has all the makings of a new rom-com classic. Insightful, atmospheric, and breathtakingly romantic."
—Ava Wilder, author of *How to Fake It in Hollywood*

"A lovingly crafted rival-to-lovers rom-com about navigating the space between traditional and modern dating! This book is a delight!"   —Farah Heron, author of *Jana Goes Wild*

"Fans of Jasmine Guillory and Sally Thorne will delight in *Lunar Love*, a deliciously romantic tale about the true and wildly unpredictable nature of attraction, compatibility, and love."
                    —Amy Poeppel, author of *The Sweet Spot*

"I dare you not to fall in love with Lauren Kung Jessen's writing. Brimming with crackling chemistry from page one, Olivia and Bennett prove that those who may appear the most incompatible on paper may just be our perfect match."
                    —Amy Lea, author of *Set on You*

"An enemies-to-lovers romance with a warm and gooey cinnamon bun hero. It was an added bonus to learn so much about Chinese culture."   —Jayci Lee, author of *Booked on a Feeling*

"*Lunar Love* is a sweet rom-com that shows that in the battle of tradition and modernity, love plays by its own rules."
                    —Julie Tieu, author of *The Donut Trap*

"*Lunar Love* is a touching tribute to Chinese-American culture and the power of family. Bennett O'Brien is the perfect book boyfriend!"
                    —Hannah Orenstein, author of *Meant to be Mine*
                    and *Playing with Matches*

"This sweet opposites-attract story shines brighter than a supermoon on a warm summer night. It has all the feels and will make you believe in soulmates. It's a match made in heaven for all rom-com fans."
                    —Elizabeth Thompson, *USA Today* bestselling
                    author of *Lost in Paris*

"A bright new voice in romance. A heartwarming debut that upends everything you know about love."

—Carolyn Huynh, author of *The Fortunes of Jaded Women*

"A delightful, sparkling romance full of family bonds, a swoon-worthy hero, and plenty of delicious food. This super-sweet read is perfect for rom-com fans!"

—Kerry Winfrey, author of *Just Another Love Song* and *Waiting for Tom Hanks*

"Prepare to laugh, cry, swoon, and rush to the nearest Chinese bakery to get your fix of Swiss rolls with vanilla cream filling!"

—Meredith Schorr, author of *As Seen on TV*

"A delightful romantic escape. Tradition and technology collide in this scrumptious match made in rom-com heaven."

—Dylan Newton, author of *All Fired Up*

"*Lunar Love* is filled with wide-eyed optimism and singular characters whose search for love will delight even the most cynical of readers."

—Lynda Cohen Loigman, *USA Today* bestselling author of *The Matchmaker's Gift*

"Lauren Kung Jessen is an author to watch, and her debut romance is both smart and swoony and will earn a place on your keeper shelf."

—Elizabeth Everett, author of the Secret Scientists of London series

"Matchmaking meets the modern age in this delicious and delightful romantic comedy."

—Elizabeth Boyle, *New York Times* bestselling author of *Six Impossible Things*

"A fun, flirty romance book with an emphasis on family, culture, and food!"
                                                —TeaTimeLit.com

Also by Lauren Kung Jessen

Lunar Love

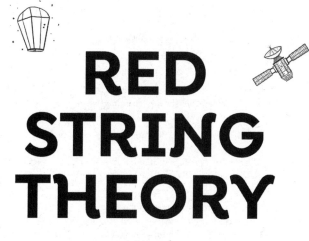

RED STRING THEORY

A Novel

LAUREN KUNG JESSEN

FOREVER

NEW YORK   BOSTON

Forever
Hachette Book Group
1290 Avenue of the Americas, New York, NY 10104
read-forever.com
twitter.com/readforeverpub

First edition: January 2024

Forever is an imprint of Grand Central Publishing. The Forever name and logo are trademarks of Hachette Book Group, Inc.

The publisher is not responsible for websites (or their content) that are not owned by the publisher.

The Hachette Speakers Bureau provides a wide range of authors for speaking events. To find out more, go to hachettespeakersbureau.com or email HachetteSpeakers@hbgusa.com.

Forever books may be purchased in bulk for business, educational, or promotional use. For information, please contact your local bookseller or the Hachette Book Group Special Markets Department at special.markets@hbgusa.com.

Interior design images © 2024 by Lauren Kung Jessen

Library of Congress Cataloging-in-Publication Data

Names: Jessen, Lauren Kung, author.
Title: Red string theory : a novel / Lauren Kung Jessen.
Description: First edition. | New York : Forever, 2024.
Identifiers: LCCN 2023036586 | ISBN 9781538710289 (trade paperback) | ISBN 9781538710302 (ebook)
Subjects: LCGFT: Romance fiction. | Novels.
Classification: LCC PS3610.E8747 R43 2024 | DDC 813/.6—dc23/eng/20230814
LC record available at https://lccn.loc.gov/2023036586

ISBNs: 9781538710289 (trade paperback), 9781538710302 (ebook)

Printed in the United States of America

LSC-H

Printing 1, 2023

For Patrick, my stringmate. I can't wait to see where our lantern will take us.

Chapter 1

ROONEY

I've always thought of Washington Square Park in New York City as a place where people say good-bye. In *When Harry Met Sally*, Billy Crystal—with a laundry bag, duffel, and baseball bat in tow—walks away from Meg Ryan as she drives off in her pale yellow Toyota Corona wagon. In *Barefoot in the Park*, Robert Redford drunkenly laughs and tells Jane Fonda that she's the one who should leave their apartment instead of him. As he shouts at her to "Get out!," this park has never looked so hopeless.

But for the past week, Washington Square Park has taken on a new meaning because I'm attempting to change the narrative. As the location for my first-ever public art installation, *Entangled*, this iconic park will be a place where people are brought together. After years of small-scale string art installations in less-frequented galleries and at art fairs, this is my big break. I stand at a distance under the giant marble arch detailed with intricate carvings and spy on my creation, just like I have each afternoon for the past six days of *Entangled* being up. Each visit feels like I'm seeing my work for the very first time.

Surrounding the fountain in the center of the park, my red string installation curves and loops past the fountain, through the grassy corner plots, under the trees, and around the globe lampposts. There's no way to identify where the beginning and end are, which is entirely the point. It's one continuous loop.

"Rooney! Why am I doing all the heavy lifting?" my mom, Wren Gao, says breathlessly before dropping a cardboard box to the ground. Her breath puffs out visibly in front of her and floats for a second before disappearing in the cold February air. "You know I'm almost seventy, right?"

"Careful!" I bend down to grab the box. "You're going to pull a muscle."

"If I didn't grab these, someone else would've. I fought off a twenty-year-old with purple hair to save that," Mom says proudly.

I give her a look. "She's one of the interns who helped set all of this up. She just picked those up from the printer."

Mom crosses her arms. "I guess that would explain how she knew my name. I thought she was clairvoyant or that she recognized me."

"Not everyone knows who you are," I say playfully. I heave the box onto my hip as Mom and I circle around the installation to a spot behind a row of barren hedges.

Mom smirks. "Maybe not, but enough do." She says it with the confidence of someone who's earned it. As a now-famous visual and performance artist, Mom creates attention-grabbing work with statements on reproductive rights and social issues. My unashamed and unapologetic mom got her career going in the late seventies, and it stayed fairly steady.

By the time she was twenty-eight, the age I am now, she had already been in the business for five years, making a decent living off her work. But it wasn't until I—an unplanned bundle of joy—was born in the mid-nineties that she catapulted to international fame. That's when everything changed for her. At forty-one years old, Wren Gao had become a name that was read aloud in newspapers and whispered about around dinner tables. Even when she toted me around as a kid from country to country, her career didn't slow down once. If it takes eighteen years and giving birth for a career to take off, then I have a very, very long road ahead of me.

I shouldn't compare myself with her. Our careers are completely different. My mom is a famous artist whose work now commands five-to-six figures at auction, and I can hardly scrape by with string pet portraits. Not that she doesn't offer to help me out. I just don't want her money or connections. My career is supposed to be something that I accomplish on my own. And when I one day match or, better yet, exceed her level of success, I'll know it was because of my efforts.

We hide behind a thick tree trunk, watching people's reactions from afar. I'm pleased to see that their attentions are drawn from their phones mid-walk, which is not an easy feat.

Mom waves her arms toward my installation beyond the trees. "How did you pull this off?" she asks.

I set the box gently onto the crunchy brown grass. "A group of students from the School of Visual Arts helped string this up. That way, no one knows it's me."

"At some point, you'll be figured out," Mom warns. "Your Red String Girl cover-up can't last forever. Certainly not these days with cameras everywhere."

"Not if I can help it," I tell her.

"Your work is imaginative. Let yourself shine, baby!" Mom says as she readjusts a wool hat I knitted her over her silver hair.

"I like being anonymous. It's more private. I can let the work speak for itself. It's not about me," I explain. "I never wanted it to be."

Mom studies me for a moment. "People like having a face to the name. If you're unknown, you're forgotten."

I wrap my arm around her shoulders. "As usual, we'll agree to disagree. Besides, I want to get people talking about something that isn't me," I justify. "With this installation, I'm creating a destination for people to go to after the rush of the holidays. There's no competition and doing this in the winter brings beauty to the gray landscape. In the summer, exhibits are expected, but then they just become any other day. This will last in people's memories."

"Yeah, well, people will also remember your installation as the day they got frostbite," Mom says, wiggling her gloved fingers.

"Hilarious. I really think we're pulling this off, though. Talia is also helping manage this. All you have to do is enjoy the show," I say, using a key to slice the tape open on the box.

"Did someone say my name?" a voice says behind us. "Wren, great to see you!"

I turn to see Talia Ma breezing toward us in a chic belted winter jacket. Talia's my best friend who I met in art school. We bonded over being mixed-race Chinese American and our belief in the Red Thread of Fate. She's one of the very few people who know that I'm Red String Girl. After years learning the ropes at Sotheby's and Christie's, Talia now owns an art gallery in Chelsea specializing in showcasing new local painters and ceramic artists with plans to open a second location on the West Coast. She was the first person to sell my string art pet portraits in her gallery when I was starting out.

Fine. She's still trying to sell them. Enough people buy pet portraits for me to get installation materials. All that string adds up. What it doesn't provide? The freedom not to have to live with my mom. Yeah. I won't accept money or connections, but I will accept a room to sleep in.

"How was your tour?" Talia asks my mom.

Mom sighs. "Exhausting, fulfilling. It's my last one. I'm done being a show pony. It did take me all throughout Asia and Europe. I sold a few paintings to wealthy art collectors and museums," she recounts. "All in all, I can't complain, except, of course, for missing Roo's opening day."

"We missed you!" Talia says.

"You're here now. That's what matters," I say.

"Nice of you to help out, Talia. Slow gallery day?" Mom asks.

"My business partner, Isla, is in town and managing the gallery while I'm here. I couldn't miss this huge moment for Red String Girl," Talia says, lifting her dark eyebrows in my direction.

My chest tightens with hope. Being able to present my work in such a public way is more than I could've dreamed of.

"Oh! Wren." Talia reaches for Mom's arm and squeezes. "I got the inside scoop that one of your pieces is going up for sale soon."

I practically leap at Talia. "Which one is it?"

Talia steadies me. "Sorry, Roo, it's not the one you're looking for."

"Perfect. Another one of my pieces trading hands, and I'll never see another cent for it," Mom grumbles. "You're still trying to find *Baby Being Born*?"

"Well, if you still don't care to buy back the video of my birth, then it's up to me." I turn to Talia. "You haven't heard anything about it at all?"

Talia's head swivels as she watches a man walk by while strumming a guitar with his gloves still on. "I'm keeping my ears to the ground," she says, refocusing on me. "I ask around periodically, but you know that the buyers are anonymous. If it ever does go up for sale, we'll at least know a couple of months ahead of time while they validate the authenticity."

"Oh, it's one of a kind, and it's real, baby," Mom says.

Talia peers into her purse. "You have the permits, right, Rooney? I also emailed you a copy."

"Permits. How by the book of you," Mom mutters. "I think you could've made a bigger statement without permits, but to each her own."

"You want me to start doing work without permits *and* share my name publicly?" I say with a laugh. "Are you personally trying to send me to prison?"

Mom's eyes widen, and she laughs. "Prison? Don't cause permanent damage to anything, and you'll be fine. It's those moments that lead to attention. And attention leads to paid shows. And you know what paid shows get you? Your own apartment. Just saying!"

Talia looks between us wearing an amused expression. "Wren, you must come with us to the Lantern Festival party tonight. You'd be a hit. The person who invited me said it's BYOWAF. Bring Your Own Wine and Friends."

"I'm not a showpiece, and I've learned long ago that it's not worth my time when I'm fifth in line to the throne of a party, especially when you have to bring your own alcohol," Mom says with a grunt.

Talia, the Queen of Multitasking, taps into her phone. "If you change your mind, let us know. It'd be nice to have more familiar faces there," she says as she looks past my shoulder. "I'm being called over. Be back in a few for those Fate Notes."

"Great! I'll get these ready for you." I lift the box lid, revealing the final pieces of the installation puzzle. The important element that makes my creation fulfill its purpose. I hold up a freshly printed Fate Note the size of a postcard from the pile.

"What the hell's a lophole?" Mom asks, eyeing the paper in my hand.

My heart stops. "It's supposed to be loophole!" I scan the cards, confirming that they've all been misprinted. "Okay, this is no big deal. It doesn't match the first batch people have been using, but it's fine. It's open-ended, interpretive. A reaction from...something. Honestly, it fits the string theory aspect of the installation well!"

Mom raises her eyebrows. "Your optimism and can-do attitude

are admirable, truly, but you can't be fine with this. They messed up your vision. They should fix it for free."

"It's really okay," I say. "But they were supposed to be waterproof."

"This is your work. You're a professional." Mom rubs the Fate Note between her fingers. "You're justifying someone else's error."

"If Christo and Jeanne-Claude can do *The Gates* in February in Central Park, I can do *Entangled* in February in Washington Square Park." I quickly problem-solve. "I'll swing by to see if they can reprint these quickly. If not—"

"Then maybe it was meant to be?" Mom says, amused.

"Smirk all you want, Mother," I say, "but all threads lead to you."

"Ah," Mom says, "there it is. The Red Thread of Fate."

"Let's not forget that you're the one who taught me about it," I say, lifting my eyebrows at her.

"You're welcome." Mom looks pleased with herself. "My story-telling abilities must really be something for you to believe it—no, embody it—all these years later. You know what? I'm glad you're not settling. That's something I can get behind. You'd be hard-pressed to find me someone worth settling for."

"Does the word 'compromise' fall within your definition of set-tling?" I ask with a laugh.

Mom lets out a huff and looks away. "Compromising is what peo-ple tell themselves they're supposed to do to feel better."

My heart squeezes in my chest. Mom's always had a fierce and strong façade with a self-attested lioness heart, but I like to imagine there's something soft and squishy deep down in there. It couldn't have been easy with me being an accident, but it's not like I would know because she doesn't talk about it.

I cross my arms, unintentionally wrinkling a Fate Note in the crook of my elbow. "There hasn't been anyone serious yet, but one

day." I narrow my eyes at her. "How about this? I'll reveal myself as
Red String Girl when you admit that you're actually a romantic."

"Ha!" Mom barks.

I double down. "You don't tell your daughter the Red Thread of
Fate myth if you don't want her to believe that their stringmate,
that their person on the other end of their red string, is out there
somewhere. And if you wanted me to believe it, then you must've
believed it, too."

Mom shakes her head. "I told you about it because it was research
for a show. That's it."

"Sure, Mom. Whatever you need to tell yourself. Did you know
Talia is also a Red Threader?" I say. "Do you think her belief in it is
silly?"

Mom smirks. "As usual, we'll agree to disagree, Roo," she says,
throwing my words back at me. She lifts a Fate Note from the pile
and focuses in on the red loopy word. "So, this lophole. What's it
supposed to mean?"

"Oh! Yes!" I say, clapping my hands together. "This installation
is my interpretation of something scientific to show how fate has
more influence than we think. When visitors come by, they're supposed to grab a Fate Note and write on it," I explain, uncapping my
red pen to write something onto the wrinkled note as an example.
"Here, I'll show you how it works. People can write a joke, a wish,
whatever they want. They slip the note between the web of string
and grab one in return. By doing this, they'll become linked with
the person who wrote the note. They'll be influenced no matter how
far apart they are."

"Influenced by...the words?" Mom asks suspiciously.

I stand from my crouched position, my five-feet-five stature towering over Mom's five-feet height. "The words, the very action of
writing a note and taking one, by fate," I rattle off. "There are a lot

of variables at play. There's some string theory sprinkled in—Hey, don't look at me like that."

"I know, I know. Fate," she says with a dramatic whisper. "It's very on-brand."

I shrug. "It's not like I'm famous or anything. Literally no one knows who I am. They just can't see me making the art, because then they will know."

"And what's so wrong with people knowing who you are?" Mom asks.

I think of how to phrase it. That if people know who I am, they'll put the pieces together that I'm Wren Gao's daughter. The infamous baby who was born in a museum. It was such a sensation that it had become my entire identity until enough time had passed and I was no longer a child.

I also don't need the literal beginning of my life on display for everyone to see. It's why I want to buy *Baby Being Born* back so no one can own something that is private and personal to me. So that a museum can't play the moment I entered the world on repeat for days on end against a large white wall for strangers to watch and comment on. Is that so much to ask?

I don't know how to explain it to her. Instead, I just ask one question. "Do you regret it? Filming my birth?"

Mom shakes her head firmly. "I don't believe in looking backwards. It gave us financial security, that video. It gave me the career of my wildest dreams. Long-lasting art imitates life."

I flip the edge of the crinkled Fate Note back and forth. "Well, I'm on a mission to get it back."

I pick up the box of Fate Notes and lead Mom to a wavy portion of the installation. With my free hand, I remove fast-food wrappers and empty cans of soda from between a stretch of string, trying not to let the misuse of my art rattle me too much. I slip my Fate

Note into a clean section. "That's how it works," I say. "It's meant to bring people together. Feel free to add one, too. Just keep it relatively PG."

"That's no fun. I'm trying to find my X-rated match," Mom says.

I watch as park visitors bundled in thick coats slow their steps to look up and around at my creation. "Do you think people are liking it?" I whisper to her.

Mom scoffs. "Who cares what they're thinking? You're Red String Girl and you're showcasing in Washington Square Park. Chin up!" She slides her hands into her pockets, puffing out the sides of her oversize, paint-splattered parka.

"Okay, easy!" I look around to make sure no one heard. "You're going to scare people away, or worse, give me away. Unless this was your plan all along, and this is one of your performance art pieces. You can call it *Daughter Being Sabotaged*."

"That's not a bad idea," Mom says with a glimmer in her eyes. "Ah, I almost forgot. I brought this back for you."

From her coat pocket, she reveals a miniature snow globe of Tokyo. Anytime we'd travel together, our souvenir of choice was snow globes to remind us of where we'd been. Mom knows I love winter, and in snow globes, cities exist in that glorious season all year round.

I shake the globe and watch as fake snow lands in the indents of the Tokyo Skytree. Yep. There's definitely a romantic bone in her somewhere. "Thank you. Maybe one day you'll be going on tour with me."

She gives me a single nod. "I would love that."

I grin at her, noting her features that mirror my own. We share square jaws and rounded noses and big smiles. Not that Mom smiles much, but when she does, it lights up a room. I place the snow globe in my bag and readjust the box in my arms, resting my free hand on Mom's shoulder. "Can you let Talia know I'm going back to the print shop to try to get these Fate Notes fixed? Or to at least get my money back."

Mom pulls a pocket-size sketchbook from her coat pocket. "I've got makeshift Fate Notes right here. Go, but hurry."

"What else have you got in those pockets? You're a magician!" I say with a gasp.

Mom's smile widens slightly. "Go!"

"I give you permission to yell at people who are using this as a garbage can. Otherwise, don't frighten people away, please!" I shout as I head out of the park and toward the print shop.

Behind me, I hear Mom laughing maniacally.

JACK

 For a print shop with a name like Sprinters NYC, they're not nearly as fast as I would've thought.

Fifteen minutes have passed since I dropped off my order for more pamphlets. Usually, an unexpected increase in crowd size is a good thing. But of course, today of all days, I only have a dozen pamphlets printed for my presentation this afternoon.

I'm sitting in the corner checking my email when congratulatory messages about the senior engineer role I had applied for multiply in my in-box. But the kind emails aren't for me. They're for a man named Marvin coming over from the Moon Mission.

A new message from my boss, Annika, appears.

Hi Jackson,

Sorry I missed you before the announcement went out about the Senior Engineer position. The decision committee typically likes to see participation in projects outside of your day-to-day work. I'd like to see you teach others about the mission and what we do and share your knowledge in a more inspiring way. Maybe letting people get to know you on a personal level might help, too. Let's keep an eye out for more opportunities for you. Maybe volunteering to serve on special committees in the company? Your presentation at the conference today will be a great starting point. Let's talk more when you're back.

Three times. That's three times now that I've been passed over for a promotion. I was sure this time would be my chance. It wasn't the title I coveted, though I can't say I hate the way Jackson Liu, senior engineer at NASA, sounds.

But more than a title, more than a raise, promotions are validating. A reassurance that you're adding value. That you're worth keeping around. Maybe my parents would notice a new title. I'm good at what I do. Why can't that be enough? Why do I have to tell people what I'm doing on the weekends or spend work time volunteering? And on special committees? What does that even mean?

The young man with curly auburn hair who helped me earlier comes up from behind the counter with an apologetic look on his face. "It's almost done. Sorry, man. You'll be out of here in no time," he says.

I look at the time on my watch. "How long do you think?"

"Another twenty minutes or so? The printer's jammed. I got this one out at least," the print shop employee says, waving my pamphlet in the air. "This is sweet. You giving a talk about Mars or something?"

"I am," I say, offering only this much information.

"Are you an astronaut?" he asks.

"I'm not."

"Oh, I know! You must be, like, Elon Musk's right-hand man. You look smart. Am I warm?"

I run my hand down my face. "Not even close," I groan, looking at his name tag for an identifier of some sort, "Dave."

Dave scratches his chin. "Jeffrey Bezos's right-hand man? Or Richard Bran—"

"I'm a systems engineer at NASA," I finally say to put an end to the twenty questions. Which is all I'll ever be unless I join a special committee or rub with the right elbows. What's so special about doing free work?

"Right on!" he says.

"These pamphlets are important," I mumble as he's still reading through one. I don't add that these pamphlets are for one of the most important missions I've ever been a part of. With the most responsibility I've ever had, with or without the promotion. If I do well at this conference, the decision committee might actually start to take notice. "Are you supposed to be reading what your customers print?"

He tilts his head. "I couldn't help but notice this sick image of the Red Planet. We're going to be vacationing there one day, you know. It says here there's ice. When this melts, we can surf those melted waves all day long," Dave states, nodding vigorously. "Oh, hey, I can give you a discount code for next time for your troubles!"

I awkwardly return his nod. "Thanks. But I'm only in town for a conference. I'll do a lap around the block until the pamphlets are done."

Dave gives me two thumbs-up. "Whatever you want. Feel free to hang out here. Looks like it started snowing."

"I don't get snow where I'm from. I'll enjoy it while I can," I say, watching through the window as small flakes plummet to earth.

"Oh, yeah? Where are you from?" Dave asks, preventing me from leaving.

"California," I say.

"No way. I've been eyeing up Malibu. Those waves are rock solid," he says enviously. "As soon as I can, I'm outta here. Just me, my board, and the swell." Dave points behind him, where there's an eight-foot neon green surfboard leaning against the wall. "I like to keep it with me so I can do my visualization exercises."

I'm getting antsy. "Sounds swell. Dave. The pamphlets?"

"Right! I'll put a rush on your travel guides as soon as the printer's unblocked," Dave promises. "Oh wait, here's the sample."

Dave slides the pamphlet across the counter to me. He cringes at his poor aim as it shoots off the end of the counter. I kneel to pick it up from the floor.

"I do hereby knight thee," a woman's voice says above me. She hoists her box up on her hip and extends a hand in an offer to help me up. She looks to be about my age, slightly younger maybe.

"Thanks, I'm good," I say, pushing off my knee to stand. With her box precariously balanced, I might pull her down with me if I accepted her hand. I slide the pamphlet into my back pocket.

I catch a glimpse of the woman's sparkling light brown eyes under her thick bangs.

"Hey, Rooney," Dave says, grabbing the box from the woman, "this guy has never seen snow before. He's from California."

"Oh yeah? What about sleet?" the woman apparently named Rooney asks, propping her elbow up on the counter. "Have you ever seen that?"

"Uh, yeah," I say, nodding.

"Fine. But have you ever seen a moonbow?" she asks like there's no way I have. I mean, I haven't. They're incredibly rare.

I shrug. "You got me there."

"Hold up," Dave says, leaning against the counter like we're all sitting down for tea and a chat. "Is that some kind of, like, rainbow at night?"

Rooney nods excitedly. "I saw my first moonbow in Iceland with my mom. It had been a long day of hot springs and more mannequins and rubber ducks than one should ever have to interact with in a lifetime." She glances up at me. "Don't ask."

"Wasn't going to."

"All of the ingredients were there. Full moon. No clouds. Dark sky. Light rain." She literally counts this out on her fingers before sighing. "Anyway. These were messed up," she says to Dave while she pats the top of the box. "I need replacements now."

"Like *now* now?" Dave asks, looking nervous.

"As now as now can be," Rooney says sweetly.

Dave looks at the clock hanging on the wall. "I've got his job finishing up at the moment, and then yours is next."

"Okay. Fine. I'll be here." Rooney exhales upward, her bangs flying up over her face.

"You doing your lap?" Dave asks me as he types something.

"Oh. It's a little too cold for me," I reply as I flip through office supplies on the nearby rack. I study the curves of Rooney's face in the fluorescent lighting before she turns back to me.

"Are you hanging around for the playlist?" she asks. Overhead, "Since U Been Gone" crackles from the speakers.

Her comment catches me off guard. "I actually chose this print shop exclusively based on the music," I improvise. Somehow, my anxiety over my upcoming presentation eases a bit as I talk to her. "It was between here and the one on Fourteenth Street. But they mostly play nineties rock. I'm more of an early two thousands pop music type of guy."

My comment draws a laugh out of her. "I knew you looked like a Kelly Clarkson fan. What's your name?" she asks, surveying me as though *I* could be a threat.

I don't answer right away. "Uh."

"I'm not asking for your social security number, just your name," she says with another laugh, her comfortable demeanor disarming me. "But I do need your date of birth and passport number."

I feel a smile form across my face.

"I'm Jack," I say a beat later. A new customer pushes open the door, blowing fresh cold air into the space. I zip my coat up higher. "Good playlists, poor heating. Noted for next time."

"I'm Rooney," she says as she moves a misplaced roll of tape back to the right hook. "You seem more like a tie guy, but that's not going to help you here." She reaches into her bag and pulls out a bundle of knitted yarn. "Take this scarf that I made."

"I can't take that from you," I say, backing up a step. "I don't even know you."

She narrows her eyes at me. "You don't trust me?"

I furrow my eyebrows. "No."

"Right answer," she says. "You're going to think this is weird, but here. Seriously. It's supposed to get even colder today." She holds up what has to be the world's longest scarf.

"Why is it so long?"

Rooney looks down at the possibly ten-foot scarf curled up in her hands and laughs. "It's my Red Thread of Fate scarf!"

I shake my head.

"It's a Chinese legend where Yuè Lǎo, the god of love and marriage, connects two people by the ankles with a red thread. Those two people are then destined lovers, regardless of place, time, or circumstances. The magical string may stretch or tangle, but never break. Romantic, right?"

I take a moment to see if any of those words spark a memory. I don't think my parents ever taught me this myth growing up. A fuzzy memory of Gōng Gong talking about string begins to take shape but doesn't grow.

I nod toward her. "And the scarf is supposed to be the…long, unbreakable red thread?"

"It's called symbolism," she says playfully. "Just let me cast off."

She does something with the last row of stitches and then approaches me again slowly. As though I'm a wild animal on the verge of fleeing. I stand very still as she wraps the scarf over my shoulders. Up close, the aroma of citrus and vanilla wafts up. It's both intoxicating and intriguing.

Rooney fluffs the seven or eight loops of knitted yarn around my neck. She takes a step back to consider her handiwork. The scarf smells like her.

"Red looks good on you," she says with a smile.

I tug one end of the scarf and consider the feel of it. "Tell me honestly. Do I look ridiculous?"

Rooney gently takes the end of the scarf from me and pulls it down farther. Her hand slides against my puffer jacket with enough pressure for me to feel it. I'm hyperaware of how close she's standing.

"I guess that was a little long. Looks like it was meant for you, though. There," she says, patting the end of the scarf once more.

"I'm not quite sure what to say here. You really want to give me this?"

Rooney smiles. "I really do. It would make me happy to know it's going to a fellow Kelly Clarkson fan."

"Okay, well, thanks," I say.

Dave lugs a box from the back and deposits it on the counter. Nodding to me, he says, "Good news! Your prints are ready."

Already? "That was fast."

"Isn't that what you wanted?" he asks, looking between me and Rooney.

I notice five small light brown moles on Rooney's left cheek. I draw an imaginary line through them, their position creating a minimal version of the Big Dipper. It draws me in.

Dave clears his throat, the noise breaking my focus.

"No. Yeah. This is great. Thanks," I say. A part of me wishes the printer would've gotten jammed again. Nerves for my presentation come flooding back, along with the surprising disappointment at having to already say good-bye to Rooney.

"Everything's breaking today," Dave says, wearing an apologetic look. "Our credit card machine doesn't want to connect with the Wi-Fi. Afraid it's going to have to be cash."

Sliding a few twenties out of my wallet, I hand them to Dave and ask for a receipt so I can be reimbursed from work.

I cradle the box in my arms and face Rooney, who's fiddling with a pack of highlighters. "Well, bye."

"May our paths cross again," she says with a smile.

I bow with a slight bend in my knee, the box bumping against my stomach. The whole thing turns out looking more like a curtsy.

Rooney laughs.

Seriously, Jack? What was that? Go. Leave. Now.

Outside, the snow has gained in size but slowed in speed. Unlike my heart. Puffy flakes float down through the air. What an odd and interesting woman. Hugging my neck, Rooney's scarf protects me against the cold.

A man stuffs a flyer into my available hand for Gray's Papaya all the way uptown and for an electronics store too far downtown. I crumple the papers into my coat pocket and turn the corner toward a park. An arch I recognize from the movie *The Astronaut's Wife* looms over a crowd of people distracted by what looks like an outdoor exhibit.

It's a peculiar sight. All this in the middle of winter. Bright red tangles of thin rope are strung across the park, like organized chaos. Up close, the string is slightly glossy. Wax coating for protection against the elements.

I slide the box of pamphlets into my other arm and check my watch. I can't linger but I can cross through the park.

The sound of ripping startles me. An older woman in a paint-splattered jacket tears paper out of a small sketchbook and hands it to a child.

"My last one. You're lucky, kid. Write something on it, slip it between the strings," she tells him. "Fate will do the rest."

I unintentionally let out a cough at this. The woman saunters over to me.

"Something funny?" she asks, examining me. "Where did you get that scarf?"

I look down at the yarn mass wrapped around my neck and think of Rooney. I've never met anyone who smiled so much in such a short period of time.

"A helpful civilian," I say.

"Right," the woman says, eyeing me suspiciously.

I nod toward the installation. "Are you the artist?"

"I'm just a helpful civilian. The artist is RSG and she works anonymously."

Exactly what someone who wants to remain anonymous would say.

"All I can tell you is that this," she says, waving her hand toward the rest of the park, "is called *Entangled*."

"As in quantum entanglement?" I ask, now slightly intrigued. I scan the rest of the installation with this new piece of information in mind. In various sections are slips of white sketchbook paper tucked into the cord. "I can see that... RST?"

"RSG," the woman repeats, elongating the "G." "'G' as in gall-bladder. Red String Girl."

"Right. Well, I can see that RSG was trying to imply that the pieces of paper, or particles, maintain separation yet still remain connected across the various parts of the string. They're influencing and being influenced by another when someone grabs one of the papers," I reason. "But when one paper is grabbed, it doesn't have a twin that's immediately affected. There's the flaw."

She rolls her eyes. "That's where fate comes in."

"And that's where you lose me," I tell her. "What does the red have to do with quantum entanglement, or as you say, fate?"

Her expression is unchanged. "This must be your first RSG installation. Congrats. Your bubble's been officially popped. More specifically, it's about the Red Thread of Fate."

"Are you serious?" I ask. Rooney must've just come from here and learned about this, too.

She looks me up and down. "You suit types never fail to amuse."

"Okay then," I whisper under my breath, checking the time on my watch.

"Are you too busy for me? Before you go, do something spontaneous and try it out. Write something down. Slip it in. You'll never forget your first time."

"Excuse me?" It's as though I've entered an alternate reality made of red webs. Are all people in New York this bossy? First Rooney. Now this person.

"Participate. It'll be good for you," she says. "I don't have any more slips, but I'm sure you have a legal notepad on you or something. You suit types always do."

"Uh." I pat around my chest and stomach, reangling the box. It's a B-minus effort to satisfy this person. I feel the flyers from my coat pocket. "I think I have something?"

"Are you asking me or telling me? Do what you gotta do," the woman says, tucking her empty sketchbook under her arm and turning to go. She proceeds to tell more people about the installation. If she's not the artist, then why does she know so much about it? She thinks she's so clever, believing she's fooling everyone. She and her work leave an impression, I'll give her that much.

I reach under the scarf to unclip my pen from my sweater's neckline. I stare at the back of the yellow Gray's Papaya flyer featuring their hot dog specials. The squiggle of mustard pops against the mysterious red meat mixture.

I settle on "Fate is the hot dog of the universe." Maybe there's a quantum entanglement special committee I can join. Something that aligns more with my interests.

I gently pull one of the red strings back and tuck my flyer in. The yellow flyer stands out against the red.

With a shrug, I reach for the nearest piece of paper without thinking too much about it. I untuck the slip from the string. The handwritten words are loopy and red, as though it was written in a hurry. The word "lophole" is printed at the top. I slip the paper into my wallet.

Now it's really time to get to the conference. I'll show the higher-ups who really should've gotten that promotion.

Chapter 3

ROONEY

Twenty-five minutes later, I'm back at my installation with my newly printed Fate Notes.

I find Mom with an empty sketchbook in hand.

"Let's see these babies," I sing, lifting the box lid. My face drops as Mom laughs.

"You went an entirely different direction, I see," she says, lifting a pamphlet with a high-resolution image of Mars on the front. "Leaning more into the science aspect?"

I riffle through the pamphlets and frown. "Dave must have mixed this up with another customer's. This is really well done. I'd hate for it to go to waste."

Mom slides on her reading glasses and holds the glossy paper up in front of her. "There's ice on Mars? Who knew."

"He was busy." I'm just talking to myself at this point. Mom's too engrossed in whatever this Mars mission is. "This is kind of perfect, right? Fate's mix-up giving me the extra dose of science for this installation."

Mom looks up from the pamphlet and shrugs. "Well, there's no time to go back now. I'm out of sketchbook paper."

"Okay. Yeah. This is good. We're all completely fine. This is a blessing in disguise! Honestly, I wish I had thought of it," I say. I track down Talia and signal for her to distribute the new Fate Notes while I stay hidden. Mom and I stroll along the winding string path, where there are more empty stretches of red than I'd prefer to see.

"How was it when I was gone? I see some white paper, but not as much as I expected," I whisper, my forehead scrunched so intensely, I can see the edges of my eyebrows.

"You're opening yourself up to new audiences, I'll say that," she says vaguely.

A shiny green gum wrapper catches my eye. "Oh no. It's official. I've created the world's most beautiful garbage net." I pluck the wrapper from the string, confirm that there are no words written on the back, and crumple it between my thumb and pointer fingers.

"Somewhere a piece of gum just felt that," Mom jokes.

I take a deep breath in, then out.

"You can't be here right now," Mom adds. "This has to exist on its own without your constant monitoring. That's art, baby. You gave it to the world when you created it. It's no longer yours."

Out of nowhere, a loud truck screeches to a stop outside the Washington Arch. Six men in bright yellow construction vests with shears in their hands march toward my installation. One rushes up to *Entangled* and opens the scissors like he's about to make a cut.

I run over to them, waving my arms in the air. "Stop!" I shout.

The man pauses, looking over at me and then over to his boss.

"What are you doing? What's going on?" I ask, looking at Mom and Talia as they run up behind me.

"Are you the artist?" a man with a hard hat and a clipboard asks. The name written in marker on his vest reads Bill.

"I . . . work for the artist. I'm her assistant," I lie. "We've been here all week. There's no opening ceremony necessary."

"Ceremony? We're not here for a ceremony," Bill says, lifting his own pair of shears. "These are Closing Down Scissors."

"Whoa! Bill, let's just talk this out," I say, panicking. "This is Red

String Girl's big moment. She worked really hard for this. People haven't been able to fully appreciate *Entangled*."

"Well, tell Red String Whatever we're real sorry, but no can do. The city told us to shut this down," Bill says.

Talia holds her hands up. "Why? We have permits for the next couple of months. You can't do this."

"A woman does something great, and then a man has to tear it down," Mom mutters. "You better be refunding us for the time and cost of materials."

Bill shrugs. "My hands are tied. It's an order coming from the top. We've got complaints about people lounging in the string like a hammock, drying their clothes, and using this as a garbage net. There's a strange smell coming from that part over there, and this definitely isn't pigeon-proof."

I shake my head. "Wait. So that man really was about to make a cut? This is art!"

Bill holds up his hands to the man with the scissors to stop him. "The permits are revocable if what you're doing becomes a public nuisance or a health hazard. This is clearly both. I got environmentalists calling me about red string and trash in the park. All I know is they're worried that, when the snow melts, the water will be contaminated. I also can't have pigeons or squirrels or, Heaven forbid, humans, eating rotten leftovers and getting sick on my watch. I'm not going down that way."

I'm starting to feel light-headed. "Why punish us and not the litterers? This installation is clearly not for the disposing of goods! Go tell *them* to stop!"

Bill adjusts his face into something that looks slightly apologetic. "Sorry, miss." He gestures scissor fingers to his crew as their signal to destroy my dreams.

With just a few snips, the entire installation will collapse. We watch, horrified, as the first cut is made on *Entangled*. The lump in my throat makes it hard to swallow. I don't want to cry here in front of everyone like this, so I hold back my tears by taking deep breaths.

I can't look at this monstrosity. I force my eyes shut and hum "My Favorite Things" to myself, changing the lyrics to match my own favorite things. But it's not fresh snowflakes falling or matcha ice cream or kittens dressed up in tiny, knitted sweaters that I imagine. Instead, it's Jack's face that flashes into my mind. I can clearly see the bottom of his lower lip with its centimeter-long scar, a pale white line in the shape of a crescent moon. My heartbeat slows, his imaginary presence slightly calming me.

"If the artist thing doesn't work out, you have a future in waste management," Mom says, patting my back. I know she's trying to lighten the mood, but it doesn't help. I keep Jack's face steady in my mind, something stable to hold on to.

As the string drapes down over itself, I realize I haven't taken a Fate Note of my own yet. It can serve as a reminder that my installation really existed at one point.

I quickly reach for the nearest note before it's too late. The string has gone slack, the notes—and all the garbage—falling with it.

The paper in my hand feels glossy and textured with wrinkles. I read the back of the note with the words of yet another person not taking my installation seriously. I tuck the note into my bag and stare one last time at my pride and joy.

I'm subject to the same fate of those before me. Good-bye, Washington Square Park.

Chapter 4

ROONEY

The Lantern Festival party is already in full swing by the time I arrive. I text Talia in the elevator to let her know I'm on my way up. She rushes to greet me at the door with a glass of Cabernet. "I'm glad you were still able to make it."

I put on a happy face. "Of course I made it. It's the Lantern Festival. It hasn't been the best start to the Lunar New Year, but we're two weeks in. There's still a lot of year left."

The host's gently restored Upper West Side apartment is two times the size of Mom's. No wonder their parties have such a good reputation. The beautifully designed space is filled to the corners with guests, everyone chatting like they know each other even though, by the sound of it, we're all friends of friends of coworkers.

The apartment glows with sparkling string lights draped from the ceilings, red paper globe lights, and gold party streamers. In the living room, people sip wine, mingle in front of built-in bookshelves, and switch out records on the turntable. I stay close to the peacock blue walls, analyzing the host's choice of art.

I admire an enameled pear-shaped vase with a pine tree and colorful clouds painted around it. "That one's from the Yongzheng period in the 1700s," Talia says, checking out the piece. "It's probably worth six figures."

My eyes pop at the number. "It's beautiful. Amazing what art stands the test of time." I frown. "What does it mean if this delicate vase survived a few hundred years, and my installation couldn't even last a week?"

Talia takes a sip of her own wine before wrapping her arms around my shoulders. "This damn city."

I lean into her shoulder, feeling utterly defeated.

"Your pet portraits are still selling," Talia says with a small smile. "I can move some artists around and make space for whatever you want to do next."

I shrug hopelessly. "Today *Entangled* became *Untangled*. I don't have a clue what's next."

"We'll figure it out," Talia says like the best friend that she is.

I slouch, hugging my arms against my body. "You have to say that."

"I really don't. Come on, let's go make a wish on a lantern," Talia says, guiding me through the living room as other guests head toward the front door, pulling their hats and scarves off the coatrack on the way out. It feels like everyone's looking at me, judging me. Then I remember they don't know who I am or what I do. I might as well be invisible.

I sigh. "It's the perfect night for a wish. I'm not going to think about today, not going to talk about it," I say with a terrible attempt at an upbeat tone. I twirl a short piece of red string around my finger, looping and unlooping it around and around.

The rooftop wasn't an afterthought. Globes of all sizes emanate soft white light around the deck while tealight candles flicker on metal bar tables. Large red- and cream-colored paper lanterns are gathered in rows on long benches as party guests cluster around them, pulling their coats closer around their bodies. It looks like there are double the number of people up here than there were in the apartment.

Lunar New Year was two weeks ago, and tonight marks the final day of celebrations. Against the starless sky and between a break in the clouds, I locate the full moon, significant for the Lantern Festival. The moon is light against the gray-violet sky, quickly growing in brightness as the night ticks on.

"We don't have enough lanterns for each person, and these are cumbersome enough to require two people minimum, so we're going to pair up," someone who I assume might be the host announces. "Preferably with someone you don't know. Make new connections!"

Guests naturally divide into couples or with friends they came with while one guy takes it upon himself to group random people together. Having invited several people, Talia spots one of her clients and leaves me for two minutes to say hello.

"Ah, you!" the self-appointed organizer calls out to a tall man coming through the entrance to the rooftop. "You're just in time. You two are paired together." He's referring to me, and before we can object, this man and I are handed a lantern.

When the man steps closer and into the light of a globe, I first notice his lip scar. I trace his lips up to his nose and then to his brown eyes, a sort of weird déjà vu overcoming me.

The word "Jack" tumbles out of my mouth. This guy has my Red Thread of Fate scarf wrapped around his neck. He's definitely the man from the print shop. And he looks equally surprised to see me.

"Rooney." He searches my face in recognition. Two times in one day in New York City, where there's nearly eight and a half million people.

"What are you doing here? Who's suing me? Am I about to be served?" I ask the series of questions dramatically, but I really do want answers. Who is this guy and why is he here?

Jack lets out a short grunt that could easily be mistaken for a chuckle. "Actually, no. I'm a debt collector. You're behind on your payments."

I hope that's supposed to be a joke. I smile, feeling some of the burden of the day melt away.

I look his face up and down, surprisingly comforted to be seeing him again. "You do have a very debt collector-y face."

"What does that look like?" he asks.

"You look at everyone like they're a liability," I say, deciphering his features. There's no doubt that Jack is handsome. His brown hair falls perfectly into place and frames his oval-shaped face.

"Wait, so why are you here again?" I ask, cutting my admiration short.

He drags his hand over his face. "I shouldn't be. My colleague said I could come by. Apparently, his wife has a friend whose cousin's partner works with the host's stylist. He has my notebook that I accidentally left behind at a work event."

I nod in understanding. "I'm here for a similar reason. My friend's friend's husband's coworker's cat has playdates with the host's cat. Or something. I only know one person here. Well, now two."

"That makes two of us," Jack says. For a split second, his eyes crinkle in what could definitely qualify as an eye smile. I'll take it. But then something even better happens. He smiles for real. It's brief, his jaw quickly settling back into its neutral position. His smile feels hard-earned, so I imprint the moment in my memory and safekeep it as a win.

I tilt the lantern on its side and reach into my bag, feeling around the bottom until I find my pen. "Should we write down our wishes? I'll write mine. Then you do yours."

Jack angles his body toward me. "Oh, that's okay," he says, looking around. His hair sticks up from the wind, giving him a younger appearance even though he must be in his early thirties. "I don't plan on staying."

"It's the Lantern Festival. I'm not letting you walk out of here without participating," I say, writing gently against the paper lantern, careful not to poke a hole through it.

He hesitates. "Okay. But then I have to get going. I've had a long day."

"You and me both," I mumble. I lift the pen mid-sentence, nodding toward the scarf I made that he's still wearing. "I hope it kept you warm."

"No pneumonia today," he says, twiddling his fingers through the yarn. "Did you want it back? I won't need this in Los Angeles. It would go better with your red coat anyway."

I hold my hands up to stop him from unwrapping the scarf. "Please, keep it. It was meant to be passed on."

"Well, thanks again. Are you a teacher or an editor?" Jack asks, nodding toward the pen. "No one I know writes in red ink."

"I probably shouldn't be," I say guiltily. "In Chinese culture, it's bad luck to write people's names in red ink. It's like writing them a death sentence. Which is why I *only* write names with this pen. Got anyone in mind?" A certain Bill comes to mind.

Jack's eyes widen.

"I'm kidding," I say, exhaling. It really has been a day. "My Pó Po was a teacher. She would mark students' papers in red ink to make sure they knew when they had made a mistake."

"Brutal," he grunts.

"Right?" I hold the red pen up horizontally, my eyes moving from the cap to the base. "This was one of her Discipline Pens. That's what I called it as a kid. Sometimes she'd grade my finger paintings with her comments, always in red. So now I use the pen to counteract all the Fs she would dole out like candy."

"She graded your finger paintings?" Jack asks with an undertone of surprise.

"I like to think she wanted me to be the best I could be." This sentiment makes me think of Mom and how hard she worked. I'm sure she felt the weight of Pó Po's criticism, too.

I breathe out, a cloud forming in front of me. "I'm changing the meaning of it and using it for good."

Jack looks impressed. "You seem like the kind of person who can take something bad and make it good."

His words are a sweet addition to this bitter day.

Jack glances around us. "Unusual that our paths crossed again."

"Maybe it's good you left something behind at your event," I reason.

"I never do that," he says.

I bounce the end of the pen against my hand. "Forget things or go to events?"

He grins. "Both. Now I'm notebookless, and you know what, I don't really want to talk about it," he says as he looks at his watch. "I should go."

I hand Jack my pen. "Not until you write your wish."

Jack pats his jacket, feeling around for something. "I always have a pen on me. I must have left that behind, too," he says with a sigh.

"Write anything but my name," I instruct.

"Well, there goes my wish," he mumbles, glancing up at me.

His words throw me off. Even though I think he's kidding, heat rises in my chest. I stay silent as he scribbles down on the side of the lantern, *Anything but my name.*

I cross my arms. "You give up on wishes that easily, huh?"

"I'm all wished out for the day," he says, the corner of his lips slightly tugging upward.

"Let's release this, then. You grab that side."

"We're not actually releasing this," Jack says flatly.

"What else would we do with it? It's tradition." Above us, glowing lanterns float into the night, paper stars rising above the New

York City skyline. Tonight, New Yorkers will witness temporary constellations.

Jack shifts his footing. "Is this legal? We're going to be arrested. Don't we need launch permission?"

"*Launch permission?*" I repeat with a laugh. "That's not how this works. But if our lantern lands on the steps of a police station, then we're definitely screwed. Our fingerprints are all over this thing. They might even bring in a forensics team to identify our handwriting. And if it's me they find first, I'm giving up your name in exchange for immunity. Of course, this is if the lantern doesn't catch on fire first."

"I didn't just hear the word 'fire' come out of your mouth," Jack says as I wriggle the fuel cell into place under the center of the lantern. "This has to be banned. Has anyone checked?"

"Fudge this city. I hope we burn it all down," I mumble.

"Fudge this what?" Jack asks, slightly horrified.

I lift my eyebrows. "Nothing. It's been a long day."

We're huddled in our corner of the rooftop, the wind blowing my hair around. I fluff my bangs back down over my forehead.

"We have to be careful that the flame doesn't touch the paper when we're lighting it." I strike a match against the little boxes provided on each outdoor table.

"I notice you said *we*. I can't be part of this. Or even witness to it." Jack turns his head and shields his eyes as I light the fuel cell.

"Why? Are you a firefighter?" I ask.

"I'm not." He says this directed away from me, his hands still covering his eyes.

"Ex-arsonist out on parole?" I add dramatically. I'm having too much fun watching Jack squirm. It's the most animated I've seen him.

Jack finally turns back to me and looks me straight in the eyes.

There's a hint of playfulness behind them, even though his lips are firm. "No."

"I hear your concerns," I say reassuringly. "Rumor has it that the host of the party worked with a local artist to make these. They may even be biodegradable and fire resistant. Once the fuel runs out, the lantern will drift back to earth safely."

Jack frowns. "Have those claims been tested? What's the plan? Do we go collect them around the city afterwards?"

"We're about to test them right now." I set the used match on the table. "The plan is this: I just lit the fuel cell, and now I'll lift this up by myself, which is, of course, even more dangerous to do alone." I peek over at Jack out of the corner of my eye.

He doesn't move.

"Your wish is definitely not coming true now," I continue, maneuvering my way under the lantern. "Only people who help get wishes."

Jack watches on stubbornly as I try to balance the lantern in my arms. I gasp at a light dent I've made in the lantern, trying to be dramatic enough so he'll help. Jack finally gives in, grasping for the lantern as it wobbles against me.

"You're a bad influence," he says.

"Am I really so bad?"

I carefully move my hands under the lantern. Jack overcompensates and extends his long arms under the entire rim to the point where we're practically holding hands. We push the lantern down low enough so we can see each other over the top of it. In the yellow glow, I see pink blossom across his cheeks. I feel my face warm in the same way, and I know it's not because of the heat from the flame below us.

"If we do this, we have to do it the right way," Jack says. "I can do some quick math. Figure out the coordinates and proper angle to release this. Preferably away from the police station. Do you know where that is?" He looks at me expectantly.

I wave one of my arms toward downtown, and the lantern is thrown off balance. "Somewhere over there."

Jack steadies the lantern and looks up at an angle. "The wind is blowing west. That's good. Let's use that to our benefit. Lift it higher. Come slightly more toward me." I shuffle three baby steps in his direction. "We can aim it toward the river and away from all the buildings and people."

Jack looks up toward his forehead doing what I assume is mental math. It's endearing watching him become this involved.

"What else are we not considering?" he asks, looking over at the other couples releasing their lanterns. "Okay, there. See? They're releasing the lantern straight over their heads. But it needs to stay low enough and at an angle. Theirs will hardly make it a mile."

"Lantern Wars. Nice. What do we win? Free lanterns for life?" I joke.

Jack shakes his head, but it's not directed toward me. "Now just look at those people," he says under his breath, leaning in closer to me. I catch a faint scent of clove on him, chased by an earthy hint of oak. Or is it cedar? Something woodsy. His scent alone warms me up.

"They've pushed the lantern out too forcefully over the edge of the building," he continues. "All that swaying is going to throw it off its trajectory."

"There's no need to overanalyze the magic of releasing lanterns. Once it's out of our hands, we can't control it anymore."

Jack furrows his brows. "We're not leaving our *paper* lantern fueled by *fire* up to...fate. Or destiny. Or whatever it is that you're referring to that is out of our control."

"Our lantern will end up where it's supposed to. Don't worry," I reassure him.

"Okay, I won't worry about fate," Jack says with an undercurrent of sarcasm. It's subtle, but I notice it. A snag in his typically calm reserve. "How about instead, I'll just worry about getting caught and spending the night in jail."

"If you have that experience, maybe you won't fear it as much."

He adjusts his footing. "That's a lesson I'll happily skip."

Within minutes, the lantern takes on a life of its own, the heat inside letting us know it no longer wants to be earthside. Our lantern floats even higher, guiding our hands up with it.

With our arms above our heads, Jack and I lock eyes under the glow of the flame. Through his dark lashes, I can see that eye-smile again.

He shrugs. "Might as well let go on three. One, two—"

At the same time, we both whisper "three" and release the lantern up toward the indigo sky. As we watch it follow its freewheeling path, we bump into each other, momentarily unaware of any unspoken boundaries.

I'm breathless and, so it seems, is Jack.

"That was thrilling," he says with a slightly confused look on his face.

"You look positively radiant," I say, mimicking his serious look.

Laughter pours out of him, unrestrained. It's the first time I've heard it from him. There's an unexpected warmth in it, such childlike joy beneath his stony exterior.

Outside, it's a low thirty degrees, and I can hardly feel my face, but hearing Jack's laugh under the brightest full moon I've ever seen thaws out all parts of me. As the moon beams like a spotlight over the Hudson River, a tingling sensation unravels in my chest. Could he be...

"Rooney, there's someone I want you to meet," Talia calls out to me.

I'm torn out of my red thread thoughts as Talia waves her arms across the rooftop to get my attention. I consider stalling, but she's too enthusiastic to ignore.

"Be right back," I tell Jack. "See you in a minute?"

"Sure," he says with a hesitant nod.

I'm introduced to Talia's frequent gallery visitors as her gallery's assistant, a cover-up we formed years ago to keep my secret artist identity intact. We make small talk about what's happening in today's art scene and how much colder this winter has been. When there's a lull in the conversation, I excuse myself and search for Jack on the rooftop and in the host's apartment. He's nowhere to be found. Gone in the wind like our lantern.

I look out the living room windows, searching the streets as if I'd be able to pinpoint exactly where Jack is. He's out there somewhere in the city.

Maybe this was meant to be our final interaction. Such is life. It's a sign as clear as the moon in the sky. I should let it go, let the thought of him go.

Just like the lantern.

Chapter 5

JACK

It's 7:01 p.m. I've been awake for over eighteen hours. When Rooney's pulled away by her friend, I use the opportunity to find my colleague and grab my notebook. My colleague is nowhere to be found on the rooftop or in the apartment. Instead, he's a couple of avenues over at a bar. I make the ten-minute trip and debate whether to go back to the party to find Rooney to say good-bye.

I should call it a night. Go back to the hotel and sleep this lousy day off. It was one thing for there not to be enough pamphlets *and* to be late for my presentation. It was another for Dave to have mixed up my order with someone else's and have to spend the rest of the day passing out menus to a local Chinese restaurant for people to take notes on.

That was followed up with fielding questions about where the information on Mars and our mission went and if the mission is still even happening at all. Repeating over and over that no, the conference was not catered, and that I will not be taking lunch orders. I rushed through the last fifteen minutes of my hour-long presentation and then skipped the networking altogether. That won't help my promotability.

Suffice it to say, today did not go well for me. But at least Noodle Palace gained two hundred new customers.

If I'm being honest with myself, assigning "lousy" to this entire day would be inaccurate. There was Rooney. Rooney who said weird things to make me laugh. Who kept me at the party far longer than I wanted to be. Who made me actually enjoy myself in a social setting. Who is unlike anyone I've ever met.

I pull the scarf over the lower half of my face and breathe in her smell. I feel a pen clipped into the neckline of my sweater. Rooney's Discipline Pen. Or her Do-Good Pen, rather. I can't steal this from Rooney. She did provide me with warmth, after all. I have to go back to the party.

Rooney isn't in the apartment. A surprise pang of disappointment jolts through me. I continue my search and walk up to the rooftop to try to find her, but she doesn't seem to be here, either. I should've said bye earlier. Covered my bases. Tied up loose ends. Now she's somewhere in the city, an unspoken good-bye between us.

"I had given you an F-minus for leaving without saying anything," a voice I now recognize says behind me.

I spin around, a smile widening on my face. Rooney peers up at me from behind her bangs.

"I have your pen," I say, handing it to her.

Rooney takes her pen from my hand. "For this, you get a B-plus. I thought you left."

"I thought *you* left," I say, relieved.

"I was in the kitchen loading up on more tāngyuán. It's red bean filled. My favorite." She dips a shallow porcelain soup spoon into a bowl filled with liquid and a small mound of perfectly round, Ping-Pong–size rice balls. "You want one?"

I shake my head. "I don't usually eat after seven thirty."

"A.m. or p.m.?" she asks, keeping her face fixed.

I let out a short laugh. Rooney seems to have this effect on me. "I filled up on the cheese and charcuterie boards earlier. I've heard there's good food here, but I didn't get to explore much. I leave tomorrow."

Suddenly, Rooney looks concerned. "Already? What were you here for?"

I feel my smile fall. "A work thing. But I'd rather not talk about it."

"Right. Long day. I get it. I don't want to talk about work, either. Can we just agree right now that anything work related is off-limits? It's officially a rule, okay?"

"Deal."

"Great." She goes in for a bite and a half-eaten rice ball rolls down her coat. "Fudge!"

I look closer at where the red bean dripped out. "Luckily it blends in. Sorry," I quickly say before realizing where I was looking. "I wasn't trying to look at your—" I clear my throat as heat rushes to my face.

Rooney smiles coyly. "I was gonna say, Jack," she teases, "it's fine. I made this. I can always make another one." She rubs at the spot with a napkin.

"I've never met someone who knits their own winter coat and scarves," I admit.

Her face lights up with a grin. She's always either smiling or laughing.

"And I've never met someone who doesn't eat solids after the sun goes down," she says. "What about liquids? Are those okay?"

I consider her question. "Depends on what kind."

"Papaya juice? There's a Gray's Papaya nearby," she says.

I nod in agreement, remembering the advertisement I was handed earlier. Those flyers really do work.

"Should we try to figure out who the host is and say thanks before we go?" I ask.

"Normally, I'd say yes, but we'd probably be here all night," Rooney says with a shrug. "For all I know, you could be the host."

In the elevator, Rooney pulls a—surprise—red knitted hat over her head.

I hold in a smile. "Do you have a fascination with crustaceans or something?"

She looks genuinely confused. "What do you mean?"

"Are you aware that you're practically dressed head to toe in red?" I ask with a laugh. "With your hat, coat, mittens, and scarf, you look like a cooked lobster."

Rooney gasps. "I was going for more of a crab look, but I'll take lobster," she says, side-eyeing me. She can't hold in her laugh. Her body forms a comma as she tilts forward in laughter. A momentary pause, as though she might keep laughing.

We burst out from the warmth of the building into the freezing cold night. In a matter of minutes, my bones feel solidly frozen.

The light of the building streaks down onto her face, emphasizing the moles on her cheek.

"What is it?" she asks, wiping her face with her mittened hands. "Red bean?"

"No, sorry," I say, breaking my attention from her face. "You have...the Big Dipper on your cheek. I didn't mean to stare."

"I do?" she asks.

"May I?"

She nods. I slowly attempt to trace one point to another with the fingertip of my glove. Time stretches with each zig and zag. I can feel Rooney's eyes on me. I focus my gaze from her cheek to her eyes, the connection a shot of adrenaline.

Rooney scrunches her nose. "Jack, when's the last time you washed that glove?"

I cringe. "I found it in a storage box, so I couldn't say for sure."

She analyzes my face. "You have the Milky Way on yours. Would you like me to show you?" She proceeds to drag her mittens across my face as she vibrates with laughter. I laugh, too.

"Yeah, that was weirder than I thought it would be," I say, catching my breath.

Something above my head draws her attention. "Look! One of the lanterns."

I follow the direction of her hand up over the nearest building and search for a bag of fire shooting across the sky like a comet. But there's no fire. Just a paper lantern bobbing up and down against the darkened ocean of a sky. Making its way...somewhere.

Everything about that rooftop launch went against how missions should be. It was the sloppiest takeoff of my life. But perhaps the most beautiful.

Rooney pivots in my direction, reaching out to grab my upper arm. "Maybe it's ours," she says excitedly. "I thought I saw a dent in it."

Where I'd typically tense at the touch, my body doesn't react. Like this is a normal occurrence. As though she's touched me there a thousand times before.

Rooney lifts her hand off my coat and takes a step back. I glance down at her, keeping my head angled up. The sidewalks are illuminated enough for me to see her blush.

"It can't be ours. We released it almost an hour ago," I say confidently.

"Let's follow it."

I should *not* go on a wild lantern chase with this woman. Especially not one without any sort of plan in place. I *should* go back to the hotel. I still need to pack for my early flight tomorrow morning.

But for some mysterious reason, I don't want to. I don't want this night to end right now.

"Unless you're too tired?" Rooney asks.

"I'm not tired at all," I lie. But it's not completely untrue. A third wave has hit me. I'm more energetic than I've been all day. I check my watch—7:35 p.m. What am I doing? "This will be like trying to find the end of a rainbow. Though now that I have an idea of who you are, I'm pretty sure you've tried to find the end of a rainbow before."

Rooney grins. "Every time I see one."

"Any luck?"

She tilts her head, indicating for me to follow. "Come with me, and we'll find out together."

Chapter 6

ROONEY

The lantern floats faster than expected. Jack and I are speed-walking down the sidewalk toward downtown, carefully dodging icy patches and people. We move as quickly as our frozen joints will allow. I keep one eye on our Paper Star guiding us where we're meant to be and one eye on Jack, who's doing a decent job at keeping up.

When the lantern disappears behind a building, I immediately turn left at the crosswalk, pulling Jack with me by his arm. It's the fourth time we've touched tonight. There are layers upon layers of fabric to prevent our skin from actually touching, but there's still something about the making contact part.

Fifteen minutes in, we've lost track of our lantern, and our fast-paced walking has made me sweaty. As soon as we stop moving, the cold sets in.

"Let's stop there," I say, pointing to a hotel.

"Yes, great," Jack huffs. "I didn't realize I signed up for a marathon."

"This is what you do in the city. You walk. This is our first hotspot of the night." We tuck under a covered hotel entrance canopy where heat lamps are mounted into the underbelly of the awning. It's like stepping under an electric fire, a heat bubble protecting us from the cold. I exhale in satisfaction. I pull up directions on my phone to pose as lost tourists instead of freezing strangers stealing free heat. It seems to work. The doorman nods to us as we linger before refocusing on the hotel guests waiting for taxis and taking the warmth for granted.

"This is strangely satisfying," Jack says, lifting his face up toward the heat lamps. "You call this a hotspot?"

I nod. "They're the spots around the city that keep you warm. I found them as a kid. I know all of the different types. When you're outside a lot, you find ways to stay warm."

"Life in Los Angeles was very different," Jack says. "My Gōng Gong took me to the beach often. We'd eat ice cream and snorkel."

"Did you wait thirty minutes in between?"

"Never. There may have been times I ate ice cream *while* snorkeling," he says, the corners of his mouth twitching into an almost-smile. "Have you ever snorkeled?"

"Once. In Hawaii. I traveled a lot with my mom. She took the afternoon off so we could try it," I recall.

Jack loosens the scarf as heat radiates down on us. "My parents traveled a lot, too. But I didn't go with them."

"What do you think we would think about each other if we met as kids?" I ask.

Jack tilts his head in thought. "Honestly? I likely would've been so focused on my studies that I may not have noticed you. But if I did, I probably would've thought you were cute." He immediately clears his throat after that last word. "Why? What would you think?"

I smile, still lingering on the idea of him thinking that I was cute. "I probably would've asked to wear your snorkel gear. Then I would've gone to an art museum to see what the paintings looked like through the goggles."

"They do give us the ability to see other worlds," he says, nodding.

I peer into the sky, on the lookout for our lantern. What I think might be our lantern appears overhead. I stretch my hands out in front of me. "Can you feel your fingers yet?" I ask Jack.

He holds out his gloved hands. "Barely."

"I see movement. You're good. Come on!" I say, pulling Jack by the forearm. He stays close as we navigate the streets.

Another twenty or so minutes later, we're in Hell's Kitchen, having sprinted down Ninth Avenue in pursuit of our lantern. Another building obstructs our view. Just when I think all hope is lost, Jack spots the lantern hovering above an intersection. We found it!

We follow its light, stopping abruptly in place when the lantern goes dark. All that's left is a shadow, the dark lantern now succumbing to wherever the wind will take it. Then, in an instant, the lantern combusts into a ball of fire, shooting through the air. It plummets to earth, leaving a streak of light in its wake. Finally it lands in a pile of slush, extinguishing on impact.

"No! Now we'll never know if it was ours!" I scream at the pile of ash.

Jack frowns at the slushy mound and then points to his heart. "We know…in here."

I raise my eyebrows. "But what does it mean that it ended like that? That can't be good."

"That was the closest meteor I've ever seen," he says. "Just a little too close for comfort."

"Yeah, it did look like a meteor, right?" I say.

Jack shakes his head. "No. Not a meteorite. It's just a meteor."

"What?"

"It's just a meteor when a meteoroid enters Earth's atmosphere and burns up, like our lantern. It becomes a meteorite when a meteoroid survives its journey through the atmosphere and hits Earth."

I stare at him for a few seconds. "You just had to explain that, didn't you?"

"I needed to make sure you understood."

"Were you popular as a kid, Jack?"

He tilts his head down. "Not even a little. Not even now."

I nod. "Just had to make sure."

He smirks. "I guess that's the end of the rainbow, then?"

I follow the invisible path from where the lantern went dark up to the building in front of it. On the street level are stairs leading to a bar below ground.

"Maybe that was supposed to happen, after all. This is where it took us," I say, grinning. "Shall we?"

Jack must be curious, because he follows me. We descend the steps to the entrance of Mangetsu Jazz, where there's an old wooden door with muffled music behind it.

"It's like a speakeasy," I whisper quietly to Jack. "How are we supposed to get in?"

Jack reaches over my shoulder and presses the button on the call box. It rings twice before a woman answers with, "Passcode, please?"

Jack and I lock eyes, as if the answer will be there.

"Full moon?" Jack says tentatively.

Two seconds later, there's a buzzing noise, and then the door clicks. Success.

My jaw goes slack. "What…how? Are you serious? We're in!"

"Mangetsu means 'full moon' in Japanese. It was a lucky guess."

"You speak Japanese?" I ask.

Jack holds the door open to let me pass through first. "My dad is Japanese and Chinese American. He tried to teach me and my mom Japanese. My mom speaks some Chinese because of my Gōng Gong, but my grandma, who was White, only spoke English. All I remember from both languages are basic greetings, numbers, and random words like 'swimsuit' and, apparently, 'full moon.'"

"Clearly words that come in handy during crucial moments," I say. "My mom and I are trying to learn Chinese. It's tough."

I squeeze past him into the intimate, dimly lit room. Even at first glance, I can tell this place is magical. Immediately, we're met with aromas of smoked wood and whiskey. The space is a saving grace for its warmth. Candles flicker in votives on small round tables covered in checkered cloth. The mirrored bar is fully stacked with Japanese whiskeys and sake. Table lamps are the main source of light, creating a relaxed ambiance for settling into the evening.

The bar is packed for a Tuesday night, but there's one last table for two. We shake off the cold and slide into chairs across from each other, amused by our good luck. I soak in the atmosphere. Squeezed into the far corner is a two-person band—one pianist and one bassist—pouring their souls into the music. It's a lively sound.

"Yummmm," I groan, flipping the paper menu over in my hands. The menu is full of small plates like Japanese-style fried chicken, curry and rice, seaweed salad, and a couple of dessert options. "If I had to eat one thing for the rest of my life, it would probably be rice."

Jack looks surprised. "That's probably the least practical food choice for a lifetime of eating," he says before pausing. "But I love rice, too."

Our first similarity. I store that piece of information in my mind, collecting details about him like rare treasures.

The waitress swings by to take our orders, depositing a metal cone filled with breadsticks on the table.

"These are sprinkled with seaweed!" I have never before been this excited over a breadstick. I twist one between my fingers and admire it, the nori as small as confetti and dotting the dough like terrazzo.

We each order onigiri with different fillings—salmon for me, chicken for Jack—yuzu and ginger mocktails, and red bean ice cream for dessert.

Having mostly thawed, I unbutton my coat and drape it across the back of the chair. Jack does the same. Without the scarf and his puffy coat, I can see more of him for the first time. He's wearing a thick sweater over a blue button-down. From what I know about Jack so far, this outfit doesn't surprise me in the slightest. He seems like a rule-following professional through and through. He stretches up straighter in the seat. Jack still towers over me sitting down, so I'd peg him somewhere around six feet. He's long-limbed, his shoulders broad but not bulky. When he leans forward to place his forearms against the table, I notice the sweater tugging against his waistline. From his shoulders to his waist looks like an upside-down triangle.

Across the room, the pianist stands while playing and turns around to the guests, a big smile on his face. The band plays a slow song and then picks it back up with a couple of fast ones. The vibe in here is contagious. Even for Jack, it seems. This is the longest smile I've seen on Jack's face. At this point, his cheeks must be exhausted.

I sneak in another few seconds of looking at him, memorizing his features. From the print shop's fluorescent lights to moonlight to this bar's warm table lamp glow, the angles of his face change in different settings. What remains the same, though, despite where we are, are his gentle brown eyes.

I tear my gaze away from him right as the waitress is back with our orders, sliding our small plates in front of us along with the fruity mocktails housed in martini glasses.

"To our lantern." I lift my glass, careful not to lose any liquid.

"We can't be sure it was ours. To *a* lantern," Jack corrects me with a charming smile, "that we assigned meaning to and followed relentlessly."

"To fate, for leading us here," I say, quickly tapping his glass with mine before he can add anything more and take a sip. It's a sweet, fizzy blend of citrus and ginger.

Jack leans back against his seat, a skeptical expression hanging on his face. "To fate, huh?"

"Why do you look doubtful?" I ask, bending forward.

"Just the whole fate thing. I feel like I've heard that word too many times today. You believe things in life are predetermined?"

"I believe that there are circumstances and situations that are beyond our control. That certain things in life are already decided for us," I explain. "Like who we're meant to be with."

Jack reaches back to lift one end of the scarf. "Right. The Red Thread of Fate."

I take another sip of my beverage. "We don't know what or who, exactly, until it happens."

"And how can you confirm that certain events are fate's doing?" he asks.

"There are signs."

"Signs," he says as he rubs his jaw in thought. "As in?"

As in us meeting on the night of a full moon. As in us being paired together for our lantern release. As in us seeing each other *again* shortly after losing each other at the party. Like we're following the same path.

But I don't say any of that, of course. It would be too much too soon. To confirm that he's the man on the other end of my red string, I need more signs.

After my stretch of silence, he asks another question. "How do you quantify fate?"

A laugh spills out of me, and I split my disposable wooden chopsticks apart with more force than I intended. "You can't quantify fate, Jack. It can't be measured."

"Sure you can," he says, like it's completely obvious. "Otherwise how do you know it's actually fate at work?"

"Fine. I'll play along. Let's take the lantern that we spotted, as an example," I say, sticking to safer territory other than love. "If we hadn't gone outside, we wouldn't have seen the lantern. The lantern could've blown anywhere, yet it brought us here."

"It could've brought us to a different restaurant," Jack says, waving his hand around. "Who's to say this is the quote-unquote fated place to be?"

"Did you just say quote-unquote?" I ask, amused. "Typically you use your fingers to convey that."

"Mine are still thawing," he says with a glimmer in his eyes.

I poke at my onigiri with an uneven chopstick. "Look at this place. You had to guess a code—correctly, might I add—to even get inside. You think that just happens?"

Jack crosses his arms against his chest, relaxing into himself. The musicians are still playing upbeat music, energizing the entire place. "We chose to go outside. We chose to follow that lantern. We chose to try this bar out. There was nothing forcing us in. I felt no tug or pull or sudden epiphany or moment of clarity."

"It's the timing of life, Jack. If you had left that print shop even three seconds earlier, we wouldn't have met." I hadn't even considered this morning until just now. More signs? "If you hadn't been late to the party and come solo, we wouldn't have been paired together. Should I keep going?"

Jack smiles like he's figured something out. "Okay. There. See. Timing is everything."

Under the small table, I can feel his knee bouncing up and down against my leg. The connection point sends a shiver down my spine. When he doesn't elaborate, I give in. "You clearly want to say something about it." I sigh dramatically for effect. "Tell me. Hypothetically speaking, how would you do it? How would you measure fate?"

Jack grins. "It's less about a mathematical equation type of measurement and more about operationalizing. In my world, we have tests. If I were testing fate, I'd say you could assess it by showing up too early or too late to a place you're supposed to be. You do that. You see what happens."

"But when you decide to show up early or late, you're making a choice. Your logic makes no sense." I take a bite of my onigiri.

"Doesn't the act of putting yourself in a situation, whether you're early or late, still have fate at play? You don't know what's going to happen when you get there." Jack lifts his onigiri with his chopsticks. Before he takes a bite, he has more to say. "Take the example you yourself gave. I showed up late to the party. You were early. We were paired together."

Satisfied with himself, he finally takes his first bite. "Wow. That's delicious," he mumbles.

I tap my chopsticks together. "If I chose to show up late after you had arrived, we wouldn't have been paired."

"You don't know that."

When I'm silent a beat too long trying to figure out his reasoning, Jack tilts his head toward me. "I hope I haven't offended you. I just think we determine the outcome of our lives. Every day, we make decisions. Every day, these decisions yield results. You call it fate. I call it choice."

"It takes a lot more than expressing your opinion to offend me, Jack. Take that last breadstick and you'll offend me, though," I say with a grin before enjoying my last bite. "But you're not changing my mind."

"I can respect that," he says.

The music increases in speed, the pianist and bassist really putting their skills on full display. It's easy being around Jack. Some could call us strangers. Technically, we are, having known each other for just a few hours. And yet there's something familiar about Jack that gives me the sense I've known him for longer, as though meeting him was like stumbling upon a new piece of art that feels like I've seen it a thousand times before.

Savory gives way to sweet when our red bean ice cream comes. I take a bite, letting the ice cream melt slowly on my tongue.

"This ice cream is thick. Very creamy. No weird aftertaste or coating on my tongue. That tastes like fresh whole milk," Jack evaluates.

I point my spoon at him. "You're like an ice cream sommelier."

He takes another bite for a second round of assessment. "It's something I like to do."

"Eat ice cream? Same," I say.

"Well, yes. Eating. But also making."

"Do you have your own shop? Is that what you do? Is that why you're here? You're scouting locations for a new ice cream place!" This excites me a lot. "You said you have tests in your world. Like ice cream taste tests?"

"Nope. Nothing like that," he says with a laugh. "I do like experimenting with making different ice cream flavors, though. Different measurements. See what results."

"Like an ice cream scientist."

He drags his spoon along the bottom of the bowl. "Let's go with that. Here's some ice cream science for you: when ice cream melts, it tastes sweeter than when it's frozen. Frozen ice cream numbs the tongue. Melted ice cream doesn't, so you taste more of the sugar when the ice cream is melted."

I stare at my ice cream in disbelief. "Now that I know that, it sounds so obvious. My mind is also kind of blown," I say, taking another bite to test out this fact.

"That's not throwaway science, Rooney! That fact is relatable to your life," Jack says, tapping his fingers against the spoon in his bowl.

I laugh while watching his fingers move to the rhythm. "Are you playing the imaginary guitar?"

He hides his hands in his lap. "Imaginary double bass."

"Don't stop! Keep going. It was beautiful."

The music stops as the band takes a break. The temporary soundtrack to our conversation becomes the sound of glassware and ice clinking against tumblers.

He raises his eyebrows. "Show's over."

I wait for his fingers to reappear. "Are you in a band?"

"Definitely not. I play on my own for fun," he says.

"So you play that," I ask, nodding toward the large wooden bass. "Or electric?"

"Yeah. Like that one," he says, slightly wavering.

"Show me."

"It's not like I can whip out a bass and play," he says with a grunt.

An idea forms. "Be right back."

When I leave the table, I watch Jack study the drink menu. With his back turned, I introduce myself to the bass player and explain my situation. She agrees to my plan, and I float back to the table to let Jack know the good news.

"Get ready to play," I say casually.

Jack looks up at me, his face unchanged. "Play what?"

"That." I gesture widely toward the band corner, where the upright bass awaits.

A mix of terror and excitement moves across Jack's face. "They wouldn't allow that. You're testing me."

I give him my best smile. "That seems to be the theme of the night. I talked to the band. The bassist agreed to let you use her bass. Just don't pop a string."

Jack wiggles his fingers in anticipation. "I didn't plan for this." He looks from the bass to the diners, his face flushed.

He'll never do it. Unless my read on him is completely wrong? Does this serious, by-the-book man actually have it in him to go up in front of strangers and play an instrument? I really hope so.

"If it makes you uncomfortable, of course I'm not going to pressure you," I tell him.

"Would going up there to play make you happy?" he asks.

"More than you'll ever know."

Jack gets up from his seat and walks over to the corner, whispering to the pianist. He positions himself behind the double bass, taking a second to admire the instrument. He avoids making eye contact with anyone as he begins to pluck.

And now the joke's on me. He commands the bass effortlessly.

Jack knows the chords by heart, his fingers moving fast and smooth across the strings. They're playing Billie Holiday's "What a Little Moonlight Can Do," and it's perfectly upbeat. Despite the catchy tune and his graceful playing, Jack still looks nervous. All eyes are on him, and it doesn't seem like this is something he's used to.

Everyone continues eating their meals while some occasionally clap and shout, "Yes!" I snap my fingers, moving my shoulders up and down to the music. His mouth forms a firm, focused line, and he keeps his attention trained on the floor in front of him.

He looks up at me for the briefest moment, and our eyes connect. Suddenly, we're smiling at each other, and I swear time slows down. The music becomes drowned out, like a passing siren moving farther and farther away.

Then, all at once, out of nowhere, like drifting into sleep or love, Jack is transformed. He and the band effortlessly transition into their second song together. The stiffness of his posture melts into a slight hunch over the instrument. He closes his eyes, and his face relaxes, the hard angles of his nose and jaw softening.

The music around me comes back in full force, as loud as ever.

Jack's not an amateur. He's good.

Within seconds, he's breathed new life into the rhythm of the bar. My heart picks up a beat watching Jack lose himself in the music. Now they're playing a double-time version of "It's Only a Paper Moon," the notes filling the air. I find myself singing along to the music with a few other people at nearby tables.

When Jack opens his eyes, he looks directly at me again. I'm still singing along to the music, knowing most of the lyrics. Jack shoots me another smile that practically screams, *How absolutely wild is this?*

And it is. Everything about this night is absolutely wild.

The man up there is not the Jack I met at the print shop or on the rooftop. This one's more alive, less reserved.

I get out of my seat to dance with an older gentleman who's swaying to the beat and clapping along. He takes my hand in his and gives me a twirl. I spin out, feeling the fullness of the chords reverberating through me.

Jack leans forward toward the microphone positioned in front of the bass and opens his mouth slightly.

He isn't...

It's a hesitation so slight, I almost miss it. Then I hear his voice singing along with my own, his low register booming out of a speaker on the bar. "It wouldn't be make-believe if you believe in me," he sings. He's off-tune, and his voice cracks every other line.

He may be a professional musician, but he is not a professional singer. It doesn't matter. The fact that he's singing at all is charming as hell and, in all honesty, might be the most enchanting thing I've ever been witness to.

Only three minutes have passed, but it might as well have been thirty years. I fully lived each second of that song. Jack looks like he's about to burst at the seams with excitement. He shakes the pianist's hand and returns to the table. He leans back in the chair and chugs half his glass of water, smiling at me with a shine in his eyes. "Thank you for that."

I shake my head at him, my cheeks aching from smiling so much. "And you don't believe in fate."

Chapter 7

JACK

Outside the jazz club, small flurries blow around in the wind. It's as though New York City has been turned upside down, and the snow doesn't know where to land.

It's 9:28 p.m.

"Do you have to go?" Rooney asks, catching me looking at my watch. A dusting of snow gathers on her shoulders.

I linger near her. "What's the alternative?"

"We can walk."

"Just...walk around?" I ask. "Do you have a plan? Are there any places you want me to see?"

"That's the beauty of the city," Rooney says, holding her hands up toward the skyscrapers. "You don't need a plan. Life will unfold in front of us, depending on which corner we turn down. I'm always discovering new places this way."

"So, no plan." I prefer plans. No, I require them. I need to know how long something will take. When can I expect to be back at my hotel? Is where we'll be walking safe? There are too many unknowns without a plan. And yet. "You're not too cold?"

She shakes her head. "Not if we walk fast enough. Trust me, this'll be fun."

I pinch my eyebrows together. I don't trust. I verify. Every last measurement. Every last approach. Every potential problem. And I have a sneaky suspicion Rooney could be a problem. A cute problem. I never know what to expect from her. But that's part of the allure. I want to figure her out, understand her mysteries and every inch of her unknowns.

I'm still riding my high from the jazz club. "Trust you? I guess I'll have to. As long as the lights are still on." I nod up at the full moon before snapping my fingers and singing, "*Oooh*." Rooney joins in on the snaps and "*oooh-*ing."

"You really can play," she says, the beginning of a smile forming. The constellation on her cheek lifts when her mouth grows wider.

I drag my focus from her smile to her sparkling eyes. "The truth is, I'm an even better singer."

"I don't know how you're not headlining concerts," she says as we stroll down the block aimlessly. "Unless you are...are you a professional musician?"

"I'm flattered," I say. "I started playing the bass and cello in high school. It's an instrument designed to collaborate. I liked that."

She nods slowly. "A real team player."

She's the only one who seems to think so.

"I like being part of something bigger than myself," I reveal.

"So there is a band."

I tuck my hands into my pockets. "Not quite. I play for me, not for others. Certainly not in public like that. In fact, I haven't played in front of anyone since I was a teenager."

She gently bumps me. "The world deserves to know your talent."

I grin at her. The buzz from the performance still has control over me. It was a bar full of people. Yet there was only Rooney.

"How far is Times Square from here?" I ask.

Rooney laughs. "You don't want to go there."

"Isn't that quintessential New York? I can't come to the city and not visit it." I soak in the view of all the buildings towering over us.

She breathes in deeply. "That's exactly what you should do. Trust me. Don't ever go there."

I stand firmly in place and cross my arms. "I want to go to Times Square."

"Jack, have you ever been punched in the face before?" She sounds serious.

"No."

"Would you ever ask someone to punch you in the face?"

"Why would I do that?" I ask.

"That's essentially what you're asking me to do," she says.

"I want to see if Buzz Lightyear is there," I insist. "Let's just swing by and check."

"'Just swing by and check,' he says," Rooney mumbles. She shakes her head and barrels past me as I follow her. "This goes against everything I know to be true."

I think for a moment, recollecting our conversation from the jazz bar. "What if your string-soulmate—is that what you'd call them?—is in Times Square at this very moment?"

"I highly doubt that," she says with a grunt. "And I call them stringmates. But not plural. Just one. One stringmate. That's it." She purses her lips and looks away from me. Is she blushing?

"Right. Stringmate. Maybe the fact that you don't want to be there means that you should be there. To see what fate has in store."

Rooney looks back at me with curiosity. "Are you back to testing fate?"

I consider this. "Why not? Another way to test fate is to...say yes to something you normally wouldn't."

Rooney is quiet for a beat. "I played along earlier so why stop now? The only way I'm doing this is if we move quickly and you don't stop for photos."

I feel a small smile form. "Sure. No photos, plural. But maybe just one."

Times Square is a vibrant and bright intersection with restaurants, theaters, and shops. It's the heartbeat of a city that I'm certain, despite the slogan, does fall asleep. Billboards featuring the latest shows and music hang above us. Digital signs flash and vie for our attention. It's sensory overload as we wind around tourists taking photographs and holding Playbills.

"I can't believe I almost missed this because of you!" I shout to Rooney over honking cars and music blasting from street vendors.

She stays close to me, keeping her arms tucked to her sides. "You're enjoying this?"

"I feel alive!" I shout, lifting my hands in the air. I take in every sign and Broadway marquee. "Rooney! Come here!"

"Do you see Buzz?" she asks, her expression hopeful.

I grab Rooney by the shoulders and spin her around to face me. "Don't look now."

"What is it?" she asks, panicked. Slowly she turns around and bursts into laughter when she sees the Red Lobster restaurant sign. "You're sick."

"You're safe with me, Lobster Girl."

Rooney smiles and rolls her eyes. "You really love this that much? If you're okay with getting punched in the face, you okay with getting kneed in the groin?"

"Let's see what you've got," I say.

Rooney leads me into a souvenir shop where the windows are lined with T-shirts featuring catchy slogans and the "I Heart New York" logo. Half a dozen racks showcase hats, mugs, stickers, license plates, and keychains, all trying to capture the essence of New York City.

Rooney holds up a pen in front of her. "I used to have floaty pens as a kid! You don't see them as much nowadays," she says as she tilts the end of the pen toward the ground. She flips it upright and turns it to show me. I watch as the Empire State Building floats from the top of the pen down toward the tip. "My two friends met when one of them returned the other's lost pen. Now they're married. It looked like this but had the Leaning Tower of Pisa instead."

"Who knew someone would care so much about a lost pen?" I shake a mini snow globe keychain. Glitter falls over New York City. "This has my name on it. Let's see if they have yours."

"You think they'll have a keychain with my name on it?" she asks. "I'll bet you a million dollars they don't have it. Easiest money I've ever made."

"There are some interesting names out there. You might be surprised. And if they don't, it's their loss in profit. You have a great name," I say, searching carefully through the rack. "I'd buy all of the Rooney snow globes if I could."

Rooney gazes up at me through her eyelashes and smiles. "Thanks. Apparently, it was an Irish ancestor's name on JR's side. JR is my biological father." She runs a finger along the metal loops of the keychains. "It was generous of my mom to give him any input at all. My first name was decided before I was even born."

This feels like a potentially loaded statement, but she's still smiling and said all of this so nonchalantly. I decide not to make it a bigger deal by asking questions.

"I have a soft spot for snow globes and actually have a pretty extensive collection," Rooney shares. "When my mom and I went on trips, we'd get one of the city we were in. Would your parents bring back souvenirs?"

"Actually, no. There weren't gift shops where they went. But that sounds really nice," I tell her. I search through each snow globe keychain. She's right. Her name is nonexistent. "I guess you're right. Sorry."

"I've accepted the fact that I'll never have my name on a license plate or keychain," she says. "Don't let that stop you from getting one, though. I'm getting this pen!"

I clutch the snow globe in my palm. "As a memento for this trip."

"Yes. A memento." Another grin takes over. Somehow seeing her happy makes me happy.

I pay for my "Jack" keychain, as well as her floaty pen. We keep walking with our new souvenirs in tow. Just a few blocks outside of Times Square, we're back in the darkness.

"Why did you bring me there? That was horrible," I joke. "Aren't you glad you said yes?"

"I'll admit it was better than I anticipated," she says, "even though we didn't get your picture with Buzz."

"Or find your stringmate," I add. Saying this out loud feels weird for some reason. I don't think I like it.

Rooney raises her eyebrows. "I don't know. Did you see Elmo? We look like we're made for each other," she says with a laugh.

"Now that's the picture we should've gotten. I guess toys and superheroes have to sleep, too," I say. "New York wouldn't be New York without Times Square. You take it for granted. It's like how we take the moon for granted. There's literally a natural satellite right there. How often do we stop to appreciate that?"

"Not often enough," Rooney says with sincerity.

When we pass by lit storefronts, I see that her cheeks are rosy from the cold and power walking. How did I end up sharing this night with a beautiful woman? I shake off the thought. She's practically a stranger. My pseudo–tour guide. My smart and charming city chaperone.

"What's something cool that you've done?" I ask her.

Rooney laughs. "Wow. Here comes the identity crisis. Uh, I once received painting lessons from this incredible artist who paints these iconic abstract landscapes full of vivid color using objects she finds in nature as her paintbrushes. She even makes her own pigments and paints using colors she finds in the wild like petals, leaves, and berries. Cool, right?"

"Sounds resourceful."

"Long story short, I now have a painting hanging in MoMA. Oh, sorry. That's the Museum of Modern Art."

I chuckle. "I may not know a lot about New York or art, but I do know what MoMA is."

I must look impressed because she quickly explains herself.

"Well, technically the piece is hers. I'm not even credited or anything," she says, waving her mittened hands in the air. "All I did was use daisies to swipe butterfly pea flower paint onto the canvas."

"To represent water?" I ask.

"It was actually for a painting of Mars," she says.

My ears perk up. "So they're not Earth-based landscapes?"

"Not always. The sunsets are blue on Mars. Did you know that? I thought that was the coolest thing," she says, her voice dreamy. "That's why I chose the pea flower."

She's clearly excited by this. I don't have the heart to tell her that I do, in fact, know this about Mars. That it's because of the iron oxide in the atmosphere that scatters the red wavelengths of light, leaving room for the blue light to have its moment.

"Sounds like not all sunsets are the same," I say.

"Like snowflakes," she says, looking up at one that's landed on her dark brown eyelashes.

"I want to see the painting," I declare.

"Too bad. MoMA is closed right now." Rooney reads the street signs. "We're not far from the museum. About eight or so minutes from here."

We pass darkened store windows with steel gates pulled down in front. I'm not used to being out past 10:00 p.m. Seeing the bones of a city without life breathed into it is unnerving. Like intruding on someone when they're not ready for guests.

We cross one avenue over and are no longer alone on the sidewalks. Rooney's pace slows. Her attention is directed toward the large white modern building across from us. MoMA. It's big but unassuming, plopped halfway down the street. Not even on a corner.

"I can't take you into the museum itself," Rooney says, tugging on her hat. "But I've decided to show you My Spot."

We walk the rest of the avenue and down one block around what would be the back of the museum. We cross the street. Rooney makes an immediate left turn into an alleyway so narrow, I almost miss it. A flimsy fence door blocks our path. We don't turn around. Rooney fiddles with the hook and opens the door wide enough for us to fit through.

More illicit activities. Before I can panic or identify security cameras, we've arrived.

It's a small opening tucked between the forgotten back areas of a restaurant and a spa. In the daylight, this space might feel less claustrophobic. In the darkness, there's only light from nearby streetlamps and store signs that probably never turn off.

Despite where it's located, Rooney's Spot is immaculate. There's an ornate metal bench lined up against the side of a brick wall. In the center of a circular patch of grass is a modern sculpture.

"It's called *X Marks The*," Rooney says with a sly smile. She watches as I survey the space.

"Hence it being your Spot."

Literally. It's an outdoor sculpture about three feet high. A steel "X" on a three-dimensional sphere. An "XO" or an "OX" depending on which way you look at it.

"The artist made the sculpture just for this secret hideaway," she says.

"Is it secret if people know about it?" I ask.

Rooney shoots me a look as she settles into the bench that looks unworn by visitors. "Not a lot of people do know. The key to this garden is the knowledge that it even exists."

"Sure. Yep. A mental key," I say. "How do you even know about this place? If it's such a secret and all."

Rooney looks around at the square cutout. "I found it randomly one night as a kid."

"You came here as a kid? Maybe no one knows about it, but there's no way that's safe."

She shrugs. "This city is my home. It's what I know. This Spot was my escape. I would come here when I needed distance from my mom."

I join Rooney on the bench and face her as she talks.

"I spent a lot of time with her growing up," she says. "It was just us two. She was—is—a force. Sometimes she's too much to be around. Topics of conversation usually end up about her." She tucks a loose strand of hair behind her ear. "She always knows what to say about things, always has an opinion. That doesn't leave much room for others who are trying to find their voice."

The veil of Rooney's confident demeanor slips. Her edges start to poke through.

"No. It doesn't," I say, knowing exactly what she means.

"Her star was so bright, sometimes I had to duck for cover. I found that here."

Instead of being a dark, dingy back alley, The Spot takes a new form. A soft place to land among concrete and steel.

"Thank you for sharing your Spot with me," I say. "I won't tell a soul."

"You don't realize how much faith I just put in you, Jack," she says. "In hindsight, that may have been too much responsibility to give you all at once. And too much trust. You're not a journalist, are you? You don't write pieces on What to Do with Twenty-Four Hours in Various Cities around the World, right?"

I lift my left eyebrow. "I can't confirm whether I do or not," I say, "but you can look out for my next piece about New York City and the hidden hideaway near MoMA. It'll be live next week. Let me just take some photos while we're here." I dramatically reach for my cell phone in my pocket.

Rooney's eyes widen, and she pushes my arm playfully. "Try it!"

The sounds of our laughter blend together.

"I can't have a photo to remember this by?" I ask. I press the side of my phone, but it stays dark. "Great, my phone's dead."

"Here," she says, snapping a photo with her phone. "I'll text it to you. But you must swear on your life you won't show anyone. What's your number?"

I tell her my number as she taps it into a new message.

"Was that a five or a nine at the end?" she clarifies.

"Nine. Ends with one nine."

"Oh, okay, hold on." She taps delete a couple of times and retypes numbers on the touchscreen. "There, sent. When you have battery, respond to my text so I know you got it."

"That's great," I say. "Now I have your number, and you have mine. If fate should have it, we'll talk again."

"Ha, ha," she says, shaking her head.

"Or I'll decide to text you back. I guess we'll see."

Once again, she bumps me with the side of her arm. I still don't mind it. "You're gathering quite the souvenirs. Top secret photo of a hidden gem, a snow globe keychain, more memories than you'll probably remember…"

"There's no way I'm forgetting tonight," I say. It's the truth.

She pulls up her own scarf over half her face, covering a grin. "Did you ever have any favorite spots when you were a kid?"

I shift on the cold metal bench. "Me? Oh. I lived with my Gōng Gong for most of the year growing up. It was mostly just him and me."

"When your parents traveled?" she asks.

"Exactly. They were away for work a lot."

She nods. "And his house was your Spot?"

I tilt my head down. "That's a nice way to put it. It was my hide-away, my favorite spot, my literal home away from home."

"Were you given a pet as a distraction?" she asks.

"I wish. I think my parents worried something like that would've fallen on their shoulders when they were home, so it wasn't even an option."

"When I pass dogs on the streets, sometimes I'll pretend they're mine and walk side by side with them for a block or two until it gets weird," Rooney admits.

I'm amused by this mental picture.

Yellow light from a window in the building next door streams down into Rooney's Spot. The light plays off the sharp edge of the "X."

"You're into art," I say, changing the topic.

Her lips form into a subdued smile. "I'm interested in the ways people choose to creatively express themselves."

"That's a fancy way of saying yes." I think for a moment. "There's a Red Thread of Fate–inspired art installation I think you might like. Not sure if you've heard of it."

Rooney's grin flatlines. "What? You saw...an installation?"

"It was near the print shop," I inform her, gesturing above us. I have no idea which way is uptown or downtown. "We can go now. But it might be too dark to see it." I check my watch.

"Oh, uh, that's okay," she says, her voice an octave higher. "I'll check it out."

"Okay. Yeah. I hope you will," I say.

A few seconds pass before Rooney glances up at me. Her face has noticeably brightened. "Jack, have you ever heard of The Dumpling Hours?"

Chapter 8

JACK

Follow me," Rooney instructs after we emerge from the subway station.

"I don't know if I want to follow you anymore. Was that a rat in the subway car?" I ask, willing myself to shake off the thought.

"Absolutely not. It was a hot dog with legs," she says with a shiver. "At least that's what I'm going to keep telling myself. And you should, too."

"I hear those are half-off on Tuesdays," I joke. "So then those weren't cockroaches but little pecans."

She laughs. "Exactly."

I spread my arm out in front of me, directing Rooney toward an invisible pathway. "In that case, lead the way." After a stretch of silence, I add, "Tonight was...unexpected. In many ways. Definitely not part of my plans."

"Or maybe it was," Rooney says, tilting her head.

"Right. Fate," I say, walking closely beside Rooney. "I have to know more about how this works. You make decisions on what food to eat. How did fate come into play there?"

She gives me a face. "Now it feels like you're mocking it. The level of belief in fate varies for everyone."

I put my hands up in front of me. "I don't mean to. I'm genuinely curious about how it works for you. You make me want to under-stand it more, even if I disagree."

"It's something that's been a part of my life from the very begin-ning," she says slowly, like she's being careful with which words she chooses. "Fate guides me in love and work."

"Love and work," I repeat. "The little stuff."

"The littlest," she teases back. "It guides the important stuff. Not what kind of tea I drink. You don't ever feel like you come across opportunities or events or people in your life because you were meant to?"

I walk around an overflowing garbage can on the sidewalk. "I think what we experience is because of decisions we've made in life. We make a lot of small choices every day. Those decisions add up. And those decisions have consequences. Decisions that we made."

"Do you believe in gravity?" she asks.

"It's safe to assume I do." I jump into the air, landing on an icy patch. My foot slides a few inches.

Rooney places her arm under my elbow to steady me, the pres-sure of her forearm on mine making me aware just how close I want her to be. She lifts an eyebrow as though quietly mocking my firm stance on gravity.

"And what is gravity but an invisible force pulling objects—oceans to the moon, you to the sidewalk, stringmates to stringmates—closer together," she poses. "You can't physically see gravity pulling items toward another object, but you trust it's there, working its magic every day." Rooney says this so confidently that it's almost convincing.

I turn to face her and walk backward for half a block. "Sure, we can't see gravity. But we can measure it. Gravitational effects are how we detect its presence. What are the gravitational effects of fate?"

She smiles. "I thought you'd never ask. People finding the person they're meant to be with."

"But how do you know?" I push on.

"Because I believe."

I can feel a frown forming. "It's the ambiguity I have a problem with. Life exists because Earth is the right distance from the sun. Any farther and it would be too cold. Any closer and we'd boil." I look up at the dark sky. "The fact we exist right now is because of the right combination of temperature, oxygen, carbon, nitrogen, and other elements. And, of course, gravity."

"And fate," she says markedly.

"With even the smallest shift in anything that makes up Newton's laws or the rules of atomic physics," I continue, "we'd all be gone or never have existed. The universe evolved in enough time for intelligent life to evolve."

"Everything you just said...how were we not fated to be here?" she asks. "You said it yourself. If anything were different, we wouldn't be here. The stars aligned, and we were destined to exist. To be here in this moment in time."

"All I can say is I'm glad to be here in this moment in time with you."

Rooney peers up at me through her eyelashes. "Even if I look like a lobster?"

I laugh with her. "*Especially* because you look like a lobster."

We cross the street to a nondescript Chinese restaurant with paper signs taped across the front. Drawn toward the restaurant like hungry tourists after a long bus tour. A red, blue, and green neon "Fried Dumpling" sign is displayed in the window. I'm immediately comforted by the thought. The awning features Chinese characters and the restaurant's telephone number, both of which are faded, making them illegible.

"I can eat Chinese food at any time of day, but it's the best late at night," she explains. "Hence why I call them The Dumpling Hours. I swear dumplings are even more flavorful and chewy after midnight... Okay, yep. Let's order a lot of them."

I hold the door open for her as she continues to talk. "Besides corner bodegas, diners, and bars, not much else is open this late. Chinese restaurants are like the North Star. They're always there when we need them. Constant and dependable. They guide us when we're lost, hungry, or just need to get our bearings."

The air is thick with the smell of garlic. "Many people think Polaris—the North Star—is the brightest in our sky," I say, unzipping my jacket to let the warm air in. "But it's not."

"It's not?" Rooney tugs off her hat. Strands of her straight brown hair stand from the static.

I shake my head. "It's also not as constant as we think, but it is the fiftieth brightest."

The constellation on her cheek lifts as she smiles. "I don't know when I can use that, but one day, I'll find somewhere to."

We settle into a vinyl booth across from each other. The yellow walls are covered in black-and-white photos, some with signatures in the corners. Cloth is draped in swoops across the ceiling, the entire place glowing a hazy red.

We're not alone in the restaurant. Two older men strategize over a game of Scrabble and refills of tea. A woman in a yellow safety vest dips a piece of chicken into sauce. In the corner, three college-age students hover over textbooks and their cell phones. It's energetic in here, despite it almost being midnight.

I skim over sections for soups, fried rice, pork, beef, and shrimp. My eyes wander up to Rooney, who's reading the menu like it's a thriller. She's intensely following the plotline of the menu. My mind wanders back to the print shop. Without the surfboarding New

Yorker, I may never have met this amazing person across from me pondering noodle selections at midnight.

"What's funny?" Rooney asks.

I realize I've snorted. "Oh. I'm just impressed by how many fried rice options there are. It's too hard to choose."

She eyes me suspiciously. "Right. Should we just do table dumplings?"

I rescan the menu, looking for what she's referencing.

"It's not on the menu," she adds.

I look at other customers' dishes. "Then how do you know they can make it?"

Rooney laughs. "It's just a double order of pan-fried dumplings. For the table. We'll share."

I flip the laminated page of the menu. "We're going to share dumplings?"

"We'll also share the soy sauce. If that's okay?" she asks.

I can't remember the last time I shared a plate of food with someone. It feels intimate. "Okay. Sure. Good with me."

Rooney lets the waitress know our order while I pour jasmine tea for both of us into little white porcelain cups.

"By midnight, I'm usually sleeping," I admit, setting down the stainless-steel teapot.

"Yeah. In New York City, even when you're at home and everything is quiet, you always know you can go somewhere, anywhere, and find another human being." Rooney slides her teacup closer. "Sure, it's the city that never sleeps, et cetera, et cetera. But you get to claim your corner of the city where and when you want it. Early morning, the middle of the night. On any day of the week. There are no rules. Does that terrify you?"

I grin. "I would rather have a routine during my preferred times of day."

"On days like today, how long will it take you to readjust now that you're off schedule?" she asks.

"I can usually course-correct within twelve hours."

Rooney snaps her fingers. "I had you pegged at nine."

"Ten when I'm feeling particularly motivated," I say playfully.

"I can imagine a routine being nice," she says. "Like the idea of having a coffee shop where they know your order. The city can sometimes feel isolating, but you're never truly alone. I'm sure even in LA this is true. People are always somewhere."

I attempt a very serious face. "You're right. People *are* always somewhere."

Rooney laughs. "Are you taking notes over there? I spew gold at this time of night." She goes quiet for a moment. "So I was thinking about something."

"What's that?" I ask, taking a big gulp of tea.

"How fate comes into play in love and work for me, and the ways you wanted to test fate," she says. "I materialize it in my own way, and you, what was the word you used? You operationalize it. Basically, we're both just trying to understand fate in our own ways. And I think that's beautiful."

"That's a nice way to put it," I say. "I think the tests were coming along nicely. You know, in case you ever wanted to really put fate to the test."

She scrunches her face. "I've lost track of what the tests were. That's not really how my mind thinks. I'm a little more abstract, some would say."

"Okay, here." I pat my jacket for something to write on. Sure enough, I still have a folded-up Chinese menu from the conference. At least it's good for something today.

"What are you—is that a menu for a different restaurant?" Rooney's eyes widen as she looks around the restaurant. "Jack, that's the competition. Do you make it a habit of carrying around Chinese take-out menus in your pocket?"

I smooth the paper menu out on the table. "You never know when the craving for lo mein will hit."

Rooney laughs.

"May I borrow your pen again?" I ask.

She reaches into her bag and holds up our lantern pen and her new floaty pen. "Take your pick."

"Ooh. The one that holds all the power. The Discipline Pen." I make dramatic grabby hands at it, which makes her laugh extra hard. I really like making her laugh.

I pop off the cap and at the top of the menu write: Red String Theory. It merges Rooney's belief and my science background. And a little bit of Red String Girl's installation.

Rooney peers over to see what I'm up to. "Wow. Am I really about to witness operationalizing in real time? I feel like once you write out whatever it is you're trying to capture, the earth's axis might shift. The construct of time as we know it will be altered forever."

"I'm doing this for you," I say, locking eyes with her. "So maybe the first test is...Times Square? Saying yes to something you normally wouldn't." I turn the menu sideways and write this down in the empty column between offerings of egg rolls and sesame chicken.

"Right. The second was...the lantern party. So...show up early or late to somewhere you're supposed to be!" she says excitedly.

I write this down next to Fate Test 1.

Rooney plays with the end of her scarf draped over the chair. "Was there a third? What about the floaty pen story? Returning something."

I flip the pen between my fingers. "I appreciate that you're getting into this," I say. "Even if it's just for fun. This helps me better understand." And I do. I want to understand something so important to her. "But of course, I hope you get to experience fate and find your stringmate in the way you always envisioned it."

Rooney's eyes search my face. "Right. Of course."

"So the third is returning a lost object. I'm still not sure how measurable these all are, but it's a start." These tests definitely wouldn't fly at NASA. But like I told Rooney, this is just for fun.

Rooney taps her finger on the table. "That's it? Just three?"

"Where else do people interact? Online?"

"Like online dating?"

"Sure. I've never done it but that seems to be successful for people," I say.

Rooney twists her lips to one side. "Is that really fate, though?"

I think through the scenarios in my mind. "Sure, why not? You have the timing of when people sign up, whether or not they're in the same city as you. The fact that they aren't too far along into a conversation with someone else."

"You make compelling points," Rooney says. "There's a timing element at play. What about social media? People slide into DMs, right?"

"What does that mean?" I ask, the neon light in the window catching my attention. It briefly flickers.

"Maybe it's better you don't know," Rooney tells me.

I nod. "Chat rooms? Do those still exist?"

Rooney's face lights up. "Probably? So Fate Test 4 can be interacting with someone online. Keep it vague."

The waitress places our table dumplings between us. After Rooney picks out her first dumpling, I lift one with my chopsticks, dip it in soy sauce, and bite it in half. I close my eyes, letting the savory flavors and crispy exterior warm me from the inside out.

"Thanks for the tour tonight," I say when there's a natural lull between dumpling eating. "Or maybe I should say food tour."

Rooney gestures around the restaurant. "For a man who doesn't eat when the stars shine, you did good. This city has a lot of great food to offer."

"It's clear you really love it here."

"I've never loved anything like I love New York City," she says softly. It sounds heartfelt and true. Rooney looks down at the glossy table. "Though I can't say for sure what love would feel like. I've never been in a serious relationship. It's the hope for love one day, though, that inspires me."

This surprises me. I say so.

Our eyes catch. Rooney studies me, her gaze intense. Like the world has been paused for two seconds. Then it speeds up, spinning faster than ever.

I inhale deeply. "I've never been in love, either." I don't say it to mock her or to fill the silence. I've never been in love. "My relationships don't last more than half a year. That's no time for love to take form, whatever love even means. Honestly, I fear it."

"You fear love?" Rooney asks.

I shrug. "Love is so unknown, and I need to know the unknown. I've never met someone who I could feel secure enough with, I suppose. Never met someone who could be there consistently."

Rooney nods, listening intently. I continue talking.

"Being in love seems like jumping into the deep end without knowing how to swim. Or going to space without a crew in Mission Control helping guide you."

"It does seem like that," Rooney agrees. "But I love the unknown because it's hopeful and explorative. You have to take a leap of faith."

I grin. "I prefer knowing where I'm going."

"You took a chance with me tonight chasing our lantern," she says.

"That was not typical for me," I explain, still amazed that I agreed to follow Rooney all over the city. I didn't think anything could distract me from this morning's news and that shitshow of a conference. But then there was Rooney.

"And yet, there you were."

I search for answers in Rooney's eyes. But I think she's looking for them in mine, too. "What if you spend your life chasing your lantern and it ends in a fiery crash?" I ask. "Was the search worth it?"

Rooney's eyebrows rise, disappearing beneath her bangs. "If you knew where your lantern was going, would it be as beautiful of a journey? I like to believe it would lead you to the right spot at the exact moment of where you're meant to be."

The restaurant is quiet, everyone focused on the food in front of them. Even the classical music playing overhead is low on the speakers.

I clear my throat. "Can I ask you something?"

Rooney sets her chopsticks down. "Of course."

I regret having made the moment more intense than it needed to be. I take a deep breath in and ask the question I've been dreading all night. "Where does our lantern take us?"

Chapter 9

ROONEY

It's the question I keep asking myself. Will we ever see each other again? Frankly, I'm surprised to hear him ask it, too. The signs aren't clear enough yet, but the obstacles are pretty obvious: thousands of miles between us and fundamental, contradicting beliefs. Yet it's been so easy being with him.

The thread may stretch or tangle but never break. When the man on the other end of my red string and I are brought together, our strings finally shortened enough to see each other, it won't be a question. When I meet him, I'll know. I thought I'd have a clearer gut reaction when I knew. Is this me knowing? How can I be sure?

I focus on my tea, my mind whirling with thoughts. What could that have possibly meant, Jack wanting to take me to *Entangled*? He didn't give any indication that he thought that I was the artist, and I didn't have the heart to tell him what happened to my art. In his memories, the installation can remain intact. It was too sweet that he wanted me to see it. He thought I'd like it, and he's right. I would've. Oddly, I feel comforted knowing that Jack has seen something so important to me, while it lasted.

Does Jack have a red string tied around his ankle? Even if he did, would it lead to me? I need to sleep today off and wake up tomorrow with fresh eyes and a clear mind. Everything will make more sense in the daylight.

"Rooney?"

"What? Yes. Sorry," I say, breaking free from my thought spiral. I bring my cup up to my lips and blow ripples into the tea, absorbing the heat from the porcelain into my hands. "I don't know where our lantern takes us, but that's the beauty of it. If we knew that everything today was leading to this moment, and we knew where we'd end up—in this exact Chinese restaurant—would you have skipped all of tonight just to be here? Would this moment mean as much? Would that change how we feel about each other?" When I say this, my chest overheats at my bold assumption.

Jack's looking at me with intensity. "You make me want to explore the unknown. I love the idea of taking the scenic route, but could we still use GPS?"

He says this softly and quickly, as though he could take it back at any second.

"We do have each other's phone numbers. Let's see where that takes us," I say, feeling hopeful. Maybe whatever this is between us really can make it to tomorrow. Maybe the daylight will shed golden lights of clarity, and maybe only then will it all become clear. It sounds too good to be true. "Maybe our paths will cross again, Times Square."

Jack holds his hand up against his chest. "That's how you're going to remember me? As Times Square? But you want to punch it in the face. I hope there's a good metaphor or deeper meaning behind that."

"New York isn't New York without Times Square," I admit.

Where Jack once looked hopeful, his expression deflates a little. "It doesn't have as nice of a ring as Lobster Girl. I just—I don't do long distance," he says reluctantly before catching himself. "Not like I was trying to imply anything, of course. Just in the grander scheme of things, it's too hard to be away from people I care about."

"I get it," I say. I have a feeling there's more to this, but Jack doesn't add anything else.

Earlier when we talked about fate, I felt so close to convincing him. If he doesn't believe in it, would we ever truly be able to be together? Really, Rooney? I think there's a world where we can be together? This man I hardly know who lives across the country? Still, I'm hung up on us meeting. Why is this man so different?

Sleep, daylight, clarity, I repeat.

We polish off the dumplings and take the last sips of our tea. Jack folds The Fate Test menu into a perfect square and slides it over to me. An artifact of our night together.

"You should keep this," he says. "Unless you'd really prefer to let fate do its thing. Then we can toss it."

My eyes could burn a hole through the paper with how hard I stare at it. I reach for the folded square, my attention fixed on the words "Hot and Spicy."

I know these Fate Tests won't actually do me any good, but I had fun playing along with Jack. In his way of understanding me better, I also got to know him better. The man who needs operationalizing and tests and measurements. No, tests won't help me find my string-mate. I'll leave that up to fate, but I'll cherish the game for giving us our own inside jokes and more time together. A set of theories that we could use to figure each other out.

I wave the paper in the air. "If only we had this much power over our destinies," I say, attempting to lighten the weight of the reality of our night ending. "I'll keep this. As a memento."

Jack smiles. "Yes. A sweet-and-sour memento."

No more time, no more tests. No more Jack. I tuck the paper into the back pocket of my sketchbook.

Jack signals the waitress for the check and pays for the food with cash, per the restaurant's rules. We head outside, where the air is still and the falling flurries have retired for the night. A light breeze blows the already-fallen snow off tree branches.

Occasional bright yellow taxis roll past us down the avenues, slowing just enough to make their presences known. There's one about every three minutes or so, its roof light blinking on for attention before it disappears out of sight. New York City's version of fireflies.

I check the time on my phone. An ache grows in my chest. Midnight has come and gone, and at some point, we really do both have to go home.

"We're fifteen minutes into tomorrow. How did that happen?" he asks.

"You and your gravity," I say with a playful roll of my eyes.

A smile flashes across his face, and the weight of the moment intensifies.

Fresh snowflakes. Matcha ice cream. Kittens in tiny sweaters. Jack.

Jack here. In front of me but for real this time. Jack with his warm brown eyes and crescent moon lip scar. No longer just in my imagination when I close my eyes. Jack, who has to leave tomorrow morning. Jack, who I know nothing and everything about.

"I guess this is it? The last stop on the food tour," Jack says. "Unless you want more ice cream?"

"You could probably churn me into ice cream right now, it's so cold out," I say.

Jack's cheeks tint. "You would be one delicious ice cream."

We linger outside. How do you say good-bye to someone when that good-bye will be the first and last? Does the situation even warrant one?

"We could walk until we get cold...er," I offer. "Are you cold?"

Jack's visibly shaking but tries to hold still. "Is—is it cold out? I hadn't even noticed."

"You're not tired of me yet?" I ask as we wander the blocks of Chinatown.

"Oddly no. At this point, the law of diminishing returns usually kicks in," he says.

I turn to look at him. "What do you mean?"

Jack moves his hands around in front of him as he speaks. "We can have a great time during hours one, two, and three. But once that optimal level has been reached, it goes downhill from there. Then hours four, five, and six are when we start to get annoyed with each other or are tired of asking and answering questions."

We walk aimlessly down the near-empty sidewalks.

"And you're not annoyed with me? We're on hour, what, five? Six?" I ask, amused.

The corners of Jack's mouth twist up. "I'm not, though that's always a fear with anyone," he says. "You see too much of me at once, I see too much of you. We're over before we even begin. Those dumplings we ate were delicious, but if we ordered another plate, we wouldn't enjoy them as much."

We turn the corner, our shoulders rubbing. "What if there is no limit? What if it's just you telling yourself there is and you set yourself up for disappointment after a certain amount of time?"

"Few things in this universe are limitless, Rooney," he says. "It's why people have coffee or dinner dates. Finite amount of time. Safe. Within the bounds of the diminishing returns. Then you have an out when you're evaluating whether or not you have anything else to say."

"When you look at it that way, everything you do is on a ticking countdown. Where's the room for spontaneity? Long nights like this?"

"Tonight's an exception," he says. "Don't ask me why. I'm still trying to figure it out."

"Well, I like every bite of dumpling equally, no matter how many," I say. "Sometimes things do get better over time."

Jack shrugs. When we turn the next corner, the full moon comes into view. It hangs like a neon sign in space.

He catches me looking at it. "You ever think about how small we are compared to everything out there? Like, we're just casually part of the universe, living on a planet."

I laugh. "I think about it a lot actually. What exists beyond the beyond? What is this all even for?" I spread my arms out, gesturing to the sky. "Our time on Earth is so short compared to the bigger timeline of it all. I want my life to count for something. I want to have an impact on people...on the world."

Jack inhales deeply, his breath visible in front of him on the release. "Yeah. Me too."

I tilt my head back and watch as occasional snowflakes drift toward me, melting on my skin upon impact. "If other life does exist, what do you think they look like?"

Jack rubs his gloved hands together. "They'd have fur covering their skin to stay warm because other planets have their own atmospheres and are different distances from the sun. They'd have big eyes so they could keep on the lookout for danger. They probably have a lot of sharp teeth because their idea of food might not be the same as ours." He says this confidently, as though this isn't the first time he's thought about it.

I nod along, grinning and processing his version of extraterrestrial life. "That was oddly specific."

Jack laughs. "And this is the point where it all starts to go downhill," he says as we find ourselves back at the Chinese restaurant.

"We basically did one big loop," I say, looking around.

"It was a pleasure to loop with you."

"I guess that's the last stop on the tour, for real this time." The disappointment in my voice is a direct reflection of how it feels to be on the verge of good-bye with Jack with no real signal for what will become of us.

I think back on the night and let out a small, sad laugh. Jack and I, we're a meteor. A streak of light burning up before it has a chance to make it anywhere at all. At least, for one night, we got to be a shooting star.

"I guess so," Jack says.

I could be hearing things, but he sounds disappointed, too.

Jack's hotel in the Financial District is in the opposite direction of my Mom's Upper East Side apartment. We agree to take two different taxis back to where we need to be.

A taxi passes by, but neither of us waves our arm. We turn toward each other on the slushy sidewalk.

"Thanks for showing this tourist all your favorite places," he says. We ignore the second cab that passes.

"Next time you're in the city, you know where I'll be," I say. "You just have to use the 'X marks the spot' photo that you're not going to let any other eyes see ever."

I cringe at the realization that My Spot will likely never feel the same without Jack.

"Cross my heart," Jack promises playfully. A third taxi stops in front of us and honks, eager for our business. "You go first." He opens the taxi's door for me.

I rest my hand on top of the door, taking in the scene. Jack's face, Jack's scent, Jack's laugh. Not another second passes before his hand is on my waist, pulling me toward him. Our lips touch gently, like a whisper. It lasts two seconds, maybe three, but it's all I need to know that this man is meant to be in my life more than just tonight.

"See? Sometimes it does get better," I mumble, touching my fingers to my lips as I sink into the backseat of the taxi.

"Maybe sometimes it does," he says.

"Have you ever wondered how many good-bye kisses happen outside of taxis?" I ask, still in a daze.

"This isn't good-bye, Lobster Girl," Jack says, looking equally stunned.

"May our paths cross again, Times Square," I whisper.

Through the back window, I watch Jack step onto the sidewalk and then peer through the glass at me. Twice in one day, I've been separated from things I care about. In the reflection, the green neon restaurant sign glows, the letter "R" blinking rapidly. It finally fizzles out, the absence of the letter shadowing Jack's face before the taxi pulls out into the road. I know I'll read too much into what the disappearing "R" means later.

Two blocks down, I reach for my phone to send Jack another message. Anything to feel connected to him. Minutes later, my phone buzzes with a text. My heart soars before I see what the message says: Thx for the pic earlier, but also weird. IDK who Lobster Girl is, but think u have wrong number.

Then my heart plummets. Wrong number?!

"Turn around!" I call out to the driver, tapping his seat. "Back to the restaurant. Hurry! Please!"

The driver does as I plead. We wind through the empty streets, but we might as well be moving in slow motion. When we round the corner back to the restaurant, it's too late.

The sidewalk is empty. Jack is gone.

I guess this really is good-bye.

Chapter 10

Five Months Later

JACK

I get 1,840,000 results for my search of "dumpling restaurants chinatown nyc open late." I sift through news articles, best-of lists, and dozens of menus. The number of restaurants with neon signs in general in New York City is limitless. At this point, my memory and the hundreds of photos I've seen of Chinese restaurants have blurred into one collage. The only concrete lead I thought I had for finding Rooney was Mangetsu Jazz. Until I remember that I paid. I scour Street View around MoMA like it's a part-time job.

When none of these restaurants jogs my memory, I try yet another search for "Rooney." "Rooney MoMA," "Rooney NYC," and "Rooney tour guide." Any combination I can think to try with her name, I do.

The results give me dozens upon dozens of articles about Rooney Mara and Sally Rooney. No leads, no clues. After the address of the party yielded no name results for owners or renters, my coworker went out of his way to track down the host through his wife's chain of connections. Rooney couldn't have been on the guest list because there wasn't one.

I at least thought Dave at the print shop would come through. But Dave wasn't kidding when he said he was getting out of there as soon as he could, self-imposed or otherwise. Apparently, the mix-up happened for more customers than just me. At the very least, I hope he followed his surfing bliss.

Even though Rooney never texted me and let me kiss her like a fool, still I search. Why did I have to go and make it awkward for everyone by kissing her like that? The way she got into the taxi, just staring at me. I scared her off. That has to be it. I terrified her with my lips and my talk of the law of diminishing returns. It's no wonder why she didn't want to text me. I wouldn't even want to text me.

I feel the start of a tickle in my throat. All of this overthinking is starting to take its toll.

I solve harder problems than this every day at work. Why is this one impossible to figure out? I just want this resolved. I should let it go.

I glance at the calendar on my monitor. Ten minutes until I have my first special committee meeting.

As soon as I got back to work after New York City, I scoured the company's internal websites for opportunities. It's what I do best: take action and put pen to paper.

Performance review feedback runs through my head on repeat. And here I am, without a promotion. The most obvious next step is to do something more social. More visible.

The description for the Artist-in-Residence Mission Liaison role was vague, but I needed to join something big. And this opportunity felt especially relevant to my time on the East Coast. I had just seen an art installation, and I understood what it was about. Art and me? We go way back. A whole five months back.

For the role being voluntary, there were a surprising number of interviews to be part of it. It's taken all the way up from when I first applied back in February until now for me to be selected as mission liaison. It felt good to be picked for a change.

I take a break to grab tea from the kitchenette before the meeting. I'm adding honey when a man I've only ever seen in the hallways reaches past me for a mug. He adds it to a collection of notebooks, figurines, and office supplies in a cardboard box. That doesn't look good.

I head over to the conference room and find a few people already sitting around a table. Behind the glass windows on the far side of the wall are the San Gabriel Mountains. This view from NASA's Jet Propulsion Laboratory never gets old. As a leader in robotic space exploration, JPL is the place where we work on spacecrafts that study atmospheric carbon dioxide and send and receive data from spacecrafts traveling beyond the moon. We run planetary defense missions and keep an eye on asteroids hurtling toward our planet. To me, this is the most magical place on earth. Here, we literally work every day to make far-fetched dreams a reality.

The mountains are brightly lit against the summer sun, the green and brown serving as camouflage. As though they hide in plain sight.

"Jackson, hello. Nice to see you again," says Kenneth Lopez, the director of the newly reinstated Artist-in-Residence program. He stands to shake my hand. Kenneth was one of the people who interviewed me for this role. Last time I saw him, he was wearing a Jupiter-patterned tie. Today his tie is covered in paintbrushes.

"Nice to see you again, Kenneth," I say, returning his handshake.

"As you may remember, this is Margie Kim and Nick Watson. They're on our Office of Communications team doing community outreach and public affairs. We'll loop in the internal communications and social media folks in future meetings. We're all looking forward to working with you as the mission liaison for this program."

"I'm looking forward to it, as well," I say, setting my tea in front of me and taking a seat opposite Margie. The ends of her brown hair are dyed pink.

"We heard you're the one who named the mission," Nick says, sounding impressed. He has a tattoo of Saturn on his forearm.

I nod and open my notebook.

"The Fuel Atomized Technology Equipment," Margie adds. "It's catchy."

"FATE has been a years-in-progress mission, with many more to go," I explain, "but recently we were able to move out of code name status."

When I don't elaborate, Kenneth nods quickly. "Okay. Well, great!"

I make a note to work on how to better explain that to the artist.

Kenneth offers me a thick packet stapled too close to the edge. Under the title page are printed-out slides of a presentation I'm sure I'll see soon.

"The board thoroughly reviewed the various missions happening, and we think FATE is an exciting one that will resonate with the public," he explains. "FATE is a critical component of NASA putting boots on Mars in the next few years. Your equipment helps make the process more efficient."

"I'm happy to hear it will be getting some spotlight," I say. "It's not the most glamorous mission."

Kenneth chuckles. "You're right. FATE itself isn't, but Mars is, and for our social channels and events, we've learned that this project in particular is something the public continues to ask about. Though the artist will be representing NASA and will have the freedom to create anything they want related to what they learn during their time here, you being the mission liaison will help get more eyes on FATE."

I can't disagree there. It's a mission I've most enjoyed working on so far. And there has been a lot of interest.

"If you remember from our initial discussion, in 1962, four years after NASA was established, an art program was created," Kenneth continues. "NASA Administrator James Webb commissioned portraits of every NASA astronaut. He had a vision of combining art and science. He figured that artists like Andy Warhol, Norman Rockwell, and Annie Leibovitz could capture the work we were doing here in a visual way."

Nick jumps into the conversation. "What we do here may seem abstract to the public, and it can be challenging to get through to people and make them care," he says. "Who better than artists to capture the abstract and turn it into something tangible, visual, and understandable?"

I remove Rooney's red pen from my button-down placket and pop the cap on and off. After writing out the Fate Tests on the menu, I forgot to give it back. Now I'm glad I didn't so I can have proof that the night was real—that she was real—and not just a figment of my imagination. I jot down notes on the front page of the packet, the red reminding me too much of her. I really should find a pen with black ink and no trace of Rooney.

I try to refocus on Kenneth talking. "We've had to scale that back over the years because of funding cuts," he says. "Recently, though, we secured grants that allow us to once again merge art and science together in a way that'll bring more attention to the missions we're working on. Artist-in-Residence program 2.0. The reinstatement of this program is a highly visible project. We're not paid, of course, and the artist wouldn't be paid very much, unfortunately, but it's a lot of exposure for the artist and NASA."

"It's hard enough to get funding for missions," I say. "We want as many people on our side as possible."

"Exactly. You'll be working closely with the artist and managing their relationships and logistics," Kenneth explains. "You'll teach them about how NASA operates, as well as the various projects and missions being worked on. You'll also join them on suit-ups. It's important that the artist gets a holistic look at JPL and NASA, and you can field the press's questions about the nuances of FATE."

Me. Mission liaison for a real human artist. For an important NASA program. With millions of eyes watching what we do. Future grants and artist residencies rest on the success of this one.

What was I thinking? There's money on the line. The reputation of the art program is at stake. I'm in this role for the science part, not the art part. I take a sip of my honey tea to ease the rising tickle in the back of my throat.

"Sounds educational," I say, attempting to exude confidence. I turn away and sneeze into the crook of my elbow. "Excuse me."

"Bless you! Now let's move into the fun part!" Nick says, grabbing the remote to turn on the projector attached to the ceiling. "The agenda for today, in addition to officially kicking off this program, is to decide on an artist. The one you recommended as part of your application looks very interesting."

Margie taps a button on her laptop's keyboard. A cover slide for their presentation appears on the screen at the front of the conference room. "Because it's important that this program is a success," she says, "and because you'll be working directly with the artist, we thought it imperative to include you in the decision-making process."

"Me?" I ask. "Like I said, I don't know much about art. I was happy to recommend an artist. I'm not sure I'm qualified enough to help decide, though."

"In a way, that's the point," Margie responds with a reassuring smile. "We don't expect the public to know the nuances of the art being created. Our job is to find the artist who can tell the story of our work here in a way they'll understand. Take a look at these images and see what speaks to you. Who would best tell the story of NASA?"

"The artist you recommended made it into the round of finalists, but you don't know the artist personally, right? It shouldn't be an issue, but this information is important to know up front so we're making a fair decision," Kenneth says.

The woman handing out sketchbook paper at the installation comes to mind. But there was no way I could confirm that she was Red String Girl.

I shake my head. "I don't know who Red String Girl is. This artist works anonymously."

Nick rubs his hands together. "NASA is all about discovery. This time, instead of discovering something new in space, we're discovering talent right here on Earth. What a thrill."

I attempt to mirror Nick's excitement by giving him a thumbs-up. It comes off as awkward as one would expect. I reach for the red pen to keep my hands busy.

"Let's review our top three contenders," Margie says, pressing another button.

I direct my attention to the screen. Margie guides us to the next slide featuring an artist who specializes in charcoal drawings. From a distance, they look like photographs while maintaining a not-quite-real quality. It's stunning how an entire image can be conveyed through varying shades of gray. But this doesn't feel comprehensive enough.

Without overthinking it, I find myself saying, "There's a nostalgic element to this artist's work. A throwback to the original astronaut portraits."

The group nods in response and take notes on their packets.

The next few slides reveal the paintings of an artist who doesn't just capture people and places but who paints their souls into them, too. I see how the vibrant colors of the paint could capture a person's imagination. This artist could be interesting.

"And now, your recommendation, Red String Girl," Margie says.

Pictures of *Entangled* shine on the screen ahead. The installation is as impressive as it was when I first saw it. A familiar sinking feeling weighs on me when Margie shows us the next photo of *Entangled* in cut-up piles. I stand and lean forward to get a better look at the images, my fingers spreading across the conference table. I look at the timestamp of the article. I still can't believe I was so close to seeing this in heaps instead of as the artist intended.

"Looks like it was taken down that same morning," she says, reading off a news article that's also projecting on the screen.

I think of sitting with Rooney in her Spot. How I encouraged her to go see it. She never would've been able to. I probably sounded like I had made up the whole thing. Sometimes it feels like I made up the entire night.

I've witnessed this piece of art in what feels like another life. No. Another dimension. But how I know it is, in fact, real is that I have a piece of the installation in my wallet, documenting that short-lived moment in time. At this point, it's probably something worth recycling. And yet, the wrinkled note stays where I put it that day.

"I saw this in person before it was taken down, which is why I recommended the artist. The piece changes as you interact with it. It's tangible," I explain. "I liked the incorporation of science into the work."

"Looks like it also integrated fate," Kenneth says, referencing his notes. "The interplay of fate with FATE is cheeky. There's something there. Maybe the artist will be inspired by that."

Next to the photograph of *Entangled* is a sketch of a different Red String Girl installation. Margie taps to the next slide with more information.

"We pulled this from Red String Girl's website. There was a list of other installations that she's done over the years, but there were only photos of *Entangled*. And there's this concept sketch of one called *Gravity*."

The sketch depicts an island platform between subway train tracks, the string forming a grid with a giant heart in the center. It hovers above a string-made dip that looks like the downward momentum of a bounce on a trampoline.

"If gravity is the curvature of time and space—" Nick starts.

"Then love is the curvature of time and place," I finish.

Margie gasps. "That's why it's at the subway station! It's the beating heart of the city."

"How very clever," Kenneth says. "Subways literally push and pull people through the city. Sometimes we just pass by each other, and sometimes we're on the same train."

The conversations Rooney and I had over the course of our night come back to me. "Gravity is invisible, but we can measure it. What are the gravitational effects of fate but people being pulled toward their destined soulmates?" I ask out loud.

"Jackson, that's beautiful," Nick says, sounding surprised.

"No, that's—" I start.

"And you said you don't know anything about art!" he exclaims with enthusiasm. "If that's what this sketch made you feel, imagine what an entire in-person string art installation will do to you."

Margie hums as she thinks. "This is compelling, but just to voice what we're all probably thinking, is anyone else concerned that Red String Girl only has photos of one installation? She hasn't done anything new since"—she checks her notes again—"February."

"Whoever we choose will need to create multiple projects over the course of the year," Kenneth says, tipping back in his chair. "We're trying to take advantage of frequent mentions in the press and have more opportunities for the public to talk about the mission and view the art. With more work, instead of just one at the end, the science and art can be an ongoing conversation."

"How do we feel about the anonymity aspect?" Nick asks, his hands loosely clasped in front of him on the table.

Margie speaks first. "The way I see it, the anonymity is actually a draw. In articles about *Entangled*, besides the trash talk, people were intrigued by who the artist was. There's a lot of chatter about it in various art forums. We'd have to figure out the logistics of how to work with the artist and protect her identity."

"Managing this artist would be like running...a secret mission," I say. I look over to see how the team reacts to this.

"Interesting! These are all stories we can play up," Margie says, documenting my contribution.

I speak again. "Red String Girl teaming up with someone who works on a mission about the Red Planet." I'm on a roll.

Nick grins. "Good one. We can work with that."

I smile to myself. Maybe talking to the press won't be so bad.

Margie flips to the last slide, detailing next steps.

"It sounds like Red String Girl is our first choice," Kenneth says. "I'll take this back to run by a couple more people and can let you know by the end of the week. Whoever we end up going with, I think it's best that you make the call to the artist, Jackson. Kick things off as our mission liaison. Sound good?"

Margie, Nick, and I all nod in agreement. We say our good-byes, and Kenneth lets us know he'll be sending out a recurring meeting invite.

Back at my desk, I exhale. A successful first meeting. I contributed about a topic other than FATE. Maybe I can do this after all. Maybe I'll even...enjoy it?

I type Red String Girl's website URL into my browser. There's a string art animal portrait section highlighting nearly a dozen different pieces. I scroll past portraits of cats and dogs. Expected. The lower I go on the page, the animals become more varied. Dragons, pigs, penguins, and horses. They're not like the string art kids make in grade school of suns and stars. This artist's work is delicate. Detailed.

The light board behind the image is almost entirely covered in string. The nails are small and silver. They complement the string instead of drawing attention from it. If I stood back, the pieces would look like shaded pencil drawings. Or photographs. Up close, the zigzagging string around nails and silver dots tell a different story. If she's this good with animals, she could probably do portraits of our astronauts and rockets. Maybe re-create some images from the James Webb Space Telescope.

Below each piece lists the materials used. Wood panel, brads, single red sewing thread. Each piece is made with one unbroken string.

In the order form on the website, the prices of each piece are shockingly reasonable for the level of quality. I surprise myself by placing an order. If she's NASA's newest artist-in-residence, one might call this an investment. I pause. Would this be considered insider art trading? I decide on commissioning a seahorse for Gōng Gong's birthday instead.

Also for research.

Chapter 11

ROONEY

How do you pronounce star A-N-I-S-E?" Mom asks from the kitchen of her apartment, enunciating each letter individually. Outside the windows of the living room, where Talia and I lounge, the upper half of Manhattan twinkles against the evening sky painted a shade of amber.

"Is this the lead-up to one of your inappropriate jokes?" I ask, taking a sip of my chrysanthemum and honeysuckle tea that I special-ordered from an herbalist who was very reassuring that the combination would help calm me.

Mom grunts. "Excuse me. I take my learning very seriously. Chinese tea eggs call for this spice in the recipe."

"I say it like 'a niece.'" I google the question on my phone. "The dictionary says it's pronounced like 'anne-niss,' with an emphasis on the first syllable. Talia, how do you say it?"

Talia looks up from her laptop on the other end of the deep-seated emerald velvet sofa. "The first way, definitely."

Mom monitors her boiling eggs. "If there's no clear answer, I'll pronounce it my way."

"Please don't," I mumble, my eyes glued to the television in the living room.

A Chinese drama plays out on the screen. A woman diagnosed with an illness has just been asked to marry a rich businessman for a marriage of convenience. She's confused why he's chosen her of all people.

"Wèishéme shì wǒ?" I ask, repeating the one Mandarin line from the show I can actually recognize and understand. I pay attention to getting the tones right.

"Did you read that off the caption or did you know that one?" Talia asks, amazed.

"When she said it, I could understand!" I say excitedly.

"Not bad," Mom murmurs, opening and closing drawers in the kitchen's built-in cabinets.

For the past year, Mom and I have been studying Mandarin together, using cookbooks, beginner workbooks, language classes, and Chinese dramas to round out our learning. Mandarin was her first language, but she moved to America from Taiwan at a young age. Once her family arrived here, they chose to mostly speak English to help their children integrate into school faster. She can still speak Mandarin, but mostly casual conversations and making plans. The cooking was a delicious add-on that we figured would help fuel the learning process.

"That's an easy one," Mom says as she removes the skin from a chunk of ginger with a spoon. "We need to be learning new words. Bigger sentences."

"Asking 'Why me?' actually seems like a pretty useful sentence. When you're having a bad day and nothing seems to go right, you can yell it into the sky with your hands up in the air," I say, thinking out loud. String moves smoothly through my fingers as I work on a lemur animal portrait.

"For you, maybe. I don't need to go around asking 'Why me?'" Mom roughly measures out the recipe's remaining spices and tosses them into a simmering pot of soy sauce, cinnamon, and Lapsang Souchong tea. The room smells cozy. "I *know* why me."

Talia and I give each other a look and laugh quietly. Mom redirects her attention to the cookbook in front of her, and I pause the TV show to skim through new orders in my shop's dashboard.

"Cute!" I say, clicking into one of the few new orders that have trickled in over the past week. "Someone named Bohai in Alhambra wants seahorses. That's a new one." I add the commission to my list of pieces to make.

"Where's Alhambra?" Talia asks absentmindedly.

I take another sip of tea, the warm liquid comforting me. "Somewhere in California. I'm switching over to a movie. I need to focus on this lemur and can't read the captions at the same time." I grab the remote and flip through the options, settling on one of my favorites, *Serendipity*.

As the movie plays in the background, I step back from the board, looking for areas where I need to layer more string.

Mom approaches with a spoonful of liquid. "Try this. I used a smokier tea. If you like it, the cracked eggs get a soy sauce bath in it, and in a day, we can eat them. These recipes require too much patience."

I take a sip. "Hot! Add a little more clove."

"What's up with all that?" Talia asks, nodding toward a corner of the apartment where my art supplies are organized into standing drawers. Next to it are poster boards with incomplete sketches of old ideas and completed pet portraits that need to be sent out. "You working on your next installation idea?"

"Oh. No. Just a few commissions for people who saw the installation on Instagram when it was still trash- and rat-free," I tell her. "The one thing *Entangled* was good for: more pet portraits. I'm in no position to be giving this up anytime soon." I rub the string-induced calluses on the tips of my fingers. "And I haven't been feeling inspired lately."

"You can't wait for the muse to come," Mom says, slurping the remaining liquid from the spoon. "You have to actively think about ideas or you'll find that you're still making pet portraits fifty years later, arguing with someone named Beth from Pensacola about whether or not you fully captured her shih tzu's personality in the portrait."

"Enlightening. Thanks." I gently push her back toward the kitchen. "Commissions are my priority until I have enough saved up. I know you were making money off your art in your twenties, but that's not how it is for me."

Mom shrugs her shoulders. "Don't wait around is all I'm saying."

"I'm blocked creatively. It happens from time to time," I lie. Never once have I ever had artist's block. "*Entangled* was my best idea, and if people can't respect an installation in a park, they absolutely won't respect one in a subway station."

Gravity came to me the week after that night with Jack. I sketched it out and everything. But then...nothing. That was it. No more ideas. It doesn't feel worth it to pursue *Gravity*. It feels as though all my creativity and energy were cut down along with *Entangled*.

I watch from the couch as Mom removes the boiling eggs from the pot and places them in a bowl of ice water. "If you want public art, you're always going to have to deal with the public. The ugly and the uglier. People can be cruel."

I frown. "I know you're right. Doesn't make it easier, though."

Next to me, Talia starts kicking her feet wildly and screaming. "Rooney!"

I jump up, pulling the string on the lemur harder than I want. I check to make sure the nail is still straight. "Whoa! Tal, what is it?"

Talia lifts her laptop up and leans in next to me. "Auction! Auction!"

I hook the red string over the lemur's half-formed eyeball. "What are you talking about? Oh! Did you sell one of your new artist's porcelain pieces? Her pieces are stunning."

"No! *Baby Being Born*! Is going to auction!" she says, twisting her laptop to face me. "My friend at one of the art houses just let me know."

"What?!" I take the laptop from her hands and read the email. I go over the words three times to confirm that what I'm seeing is real. "It's happening in eight months," I say. "And there's no way to know who has it?"

"It's as anonymous as you, Roo," Talia says, her eyes bright. "But how great is this? They'll still need to verify it and make sure it's the original, and it'll take some time to gather more video art to complete the theme of the auction, but yay! It's what you've been waiting for!"

Mom cackles while she wipes her hands off on a towel. "Are you really going to try to buy it back? How are you going to do that?"

I break out in a full-body sweat when I think about how many pet portraits I'd need to commission to be able to pay for the piece. It last sold in 2010 for $15,000. I hope it hasn't tripled in price since then. "I haven't thought through the money piece yet."

"We have some time to figure it out," Talia says calmly. "My source will try to find out more information, but this is huge."

She's right. Next March, I'll have the chance to buy back *Baby Being Born*. Finally.

An idea forms. The only thing I ever want to accept from Mom is a room to stay. I want to be financially independent, but this shot might come around only once.

"Mom," I say slowly, "you want to go halvsies on it? Didn't you just sell some pieces of your last collection?"

Mom grunts. "You're out of your mind if you think I'm going to buy back my own art for double, triple the cost. And you. You should not be going into debt for this video."

I make a face. "You're right. I want to do this on my own anyway. The buying-it-back part, not the debt part." I pull a pillow onto my lap and study Talia's expression. "You think it's really going to sell for that much?"

"The value of art depends on what someone is willing to pay for it. And this is the video that made your mom famous. Not like I have to tell you that, but with your mom taking a break from making art, her pieces will become more valuable," Talia says. "Even this one. *Baby Being Born* has only been sold once since the first time your mom sold it."

"Yeah, I'm still taking a break," Mom calls out preemptively from the kitchen. "I need some me-time."

Talia's cell phone vibrates against the glass coffee table, startling all of us.

"Who's calling at six fifteen on a Friday night?" Talia asks. She lets the call go to her automated voice mail. "We have more important things to discuss."

"Totally. Like how we're going to get approximately thirty thousand dollars by March," I say with a groan. "Casual Friday night chitchat."

Talia's cell phone buzzes again. Restricted number.

"Maybe this is something about the gallery. California's three hours behind us. One sec." Talia has her gallery phone calls forwarded to her personal cell phone when she's not there so that she never misses an interested client. She taps the green button on her screen. "Hello?"

While Talia's on the phone, I help Mom in the kitchen. We lightly crack the hard-boiled eggs and roll them against the wooden cutting board.

Talia hangs up and looks over at us. "Scammers are getting way more creative. Have you ever gotten one claiming they're from a space agency?"

Mom groans. "Maybe they're offering seats to the moon for two hundred and fifty thousand dollars apiece. You just missed out on a trip of a lifetime."

Her phone rings a third time.

Once again, Talia answers. "The NYPD are on the line with me" is how she answers this time. A trick we learned that tends to freak out scammers.

After a few seconds, Talia still hasn't hung up.

"Who is it?" I shout-whisper.

She shakes her head and puts the phone on speaker. "How did you get this number?"

The voice on the other end comes out warbled. "I found this number on Red String Girl's website. It was the only contact information listed."

Talia shoots me a look when she realizes that I made her gallery my contact number.

"Sorry," I mouth and give her an apologetic look.

She rolls her eyes. "It's fine," she mouths back. "Okay. Yeah. I'm her...assistant. Um...Officer, you can hang up now. How can I help you?"

I laugh quietly while I crack an egg gently under the weight of my palm.

"Uh," the man says, sounding nervous. "Like I mentioned, I work at NASA. My apologies. I failed to remember the time difference. If this is too late to be calling, I will try again on Monday. I was looking for Red String Girl?"

This gets my attention. I gesture to Talia to keep talking.

"Wait. Red String Girl is unavailable at the moment." Talia clears her throat. She lives for a good improv moment. "I handle all of Ms. RSG's affairs."

"Right. Ms. Sorry," the man says.

Talia stifles a laugh. She is enjoying this way too much.

As Talia talks, Mom and I transport the cracked eggs into the cooled soy sauce and spice bath to let them soak.

"As I said, I'm calling from NASA." He sounds stuffed up, like he's in the height of a cold. The speaker makes him sound like he's underwater. "I'm calling because NASA is reinstating its Artist-in-Residence program. We choose one artist to create art to represent the work we're doing. The pieces are then displayed in museums throughout the country."

"I'm listening," Talia says to signify that she's still there.

"We're excited to share that Red String Girl has been chosen as our first artist," he says in a professional, neutral tone that doesn't match his choice of words. "Would this be of interest?"

My mouth falls open at the same time that Talia's jaw drops. Despite bouncing on the couch, she manages to say coolly, "This might be of interest to Ms. RSG."

I dry my hands and join Talia on the couch. I crouch forward over my crossed legs, eagerly listening.

"I'm told you'll work out the details with the program director, but the artist...compensated...for the year," he says, the line crackling.

"You broke up there for a moment. Could you repeat that?" Talia asks, leaning closer to the phone.

The static clears as the man says, "She'll be compensated twenty-two thousand dollars for the year."

I widen my eyes. Wow. That's a lot of pet portraits.

Mom fast-walks over from the kitchen and lunges toward Talia's phone. "Bullshit! You come at us with that number? We've got offers for days," she says.

"Shh! Don't you dare," I whisper, pulling on her arm. "If you negotiate, they might not want to work with me anymore."

Mom balks. "Multiply that number by six, divided by three, multiply it again by two, and add ten. That's the number we want to see on a piece of paper."

"I'm sorry. Who is this?" the man asks.

"Sorry about that. This is my...coagent," Talia makes up. She shoots Mom a look.

"Names aren't necessary unless we talk real numbers," Mom says.

Talia covers the phone with my hand. "Are you trying to do an accent?"

I grab Mom from the waist and pull her back farther. "You sound like Keanu Reeves in *Bram Stoker's Dracula*. You're not convincing anyone."

"I'm aiming for Elizabeth Hurley," she whispers.

"As Vanessa Kensington in *Austin Powers*?" Talia asks, still covering the phone.

Mom grins. "As the Devil."

"You're both awful! And don't you dare insult Keanu!" Talia whispers. "Sorry about that. Please, go on."

NASA Guy continues. "Unfortunately, I don't have the power to increase that number. We rely on grants for the money. But the attention your client should get will be significant."

"We can't pay rent with significant," Mom says, pouting her lips Liz Hurley style. "How about less tellys and more monies for your artists."

"Televisions?" the man asks. He sounds so confused at this point, I almost feel bad for him.

Mom exhales audibly. "Telescopes!"

NASA Guy sighs. "I hear you. I do. I wish I could do more in that regard."

"Wishing is nice and all, but what *can* you do?" Mom smirks.

"I—I guess I can try to get a cafeteria card for Ms. RSG," the man offers. "I can't guarantee an amount. But it should cover or at least subsidize meals."

"There we go. Next time lead with that," Mom says bluntly. Her accent slips into something more like Lindsay Lohan's version in *The Parent Trap*. It doesn't know what it wants to be.

"NASA will also offer housing and travel allowances for the living and moving arrangements."

Mom raises an eyebrow. "Better."

I wave her off.

"How did you say you got Ms. RSG's name? She didn't apply for a NASA program," Talia says.

There's a long pause. "The team saw her *Entangled* installation."

Hearing my installation name in this context hits differently. Instead of a pile of string, I remember the installation as it originally was. I feel a spark of excitement again.

"What is it about her work that you liked? I mean, enough for being picked as the artist-in-residence?" Talia pushes on.

He doesn't respond for a few seconds but then finally says, "We think her ability to intertwine—excuse the unintended pun— science and...high concepts...works well for our ongoing missions. Her work is creative. She brings an interactive sensibility to ideas that often feel too far out to grasp. She'd help us convey high-level ideas visually and in an approachable way."

"That's right!" Mom shouts. "Our girl can do what you need." She's transitioned from the Devil into someone so posh, she could be a shoo-in for one of the Bridgertons.

Talia waves Mom off. "What kind of high-level ideas exactly?" she asks.

For a second it sounds like NASA Guy is blowing into a tissue.

"Excuse me. Apologies for that. Unfortunately, I can't give specifics until the agreement has been made. Confidentiality. I'm sure you can understand."

"Me?" Talia asks.

"With your client's identity remaining a secret," he says, his congested voice blaring from the speaker.

"Yes. Oh! Yes," she says, almost forgetting herself.

I stand to pace the room and process everything. I need to be doing something with my hands. I make my way to the kitchen and grab the ladle to push the marinating eggs back and forth in the mixture.

"Accepting this position would require living in the Los Angeles area for a year as Ms. RSG creates her art. I'd be her liaison, teach her about the work we're doing. There's some travel involved. As well as several showcases throughout the year."

"Los Angeles? Multiple showcases? And for a year? A year is a long time," I whisper to myself, not realizing Mom has joined me in the kitchen.

Mom makes a noise. "A year's a drop in the bucket."

"Not when you're creatively blocked," I tell her before turning away and watching as Talia remains impressively calm. She delivers good news all the time to artists she wants to represent. And bad news to clients whose work doesn't sell.

"Ms. RSG will be fully integrated into our work. It's a once-in-a-lifetime experience and opportunity," NASA Guy adds, the line cutting in and out with more static. "It will be a lot of exposure."

Talia watches me. "As you said."

The pounding in my chest deepens.

"My understanding is that Ms. Red String Girl doesn't want too much...personal publicity. We would honor her anonymity with nondisclosure agreements with people she meets around NASA. I will be the one to communicate with the press and working with Ms. RSG on what she wants to convey. At NASA, we put the missions—in this case, the art—first. It's not about any one person," he says with a sniffle. "Her anonymity is actually a compelling factor."

Talia switches positions on the couch and leans against a pillow. "That's all great to hear. When would this start? Ms. RSG is a very busy, in-demand artist," she says with extra emphasis on "busy" and "in-demand."

I nod dramatically, pretending it's true. It's literally the furthest thing from reality. But as I stare into the dark brown tea egg liquid, the cracked eggs bobbing up and down, it occurs to me that this could be how I buy back *Baby Being Born*. Not with the NASA money entirely, of course, but with the exposure. I can sell more pet portraits and maybe some bigger pieces with this type of coverage in the media. Maybe even line up more shows.

I ignore the pit in my stomach about the whole creative block thing. I'm sure I'll figure it out. A lack of ideas has never been a problem for me before. Maybe this is the push that I need to get myself back on track.

"That's another topic of discussion," the man says. He's so professional. "Because we're reinstating the program, we don't have an artist currently at work."

I wave a hand in the air to get Talia's attention and rush up to her, abandoning the eggs.

"Tell him I'll do it, and I can be there in August," I whisper.

"You've got yourself a deal," Talia says quickly. "She'll be there next month. Please email me with the details." She ends the call, and we release our pent-up screams.

Mom brings over a bowl of mixed Asian rice crackers and cringes at the noises we're making.

"Wait, what am I doing? I should think about this, right?" I say, my heart pounding. I drop into a wide, cushioned chair opposite the couch.

"Don't you do that," Mom says.

"It's across the country," I say, scooping out a handful of rice crackers. "How could I leave the city?"

"It's a year," Mom says.

"I don't even drive," I add.

Mom grunts. "You can learn when you're there. They say it's like learning how to ride a bike." She thinks for a moment. "A three-thousand-pound bike, but still."

"This skin doesn't do well in the sun," I say, rubbing my forearm. I pick out the flower-shaped rice crackers to eat first.

"Knit yourself a long-sleeve sweater or buy some sunscreen," Mom responds.

I gesture around the living room. "All of my supplies are here."

"They have art stores in California," Talia jumps in. She crunches down on a handful of Wasabi green pea crackers.

"You're both here," I reason.

"I'll make stops in LA to visit during my time off," Mom promises.

I hold back my last question.

"Out with it," Mom says, tossing a sesame stick at me.

"What if I run into Jack?" I whisper.

It was a night that changed everything and nothing. It felt possible that, even among shreds of string and trash and ugliness, something beautiful could still come out of that day. But ever since then, the signs have practically disappeared. There have been barely there moments, but they didn't lead to the person on the other end of my red string.

I sink lower into my seat. "Somehow my signals got crossed," I say. "I misread the meaning of the night. I misread the meaning of him."

Even though he gave me a wrong number, or I mistyped it, I tried texting as many variations of the one he gave me that I could think of until one of those numbers threatened to report me for spam. Then I turned to Google, but by now the J-A-C-K letters on my keyboard are all worn out from the different search combinations. Dave no longer works at Sprinters, which felt like a really big sign. I even called every hotel in the Financial District to ask if Jack stayed with them, but they weren't allowed to reveal their guest list. All I know is that he was in the city for work. That's it. That can mean anything! It's become very clear that I wasn't meant to get in touch with this man. Maybe it was meant to be one magical night sealed with a kiss. Ugh. That kiss!

"Los Angeles is a big place, Roo," Mom says, interrupting my thought spiral. "Trying to locate him would be like trying to find other life in the universe." She looks surprised. "That was pretty good. If you don't want this gig, recommend me for it."

"It's true. He's a hard man to find," Talia says. "Even after I finally got the name of the party host, you explained what Jack looked like a thousand different ways and they still had no idea who you were talking about. Apparently, that was their biggest party to date."

I gasp. "That's where I went wrong. Maybe I could hire a sketch artist and—"

"And what?" Mom asks. "Post a thousand sketch photos of Jack up on news outlets? You'll make the man look like a criminal! It would become a different kind of manhunt."

I exhale slowly. "It's clear I wasn't meant to find him. Mangetsu Jazz, the souvenir shop, and the Chinese restaurant we went to were also dead ends. Apparently businesses value people's privacy, and he paid for the dumplings with cash."

Mom scoffs. "Privacy? Who do they think they are? Apple?"

"I'm just trying to let this sink in. This is a big undertaking. Probably bigger than I could even imagine. The first artist in their new program? I'm nowhere near experienced enough. I still make pet string portraits," I say, holding up a tangled wad of red string. "What if I fail? What if I don't make what they want? I'll be done before I've even started."

"What if a bird flies through that window and pecks your eyeballs out?" Mom lifts another handful of crackers from the bowl. "You've already had a public installation in an iconic park. You have commissions coming in. Give yourself a little credit."

"How did this even happen? Wèishéme shì wǒ," I ask. "Huh. That actually is useful."

Mom throws her free hand up. "Why you? Why *not* you?"

Talia echoes Mom's last question. "You're never this fearful," she says. "You're the say-what's-on-your-mind-act-before-you-think girl. Where did she go?"

"I'd love to know," I say honestly, pinching the bridge of my nose. My theory is that that version of me went away when I became creatively blocked. When I felt like a complete imposter after having my installation cut down. When I had to say good-bye to Jack permanently. "Maybe doing this will help me find myself again, but I don't know if I can do this alone."

Talia's eyes widen. "I don't know if that's an invite, but if it is, I'd love to come. I can work on the final touches of our gallery in LA and spend time with Isla. The gallery needs some love and attention from me."

"I can't ask you to do that," I say, peering up at her.

Talia waves me off. "You're not asking. And I don't know, I feel like there's something for me there, too. Plus, I can coordinate with the communications team and help you install your showcase. Make RSG look legitimate."

"I can't believe you. If you're sure, then yes a million times! I owe you forever," I scream, leaning over to hug her.

"And we can showcase your pet portraits at the gallery. Do some other exclusive exhibit maybe? Definitely up the prices. It's Los Angeles. They'll fly off the walls like an Andy Warhol Marilyn Monroe silk screen. Use the NASA exposure to start making money for the auction." Talia's laugh is filled with excitement. "This will be a fun new chapter for both of us."

After everything that's happened, it's time for a change. A new start. And that can only happen in Los Angeles.

I stand with newfound resolve, feeling lighter than I have in months. "Sounds like we're going to California."

Chapter 12

One Month Later

JACK

It's Day One of the Artist-in-Residence program, one of the most high-profile projects that I've ever worked on, and I'm running late. Or rather, Red String Girl and her team are early. Very early. I timed it so I'd be the first one there. Now I just look bad.

Sweat trails down my back as I open the gate to the Mars Yard, where we're all meeting. Why did I think it would be a good idea to have our first team meeting outside at the end of August instead of in an air-conditioned conference room?

The Mars Yard at the Jet Propulsion Laboratory is a simulated Martian landscape for testing robotic prototypes and applications. I figured that'd be fun. A visual, hands-on place that an artist might love to see.

But now that I'm going to show up drenched, I am cursing Past Jack and his decisions.

I slow from a run to a jog up to the group of people huddling in the Yard. Did everyone get the memo to be extra early today? It looks like Kenneth, Margie, and Nick are already here. So the other two must be Red String Girl and her assistant.

My already-pounding heart picks up speed at the thought of meeting Red String Girl. Do I tell her I'm sorry that her installation was cut down in the way that it was? Or ignore it altogether? Probably best not to say anything. No one wants to be reminded about things like that.

"There's Jackson Liu now," Kenneth, who's facing me, shouts. He gives me a tight smile.

I wave my hand in the air. "Apologies. But I come bearing Welcome Packets," I say between breaths as I run over. I spot who must be Red String Girl from behind. She's in a sweater and a red skirt. A sweater in August? I hope she doesn't get too hot. I'm now realizing it might've been nice to bring water for everyone.

I continue with my apology as I near the group. "I really am so sorr—"

As Red String Girl turns around, a sharp pang shoots through my chest. My entire body goes numb in a split second. It's only when Kenneth is profusely apologizing that I realize I've dropped the stack of Welcome Packets mid-jog. In my peripherals, I see packets on the ground covered in dust. But in my direct line of sight, all I see is red.

And by red, I mean Rooney. Why is Rooney here? Unless...

I run my hand down my face, rubbing my eyes to make sure she's not a figment of my imagination brought on by heat and exertion from my midday jog.

My mouth goes dry as I try to find the words. She looks exactly the same as she did six months ago, just with slightly longer hair. She's in a red knitted sweater and skirt, her lips painted a striking shade of ruby. She's both familiar and a complete stranger.

At the sight of me, Rooney's face pales, and her smile morphs into a frown.

"Jack?" she finally whispers, so low I almost miss it. She looks at the woman to her left, who has a day organizer tucked into her arms, a pen at the ready.

Rooney's voice is so familiar, having become deeply ingrained in my mind. In hearing it, I'm pummeled by a wave of memories. They happen in glimpses. Her wrapping the scarf around my neck at the print shop. The fire from the lantern casting shadows across her face. Her dancing to my music. Sitting under the moonlight on the bench at her Spot. Sharing dumplings at midnight. An entire night plays out in front of me. I'm right there, and I'm right here.

After months of searching and troubleshooting how to find her, here she is. Problem solved. I thought it was easier to find life on another planet than it was trying to find Rooney. The discovery releases something tight and anxious inside me.

Kenneth takes a step toward me and hands me the dusty packets. "This is Jackson, the mission liaison. He's a systems engineer on the mission you'll be learning about."

At this, Rooney's eyes grow wider.

"Are you okay, Jackson? You look queasy," Margie says.

I cling to the Welcome Packets so tightly that they crease. I'm supposed to be a professional here. "Sorry. This is just so...a lot. It's not every day you meet someone whose art you've seen in real life."

The woman next to Rooney extends her hand first. "I'm Talia Ma," she says. "My gallery represents Red String Girl."

I mirror her actions, too stunned to think one step ahead. "Right. Sorry. I'm Jackson Liu."

I slowly move my hand from Talia's over to Rooney. She looks at it like I've just sneezed into it.

So if Talia is Red String Girl's representative, that would make Rooney...

Red String Girl.

In my mind, I hear the clicking of pieces into place. This admission doesn't feel like a surprise. It feels obvious. Because of course she's Red String Girl. It's all so clear now. Her knowledge of the Red

Thread of Fate, all of her red knit clothing, her interest in art. So then who was the woman handing out paper? Add it to the list of unknowns.

It's subtle, but I notice Talia nudging Rooney. It's as though she's snapped out of a trance. She places her hand in mine slowly. We squeeze at the same time and a chill runs up my neck.

Our eyes lock, and her lips part, as though she wants to say something. "I'm Rooney Gao."

There could still be a chance that she's not Red String Girl. That they're both assistants. Would that make this any less weird? Highly doubtful.

"I'm Jackson," I say, sharing with her the name I use at work.

Rooney pulls back from me. The absence of her hand in mine is noticeable. I grip the Welcome Packets with both hands now to fill the void.

"We're all very excited, and a little starstruck, clearly," Kenneth says, jumping in to keep the afternoon moving along. His tone of voice tells me that this is a warning and it had better not happen again. This program is too high-profile to get off on the wrong foot with our guests. No, NASA's guests.

"Here at NASA? You'd think you see enough stars," Rooney jokes, gesturing up toward the sky.

The comment takes the attention off my clumsiness. Luckily for me, the team moves on.

"I want to assure you, Rooney and Talia, that you're in great hands," Kenneth adds. "Jackson's knowledge about the mission is vast."

I nod, unable to form more words.

"As I understand it, Talia, you'll be fairly hands off," Margie says, checking her notes. "And Rooney, thank you for deciding to trust us."

I look from Margie to Rooney. "Trust us?"

"Jackson, before you arrived, Rooney let us know that she's Red String Girl," Margie tells me. She looks excited. Probably not at all what my face looks like right now.

There it is. Confirmed.

"Red String Girl." I take a deep breath in to steady myself. "I see. Well, thank you for trusting us."

Rooney winces at this, and I don't know what's more confusing. The fact that she didn't tell me who she was that night or that I understand why she didn't so I can't even be mad.

I want to be careful here. I told Kenneth that I didn't know Red String Girl. Which was true at the time. But now…now I realize that I do. But how much of someone can you really know in one night? If I say that we know each other, I might compromise her position. After what happened to *Entangled*, I wouldn't risk taking anything else away from her. And the fact that Rooney hasn't said anything either must mean she's thinking the same. So I stay quiet.

"In return, teams she meets here must agree to keep her identity private. To the public she will remain anonymous," Margie finishes explaining.

I nod. "We'll make sure everyone you meet at various centers around NASA signs nondisclosure agreements," I say. "We'll also make sure you have access to buildings to create your installations in the off-hours."

Rooney's eyes soften, and she seems to relax a little. "Thank you. Hey, I have to know, who chose Red String Girl to do this?" she asks the group. "It's still pretty amazing to believe that Red String Girl, um, that I will be creating something for NASA."

I let someone else on the team take this one. They can explain how we narrowed down artists and more about the responsibilities.

Instead, Nick decides to jump in and say, "Oh! Jackson put your name in."

In hindsight, not speaking first was a bad idea. I blow out a breath of air.

The look of shock has resumed its position on Rooney's face. "Oh…"

"You're kidding," Talia says, crossing her arms. Why does she look amused?

"Your installation," I interrupt in my defense. "What you do. It's unique. *Entangled* showed what you could do with science and art. The literal merging of the two. We thought you could potentially do something interesting with FATE."

"Well, yes. Fate is at the core of my installation work," she says, nodding in understanding.

"But also with FATE, the mission," Nick clarifies.

I dip my head and groan silently.

"Wait. Your mission is named, what, FATE?" Rooney's eyes sparkle. "No way. Who did that?"

I stuff my hands into my pockets. "I actually named it. It stands for Fuel Atomized Technology Equipment."

She puts her hands up on her hips and smiles so hard that the constellation on her cheek morphs into a new shape I've never seen. I've fallen out of the habit of connecting the dots. I have a sinking feeling it's a habit that will come back without any effort at all.

"You believe in fate," she asks. "And you made it your mission."

Rooney is warming up. She feels as familiar as she was that night in the city. It's unnerving.

I shake my head. "It's not *my* mission. It's my *team's* mission."

"This guy! Team player right here!" she tells the team, pointing at me. Her word choice hits deep. Am I really a team player, though? Feedback in my last performance review would indicate otherwise.

Kenneth, Margie, and Nick all laugh. Talia gives a smile like she's playing along, but I can tell she's analyzing me. I don't like being analyzed.

I check my phone for the time.

Talia grunts. "Oh, good. Glad to see you have a phone in working order. You can communicate with us, like you're expected to," she says. This feels loaded somehow.

Rooney nudges her and whispers something.

I attempt to redirect everyone's attention. "Anyway. We're looking forward to your time with us," I say in my most professional tone. "As you can see, we're in the Mars Yard."

Rooney looks around, confused. "Where's the ice?"

I sigh. The pamphlets.

Rooney walks over to a large rock and attempts to lift it. "Those aren't very heavy," she says.

I join her and tap the rock with the palm of my hand. "They're volcanic rock," I inform her as I bend down to lift a smaller one. "They help create a more accurate environment of the Red Planet."

I place it back onto the dusty ground, a mix of beach sand, brick dust, volcanic cinders, and decomposed granite. The overall terrain takes on a tint of red. For a moment, if I ignore the houses on the hills and deer-crossing signs and the sounds of cars driving by on the road, I could pretend that I'm on a different planet.

Right now it certainly feels like I'm existing in an alternate world or plane. Like at any moment I might wake up and it will all have been a dream. Just like the way that night in New York felt.

Something catches Rooney's attention. She kneels to the ground, looking excited.

"I found life! Our job here is done," she shouts, pointing to a small green weed poking out of the soil. When she lifts her head, her bangs fall across her forehead, accentuating her eyes. It stirs something deep in me that I haven't felt in six months.

I pluck the weed out of the ground. "We can try to leave this planet, but problems will follow us wherever we go," I say grimly.

She must think I'm joking because she laughs. It's the laugh that has accompanied—no, haunted—my dreams for half a year.

But this isn't a dream. Rooney is really here, and we need to work together. There wasn't enough preparation in the world that I could've done to ready myself to ever see Rooney again.

It's not like she's going to require hand-holding every single day. I shake off my poor choice of words. There will be no hand-holding, obviously. Rooney will spend time with other teams in the agency, so it won't be a twenty-four/seven situation. I'll simply provide information about the mission. Answer questions. Offer more space facts. Ensure that this program is a success and get a promotion. Rooney has spent six months existing in my head. I can spend twelve months with her in real life. Then she'll leave.

It's going to be fine. This year is going to fly by.

Chapter 13

ROONEY

This is going to be the longest year of my life. I already thought it was going to feel like forever trying to get creatively unblocked. Now this.

I laugh so I don't have an emotional breakdown. No. I am completely and totally fine.

"Definitely. The problems follow wherever we go," I respond to Jack, who's holding a baby weed between his fingers. I could sketch those hands from memory. I'll never be able to get the thought of him playing bass out of my head. With those eyes. With that voice. With those fingers.

"Rooney!" Talia calls for me. I snap out of my thoughts and stand. "*Jackson* is going to take you on a tour. I'm heading back to the gallery, but text me later. We have a lot to catch up on."

I haven't even had a chance to freak out to her about this—seeing Jack again, him being here of all places. I plaster a smile on my face and nod.

"If there's anything else you need, please let us know," Kenneth tells us. "Jackson, we'll let you take it from here."

Kenneth, Margie, and Nick walk with Talia out of the yard, leaving Jack and me behind. Just the two of us alone together.

"This way," Jack says, pointing to a side gate in the chain-link fence.

"Great. Thanks, Jack," I say with one eyebrow raised. "Or should I call you Jackson?"

He lets me exit the yard first. "Jackson is my full name. It's what colleagues call me. But you already know me as Jack, so that's probably fine."

I nod. "It won't be weird that I'm the only one calling you by your nickname?"

Jack wrinkles his nose. "I think it would be weirder if you called me Jackson."

"Fine. And true. How about this? I become the offbeat anonymous artist who gives nicknames to everyone. That way you don't stick out." I nervously laugh to myself as Jack continues marching forward.

We begin crossing the campus to start the tour at what Jack explains to me is the Space Flight Operations Facility. Large buildings surround us. JPL, short for Jet Propulsion Laboratory, is practically its own little city within La Cañada Flintridge, though most people credit Pasadena as being JPL's home, Jack explained. "It's a whole thing," he said with a shrug.

As we walk, my mind races with questions but nothing comes out. It feels like running into an auntie you haven't seen since you accidentally broke her porcelain vase when you were thirteen years old but still to this day act like it never happened.

"Jack," I finally say.

"Yes, Ms. Gao?" he says courteously. "Or Red String Girl? Which do you prefer?"

I make a face. "With you? Neither. Just like I know you as Jack, you know me as Rooney."

"Rooney" is all he says. It's been six months since I last heard my name on his lips, and after all this time, it still sounds sweet.

I smile. "That's better."

"It's you. I can't believe it," he adds. Jack's posture loosens, the muscles in his face relaxing.

"It's me. Glad you remember," I say. Honestly, it's a relief to know he's as shocked as I am.

"I knew it was Roo-something, so I took a wild guess," he says clumsily like he's trying to make a joke.

"You're actually spot-on. My name *is* Rooney Something. Good memory, but I don't remember telling you my middle name," I say with a smirk.

Jack's eyebrows pop up. "Yeah, and my middle name is N slash A for Non-Applicable."

"No, seriously. My middle name is Something," I say. "When my mom was asked what my middle name was, she was deciding between Something and Whatever."

"Oh," Jack says neutrally. "Sorry about that. In all honesty, I don't have a middle name. I guess Something is better than nothing."

I grin. "Only if you like that something."

Jack pinches his eyebrows together. "So, Rooney Something Gao. RSG. Red String Girl. That's very…what did you call it in the print shop? Symbolic."

Jack mentioning the moment we met throws me off. I've longed for this since that night, but we're not in New York City anymore. We're walking and talking but the context couldn't be more different. The lit-up skyscrapers that surrounded us have been replaced by olive trees that confidently take up space. We shift awkwardly as the tension builds in the silence.

"I'm sorry about *Entangled*," Jack says as we cross the street. "I had blabbered on about it to you that same night that, well, you know. I thought the artist was someone else."

"You don't need to be sorry—" I stop in my tracks. "Wait. Who did you think the artist was?"

Jack hesitates. "I met this blunt older woman at your installation. She was handing out sketchbook paper. Her clothing was covered in paint," he reveals. "She knew a lot about the art and its themes, which is why I thought it was her."

My jaw drops. "You met my mom," I say, covering my face with both hands. "What did she say? Actually, it's better if you don't tell me."

"That was your mom?" Jack asks.

"The one and only."

Jack grimaces and runs a hand through his hair, the ends sticking up a bit. I'm tempted to reach out to flatten the strays, but I'd like for this moment to be less awkward.

Instead, I hold out my hands in front of him, just close enough to touch. "Jack, you clearly didn't know about *Entangled*, and you were right that I would've loved it. Besides, I have a different perspective about it now. Look where it led me," I say, lifting my arms up toward the sky. "I'm in California!"

"That you are," Jack affirms.

"I'm sorry I didn't say who I was," I feel the need to add. "It didn't feel like the right time."

"I get it," Jack says. He looks like he means it. "You're anonymous to the public. It makes sense you would tell us who you are now that we're working together. Otherwise, it's a logistics nightmare."

"Thanks for being so nice about it," I say.

"I'm Jackson at work," he says with a smirk. "I kind of live a double life, too."

I catch up to Jack and reach for his arm, stopping him in the middle of the sidewalk. Since the Mars Yard, he's folded up his sleeves. My fingertips prickle when it strikes me that I'm touching Jack's forearms. In New York, he was in a sweater and a coat. It was too cold to have any skin exposed. The friction of us touching sends tingles up my own arm.

"I don't want you to think I don't trust you," I tell him, still holding him. "Because I do. And if you recall, we agreed not to talk about work that night."

His eyes move to where my hand is, and his expression relaxes. "Rooney, I'm not mad. And don't worry, I remember it well."

After a second too long, he pulls his arm away. I fiddle with the visitor badge hanging around my neck, twisting the blue lanyard with "JPL" printed on it.

We continue walking. Jack's long strides mark the pace as I trail behind.

"Who was it that I spoke to on the phone?" he asks, looking over his shoulder.

"That was Talia and my mom," I admit.

Jack huffs out a laugh. "They were entertaining."

"That's one word for them," I say.

We take a few steps up shallow, concrete stairs. By now Jack has slowed down enough for me to catch up with him. We're back in rhythm, walking side by side.

"FATE, really?" I ask. "And I mean the mission, not destiny."

Jack looks like he's gathering his thoughts. "We're building equipment that will serve as fueling stations in space. For spacecrafts heading to Mars and deep space. We're making reaching Mars a more consistent and frequent reality."

"Okay. That's super interesting," I say. "But why FATE?"

"The letters ended up working well together."

I tilt my head toward him. "Come on."

He hesitates. "Fine. Maybe I was inspired in an ironic way by what you told me about it. This equipment is how we take fate into our own hands if you will. Distance becomes irrelevant. We'll speed up progress."

I smile. "Ah. *Verrrrry* interesting. Admit it. You've got a little thing for fate, huh?"

Jack raises his eyebrows. "The only fate I believe in or care about is this mission. And the fate of the earth and how it'll all end."

"Sure. So then tell me. How does FATE work?" I remove my sketchbook and a pen from my bag to take notes as we walk. I catch Jack looking at my pen, and I realize which one I'm using. The floaty pen from our night together.

"I—"

"It's nice that you use it," he says softly. "A memento. Um, so with FATE, we won't have to wait for Mars to align with Earth anytime we want to send rovers. Eventually humans. There's less of a risk of missing that short window of alignment, as long as we have the equipment ready. You don't necessarily have to create something about FATE. It's one of the many missions happening here."

"I'll keep that in mind," I say.

I balance my sketchbook on my arm, jotting down keywords that I hope will inspire ideas later. While I typically fly through sketchbooks, this is the same one I've had for over a year. I don't dare flip the last page over. I know what I'd see: *Gravity*, the last idea I had the week after my night with Jack. The remaining blank pages a direct reflection of my lack of ideas and drained creativity.

Jack opens the door to the Space Flight Operations Facility. He tells me this is home to Mission Control for NASA's Deep Space Network. I notice his tone shifts into something more professional.

We step into the back of the room. Ahead of us, computer banks stretch horizontally while large screens overhead showcase images of satellites with data moving in and out of the dishes.

"This is the center of the universe," he continues, pointing to a plaque on the floor that says just that. "Data from deep space comes through Mission Control first. Then it's shared with the operators of the mission and teams so they can use the information to guide their work."

I spin, slowly observing everything around me. In the blue glow of the room, my sweater looks purple.

"It's like I'm in NASA's brain," I say, loosely sketching the scene in front of us. Drawing something that exists? Fine. Creating something from scratch? May never happen again.

Jack smiles and looks around, too. "Something like that. The data and images that come through here help us improve our understanding of the solar system and universe."

"Why are these here?" I ask, lifting a bag of peanuts.

"They're good-luck peanuts. After six failed missions in the Ranger program in 1964, there was a lot of pressure for the seventh mission to be a success. Peanuts were passed around to everyone to relieve tension. To give people something to snack on. Take their mind off the pressure. As you could probably guess, the seventh mission was indeed a success. From that point on, peanuts were designated as lucky."

This information pleases me to no end. "NASA is superstitious!"

"It's more of a tradition," he corrects.

I shake the peanuts. "What if someone's allergic to this tradition?"

Jack grows quiet. "Hmm. We don't always leave them lying around. But that's a good question." He points out the other people in the room, who are closely monitoring their screens. "There's always at least five people here at all times."

"Every day?"

"Twenty-four/seven. Since 1964," he says, facing me.

In Jack's eyes are small white rectangles, the monitors in the dark room reflecting off his pupils. Knowing that he works here is like a block falling into place in a Jack-shaped Tetris game. His comments in New York about Polaris and the moon being a satellite pop into my head. It makes so much sense now.

I whistle quietly. "That's one high electricity bill."

We peek through the windows of the Multi-Mission Support Area and then make our way up to what Jack explains is the Viewing Gallery.

Peering down over Mission Control, I etch a darker line around the curve of a peanut I've drawn. Then, without warning, I poke Jack in the shoulder with the end of the pen.

Jack looks at the light indent in his button-down. "What was that for?"

"Just making sure you're real," I say, twisting the pen between my fingers. "I can't believe I'm here right now. That *you're* here right now."

Jack angles his head up, gazing toward the ceiling. In the few seconds that he's not watching me, I steal a glance at the face that fills my day- and night dreams. Seeing the crescent moon on his lip sends chills down my spine, a sliver of a reminder from when he kissed me.

He holds his hand against the back of his neck. "I'll say this: I really never thought I'd see you again."

"Lightning doesn't strike twice," I say, swallowing down unexpected emotion that rises to the surface. It's nice seeing him shocked. I imagine it takes a lot to rattle him, but he's not as surprised as he should be. Because this is a Holy-Shit-What-Does-It-All-Mean level of surprise. I keep an awkward grin plastered on my face, smiling through the confusion and absurdity of the situation.

Jack. As my liaison. He was supposed to be someone I could recall stories about when I wanted to share what wild chance encounters really looked like. A What-If who I could feel the low ache of sadness over. A mirage in my memory, wondering if it really happened.

He wasn't supposed to be someone I have to work with for an entire year.

Jack crosses his arms. I notice that his sleeves are rolled down again. I also realize that this disappoints me. "I am looking forward to seeing what you create. Though you're unknown to the public, your art is really truthful."

I inhale deeply. "Thanks. I'm thrilled about my work being seen on a national level, and it's neat that there's history and legacy behind this program. I hope to teach people about something abstract and bring them together around one exciting moment or cause or concept or purpose. Like FATE. The mission, of course," I say with a grin.

Jack dips his head and smiles.

"With my art, I want to create what I care about and what I believe in. There's more overlap with fate and science than you might think," I add.

"You're going to have to explain that to me sometime," he says.

"You'd be surprised. My work isn't so black and white."

Jack lifts his chin. "No. It's red."

My work *was* red. At this point I'd take blue, green, yellow. I'll drop the R from my name and become Ooney, Orange String Girl. I'd work with any color, if only I could think of new ideas.

I don't share with him that I've been feeling creatively blocked. I can't just tell the mission liaison of NASA's new art program on the first day, "Hey, great to be here. I know you're taking a chance on me and that it's imperative this does well so you can continue to get funding in the future. Oh, by the way, I haven't had any new ideas in six months. Want me to make a pet portrait of your dog until inspiration strikes?"

Instead, I give positivity a shot. "Perfect for the Red Planet," I end up saying.

When it becomes unusually quiet, I realize it's just us in the Viewing Gallery. The glowing blue room feels like a futuristic confessional, so I continue.

"My mom, Wren, you know the one," I say, attempting to make Jack laugh. When he huffs out a small puff of air, I smile in return. "Your suspicions weren't far off. She's also an artist. A pretty famous one, too. I hope this opportunity can do for me what one of her video art pieces did for her. Not the making-me-famous part, but the part that gives me enough exposure to help me branch off on my own. Financially, I mean. I want financial independence, to be a working artist."

I purposely don't mention *Baby Being Born* and needing money fast so that I can buy it back. It's too weird to try to explain.

"I think that's great," Jack says. "And this should definitely bring Red String Girl more exposure. Especially with several showcases throughout the year. More touchpoints for you to have work for people to discuss. The first one will be in January."

"So that means I need to have an installation ready in...five months." I write the month down in my sketchbook and circle it a couple of times. "Easy peasy lemon squeezy."

"Your work really is incredible, Rooney. I think what you do here is going to impress people. NASA isn't limiting you, either. You can create installations around whatever you learn that you find interesting. And you can still make your own art and put on shows, of course. It was in the contract so I'm sure you know all of that."

"Thanks," I say, nodding and forcing a smile. Before we go down a rabbit hole of questions like where I usually get my ideas and inspiration from, it's time to change the subject. "Why are you doing this program?"

Jack shifts his weight from one foot to the other. "Oh. It was a unique opportunity to resurrect the Artist-in-Residence program. It's an honor to have a small role in it."

I lean against the railing. "Right. You trying to be promoted or something?"

In the blue light, I can still see Jack's cheeks grow a shade darker. "What? I didn't say that."

"There's no shame in trying to get ahead, Jack. I'm curious to know why you're part of this."

He lets out a long breath through his nose. "I've been told that I don't inspire. That I'm too transactional. That I do the work but don't know how to teach it. People need to see that I'm a person and not just a coworker, I guess. Something about emotional connection. On that day in New York, I learned I was passed over for a promotion for a senior engineering role. For a third time."

I let out a small gasp. "I'm sorry, Jack. That's why you didn't want to talk about work that night."

Jack stares down over the blinking lights of the computers. "We don't usually have to discuss our work with the press or anything on this scale. Only at conferences and with other teams."

I wait for him to elaborate, but he doesn't. "This might be one of those teaching moments you can practice," I say. "Take it from the top. Systems engineer. What do you do? Go."

Jack's mouth quirks. "Oftentimes, early in the development life cycle of a mission, we live in the gray. Develop mission concepts. Do systems modeling and analysis. We're like producers managing a lot of moving parts and numerous teams trying to keep everyone happy and working in sync, all within a tight budget and timeline."

"Sounds like you really know what you're doing," I say.

"Apparently that's not enough," Jack says on an exhale. "The role went to a guy who's the total opposite of me. Social, involved, inspirational. A real team player. I thought I was a team player because I do my job well. When the next promotion cycle comes around, I need to be ready."

I nod along. "Hence doing things like this program."

"I can get really into the weeds, and my manager wants me to see the forest," he says. "And teach my team about the forest in an inspiring way. That's the best idiom I've got."

"I was hoping for something space-themed, given where we are, but I get it," I say, nudging him.

A bigger smile forms on Jack's face. For a few seconds, we're just there, frozen in the moment. Staring at each other above the center of the universe, where there's beeping and blinking lights, the cosmos at people's fingertips. I take a deep breath in, steadying myself.

And then I have to ask. "Why did you kiss me?" I whisper.

Jack inhales quickly and looks around. "Rooney, we shouldn't be talking about this here. I—"

"I just want to know what it meant." I tug at a loose thread on the waistline of my sweater. "What it meant to you."

"Honestly? I don't know what it meant anymore. I've never done anything like that before. And now it's more complicated, especially since we work together." He pauses. "But while we're on the topic, why didn't you text me?" he asks, his tone flat.

"Why didn't I text you?" I whisper. "If you had given me the right number, you'd know I tried contacting you."

"You must have gotten the numbers mixed up," he says, his steely reserve softening.

"I texted you on the number you gave me," I explain. "When I realized it was the wrong one, I texted dozens of versions to try to get it right. When that didn't work, I called every downtown hotel looking for you. I even went to see if Dave might know how to reach you."

His eyebrows shoot up in surprise. "Yeah. Dave is long gone. I tried to find the painting you were a part of at MoMA. Can confirm that you are uncredited. But that pea flower sunset? Wow."

The fact that he remembers this small detail makes my heart swell.

"I must've searched for the Chinese restaurant we ate at thousands of times," he adds. "I couldn't for the life of me find it."

"Oh, yeah. It closed down a month after. Now it can only exist in our memories." Just like how I thought you were going to exist, I don't say. Instead, I just keep smiling and pretending everything is totally fine, but there's a sadness deep down. "I spend months searching for you, and you searching for me. Then suddenly we're both here. Isn't that amazing?"

"I never thought our paths would cross again," Jack says.

"And now they have, but things are...well, they're different, aren't they? We work together now." I think for a moment, trying to untangle the thread. "We have new knowledge. Like how you want a promotion and need this program to do well, how I want to get my art career off the ground in a big way, how this knit blend does not work in the desert."

Jack looks at my sweater and smiles. "Give it a few months and it'll be perfect."

I keep my smile in place. "Regardless of everything, it's nice to have a friend here."

"Yes. A friend," Jack says skeptically. "I don't really have friends at work."

"Now you do."

A small sense of closure washes over me. Closure for that night but also for my wavering belief in the red thread. After that night with Jack, I felt like it had fizzled out. Everything felt hopeless in love and work. At certain points of our night together, it really felt like this man in front of me could be my stringmate. And when that night ended, it took part of me with it.

Now it strikes me that, if that night meant anything, maybe it was ultimately about bringing us here together now, at NASA. Jack saw my installation and didn't get a promotion. People littered in my garbage net, and it got cut down. We were brought together so that we could help each other in this way. Professionally and not romantically.

It could be that my string and Jack's string are overlapping, but they're not connected. This is all just part of the process. There must be something—or someone—else for me here.

Jack looks down at the ground. "Rooney, can we not let that night affect our working relationship? There was this guy who was recently fired for having an intimate relationship with one of the vendors he worked with. He showed preferential treatment. With my job, the promotion, I can't risk it. New York has to stay in the past."

I wave my hands. "I don't want you to lose anything, Jack. I don't want me to, either."

His jaw flexes as he clenches it. "You're here for a year, and then you'll go back to New York City. I know this is unusual. That night we met, we agreed not to talk about our work. Now we're at work. Together. The irony."

"Alanis Morissette would have a field day," I joke, trying to relieve some of the tension. "But this does feel like a big sign."

Jack rocks back on his heels. "A sign for what?"

The start of something that will either make me or destroy me.

"I don't know yet," I finally say. "But I can feel it."

Chapter 14

JACK

Welcome to your first suit-up. This is the clean room at the Space-craft Assembly Facility, or SAF," I explain as I join Rooney outside the doors of the gowning room. After a couple of weeks of orientations and trainings, Rooney finally gets to experience what we do here.

We're both covered head to toe in white bunny suits. She pulls at the protective thin material. "Think NASA will let me keep one? You know, as a memento?"

"I can't endorse that," I say. "We wear these to help minimize pollutants and airborne particles in this room. Dust, hair, fragrances, body oils. All of these things run the risk of contaminating the spacecrafts and potentially the environment we're trying to study in space."

"Isn't that what the air shower was for?" Rooney asks, tucking her red sketchbook under her arm. "Because that was life-changing."

"Exactly. It's the last chance to get dirt, hair, and any remaining debris off before entering the clean room. Sometimes after, I feel cleaner than if I had showered with water," I admit.

"What brand of air shampoo do you use?" she asks with a smirk.

"I prefer the one that makes the air body wash–shampoo combo. It saves time." The joke slips out before I fully process our conversation. This is absolutely not the place for jokes.

"We're cleaner than surgeons before they operate," she continues. "It makes you wonder why doctors don't have air showers, doesn't it?"

I resist the urge to joke again.

"We have to do everything we can to avoid system and instrument failures," I explain. "It's very serious."

"That would be so typically human of us to bring bacteria from Earth to another planet," she says bleakly.

I cast a sideways glance at her, slightly amused. "Here we build and test most of our robotic spacecrafts. High Bay 1 is JPL's largest clean room. It's about eighty feet by one hundred and twenty feet. Forty-four feet high. I'll be showing you around."

Rooney rubs her gloved hands together. "Will I get to touch a spacecraft?"

"No."

"One of the FATE gas stations?" she asks.

I shake my head. "Unfortunately not. But you can touch it with your eyes."

"That's my favorite way to feel," she says sarcastically.

I watch her explore the all-white, warehouse-size space. Her gaze passes over the equipment, the Wall of Fame with images of previous missions, and the silver film spread over machinery and objects in the room to prevent contamination and transmission of electric charges.

"Can I do one of my installations in here? This space is incredible," she asks.

I snort. "Dusty, the contamination control engineer who manages the clean room, would never allow it."

"Wait. The guy who manages this place, his name is Dusty?" Rooney asks. "That's perfect."

"It's actually Dustin. He prefers Dusty, though," I clarify. "He thinks it's pretty funny, too."

"What do those vents up there do?" she asks, pointing toward the far end of the room.

"The air is kept clean by a special ventilation system. Clean air blows in from there, and the old air is sucked out and processed through filters before being blown back."

"Forget nature. This is the cleanest air I'll probably ever breathe." Rooney deeply inhales. "Yeah. That's good stuff. My New York City–born-and-bred lungs can't handle such pure air. Can we pollute the air a little? I don't want my lungs getting too comfortable."

I smile. "Sure, no problem. I'll sabotage the missions for you. Grab some soil from the Mars Yard. Throw it into the air. Dusty will kill me, but it's worth it if it means saving you." I catch myself, as though even the slightest impure thought might contaminate the area.

Rooney places her gloved hand on my upper arm. "That's the most romantic gesture anyone's ever offered me."

"Here. Let me help you with your grounding strap," I say, noticing she's not wearing it. Rooney steps closer to me and holds her wrist out. I pull back her sleeve until I find skin. I fumble with the coiled cord, wrapping the wristlet around her arm.

"That's not too tight?" I ask.

"Just right," she says quietly. With her hair under a hood and the face mask covering the lower half of her face, her eyes are all I can see. When framed by white cloth and without bangs falling over them, they look like a richer shade of honey. Dark amber.

I hold her eyes for a few more seconds.

"Is that it?" she asks.

I pull my gloved hand away from her wrist. "Yeah. Yes. We, uh, we clip this end to the hardware when we're working on it. This is to prevent the buildup of static electricity. We can't risk damaging these spacecraft electronics with an electric shock."

Rooney confidently gestures toward the others in the room and calls out, "You're all unsung heroes. Without you, this room, your brains, and these little black wrist cords, astronauts would go nowhere." They laugh.

Everyone in here today has signed NDAs so that Rooney can ask them questions. If there's anything I've noticed about her so far, it's that she's observational. Rooney notices something unremarkable about a place and expands upon it, providing a new perspective. No wonder she's a great artist.

Dusty approaches us with a clipboard in hand. I estimate that he's in his mid-sixties. He's clean-shaven and detail-oriented, which I've always appreciated. He's also worked his way up at NASA, which is an inspiration in and of itself. He's been here longer than I've been alive.

"Welcome, Rooney," Dusty says before introducing himself. "If you have questions I can answer about the clean room, I'll be around."

"Actually, I do have a question," Rooney says, smiling sweetly and pointing to me. "He won't let me touch anything in here. Do you have the power to do something about that?"

I cough out a small laugh.

"No coughing! I'll apologize for him, Dusty," Rooney says, patting my back.

"Your DNA is getting all over," Dusty says dramatically. "We can't risk little Jacksons popping up on Mars."

Rooney laughs hard at this.

Dusty chuckles, too. "But no, I'm afraid you'll have to blame me for that one," he says, answering Rooney's original question. "I assure you we're excited to have you here. I'm personally a big art fan, so this was happy news about the Artist-in-Residence program coming back. Have you been enjoying the area?"

"So far I've only visited the Norton Simon Museum," Rooney informs him.

"That's it? Has Jackson planned anything fun? A team welcoming of sorts?" Dusty asks, turning his focus on me.

Rooney shakes her head. "Afraid not, Dusty. We've been focused on work, but a little team event sounds like a great idea. Nothing like a little NDA-signing party to make everyone feel bonded."

Dusty leans back and crosses his arms. "You have your reasons, I'm sure." As he turns to leave, he adds, "If you ever want to come to Social Science, Rooney, do let me know. It's our biweekly happy hour. There's also the Cacti Council, of which I am the chair. We discuss very important topics like what type of cacti is trending. There are a couple of events coming up you might want to keep on your radar."

"Dusty apparently has an extensive cacti and succulent collection at home," I explain, recalling what he's shared with me during an earlier invite.

"They're my children," he says. "I put all my money into them and love them equally."

"Kids. You have to love them even when they're prickly," Rooney says, straight-faced.

Dusty chuckles and tilts his clipboard toward us. "And Jackson, the invite always stands. It would be great to see you there sometime."

"Invite still stands?" Rooney asks when Dusty moves on to the next team.

"I haven't had time to go," I inform her.

Rooney arches her eyebrows.

"What?" I shrug. "I'm not here to socialize."

"Do you know anything about the people you work with?" Rooney asks. "What about barbecues or office parties? Aren't you angling for a promotion?"

"How do grilled meats have anything to do with that?"

"Dusty seemed to appreciate that you know about his cacti," Rooney says. "It shows him you're interested. That you care. It's nice to have people on your side, Jack."

"It's just not something I'm used to. My inner circle is...small. As for my colleagues, I know what they do here and how we need to work together," I say. "I don't see how needing to know who's married to who or who does what for fun on the weekends really matters."

I can see Rooney studying the side of my face as I guide her through the room so I feel compelled to add, "When the team needs something, anything, I will do what I have to do to get it for them. To ensure the mission is a success. I like to focus on the work. Besides, now I'm mission liaison."

"Exactly. You're the mission liaison. You'll be talking to the press about your mission but also about the team behind it, right? They'll want to hear how you all work together to accomplish this massive undertaking more than they'll want to know about the technicalities."

I shake my head. "I bet people are more interested in how it works than you think. That's why I'm the one who has to liaison and explain it. And I'll be using your art to help me communicate the big ideas. People want to know how we're actually going to get to Mars, not about the people behind it like me."

Rooney gently places her gloved hand on my shoulder. "They definitely want to know about people like you, the people behind the machines. And absolutely they want to hear from the ones who are doing the work more than they want to be marketed to by a communications team. You and your team do challenging things every day here. Tell people who you are."

I let Rooney's words sink in. When she doesn't say more, I lead her to the airlock, the area attached to the clean room where spacecrafts and equipment move in and out without exposing the clean room itself to the outside air.

"Once the spacecrafts leave the airlock, they're on their way to the end destination," I explain. "People think it's once the spacecrafts have taken off at the launch site that the journey begins. But no. This is where it all starts."

"It's fun to watch you do what you love," Rooney says as she hugs her sketchbook to her chest. Her papery-thin suit makes a soft crinkling noise.

"How can you tell I love it?" I ask.

She hums. "The way you talk about it. How your voice softens. Your thoughtful movement in the room. Your patience with me."

"Being in here never gets old. This is where history is made," I say matter-of-factly.

"Literally. It's *made* here," she says, looking around at all the shiny equipment.

Behind my face mask, I smile at her.

We quietly walk past teams working on spacecrafts for their missions. Finally, we reach one of the parts of the FATE mission equipment. My colleague, Maria, is already there working on troubleshooting potential problems.

"You grounded?" Rooney asks, looking carefully at their wrists.

"Fast learner," Maria, the team's instrument systems engineer, says with a laugh. She holds up her wrist to show us that she is.

"So this is it, huh?" Rooney says, eyeing up the craft.

"One of the FATE spacecrafts, yes," I say.

"How would fuel actually get to the equipment?" she asks.

"We're working on a couple of different options," I explain. "There's one way of thinking that uses the moon's water ice from its lunar craters to convert into rocket fuel. But our mission focuses on alternatives to moon mining."

Maria climbs down the ladder. "We want to build stations like the International Space Station, or ISS for short. Not as large, of course. Just big enough for docking and fueling," she adds. "Jackson, if you need me, I'll be back from lunch in a bit."

I nod to acknowledge her.

Rooney watches us curiously. "So you launch these into space. Then they just stay where they are?" she asks me.

"Good question. The ISS orbits Earth at seventeen thousand five hundred miles per hour to stay in orbit. The equipment of our FATE mission would also always have to be in orbit. We would manage them and their locations within the solar system from Earth."

"It's like stepping stones," she says. "To Mars."

"That's a nice way to imagine it," I say.

"Lily pads in a pond that frogs use to cross over to the other side."

"Anything else?" I ask.

"I prefer not to give spoilers. I need to save them for my creations," she says. "Next question: How far away is Mars?"

"Depends on where it is in its orbit around the sun. They have elliptical paths, so their minimum distance is never the same," I say. "And gravitational pull affects their orbit. And other planets, like Jupiter, influence the orbit, too."

"I should've known better than to have expected a simple answer," she says, starting to move in her own orbit around the equipment.

I climb the ladder next to the spacecraft to check out the machinery. I clip myself to the hardware and evaluate the work that's been completed today to determine if there are more tests to run this week.

It seems that Rooney and I share a similar process. Below me, she crouches to look at the hardware from a different angle. For a moment, I see the equipment in front of me through Rooney's eyes. I follow the sharp angles of it until Rooney is back in my view. Her knees have become a makeshift table for her sketchbook as she holds her pen an inch above the paper. She doesn't make a mark and instead stares at the empty page.

"Do you want to see this up close?" I call to her. "The inside is more interesting than what's underneath."

Rooney looks up and nods quickly. "I want to see how the space sausage gets made."

She holds the base of the ladder still as I slowly step down. We switch places at the bottom. Move clockwise, our covered feet in sync. The dances of the sterile chamber.

I grip my hand over the side of the ladder. She hands me her sketchbook before climbing. Her leg sweeps my arm, our bunny suits rubbing gently against each other. The spark of an electric shock runs through me, my grounding strap not protecting me from the charge.

"I've never seen anything like it." Rooney peers into the body of the craft when she reaches the top. "Scalpel," she says, holding out her hand.

I laugh and shake my head. Her sketchbook flips open. While she's busy looking at my work, I can't help but glance at hers.

"No, don't look!" she calls out.

I'm mid-flip when she says this and have already looked at a few pages. But there's nothing there.

"Jack!"

"Sorry! I didn't see anything. See?" I turn the sketchbook toward her. "It's blank."

"Exactly," she says with a dramatic huff. She unclips herself from the machine and climbs down the ladder. "That's what I didn't want you to see."

"I sincerely apologize. I had something in my possession that gave me direct access to your brain. It drew me in." In her eyes, I can see that she's sort of smiling. "What did you not want me to see?"

"That I have," she starts, looking around and lowering her voice to a whisper, "artist's block."

I close the sketchbook. "This is all so new. That would be pretty unusual to have ideas for intricate installations on your first suit-up," I say, trying to reassure her.

She keeps her eyes trained on the large piece of reflective metal in front of her. "I appreciate you saying that, but even still. This place is artistically ripe for something incredible, yet the information just passes through me. Nothing is sticking. There's no significance. Without deeper meaning behind my installations, it's just...string. I've really fooled everyone, huh?" she asks, her arms wrapped around herself. "This opportunity is the biggest heist of my career."

I arch an eyebrow. "How do you figure? You were chosen to do this. You were picked because of your work."

"Jack, I haven't had a new idea for an installation in six months. Inspiration? Motivation? Who are they? I don't know them anymore." Rooney fiddles with the cap of her pen as she laughs humorlessly to herself. "My liaison is the last person I should be admitting this to."

"Anytime you feel unsure, you can talk to me," I say. "That's why I'm here. You can tell me things you don't want NASA knowing." This block must be why there aren't any other photos of work on her website, just *Entangled* and sketches of *Gravity*.

Rooney's eyes glisten under the bright lights. "I just don't want to let anyone down. This is too important. I need this to work and get exposure. I need the money. The auction is only…"

She squeezes her eyes shut.

"Hey, it's okay. What auction?"

"Jack, I'm going to come clean to you. And be warned that this is not proper clean room talk." There she is.

"Okay. Yeah. Welcome to Clean Room Confessions," I say, suddenly realizing how hard I'm trying to make her feel better.

She inhales deeply. "I was born a piece of art."

"You are pretty great," I start, not knowing how to respond to this.

"No, like a literal piece of art," she clarifies, her tone unenthusiastic.

I'm confused. "Like your mom painted a portrait of you after you were born?"

Her posture deflates. "More like I was born in front of people, and it was recorded and subsequently sold for a good amount of money. Literally. My mom birthed me in a museum as part of a one-time be-there-or-you'll-miss-it art exhibit."

My jaw drops, and I'm grateful for the mask to cover it. "Seriously?"

"It's called *Baby Being Born*. I'm…the baby that was born. Her goal was to celebrate birth and women and to show the types of things you rarely get to see. Expensive art, people giving birth," Rooney explains. "Long story short, it's coming up for auction and I want to buy it back. For my entire childhood, it was the most interesting thing about me. I was always that baby, an exhibit."

I'm exposed to big, new ideas every day at work but that is definitely something I haven't come across before.

"Talk about being put on a pedestal in life. That must've been tough," I say.

"People wanted to meet me because of it. It's partly why I went into hiding as an artist. I didn't want my success to come from *Baby Being Born*. I wanted it to be because of what I create."

"That's why you go undercover as Red String Girl," I say.

She nods. "If no one knows it's me, daughter of Wren Gao, then I can find success on my own," she says. "And they won't rename the piece *Nepo Baby Being Born*. Anyways."

I know she's trying to make light of the situation, cracking jokes at her own expense. I clench my jaw. I don't like seeing Rooney sad.

"It happened after our night in New York," she continues. "Losing inspiration. All that talk about fate, us meeting in the way that we did, the destruction of *Entangled*, it must've thrown me off. That was the installation that was supposed to change the course of my career. And maybe in a weird way it did, because now I'm here. I got a second chance for a big break, and I'm creatively blocked!"

I nod, understanding the feeling of having been thrown off after that night. "And our talk about fate impacted you? You don't believe in the Red Thread of Fate anymore?" I ask.

"Of course I still believe in it...but the spark feels gone. Everything feels flat, empty. For my work, for any new ideas, and yes, sometimes even for fate," she says, glancing up at me. "I've never been creatively blocked before. I just haven't felt like myself in a long time, and now meeting you here just makes everything more confusing. Like I said, nothing is sticking. It's difficult to know what anything really means right now."

I look around to see who might be able to overhear us. I'm not used to having these types of discussions in here. It's mostly empty, except for Dusty and another team at the computers. We walk around the equipment toward a different piece of machinery.

"I don't know what I'm going to do," she says, staying close to my side. Her defeated tone of voice makes the center of my chest tighten.

I can problem-solve this. Fix this. That's what I'm good at. Talking about the technicalities and working through complicated issues. But my manager has been saying that there are soft skills involved, too. That I need to inspire. Maybe this is one of those moments.

Think, Jack. If this was a challenge on your mission, how would you find a solution? What can you say that might help? What can you do?

It comes to me so suddenly, I almost want to laugh.

"We'll test it," I say.

Rooney shakes her head. "What?"

"We're going to get you creatively reinspired," I tell her.

"I wish it were that easy," she says.

"Would you be willing to try?"

"I don't agree to anything without reading the fine print first, but at this point, I'll try anything," Rooney says. There's intrigue behind her eyes.

"Red String Theory. The fate tests we came up while eating dumplings. We're going to follow the list."

Rooney lets out a short laugh. "You're not serious…"

"You said you want to become creatively unblocked. And your belief in fate helps you do that. It's what inspires you in your work."

"And in love," Rooney adds. "They're both intertwined."

"Yes. Right," I say. "Your first showcase is in less than four months. Let's get you your spark back. I think a little perspective shift is needed. We'll take classic fate moments, do them in real life, and observe what happens."

Rooney pulls at the grounding strap on her wrist. "I don't see how that's going to work. Especially here of all places. You want to test fate…at NASA. I'm sure I'll feel creative again soon. There's still time." She doesn't sound very confident.

"Rooney, there's no time to wait around for inspiration. Or fate, for that matter. NASA is literally where people come up with new ideas and make them happen. We're in a room where spacecrafts get made," I say, gaining enthusiasm as I go on. "You think we get to space by waiting until motivation strikes? No! It's because we have an idea, a goal, a dream, and we make it happen. We form hypotheses, test them, and try different variations when the first time doesn't work." I'm breathless after my pep talk.

Rooney's eyes are scrunched up. "I hear you. That was very convincing, but—"

"No buts. You were willing to play along in New York. Will you now?" I ask. "Do you trust me?"

She's quiet, though I can tell Rooney is smiling by the way her cheeks push up over her mask. "Now you know all of my secrets, so yeah, I guess I do." Rooney tilts her head back. "I'm doing this for both of us, though. I know how important this promotion is to you, and I'm not the only one who wants the program to be a success."

"Yes. Great. Okay. We'll keep it simple. Here's the hypothesis," I say excitedly, piecing the words together in my head. "If you follow these Fate Tests, then you will be reinspired."

Rooney's eyes are fixed on mine. "Where do we start?"

"Do you have the list from that night?" I ask. "If not, we can try to piece it back together."

Rooney glances down at her sketchbook in my hands. "Check the back pocket."

I reach into the attached folder and pull out the creased Chinese menu from our night together. In the corner is a splash of soy sauce that I hadn't noticed earlier.

I unfold it, and for a brief moment, I'm back in that Chinese restaurant at midnight. I'm warm and eating dumplings while the snow falls outside. I snap out of it and back to the present moment. I run my eyes down the list.

> Fate Test 1: Say yes to something you normally wouldn't.
> Fate Test 2: Show up early or late to somewhere you're supposed to be.
> Fate Test 3: Return a lost object.
> Fate Test 4: Interact with someone online.

Rooney peers over the edge of the menu. "This is a good start, but we need one more. Four is bad luck. What about 'Follow the signs'?" she offers. "Like when I notice something that feels like a sign, to pay attention and…follow it?"

"That's too abstract. What about directions and knowingly not following them? Like with maps. Something like that?" I think out loud.

"Yeah, that's not bad." Rooney points at me. "You might be a little too good at this, Jack."

On the menu, below Fate Test 4, I write:

> Fate Test 5: Go the wrong direction on purpose.

"Now what?" Rooney asks.

I smile. "Follow me."

Rooney stays where she is and narrows her eyes at me. "Is this part of the test? Should I walk in the opposite direction of you?"

I shake my head and wave the menu. "I can't rip this in the clean room. Fibers from the paper and all that. Come on."

Her curiosity gets the best of her. "Rip? Rip what?" Rooney asks as she traces my steps.

"After you," I say, opening the door to the air shower. "We're going into the shower together. Air shower! That's where we're going together. That's not how I meant that to sound." My face feels as hot as the sun. "I apologize if I made that weird."

Rooney bursts into laughter. Her laugh is as easy and loose as it was in New York. That night is a memory I've sealed shut in the airlock room of my mind. A place where no other thoughts can touch or alter it. That night is its own standalone event. So out of the ordinary for my life that it requires careful handling because it's once in a lifetime.

"I'm going, I'm going. Just promise you'll share the hot air." She steps inside the enclosed room.

I take the menu between my fingers and tear along each written Fate Test until we have five strips with one test per slip. I open and close the entrance door to activate the high-velocity air. From the jets in the side of the wall, air pummels us from all sides. Rooney holds her hands up, waving them vigorously as her suit puffs out.

"Grab one!" I shout to Rooney. Then I let go of the strips of paper.

The Fate Tests blow around us, being pushed every which way like we're in a money-blowing machine. But right now, these Fate Test strips are better than dollars.

Rooney closes her eyes and leans her head back. She spins slowly, like she's letting the air blow her worries away. I've never seen anyone so moved by being cleaned. She keeps her fingers spread out until one of the papers flies into her hand. She makes a fist around it.

As cool air expands my suit, I realize that this is a total misappropriation and misuse of taxpayer dollars. But for her, I would do it over and over again.

For her, I am going to test the hell out of fate.

Chapter 15

ROONEY

I'm staring at one of the Fate Test slips when Talia rolls to a stop in front of the entrance of The Huntington Library, Art Museum, and Botanical Gardens in the car we leased together. Well, Talia paid for most of it, and I'll pay the rest of my half as soon as I can.

"You're sure you want to be forty-five minutes early?" Talia asks. "What are you going to do while you wait?"

"Being early gives me time on the front end to see what happens," I tell her, waving the slip with "Fate Test 2: Show up early or late to somewhere you're supposed to be" written on it. "And I'm meeting the FATE team and want to make a good first impression."

"You're going to have to explain this whole test thing again to me later," Talia says, checking her eye makeup in the visor mirror. "Text me when you're done."

I step out of the car and make my way to the check-in kiosks to present my e-ticket.

Tucking the slip into my bag, I take note of my surroundings. The entrance to The Huntington is lush and beautifully designed. Olive trees and succulents line the walkway, which leads out to buildings containing art and rare books as well as gardens of all kinds, like Chinese, desert, rose, Japanese, and camellia. This place is an installation heaven.

I could start in the café and grab a beverage. Or I could go see the garden sculptures and fountains while I wait for the team. There's a large group wearing cloud-covered shirts taking over two tables in the courtyard. In theory, the Fate Tests sounded compelling, but now I just feel silly. What am I even supposed to do?

After I look around, unable to figure out where to start, my attention is drawn to a family coming out of the gift shop. A tall man in dark jeans and a blue T-shirt with clouds on it, like the group in the courtyard, holds the door open for them. It's like he knows I'm looking at him because his eyes find mine, and we smile at the same time. He stays where he is, so I walk over, lingering a few feet before him.

I look at him expectantly, taking note of the way his blond hair shines in the sun. I'm quiet, willing him to be the first to speak. It works.

"So...are you going in or staying out?" he asks kindly.

Okay. Not quite what I had in mind.

"I could ask the same thing," I say with an awkward laugh. I notice the words on his shirt spell out "Cloud Lovers League."

"I'm going in," he says, removing his hand from the door but keeping it propped open with his foot.

I take this as a sign that he's trying to free up his hand to shake mine, so I extend my arm out first. As I do this, the man's hand is halfway to his back pocket where he reaches for...his phone.

My hand morphs into a pointing position without me having to think too hard about it. I love when reflexes do their job. "There. I'm going in there," I say, exaggerating my pointing finger as though that's what I had intended to do all along.

The man nods curtly. "Uh, great. After you. Have a nice day." He follows me in but quickly turns toward the opposite side of the gift shop.

That went well.

The store is spacious and colorful with autumn-themed decorations, little bundles of hay lining the windows with stuffed pumpkins on top. At first glance, it's well curated with themed tables scattered throughout the shop. One has a topical selection of books, teas, and accessories related to forest bathing. Another is all about apples.

I look at my phone to check the time. Still thirty-five minutes left until I meet up with the FATE team. I'm starting to regret having agreed to tests of any kind. I despised tests in school. Why did I willingly sign up for more? And why am I doing them alone? Regardless, I don't need tests to find inspira—

"Rooney," I hear a voice say.

I spin to find Jack wearing a lightly faded, short-sleeve maroon polo with sunglasses tucked into the unbuttoned neckline. It surprises me that he's in khaki shorts, a garment Jack would consider unprofessional in a work setting, but it's a Saturday and we're technically not at work. What a relief it is to see his face.

As I take note of his outfit, my eyes slip farther from his shorts to his shoes, along the way catching sight of his legs, the curve of his calves making their firm appearance as he takes each step. My ears lightly throb as my heartbeat quickens. I must be nervous to meet the team.

Jack's coming toward me, so I redirect my eyes, running them along the lines of the carpeting and up the nearest bookcase. Finally, after enough time has passed, I look back at Jack, but at his eyes this time.

"You're early," we both say at the same time.

"Did you know that man at the door?" Jack asks with a quizzical expression.

I peek back toward the entrance, where fate did not have plans for me. "You saw that? I don't know him. I was trying something out," I explain. "In my head, it was supposed to be more romantic than that."

"That didn't look even the slightest bit romantic, I'm sorry to say," he says, looking like he's holding back a laugh.

I groan. "That bad, huh?"

Jack smiles and points at me. "I'll say this: you have a great reflex."

I tug at the neckline of my cropped knitted red tank top and distract myself with a soy sauce bottle ornament, focusing on the shine of the red glittery cap. We walk slowly through the store, picking up small items here and there.

Jack turns to face me, looking excited for some reason. "Speaking of stringmates, if I may...or is it too soon?"

I huff out a tight laugh. "You have something to say about stringmates? I have to hear it."

"I watched *Serendipity*—" he starts.

"Wait. You watched *Serendipity*? Without me? That's my favorite."

"It was in the name of research," Jack explains. A flash of what looks like regret crosses his face. "Sorry. I didn't know. But I got an idea from it."

I sigh. "Don't tell me you want me to write my name on a dollar bill," I say at the same time he says, "You should write your name on a dollar bill."

"Jack," I say, crossing my arms, "really?"

"Okay," he says. "Maybe not a dollar. Statistically speaking, there was no way Kate Beckinsale would've ever gotten her money back. But for the purposes of this, we can find something unique to you and put your number on that. See who calls. I was thinking it could be Fate Test 6."

"Look, I've been thinking about these Fate Tests, too, and I don't want to do them alone. I've clearly proven how awkward it is," I explain, gesturing toward the door. "I'm only going to do them if you come with me. This is how you're going to learn how to inspire. Didn't your boss say you needed to be better at that? So guide me through these tests. You're too much on Earth. You need to think like you're on the International Space Station looking down at Earth. I've been working on space figures of speech for you to use instead of your forest one."

Jack smiles, his crescent moon scar rising up with it.

"Let me put it this way: If you join me on the Fate Tests, then both of us will benefit in our work," I articulate, giving him a taste of his own hypothesis.

Jack's eyebrows pinch together. "This could be a fertile sandbox to test and practice my motivational skills."

"It might mean spending time together outside of work," I say hesitantly.

Jack thinks for a moment. "This is work, though, right? You can't do what you do unless you're inspired."

"Exactly. So we'll do Red String Theory together. The Fate Tests will hypothetically creatively unblock me. I'll design installations that will make everyone happy. Ideally that brings exposure, I get more shows, make money, and buy back *Baby Being Born*. If we pull this off, you'll have successfully inspired me, and we'll have worked together to do it. I'm your experiment to do with as you see fit." I frown. "I just heard that out loud."

Jack clears his throat and lifts a mug that looks like a terra-cotta pot. "Okay. I want to help."

"Great! So Fate Test 2 is checked off the list. Seems a little short-lived."

Jack sets the mug back down on the shelf slowly. "The day is still early. Maybe that guy in the blue shirt will come back for some more sweet romancing," he says, finally releasing his laugh about it.

"Hilarious. I'd love to see you out there sparking up conversation with a stranger." I say this with an attempted tone of confidence, but I find I'm failing at that. "How will this work? How do we handle the other Fate Tests?"

"We don't have to go in order. There might be a natural progression that we can follow. I may have an idea for 'Fate Test 3: Return a lost object.' Others we can act on whenever we want, like the interacting-with-someone-online test."

Heat rises in my chest as I notice his use of "we." "That works. What's your idea for 3?" I ask.

"This guy I know, Bennett O'Brien, is having a birthday party for his daughter in a couple of weeks. She's turning one," Jack says. "I wasn't planning on going but apparently they're doing something with objects. I was thinking you could come with me?"

My hand flies to my mouth to cover my gasp. "Are they having a zhuā zhōu ceremony? It's a Chinese tradition for children's first birthday parties."

Jack shakes his head. "It could be? Bennett said to bring an object for the ceremony."

"It sounds like it is!" I squeal. "That's a very fate-itious tradition."

"If objects are there, I'm sure we can think of something for Fate Test 3. There should be a good number of guests. Bennett and his wife, Olivia, are well connected in the city."

"Sounds great. I'm excited to meet them," I say.

"I know it's on a weekend. But this is work. We have to get you inspired."

I laugh. "Jack, I've already said yes."

"Okay, now that that's settled, is anything inspiring you in here?" he asks. "That's the whole point of this. What about these?" He holds a pair of opera glasses against his face and looks in my direction. "Wow, that's close. Your eyes are even lighter when magnified."

I open my eyes wider and step closer to him. "Okay, now they're terrifying," he says with a laugh.

I make a silly face, and he laughs harder.

"Jackson!" a deep voice calls out.

Jack jumps back and sets the opera glasses down on the table a bit too hard, sending a stack of jeweled bracelets scattering. I lunge forward to help Jack restack them, but there's nothing to be done about the loud noise the bracelets make against the wood.

"Dusty, hello," Jack says, his professional tone of voice on full display. He clears his throat. "We were just...We were early."

Dusty looks between the two of us, amused. "Well then, shall we? The team's outside," he says, waving us along. "We have cacti to get to."

⁓

The Huntington Desert Garden looks like a dry, magical fairyland with hundreds of golden barrel cacti sprawling across the ground among thousands of other desert plants and succulents. They practically glow with their yellow spikes uniformly protruding from their short and round bodies. Like poky watermelon. We're definitely not in New York City anymore.

In every corner of the landscaped beds, thousands of species of desert plants and succulents multiply and expand. Even in all of my travels with Mom, I've never seen anything like it.

Jack looks equally enchanted as he crouches to get a closer look at the smaller cacti growing in front of the golden barrels.

Not all of Jack's team could make it to today's outing. I formally met Maria, but Toby, Brian, and Nell are new to me. They're the team's verification and validation systems engineer, project manager, and mission assurance manager, respectively.

"Thanks for setting this up, Jackson," Dusty says. "I'll be rambling on about cacti, but please chat with each other along this tour. That's the point of this."

"You set up a walking tour about cacti...as a way to get to know the team?" I turn to ask Jack, who's trailing behind the group.

"What would've been better?" he asks.

"I don't know. I've never worked in a corporate setting before. The typical things people do in team bonding. Bowling? Dinner? Paintballing? Definitely not cactus tours."

"Bowling is loud. You're just watching people roll balls down a lane. At dinner you have to eat in front of people, and you're stuck talking to whoever happens to sit next to you. When you're paint-balling, how do people get closer when they're running around trying to hide? With a cactus tour, there's movement but in an inter-active way. And where else do you get to talk about cacti that look like old men?" he says, sweeping his hand toward what Dusty called the Old Man Cactus.

My gaze lingers on the grouping of stick-straight cacti covered fully in white fuzz that Jack's gesturing to.

"That one looks particularly grumpy," I comment.

"That one's probably a hundred and five years old. Of course he's grumpy," Jack retorts.

I laugh and then take a photo of the bunny ear succulents, which look exactly like what they're called.

I nudge Jack. "It's time to start bonding. Honestly, this team meet-and-greet is more for you than it is for me."

Jack speed-walks to catch up to his colleagues. While Dusty scribbles something in his notebook, I hear Jack ask Nell, "Do you come here often? To the desert garden, I mean."

It's not the worst start, I guess.

Nell greeted me earlier with a hug, which immediately warmed me to her. She's wearing big silver hoops and purple overalls, and before I even had to ask, she informed me that yes, they did come in red.

"I actually love cacti because I've killed every houseplant I own," Nell says. "Well, I've killed cacti, too, but it's harder to do."

My attention is pulled away by Maria, who sidles up next to me. "It's so cool that we get to hang out with you. How does it feel to be NASA's artist?"

"Can I tell you the truth? It's slightly intimidating to be working on something on such a big scale, but I'm excited," I admit.

"I can relate," Maria says. "If you ever have questions, feel free to ask anytime."

"I appreciate that. And in even more honesty," I say, "it's cooler that I get to spend time with you all."

We fall into easy conversation about how Maria got started at NASA, the difficulty being away from her family in the Philippines, and how she regrets getting her pet hamster an exercise wheel that looks like a car because he's been pulling all-nighters "driving" it. I tell her about how I'm on the hunt for a complicated knitting pattern and how much I miss walking to places. When she asks if I've been inspired by anything yet for an art piece, I keep up appearances and pretend that I am a capable and confident, creatively fulfilled artist.

Ahead of us, we hear Nell inform Jack that her favorite cacti so far were the golden barrels. Are they still talking about desert plants?

"They look like scoops of ice cream," Nell says, and it activates a memory.

"Jack makes ice cream," I blurt out, intruding on their discussion.

Jack and Nell glance back at us, both looking relieved by the interruption. This is what the walking tour is for, I figure. Interaction and a seamless flow of jumping in and out of conversations.

"So cool!" Maria contributes. "What flavors do you make?"

Jack looks at me, and his shoulders drop an inch, a small gesture hopefully confirming that this is safe discussion territory.

"I make a variety of ice cream flavors," Jack says, looking between his team members. "Matcha, black sesame, chocolate. I make the cold kind you're used to, but I also make freeze-dried ice cream."

"Freeze-dried? What? How!" Brian asks, joining us.

Jack has caught the attention of the entire team, the people in front slowing down to hear him.

The realization that I don't know these details pricks at me deeper than any of the surrounding cacti could. But how could I know things like that? We spent less than six hours together that night in New York. There's an ache of sadness inside me, and I remind myself that there's a year for me to get to know Jack. There's still time.

Jack looks content as he talks about how the process works, complete with vacuum chambers and removing ice crystals. His team asks questions about temperatures and timing.

This is an opportunity for Jack to be inspiring on an emotional level, but instead the conversation is turning into Ice Cream Making 101. I'm about to say something when Brian beats me to it.

"That all sounds cool, but I think I'll stick to eating the ice cream," Brian says with a polite laugh. "Some things in life are better left mysteries."

"Except the mysteries in space, of course," I joke as the team laughs. "Jackson, what inspired you to start making ice cream?"

Jack looks surprised by my use of the name he uses at work. "My Gōng Gong—my grandfather—taught me. We built our own freeze-drying machine," he explains. "It was a lot more cost-effective."

This gets the team's attention again, and I nod to Jack to keep going.

"My Gōng Gong worked in an ice cream shop. It's how he met my grandmother, actually. They grew up in the same town but never knew each other. Turns out that they had worked at the same ice cream shop, him during the off-season, her during the summers. They had always been near each other in proximity, but it wasn't until her mother came down with the flu that their paths finally crossed."

"How?" Dusty asks, resting his clipboard against his chest. He's as captivated by this story as the rest of us.

Jack smiles. "He was covering for someone at the shop when the phone rang. A girl asked to have two scoops of chocolate delivered for her sick mother. He dutifully did as she asked and added an extra scoop for her. He delivered it, and that was the first time he met my grandmother."

It's stories like these that make me emotional but also kind of freak me out. Jack's Gōng Gong wasn't even supposed to be at the shop to receive his future wife's call. If he had never covered for someone, he may never have met Jack's grandma. And then Jack wouldn't be here. It's downright scary sometimes how close we are to alternate life paths without even knowing. It's a story that reminds me how powerful the red thread can be. At Jack's words, there's a tingling sensation in my fingertips so slight I almost hardly feel it, but it disappears within seconds.

"He was at the right place at the right time," Jack says.

He looks up at me when he says this last part, and I blurt out, "Timing is everything," even when I know he'd explain it as a choice. He'd say his Gōng Gong chose to cover for someone, chose to add the extra scoop of ice cream, chose to go above and beyond and make a home delivery. Still, it's an inside joke, something no one else will ever know. New York City is a secret just for the two of us. It comforts me to have this invisible connection with him. We'll always have that night.

"And where does the freeze-dried ice cream come in?" Toby asks.

Jack leans back on his heels. "Ah, yes. My Gōng Gong was an ocean engineer. Sometimes he'd be out on ships and want ice cream as a snack. A snack, not a dessert. Important distinction. To him, snacks were something he could keep in his pocket," he says with a grin. "So he and my grandma learned how to make freeze-dried ice cream using the appliances at her job. She was a design engineer for a kitchen equipment manufacturer. Years after she died, Gōng Gong taught me how to make our own machine using more updated parts."

"I change my mind," Brian says. "I want to learn how to make freeze-dried ice cream."

"It's a pretty sweet story, right?" Jack asks. "No pun intended."

His team laughs.

I look around dramatically for effect and say, "Now I'll only remember this place as the Dessert Garden."

Nell hooks her thumbs into the pockets of her overalls. "Sometimes, after working late, we go to the ice cream freezer outside of the mission control room. Jackson, you should come with us next time," she offers. "You too, Rooney."

"That would be fun. Thanks," I say as Jack nods.

When no one else is looking, Jack dramatically wipes his forehead with the back of his hand. I give him a discreet thumbs-up.

"This was a pleasant surprise," Maria and Nell say to me as we continue to follow Dusty's guided tour. Jack, Brian, and Toby stay close to him as he talks about an aloe vera plant.

"This outing?" I ask.

"Yeah, we thought it was going to be awkward," Maria says. "We've never spent time with Jackson outside of work. We all go to Dusty's Social Science happy hour, so we know each other fairly well, but Jackson? I don't even know where he lives."

"That was the most I've ever heard Jackson say about nonwork topics, and I've worked with the man for two years," Nell chimes in. "He's definitely gotten more comfortable since becoming liaison and you being here. It's nice."

I don't quite know how to respond. Up until recently, Jack and I have only ever talked about things other than work. Even here in California, it feels like we can pick up where we left off. Talking about work doesn't feel like work. I'm glad the Jack from New York is starting to show, but I'm also glad I get to know him in his work element, reserved and all. It's every side of him that makes him who he is, and it's really something to see.

I turn to Maria and Nell and smile. "I agree. The man's got layers."

Chapter 16

ROONEY

I brought this as my object," I whisper to Jack as I pull a red thread between my fingers.

"So that she'd be a string artist like you?" he asks.

"So that she'd have a long life, but I like the way you think," I say. "Your rocket ship was very on brand."

Jack gives the plush a light squeeze. "We're on a mission here. Find a lost object."

"Vague," I say. "And difficult. I don't know if that's more inspirational or anxiety-inducing."

"We have to keep our eyes out for something. There's a pile of things sitting over there. You think all of them have an owner?"

"Probably since people were told to bring them," I say.

"We may need to rethink how we go about testing," Jack says with a frown. "Reconsider some variables."

"Okay, it's fine. Let's see what happens."

We're at Olivia and Bennett's house in a part of town called Silver Lake. Their living room contains furniture in various earth tones that complement each other nicely. Hanging on the walls and resting on tables throughout are photographs and various mementos that naturally get collected over the course of a relationship. The observation sends a pang of longing through me.

"Rooney! So great to meet you," Olivia says, bringing me back to the moment. She embraces me in a hug. I've never been hugged more in my life than I have here in Los Angeles. "Have you met my husband, Bennett, yet?"

After picking me up for the party, Jack prepped me about the hosts. He knows Bennett because they volunteer together in the same Shoot for the Stars group where they work to get kids interested in STEM. Olivia took over Lunar Love, her Pó Po's matchmaking business, at the same time Bennett was launching his matchmaking app, ZodiaCupid. When they teamed up, business boomed, and they became a highly rated and sought-after matchmaking service.

A tall man with a friendly smile approaches us and nods to Jack. "Hi, I'm Bennett. You're Rooney, right? This is baby June."

"Nice to meet you both. Hi, baby June," I say, looking up at her in Bennett's arms. I lift a knitted stuffed tiger out of a glittery gift bag. The tiger has small bead eyes and a floppy long tail hanging off the back. "Chinese folklore says tigers are the king of all beasts. They possess protective powers to keep you safe." I lean back. "I've said a lot of words that June can't understand. Here."

Olivia takes the tiger from my hands and offers me a big smile. "This is adorable. Thank you, Rooney." She leans over to pick up a rust-colored cat and lifts his paw as though he's waving to us. "This is Pinot."

I proceed to talk to Pinot as though he, too, can understand words.

"Thanks for bringing objects," Olivia says to us. "We thought this tradition was really special but wanted to incorporate everyone more by having them bring items that are meaningful to them."

"I wouldn't be mad, though, if June picked a calculator," Bennett says, bouncing his daughter in his arms. She blinks up at us through brown eyelashes, her cheeks wide in a huge smile.

Pinot jumps out of Olivia's arms when Olivia looks up at Bennett, her eyebrows raised. "What would you be mad at her picking?"

Bennett thinks for a moment. "I guess nothing. Because whatever she picks will be perfect, isn't that right, June?" He boops her nose with his.

"Exactly. She'll pick what she wants, but preferably she chooses the Chinese zodiac chart," Olivia says playfully. She wraps her arm around Bennett's waist and leans in to brush wispy hairs off June's forehead.

"So you both teach kids about STEM?" I ask, looking between Jack and Bennett.

Bennett gently bounces June as he speaks, swaying side to side to the music lightly playing in the background. From small speakers in the corner of the room, Ella Fitzgerald sings about the moon.

"Every month we get together at Griffith Observatory. The kids call Jack the Star Guy," Bennett says. "It's sweet."

A blush spreads from Jack's cheeks to the tips of his ears.

"How adorable," I say.

"And it's not only because he has this shirt that's covered in glow-in-the-dark stars," Bennett elaborates. "This guy's great at breaking down complex topics and making it interesting for these kids. Supernovas, black holes, weather on other planets, you name it. Did you know that, on Mars, sunsets are blue?"

I look up at Jack, and though his expression is neutral, his eyes are creased upward.

"That sounds beautiful," I say.

Guests approach with objects in hand, trying to get Olivia and Bennett's attention. Olivia accepts some objects, redirecting people when her arms are full. "We have to go get everything set up," she says. "Nice to meet you, Rooney. See you, Jack."

As she and Bennett move to the center of the living room, Jack leans closer to me. "Explain to me what this is again? I think I remember Gōng Gong talking about wishing my parents had done one for me. But I can't remember specifics."

"It's a Chinese traditional ritual called zhuā zhōu. When children turn one, they pick one item from a variety of objects in front of them," I say, watching as Olivia and Bennett try to figure out how to organize the objects.

"To play with, or?" Jack asks.

"The idea is that what June picks will determine her future, what she'll be when she grows up. The calculator represents numbers and accounting, something entrepreneurial maybe. If June picks the pencil, maybe she'll be a writer or lawyer. The tennis ball could mean she'll be an athlete or coach. The keyboard for a software engineer, maybe. The apple for a chef, toy stethoscope for a doctor, building blocks for an architect. Your rocket plush for a systems engineer. And they included the phone, which for them probably represents the Lunar Love app. It's all slightly interpretive."

There's a trace of a smile at Jack's lips. "How symbolic."

I nudge him with my shoulder. "So your Gōng Gong wanted you to do this, but your parents didn't. Why?"

"They already knew what they wanted me to be," he says.

After Olivia lines up an array of items, June is placed in a sitting position on a pink fuzzy blanket two feet away. She'll crawl to whichever object she's destined for.

"Thanks, everyone, for coming!" Olivia says, speaking loudly so we can all hear her from her kneeling position. Guests are sitting in the chairs and couches in the living room, with many of us standing behind the furniture to catch a glimpse of fate at its finest.

"We have so many wonderful items here. We eliminated duplicates of things like stethoscopes, calculators—two of which came from Bennett—and piggy banks. Everything you see came from someone here, except for this," Olivia explains, holding up a tomato pin cushion. "This has been in Lunar Love's lost and found for years now, which I thought added a fun element of surprise."

Next to me, I feel Jack straighten his posture. He watches where Olivia places the object and looks over at me. "We need that pin cushion," he whispers. "That's it. For the test."

"Sometimes," Olivia continues, "we don't realize we're lost in something we believe in so deeply, but that doesn't mean you still can't be found." She looks up at Bennett and smiles. His whole face lights up looking at her. I'm intrigued by their connection and the love between them. They're stringmates, no doubt about it. The tingling sensation in my fingertips returns, a little more noticeable this time.

"How did Olivia and Bennett meet?" I whisper to Jack.

He steps even closer to me to answer, and I catch a whiff of his signature clove and forest scent. "I'll tell you later. It's a long story and involves a bet."

Around us, guests take guesses about what June will pick from a variety of objects in front of her. When June makes her first crawling movement, everyone grows quiet in anticipation, all of us watching with eager eyes to see what she'll do.

June moves her left hand forward, and there are a few gasps in the crowd.

"She's going to be an editor!" Olivia's sister Nina whispers to her husband when June inches closer to the pencil.

"Come on, June, don't pick the tomato," Jack says under his breath.

June turns to the right, instigating more chatter. She propels herself forward, grabbing the tomato pin cushion. She clings to it, her grip tight. Then, in a final burst of energy, she bolts through the line of objects and makes her way to the coffee table. She thrusts her arm toward a set of keys and pulls them down to the ground. Settling back into a sitting position, June has the tomato and keys in her lap.

Olivia and her auntie squeal with delight. "It's the keys to Lunar

Love!" Olivia tells everyone. "She's going to take over Lunar Love one day and be a matchmaker like her mama, Auntie, and my Pó Po! And be a fashion designer. She's a person of many talents!"

Jack lets out a long exhale and rolls up his sleeves. "Ready? You distract Olivia and baby June," he whispers.

I hold my hand out to stop him. "Jack! We're not stealing an object from a baby. We'll need to find something else, but first can we acknowledge how unreal that was? We witnessed fate at work."

"Are you crying?" Jack asks, turning his focus from the lost object back to me.

I wipe a tear from my eye. "Truthfully, I wish I had more tears in me to shed. It's overwhelming to see something like that."

A smile plays at the corner of Jack's lips. "It's overwhelming to watch a baby pick up something? Technically, she picked up two things. Does she at least now get to have a choice? This can't possibly dictate the course of her life. All of those objects didn't even account for every career possibility." Jack shakes his head. "She probably went for it because it was shiny and in her line of sight. Why are those keys even within reach for a baby? Those can be used as weapons."

I make a face at him. "Do not ruin this for me, Jack. I love this tradition. I did it as a baby."

We head out to the backyard, where there are long-life noodles, dumplings, cut fruit, and Ox-shaped cake being served on Chinese zodiac–themed plates for June's party.

"Are you serious? That actually makes a lot of sense. What did you pick? Wait, let me guess. You picked a sketchbook," Jack speculates.

"Close! I picked a paintbrush," I reveal. "My mom did it as a baby, too. She picked a tube of paint. We were both destined to become artists."

"You don't think you became an artist because you were around art all your life? Saw your mom as a working artist?" Jack asks.

"It's not like my mom only laid out art supplies to choose from," I say. "I had an assortment of objects, apparently. I don't remember the specifics because, you know, my brain couldn't form memories."

Jack laughs. "Sounds like a momentous day."

I place my hands on my hips. "What do you think you would've picked if you'd had a zhuā zhōu ceremony?"

Jack shrugs. "I can't imagine my parents doing anything like this."

"But if they had?"

"It would've been biased from the start," he says, convinced. "They're astronomers. There'd have been telescopes and star charts exclusively. Fate didn't stand a chance."

"I see." I nudge Jack's arm and nod toward the cake. "What's your sign?"

"I think I'm a Goat. You?"

"Interesting. I'm a Pig. Do you relate to your traits?" I ask.

He shakes his head. "I have no clue."

"Me neither. Want cake?" I reach for the piece that looks like the Ox's ear. Jack grabs what appears to be the nose.

The cooler September temperatures are much more appropriate for my knitwear. Still, it's no New York City fall. We spot a couple of yellow chairs to sit in positioned under red- and cream-colored lanterns swaying from an olive tree. I'm watching guests mingle in the yard when something reflective catches my eye in the grass.

I stand to pick it up. It's a Natural History Museum ID for someone named Lucy. "Unless this person is still here, this can be our lost object!"

Jack doesn't look impressed. "It's too easy. We know the who, what, where."

"Sometimes it really is that easy." I don't see Lucy anywhere among the guests. "She might've left. We'll have to return it in person."

"It's a start," Jack says.

I take a few seconds to visually trace the outline of Jack's face when he's not looking. "So, Star Guy, huh?"

Jack quickly inhales before plunging his fork into the corner of the chocolate cake. "Seems so," he says with a small grin.

"You let Bennett and Olivia call you Jack. You're good at teaching. Is it only at work that you're not as comfortable with those things?" I ask.

Jack wipes his lips with a napkin covered in the moon phases. "Work is meant to be professional. And teaching kids versus adults is very different. One is for fun and pure education. My colleagues don't need me teaching them anything. They know how to do their jobs."

"Maybe the teaching is more of a mentorship-type involvement, like the kids you educate?" I pose.

Revelation flashes across Jack's face. "That's a good point. I hadn't thought about it like that. Mentorship also does look good on a résumé."

"It can also be something you do for fun, you know," I tell him. "Kind of like how you don't tell anyone you volunteer."

Jack looks down at his plate. "That's different. I'm used to tracking my work achievements and using them to..."

When Jack trails off, I insert words to try to keep his momentum going.

"To be paid handsomely so that you can buy your own island? To create a list that you can read off every morning to self-motivate?"

Jack laughs at my attempt to make him smile. "To be seen. Achievements were how I was seen by my parents. Still are."

I nod knowingly. "Ohhh. Yes. I get that."

Jack locks eyes with mine. "Do you ever feel like people want you to be something you're not?"

I raise an eyebrow. "Definitely. My mom thinks I should stop hiding behind Red String Girl."

He nods. "With my parents, I always had to be on top of my game. I was supposed to listen to them because what they knew was best." Jack blows out a breath. "You know how in school you're taught to be well rounded and to involve yourself in a variety of activities?"

I shake my head, drawing lines across the icing with my utensil. "I don't. All I did was art, but I hear you."

"Well, my parents didn't want me to bother with other extracurriculars, either. They wanted me to be excellent at one thing: astronomy, like them. Become an expert in the field, like them." Jack pushes back a strand of hair that's fallen in front of his eyes. "They're not big fans of everything we send into space. They're observers, so anything we put up there, like satellites, only disrupts their view. If I can get this promotion, though, maybe they'll take a second to see what I'm working on and think differently about it."

"Yeah, maybe," I say. "Oddly, I can relate. I'm an artist like Mom, but I'm still not visible enough, not daring enough."

"She wants you to follow in her path, too?"

"It's the only version of success she knows. It worked for her, so it might also work for me."

"Right. Yeah, you get it." Jack shifts in his seat.

"What does your Gōng Gong think?" I ask.

Jack's eyes light up at the mention of him. "Oh, he's the best. Besides Gōng Gong, there hasn't been anyone else in my life who's been interested in knowing what I think purely for the sake of wanting to hear my thoughts. No hidden agenda of sparking a debate. No manipulation to make me think the same way. Gōng Gong always saw me for who I was. With my parents, it's like their love was—is—conditional. I have to earn it."

I nod along as he talks. "Gōng Gong never pushed me into being an ocean engineer," he continues. "I think that's because it wasn't his whole world. He was in the Marines and lived a lot of life before transitioning careers. He always supported me, took me to the aquarium, made ice cream with me. I'm lucky to have him. Sometimes I feel awful that my desire to connect with my parents outweighed his influence and opinion."

"It sounds like the relationship you two have is strong," I say, "but it can be different with parents. Their influence is like a gravitational pull."

He grunts. "Yeah. It really can be," Jack says. "My parents would go away on months-long expeditions for work, which didn't leave them much time to spend with me. They didn't take me along."

"Never once?" I ask.

"They were remote sites without much for kids to do," Jack explains. "They wanted to focus on their work. I get it now as an adult, but it was hard as a kid to be away from them for long periods of time and not really understand why. Looking at the stars sounded fun."

This I don't relate to as much. I went everywhere with Mom.

"I doubled down on learning a lot about space so I could impress them," Jack adds. "I thought that if I could connect with my parents, be interesting enough to them, then they wouldn't go away so often. But...people leave."

"Yeah," I say, pulling at a string on my sleeve. "People do leave."

Jack sets his plate of cake down on the grass. "I want these kids learning about STEM to know that they have options. I don't want them to feel pushed in one direction or another like I did as a kid. There's a whole world out there to explore. They show up every month eager to learn."

"Like how you were as a kid," I say, feeling emotional about the thought of a curious young Jack enthusiastic to learn as much as he could. I imagine he had a lot of questions growing up. And that he liked to test things.

"Right. They listen, they're open-minded, they want to know everything," Jack says, dragging his fork across the plate to scoop up the remaining crumbs. "And I want to help them understand all of it. I want to inspire them."

"Maybe you don't think your team needs the inspiration in the same way that the kids do. But what if they do?" I ask.

Jack goes quiet, but there's a trace of a smile. He takes my plate from me, gathering it up with his own.

"All I know is that there's one person in particular who does need inspiration," he says, locking eyes with mine.

A meow from behind Jack startles us both. A white cat with gray dots appears, rubbing up against Jack's leg.

"Pinot, how did you get out here? You're going to get eaten by coyotes," Jack says, lifting the cat into his arms.

I grab our plates from Jack and follow him into the house. "Olivia, Pinot was outside. The doors must've been left open."

Olivia looks confused. "Not sure who you're holding," she says, pointing over to the real Pinot with rust-colored fur sitting protectively next to June. "That's Pinot."

Jack's eyes go round as he looks at the cat lying calmly in his arms. "Then whose cat is this?"

I look at the collar. It says Sprinkles with an accompanying phone number. Jack dials the number a few times, but no one answers.

Jack furrows his brows. "I don't feel good about leaving her outside to fend for herself. We need to find her parents."

Seeing Jack being overly protective of this cat is incredibly endearing. My heart squeezes in my chest.

"How perfect that a cat named Sprinkles found you. You love ice cream, and cats love milk. What is ice cream if not frozen milk?" I ask.

He frowns. "Most cats are actually lactose intolerant."

"Look at that! You're already an incredible temporary cat daddy!" I say.

A small grin cracks through Jack's look of concern. We make a game plan to continue calling the number on the collar, check in with the local shelter, put up flyers, and talk to neighbors. I reassure him that we'll get Sprinkles home. In the meantime, Jack will take his new pal back to his apartment since mine doesn't allow animals and Talia is allergic.

"How did we go from zero lost things to two?" Jack asks, shaking his head.

I pet the top of Sprinkles's head. "In time, I think we'll know why."

Chapter 17

JACK

Rooney's staring into the open jaws of a T. rex. Her head is angled, like she's trying to figure out something.

"He could've put his entire mouth around my head and plucked it off like a grape," she says.

"Add a little cheese and salami, and that dinosaur's got himself a nice afternoon. Okay, we should probably give the ID to the Lost and Found," I say, analyzing the map to the Natural History Museum of Los Angeles. "Olivia said Lucy has been on vacation for the past week but she's back today. We passed the Help Desk on the way in but if we go back—"

"We love trying to understand where we came from," Rooney says, clasping her hands behind her back. She's clearly ignoring our mission. Which should be okay. That's the point. To see where each Fate Test takes us.

I nod. "It helps us understand where we're going."

"Does it, though? How can we really know? Doesn't all of this," she says, gesturing around us, "feel like we're trying to have control over something that we can't? All we can do is let whatever's meant to happen happen and then try to understand the meaning of it after the fact."

I shake my head. "I don't subscribe to the belief that we should be passive in life. If we want something, we have the power to go get it. To make it happen."

Rooney reads a placard in front of a triceratops. "Sometimes things in life happen without us having to try very hard," she says. "I think it's those outcomes that are the most meaningful. We don't even see them coming, like the dinosaurs. Not that I want their fate."

"Between the volcanoes and asteroids, they certainly didn't have it easy," I say.

Rooney purses her lips. "Maybe it all happened as it was supposed to, and we were meant to be here."

I cross around to the side of the assembled dinosaur skeleton. "Fate implies that it was intended to happen. That was another result of gravity."

"We already have so many awful things to deal with as it is on Earth. Now we have to be on the lookout for asteroids?" Rooney asks with concern.

"Don't worry," I say with a tone of reassurance. "At NASA, we track near-Earth objects that pose a risk."

"You can't stand the thought of being out of control, can you?" she says with a grin.

I narrow my eyes at her. "Just like you can't stand the thought of being in control."

"We have different thoughts on how the world works. Try keeping your eyes open for the signs, Jack. That's what I'm trying to do. That's where the inspiration will come from," she says, pulling her extra-long sleeves over her hands. It's cool in the museum but eighty degrees outside. And yet, she's still in a red sweater, though this one looks like it's made of cotton. I've learned during our time together that she runs cold. She's either wearing a sweater or carrying one with her, just in case.

"Have you ever considered not wearing red outfits made of string out in public?" I ask.

"Never. I like living on the edge," she immediately responds.

"I guess it is practical. If you ever run out of material, you always have a spare roll or two."

Rooney threads her fingers through her sweater's knitted loops. "Oh, I've definitely had to unravel a sleeve before."

I imagine it and laugh. These days, I'm laughing a lot more. And I know it's because of Rooney.

"Besides, if I didn't wear red," she adds, "I'd be...String Girl."

"That's not as catchy," I admit. "So these signs. How am I supposed to know when one happens?"

"They're often personal so I won't be able to say exactly what something might mean to you," Rooney explains. "But pay attention to meaningful moments, big and small. Be observant to what's happening around you. It's like Jewel sang, you have to listen to your intuition."

"Personal, observant, intuition. Got it."

"Good. I think you'll start to see signs in the most unexpected of places," she says. "Speaking of places, wouldn't this museum be perfect for an installation? Let's make sure we check out the Rotunda."

We leave the dinosaurs behind and head down the halls of the museum toward the Help Desk. Before we reach it, a woman in a khaki vest waves us over as we pass her, asking if we'd like to see some butterflies.

I slow my steps. "If I'm following the winds of fate, then yes, we would love to see some butterflies today. You did pick us out of all these other visitors, so...that makes us the chosen ones?"

"I never saw my job in that way before," the Butterfly Lady says, noticeably happier. "Thank you. We're having a special monarch butterfly event."

"Oh, we really need to get to the Help Desk," Rooney says to me with urgency, her eyes wide. She grabs my hand to try to pull me away.

Rooney scans the lady's vest covered in colorful flying-insect pins. The Butterfly Lady looks between the two of us. "So is that a no?" she asks.

I pull Rooney back to me. "This feels like a sign. Bring us to the monarchs," I say before turning my head toward the woman and adding, "please."

She leads us toward the door. "Wonderful! Right this way."

Rooney exhales. "You first."

"After you," I say, regrettably dropping her hand so I can gesture toward the butterfly entrance.

She takes a step back. "Lead the way."

Rooney and I are at a standoff. Butterfly Lady doesn't notice.

"Okay, sure," I finally agree, jogging to catch up to the woman. I'm a few steps ahead of Rooney, keeping an eye on her in my peripheral vision.

We're guided into an arched greenhouse and then left to explore on our own.

"Wait, you're leaving?" Rooney asks the Butterfly Lady.

"I'm simply here to welcome people into the event. Enjoy!" she says, closing the door behind her.

Rooney stays close behind me. I feel her breathing on my upper arm.

"I am not used to this air density," I say, turning around to face her.

"Did you say destiny?" Rooney asks, circling me and staying close.

"Density. What are you doing? Why are you so close to me?" I ask, taking her by the shoulders and guiding her a step back.

She looks on the ground behind her before putting a foot down. "Sorry! I didn't realize I was too close."

"Not *too* close," I mumble, "just...close."

She tiptoes over to a bench, keeping her body compact.

"What's all this?" I ask. "Why are you crouched?"

"I don't want to step on a butterfly," she says. A monarch butterfly whizzes past us. Rooney yelps and ducks, grabbing for my waist.

"Are you...scared of butterflies?" I ask, looking down at her face near my stomach.

Rooney looks up. "Are you talking to me?"

"Nope. I'm talking to the other person attached to me."

Rooney straightens. "Oh, no. I'm cool. Just wanted to feel what that felt like," she says awkwardly, moving her fingers around animatedly. "It's nice and tight."

I cross my arms. "If you're so scared of butterflies," I say, more entertained than I intend, "then why did you come in here?"

"This is me saying yes. Fate Test 1. Check," she says with a pained smile. A bright orange monarch flies by her head. She lifts her shoulders up to her ears, as if to protect the vulnerable parts of her neck.

"What is it about them that terrifies you so much?"

She blinks a couple of times as though she's piecing together her thoughts. "They're erratic. They fly without any sense of direction. That one almost ran into me!" Rooney hugs herself. "Some look like they have eyes on their wings. They're insects that can land wherever they want. I've only seen a butterfly once in New York City and that's when it followed me down an entire avenue. Pretty sure he had it out for me."

I laugh and shake my head. "Okay, come closer."

She takes a step toward me. I pull her in the rest of the way until we're inches apart. "Stay near me. Any butterfly that tries to mess with you has to get through me first."

She shakily laughs.

"I'll do it, too," I say sternly. "I'll fight a butterfly."

This makes her laugh harder. And for the first time in my life, I think I really would wrestle a butterfly if it meant she felt safe.

"Butterflies are actually in control of how they move," I explain. "They bob and weave to trick predators. Their flight path is unpredictable on purpose. That does make it feel like a butterfly's wings are going to slap you in the face. But their control means their survival."

"So what you're saying is they won't run into me?"

"That's the last thing *they* want." Of course, as I say it, a monarch butterfly lands on my sleeve.

Rooney gasps, watching the butterfly on my arm stay perfectly still. It lingers for a few seconds before fluttering away.

I drop my arm. "That wasn't so bad, right?"

"It felt like there was a real connection there," she says. "Good thing butterflies aren't the size of birds."

I laugh at the absurdity of this image. "And they run cold, too, like you. They need warmth to fly. You're my—a butterfly. You're *a* butterfly. Out in the wild. Because you belong to no one," I say, tripping over my words. What I say next flies out of my mouth on its own unpredictable flight path. "Maybe you can knit them little sweaters." I close my eyes in horror.

"Don't be ridiculous, Jack," Rooney says with a smirk. "Little scarves, maybe." She takes a half-step closer. "What else about them?"

I cross my arms in thought. "Legend has it that when monarch butterflies migrate south early, they're letting us know it's going to be a rough winter."

"Do you believe that legend?" she asks, looking surprised.

I snort. "No. I also don't believe that Punxsutawney Phil can predict the start of spring."

Rooney smiles. "Figures."

"When I was younger, my mom taught me that butterflies represent long life in Chinese culture," I share. Warmth fills my cheeks. "And love."

Rooney glances from the ground up to my eyes. "So that means we're surrounded by love right now."

"It would appear so," I say, blinking slowly.

Rooney holds her fingers to her neck. "Okay, I feel better," she says, breathing out.

We take slow steps in sync down the concrete pathway. Butterflies with stained-glass wings perch on flowers and leaves.

I lean closer to observe a butterfly's white spot patterns. "They don't have long life spans. They experimented with this one in space."

Rooney follows my gaze to the butterfly. "That exact one?"

I hold back a laugh. "Yes! Isn't that wild?" Rooney smiles as I go on. "They brought larva up to the International Space Station," I explain. "They live about two weeks on Earth, but one week in orbit. They were studying their ability to grow in microgravity."

"Wow. They start out so unassuming," she says. "Minus the whole life span thing, you're kind of like a butterfly. I think your colleagues see you in your chrysalis." Rooney faces me and smiles. "I see you as a free-floating butterfly. You've got a gorgeous pair of wings on you."

I'm not convinced of that. Only with Rooney do I feel like there's been a crack in the shell. But mostly because she's the one breaking it open. She reaches in and forces me out. Ever since New York, she's been doing that. Even so, I'd hardly call it a metamorphosis.

"I think it's because of you," I accidentally say out loud.

"Me?"

"I mean us working together. Being your liaison."

She smiles, and I connect the imaginary dots on her cheek constellation. The habit is officially back.

We pass various species of flowers. It's a completely different world in here. It's almost like being in the clean room. Both require heightened spatial awareness and remaining calm. But here anything goes. There are hardly any rules despite this being a home to living insects and bugs. Spending time with Rooney is still surreal, but there's nowhere else I'd want to be.

"Think any other species snuck in?" she asks. "If you see one that's black and white and slightly translucent, it's the *Idea leuconoe*, or the rice paper butterfly," Rooney says, reading off the butterfly identification board mounted into the ground. "Pretty."

"I don't know if the ones in here are, but in the wild, those are supposed to be poisonous," I say. "So maybe avoid touching them."

Rooney makes a face. "It's like we're back in the clean room. Look, but don't touch," she says, reading my mind.

"Exactly! But worse because you in a bunny suit is quite the sight," I tease.

"Like in a Miss Bunny ooh-la-la way or Bette Midler as a singing telegram bunny kind of way? Because honestly, I'm good with both," she says, fluttering her lashes and striking a pose with her hands bent in front of her. Though she's much calmer than before, she still stays close.

"I was thinking more like Bugs Bunny," I say with a smirk.

Rooney laughs and gives me a gentle push on my shoulder. When she removes her hand, a monarch lands in its place. Suddenly, it flits up to my neck.

"Oh, no. Where is it?" I say, angling my neck away from the insect.

Rooney holds up her hands. "Just give him the money, Jack, and do what he asks!"

She pulls out her phone and snaps a picture. She turns the screen toward me. I almost don't recognize myself. I'm mid-laugh, a version of myself I rarely see, let alone in a photo.

"Cute," she says. She avoids eye contact and turns away from me. The hair on the back of my neck rises, tingling in the humidity.

"So these Fate Tests," I say, remembering the reason why we're at the museum. "You've shown up early somewhere. And you completed Test 1 by saying yes to this. We're returning the ID, so Test 3 is in the works for you. As long as we make it out of here alive."

"Ha, ha," Rooney says with a roll of her eyes. "You think it's funny until you're a death-by-butterfly statistic."

I stifle a laugh. "I'll take my chances."

Rooney casts a side glance at me. "We need to get 'Fate Test 4: Interact with someone online' going. At The Huntington, the guy who opened the door for me had a Cloud Lovers League shirt on. I looked it up and it's this online forum where members share photos of clouds. That sounded sweet."

"Yeah. Good idea," I agree.

Rooney ruffles her bangs, letting them fall casually over her forehead. "I'll download the app and add my first photo later." She turns her phone toward me again. "Here's one I took already. Doesn't that cloud look like a dumpling?"

Against a bright baby blue sky, an oblong puffy white cloud hangs in the distance. The sides are slightly turned up.

I analyze the photo. "Yeah, there are the pleats. Yum."

"What do you think clouds taste like?" she asks.

"In Los Angeles, smog with a side of avocado."

Rooney smiles at me, and for a moment it's only us in the room. Well, us and about a hundred butterflies.

Rooney slips her phone into her bag. "Any word on Sprinkles's owner?"

I sigh. "Nothing yet. I've left a dozen voice mails and text messages by now. There's no address, either, so I can't swing by."

"Maybe Sprinkles's parents are out of town," Rooney reasons. She's still laser-focused on where she steps. "Someone will miss her and get back to you. Hey, I was thinking about something you said about your parents going on their expeditions and not taking you." Rooney threads her fingers through her sweater. "It's so interesting, how different our childhoods were. Yet I relate to so much about the way you felt."

"It sounds like your mom kind of did her own thing, too."

"My mom had me in her early forties," she explains. "By that time, she had lived a good amount of life. She had settled into her routine. She was used to doing her own thing."

"You mentioned a person named JR," I say, hoping it's not too nosy of a comment.

She looks surprised that I remember this detail from New York.

"Oh, he's who my mom slept with to create me," she simply states. "They weren't romantically together ever. Just physically the one time. Neither had ever thought about kids for themselves. Truthfully, I was more like a friend than a child."

"So you were a surprise for them."

Rooney stops to watch a caterpillar munching on a leaf. "I wasn't unwanted, per se, but I definitely wasn't planned. My mom and JR had been friends in the art world. People always envision that I'm the result of a drunken wild night, but it wasn't like that. They had been working on curating a show for his gallery, and one night they got together. I was made from mutual respect and attraction. But it wasn't love. He wasn't the man on the other end of her red string. My mom knew that."

"So what happened?"

"Mom decided to have me, and here I am," she says, raising her arms. "She didn't want to force JR into something he didn't want to be a part of."

"How do you feel about it?" I ask.

My question seems to catch her off guard. "It was lonely sometimes," she says. "JR's identity was never a mystery to me, but I don't know the man. He wasn't involved. It was always me and Mom. I had a lot of independence at a young age, especially when Mom was working, even though I'd be with her on location. My childhood was a blur of new cities, paintbrushes and oil paints, and galleries and museums. We were always on the move, but that made us close."

Rooney looks up at the leaves on a tree branch and adds, "Mom had me, but she also lives so much of her life independently. It's one of the reasons why the Red Thread of Fate is important to me. Because of it, I never felt alone. I always knew that I was connected to someone out in the world, and that thought comforted me. It still does."

I nod. "As a kid, when my parents were on the go, I felt like I was spinning in place."

"Maybe it's all that spinning that kept you together," she says thoughtfully. "Like if the world stopped spinning, everything would go flying into chaos, right?"

What she doesn't know is that all I wanted was to have time stand still. Just like I did that night in New York. Just like I do right now.

"I experimented with different ways to keep my parents with me," I share. "I started getting in trouble at school. Speaking out to teachers, cracking jokes in the middle of class."

Rooney raises her eyebrows. "You strategically planned out ways to get what you wanted? I'm impressed."

"Experiments made me feel in control. They made sense. There's a cause and an effect. I could hypothesize something and make it work. Except with my parents, it seems."

"Parents are hard to change," she says. "My mom is so confident in her beliefs, and she doesn't have regrets. I admire the way she refuses to diminish or devalue her work. Which experiments of yours worked?"

"Getting in trouble at school got their attention. But what really made them notice was when I did well," I share. "Getting good grades. Being well behaved. Studying hard. Advancing in my career."

Rooney nods her head slowly.

"I'll feel bad if I sound like I'm complaining. Is that how I sound?" I say. "I'm really grateful. My parents weren't neglectful. I had everything I needed. Maybe I would've liked a pet. But they paid for all of my education and hobbies."

"It sounds like you needed more from them emotionally," she says, seeming to fully understanding where I'm coming from. "That's a need, too."

I nod. "Yeah, you could be right. The cosmos was my space blanket. It protected me when I felt vulnerable. How's that for a figure of speech?"

Rooney maintains an even expression, but her eyes are playful. "They're not your strongest skill," she admits. "But I can see how the vast emptiness of the universe would make you feel safe."

I try to mirror her neutrality. "Exactly. You know, with its lack of oxygen, balls of gas, and black holes."

Rooney lets her grin grow.

"Though there are many unknowns, there are also a few things that are for certain. The universe is constantly expanding," I add, counting off on my fingers. "Faster than predicted, in fact."

"Excellent," Rooney says.

"One day the world will end," I tell her.

"I'll be sleeping well tonight."

"And every night, no matter what happens in the day, the moon is always right where it should be in the sky."

A gasp escapes from Rooney's lips. "That was really beautiful," she says, placing her hand gently on my shoulder. I can feel her warmth through my sweater.

I can't stop the grin that spreads on my own face.

That's when a monarch flies straight at us, disrupting the moment between us.

"Come on, let's go try to find that poisonous butterfly," I say, extending my elbow. "And then we can go return the ID."

Rooney nods, patting her bag where she's put the lost object. "Right. The ID. That's why we're here, after all."

She loops her arm through mine. We walk together slowly, tiptoe-ing around and dodging butterflies, on a mission to find one that looks like rice paper.

Chapter 18

ROONEY

The man was going to fight a butterfly for you?" Talia shouts as she hangs my latest string art piece up on a freshly painted white wall in her new gallery. She and her business partner, Isla, who's based in LA, have officially opened and have even sold a few paintings and sculptures already.

"If it came down to it, yeah. You know how I get with butterflies," I say as I sprawl on a light brown velvet couch in the shape of a croissant. I'm taking a break from stringing a small-scale installation in the gallery for someone to hopefully buy. It's one of my older ideas that I've done before in art school. I hate recycling ideas, but these are desperate times.

"I thought you were there to return a lost ID?"

"We were, but we took a detour. It happened so fast," I tell her.

"And he took a cat home for you?" she asks.

"It's not for me. I think Jack has a secret soft spot in his heart for cats. He's been going house to house around the neighborhood asking about her. The microchip wasn't useful because it wasn't registered to anyone."

Talia makes a sad face. "And I take it those sweaters are for Sprinkles?"

I lift my knitting needles in the air to show off my handiwork.

"She'll have one for every day of the week. Can I ask you a question now? Do I go short sleeve or long sleeve?"

"Short and above the elbow. Makes it easier to jump," Talia says as she joins me on the croissant couch. She comes bearing two individual chicken pot pies for our lunch.

"Was this meant to look like a French pastry, or…" I ask, running my hand along the back of the couch.

Talia laughs. "You should always be surrounded by things you love."

"It makes me hungry, but I do love it." I squeeze the yellow pillow next to me. "This also looks like a pat of butter. Really completes the look. This place is coming together. How are you feeling?"

Like many galleries, the architecture is understated, and the walls are bare so that the art stands out. Unlike many galleries, Talia and Isla wanted the space to feel cozy and welcoming. The concrete floors are covered in layered rugs and there are sheer linen curtains draped over the ceiling-to-floor windows. It's a place where you can sit back on a croissant-shaped couch, have a warm cup of tea, and envision the art on the walls being in your own home.

"There's such a different vibe on this coast," Talia says, opening her box of pie. "It's been great being able to work with Isla again in person and to dream about expansion plans. I can't believe we're here."

"It means a lot that we get to be here together," I say, lifting the lid on my own pie to let it cool.

"And I'm glad you're still working, even if they're not new creations," Talia says, nodding toward my string art hanging on the wall. Even from across the gallery the red string really pops. "I think they're going to sell well here."

"I can only get away with repeat work for so long," I say, locking eyes with a hound dog made of string. "I've been spending time with

different teams and learning a lot. Still no breakthroughs for installations, but we're working on it."

"We?"

"Jack and me. With Red String Theory," I say, focusing a little
too intently on one stitch.

"And Red String Theory is…the name of those Fate Tests,
right?" Talia asks. She sweeps her long, curly brown hair over her
shoulder. "You think they're going to work?"

"It's too soon to tell, but I hope."

When I'm not at JPL, I'm working around the clock to make as
many generic animal string art pieces as I can, so Talia and I haven't
had time to update each other on our lives. I quickly catch her up on
what Fate Tests we've completed so far, what's in progress, and what
we still have left to do. Since telling Jack about the Cloud Lovers
League, I've signed up for an account and posted several photos of
clouds. I tend to mostly see the food-shaped ones for some reason.

"The Cloud Lovers League has actually been fun," I share. "In
fact, I'm in talks with a couple of people in the LA area. I made
plans to meet up with a group next week. One of them thought my
dumpling cloud looked like a—you'll never believe it—he thought
it looked like a croissant," I say, gesturing to the couch we're sitting
on. "They're everywhere!"

Talia and I laugh together. "You can never have too many crois-
sants!" she says. "And Jack is doing all this to help you get inspired?"
She narrows her eyes at me before proceeding to scoop out a bite of
chicken and potatoes.

I take a break from Sprinkles's sweater and set my needles down.
"What's that look for? The success of the program is important to
him. I told him about the auction and being creatively blocked. He
wanted to help. He also has a promotion on the line."

"Uh-huh," she says with a roll of her eyes.

"What?" I ask, nudging her leg gently with my foot. "You don't think the program being a success is important?"

I watch intently as Talia mixes the crispy pie dough with the chicken filling. "Jack obviously wants to spend time with you outside of work. What did your mom say when she learned it was *the* Jack?"

"It's Wren, so you know, she questioned how a man who works at NASA could improperly provide something as basic as a phone number, though it was me who got the ones, fives, and nines all mixed up," I say. "I think it's all a disguise for her being as shocked as I was. If you can believe it, she gets more freaked out by fate-itious moments than I do. There's nothing to get weird about, though. Jack and I agreed to keep our relationship strictly professional."

Talia laughs with a hint of disbelief behind it. "And how's that working out?"

"Everything that we're doing is for the benefit of our careers, so it's great," I say, swallowing down a bite. "We have our trip to Florida and Texas at the end of the month. I'm hopeful that an idea will come to me in time for the first installation. I don't want to continue having to re-create things I've done in the past. That is not what NASA is paying me for."

"I have an auction update, but when I say this, don't freak out," she starts.

I break out in a full body sweat. "Never start sentences like that! What is it?"

"The auction is being moved up by two months. It's now happening on January twenty-third," Talia says, glancing up at me to gauge my reaction.

My spoon pierces through the puff pastry, sending crumbs all over the velvet. It's looking more like a real pastry by the second. I try to wipe the flakes off, but they bounce in place. "No! That's the day of my first showcase! We needed to use that exposure to drive sales of portraits. Hopefully get some more shows in local galleries and museums. Maybe even some private commissions on a larger scale." I roll the ball of yarn for Sprinkles's sweater back and forth across the width of the couch. "Now what?"

"Will NASA be posting behind-the-scenes photos on social media of your suit-ups?" Talia asks. "Without your face in them, obviously. Maybe that will remind people that the idea of you exists. That art is on the way."

I pull up their Instagram feed and scroll through recent posts. "There are a few pictures here and there, though that's clearly not helping much. Do you know the range of what the auction house thinks it'll sell for yet?"

"I spoke to someone, and they're estimating that it could be double or triple what it sold for last," Talia says, doing an admirable job of remaining calm. "There's a resurgence in video art interest."

I balk. "They think it could be twenty to thirty thousand dollars? I won't have that in three months. NASA gave me half of my payment up front, but that plus my savings won't cover it. I have fourteen thousand right now."

"I've doubled the price of your commission pieces now that you have NASA to your name. That's been a draw when I tell people. I'm featuring your work in our next newsletter. Can you create more pieces to have ready for when your showcase happens?" Talia asks. She lifts the half-formed sleeve of Sprinkles's sweater. "Think there's a market for hand-knitted animal clothing?"

A small laugh escapes my lips. "Don't tempt me," I say, a capsule collection of pet knitwear already forming in my mind. The joke helps relieve some tension, but the stress returns when I attempt to do mental math. "My prices weren't very high to begin with, but raising prices could still help. I need more collaborations and shows with other museums, if possible. Maybe more pressure is what I need to jump-start my inspiration. In the meantime, more string cats and dogs."

"Once the first showcase happens, you're going to explode." Talia gestures with her hands for effect. "People need to see what you're about first."

"Right now I'm all about my past work," I mumble. "I'm not going to be able to buy this piece back, am I?"

Talia pats my knee. "It's going to be great. It'll work out. We got this. Don't lose hope. Ideas are going to overflow on the trip, and you'll come back to LA reenergized and reinspired. Especially since you're going with Jack," she says, wiggling her eyebrows. She's trying to comfort me by using Jack's name and it's kind of working, even with her insinuations.

"Talia! Jack is, well, I don't know what Jack is. My liaison. Some might even call him a colleague. A coworker." I move the spoon back and forth in the dish. Eating is the last thing I want to do right now. I need to get back to work.

Talia throws her head back. "Oh, please! He's hardly either of those things. Your situation is different than if he was someone you met at the office. You knew him in a different way before working together ever came into the picture."

"Maybe us meeting in New York was so that we would ultimately come together now. Maybe it was never meant to be romantic," I say, not fully believing my own words. "Our belief systems about love are different, too. It's not that I was expecting my stringmate to believe in the Red Thread of Fate, too, but maybe being open to the idea that there's something bigger at play would be nice? At least some common ground there?"

"You believe it. Isn't that what matters?" she says, setting her empty pie dish on the glass coffee table in front of us. "But also, as a fellow Red Threader, I completely get it. That pull, that feeling, the signs, that can matter, too."

I nod, feeling seen in her validation.

Talia makes a face and pokes at her pie. I can tell she has more thoughts.

"It's too weird, right? Jack and I finding each other again," I say. "Ever since that night, I feel like I can't get a good read on any of the signs. What do you think it means that Jack and I were lost to each other?"

Talia considers this. She opens her mouth and then closes it. Then she shakes her head and says, "You know what? Forget being neutral. Your fated night in New York? The party? And let's not forget how he kissed you..."

"I know!" I bury my face in my hands. "Believe me, I've thought about that night every which way. Broke it down, tried desperately to understand what it all meant. But it was six hours! That's hardly any time to make big, important life decisions," I justify. Who was the last man I spent that much time with? No one comes to mind. "It's not like we didn't want to stay in touch. He gave me his number, and who knows where we'd be right now if I had typed in his number correctly. It's pointless to speculate because the fact remains that it didn't work out."

"But you like him," Talia replies. I can't tell if it's a question or a comment.

"Of course I like Jack. Ever since New York I've liked him," I admit. It's the first time I'm saying this out loud. Thoughts can remain in my head without consequence, but now they exist in the world. Like with everything else in my life, it's easier to stay in hiding and keep emotions like these concealed.

Talia reaches for Sprinkles's sweater and gives it a little stretch. "You're happy when you're around him. Carefree in a way I've never seen before, especially with your entire life hidden from the public and most people. I think you're in too deep, but you don't even know it."

"Like how if you're on the moon, you can't see its phases," I say, testing out another forest replacement idiom for Jack.

"Totally," Talia says. "You're too close to the situation. That's probably why everything's confusing."

I groan. "Jack knows practically everything about me, and I've only known him for, collectively, eight weeks, five days, and one night. Less if you count the time we've actually spent together. There's too much at stake for us both for me to follow a thread. Especially if it leads nowhere. And especially because we go back to New York in ten months."

I think about what Jack's told me and how hard it is for him when people leave. I can't imagine what he must've felt when he believed that I purposely hadn't texted him after our night together.

"Maybe it's worth tugging that thread a little, to see what happens," Talia says as she runs a hand through her hair and flips it to the other side. "And I did not mean that in a sexual way. Then again..."

My jaw drops. "Tal!"

"For this trip, are you both staying in different hotel rooms or is this going to be a One Bed type of situation?" she presses.

I roll my eyes and whack her with the butter pillow. "This is real life. Not a rom-com novel. We'll each have our own separate rooms on this *work trip*," I say, carefully articulating the last two words.

Between us on the couch, my phone lights up with a text message from Jack.

Talia peers over to see who it's from. "Looks like you got that phone number situation sorted out," she says, raising her eyebrows.

I grab my phone and hold it close to my chest dramatically. "Your point has already been made."

Before Talia gets up from the couch, I reach for her. "Hey. You know you're the best friend ever, right?"

"I mean, I know it, but it's nice to hear it," she says, flipping her hair back over her shoulder dramatically.

"Thank you for being here for me," I say.

"I'm not here for you. I'm here with you," Talia says, pulling me in for a hug. "And I know it feels like I'm helping you, but the RSG name has drawn a lot of attention to the gallery. That's helped sales in general. Your time will come."

While Talia makes tea, I read what Jack texted.

Sprinkles has landed.

I smile at the attached photo of Sprinkles peeking out from a cardboard box with a rocket-shaped cat house printed on the side.

Another text comes through. He likes the box the cat house came in more than the actual house.

In the corner of the picture, I spot a stuffed star and a tub of catnip. The thought of Jack shopping for cat toys makes me smile harder.

I flop back against the croissant. It's official. Wherever it is I am, a dense forest or a phaseless moon, I'm in too deep and am way too close.

Chapter 19

JACK

W ho decides to meet at the beach on a Friday night at rush hour?" I mumble.

Rooney's sitting in my passenger seat rattling off directions even though we're at a standstill.

"Once we get off the 101, we need to get onto the 405," she explains, pinching and zooming the map on her phone. "Thanks for driving me, by the way. Talia has the car tonight. Now that I'm seeing it on the map, though, I'm realizing this is pretty inconvenient for you."

"It's no problem." I stare straight ahead at the row of red taillights. "Can you tell me the exit once we get closer, let's say, in an hour or so? If we're lucky."

Rooney shoots me a concerned look. "An hour? Jack, it's four forty-five. I'm supposed to meet the group at six. The sun sets at six twenty. Google is saying there's still…an hour and a half to get there? How is that possible?"

I glance at her phone screen. We're north of Glendale. "There must be a concert tonight or a game," I say. "Or nothing at all. This is LA."

"When my mom comes to visit in a couple of weeks, she is not going to like this. The art show she's taking me to is also in Santa Monica. We're going to need to leave three hours early."

"That would probably be best," I agree.

She throws her hands up. "We haven't even moved a car length, and it's been fifteen minutes. What are people doing?"

"Exactly."

"We should've left earlier," she says. "I'm not going to make it."

"I'm not a doctor," I say, pressing the back of my hand to her forehead. "But I think you're going to make it after all."

"Are you...joking right now?" Rooney asks. "This is my first meet-up for the Cloud Lovers League, and you're cracking jokes. Remember, doing any of this was all your idea."

"We already left work early," I reason. "I don't want you to miss the sunset, either."

"We're actually going to watch the cirrocumulus clouds as the sun sets. Not the same thing. Those type of clouds are the ones that look like rows of small puffs," she says excitedly. "It's supposed to be a fuchsia sky tonight, which I now won't see."

I gesture toward the windshield. "Oh, you'll still see it. That's what's great about the sky. It's everywhere."

Rooney turns to face me in her seat, her expression more thoughtful. "That's the thing. It's everywhere, and yet how often do you notice it?"

"What do you mean? I see the sky all the time."

"Yeah. We see things all the time, but how often are we really looking? And it's bigger than simply seeing shapes. Take those clouds, for instance," she says, pointing to an extensive patch of cloud covering. "Doesn't it look like the ripple of the surface of the ocean, but from below? It's like we're all underwater."

"Sounds like Fate Test 4 is working," I say. "You interacted with someone online, and now you're noticing these beautiful things."

"Time will tell if it's actually working, but I do feel like I'm noticing these small, fleeting moments," she says. "What's incredible is that it's ever-changing. Those clouds we just looked at? They're darker and more scattered, and it's only been a few minutes."

I glance back up in the same direction. It's true. Their color has taken on a bluer hue.

"It's art created by the elements," Rooney says, sounding amazed. "These magical moments are happening around us all the time, formed for no other reason than because invisible water vapor condenses into something visible in the air. They're existing exactly as they are, but it takes focused observation to really give them meaning or purpose."

"It's like they're hiding in plain sight," I say.

This gets a smile out of Rooney. "I think you're going to start noticing clouds now, too."

I direct her attention to a cloud hovering above us. "That one looks like a paw."

Rooney angles her phone up toward it to take a photo. "That's for you to show Sprinkles later."

"She'll love it," I say, catching myself smiling. I should not be bonding with this animal that's not even mine. After nearly three weeks since finding Sprinkles, a neighbor finally called with information. Sprinkles's previous owner moved out of state last month. Which means he left her behind. I tighten my grip around the steering wheel. Some people don't deserve animals.

"Do you know what you're going to do with her yet?" Rooney asks.

"The neighbors don't want her. And I can't put her up for adoption, either. I drove all the way to the shelter. Couldn't bring myself to take Sprinkles into the building. You know she's already found her favorite spot under the coffee table? And at night, she lies on my pillow and kneads my hair."

"Jack, have you thought about keeping her?" Rooney asks softly.

"Me? Oh, I can't have a cat. I work long hours. And we have our trip in a couple of weeks. I already feel terrible leaving her," I say. "I've never had a pet. I wouldn't even know what to do with one."

"You'd do exactly what you're doing now. Cats are generally pretty easy to care for. You can think about it over the trip," she says. "She's safe with you for now."

For now. Those words linger longer than they should.

"What would you create if this were one of your installation themes? How might clouds play a part?" I ask, changing the subject. "It doesn't even have to be for NASA."

Rooney looks out the window and sighs. "I like to think it would be less about the clouds and more about nature. So much exists that we have no influence over. It's like everything you've described about the universe, Mars even. We had nothing to do with that, and yet it's stunning. I wish I had a better answer."

"Let's hope tonight's fuchsia clouds help."

"If we get there." Rooney pulls the sleeves of what she calls her "chunky knit" sweater over her hands. She sinks lower into the seat, crossing her arms. "There's still time. Let's wait and see what happens. Maybe traffic will clear out."

I pull the sunroof covering back so that the window is exposed above us. "You can get a better look this way."

Rooney moves closer to me to lean her head back. Her bangs fall to the side, and I sneak a look at her eyes. At the same moment, she's looking up at me. Heat shoots through me quickly, my cheeks the last to feel the effects. But even as my face burns, I keep my eyes trained on hers. In my peripheral vision, I can see the rise and fall of her chest quicken. It matches the pace of my own breathing.

My gaze slowly falls to her lips. They're Mars red tonight, the curve of her bottom lip accentuated. If I knew anything about art or how to make it, Rooney's lips would be my main source of inspiration. I shake the thought loose. I'm driving Rooney to the beach so that she can be inspired to do her work for a program that I'm a part of. I can't be thinking these thoughts.

A honk from a couple of lanes over breaks my attention. I face forward, hoping Rooney didn't see me staring at her. How long was I looking at her mouth?

I redirect my attention to the music and adjust the volume. "Here, pick a song," I say, handing her my phone. "It's connected to Bluetooth."

She scrolls slowly, her red-painted nails moving up and down. "I'm going to put it on shuffle, and your playlists can decide," she says, wedging the phone into the cupholder before rummaging through her bag. "Thank goodness I brought car snacks. We might be here all night."

Rooney sets a bag of mixed Asian rice crackers between us. We alternate reaching in for handfuls, and I become hyperaware that our hands could collide at any moment. The first few songs are jazz. The sounds of crunching fill the silence in the car as the sun drops slowly. Another thirty minutes pass, and we're only north of Griffith Park. We're zoned out staring ahead at the sea of lights when Queen's "Under Pressure" comes on. At the first few beats, Rooney springs to life, her initial reaction to turn up the volume.

"Timely!" she shouts while she sways side to side in her seat. *"Pressure! Pushing! Down! On! Me!"*

I tap my finger against the wheel.

Rooney takes her sunglasses out of her bag and sings into them. "Sing it if you know it, Jack! And I know you know it because this shuffle is on your playlist."

She holds her sunglasses in front of my mouth, indicating for me to sing.

I lean in. *"Dee-day-da"* is what comes out right as Freddie Mercury sings it.

We both laugh at the perfect timing. A knot of tension releases in me that feels familiar from our night in New York. Before I can fight it, we're both dancing in place and sing-shouting, "*Let me out!*"

I can say with clarity and certainty that traffic has never been so fun before. And it's because of Rooney. The heat from before comes rushing back, a mixture of my heart racing from all the movement and the sudden realization that I like her. Like her in the way that I shouldn't. Even though I'm her liaison and even when she's leaving in ten months. These feelings I have toward Rooney are already set in motion. All I can do now is try to stop them from developing into something bigger.

Naming this feeling is freeing in a way. In this moment, I am at ease. We could not move another mile for the rest of the night, and I would be okay with that. No, not just okay. I would be happy about it. Ecstatic, even. A part of me hopes that they shut the entire highway down right now, and we can be here. Stuck together.

"It's almost six, Jack, and we're nowhere near the exit we need to take. I'm supposed to be meeting them right now," Rooney says with a whine. She stuffs a handful of crackers into her mouth. "I hate bailing on people."

I wonder if going off-highway would be faster. But we're already late. Getting from here to the beach isn't going to happen in twenty minutes.

"Are there night clouds you might be able to look at?" I ask.

"Not the kind I'd want to see. Noctilucent clouds are rare," she says with a sigh.

"It sounds like you're learning a lot from this league. That's cool." When she doesn't say anything, I add, "I'm sorry, Rooney. I don't like canceling plans, either."

Rooney gives me a look of appreciation. "Fine. You're right. I'm calling it." She types something into her Cloud Lovers League app.

"I let them know I can't make it, and we can turn around. I'm sorry for wasting your time. I hope you didn't cancel plans for this."

If canceled plans means watching a new space documentary with Sprinkles, then yes. Plans were canceled.

Rooney directs me to the nearest exit.

"This is wrong. We should be going east," I tell her. "Is your GPS redirecting?"

I see a sly smile on Rooney's face. "It's time for me to do Fate Test 5," she says. "'Go the wrong direction on purpose.' Let's see where we end up."

Once we're off the exit and free from the standstill, Rooney randomly calls out left or right, and I follow her instructions. We weave through roads and into different neighborhoods. Fifteen minutes and several winding roads later, there's a sign for the Hollywood Bowl Overlook off Mulholland Drive. I turn my car into the parking lot.

"You can't see the beach. But you can see the clouds," I say, putting the car into park.

"And really, that was the whole point," she says, grinning. "Right on time, too. We're even closer to them up here."

We get out of the car and climb the stairs for a better view to take in the sights. There's a look of amazement on Rooney's face. The terrain rolls out ahead of us, the green of the treetops blending into the concrete of the city. We loom over the Hollywood Bowl as our eyes follow a natural path leading out toward a miniature version of downtown resting on the skyline.

"It's so expansive," Rooney says, leaning forward against the railing. "I almost didn't even see the sign."

In the distance, the Hollywood Sign looks like a speck, a star against a mountainside of sky.

"The Hollywood Sign is like clouds. You get used to it and forget it's even there," I say.

"Hiding in plain sight," Rooney says, bumping me with her shoulder.

Above us, clouds are lined up in rows of small puffs like strings of popcorn. Closer to the horizon, the sky is bright orange. It gradually builds in color above it, from yellow to the fuchsia Rooney was eager to see. The clouds nearest us are teal, their shapes more pronounced.

The sky cracks open, revealing a burst of unexpected light blue as the last rays of sunshine take one last stretch. We stand there side by side, the heat from our bodies radiating between us. Before we know it, night has taken over. I sneak one more look at Rooney's content face, the Big Dipper on her cheek elevated from her smile. I breathe out with a sigh of resignation.

If I don't get a grip on these feelings, I'm in big trouble.

ROONEY

Mom and I left three hours early for the art show, and we arrived minutes before it started. This city is too much sometimes. We're among hundreds of others waiting for Arlo Hart to make his appearance. The son of a famous photographer, Arlo is a twenty-year-old aerial photographer whose work goes for five figures and hangs on the walls of celebrities' homes. People love sharing on social media that they own one of Arlo Hart's pieces.

Mom and I stand shoulder to shoulder on Santa Monica Beach, a beautiful location for a show of this size. The warm October air hasn't gotten the memo that fall is here. In front of us, a helicopter makes lazy circles over the ocean.

"Quite the showman, isn't he?" Mom asks. "Has the ocean always been this loud?" Waves crash down in front of us, leaving a reflective seismogram of foam as the water pulls away from land.

"This is what nature sounds like. You've gotten too used to sirens and honking," I say.

"At this point, that's white noise. This is a different beast entirely."

"The noise is relaxing. It's supposed to be good for your brain," I inform her. "You know people pay hard-earned money to have machines that make this sound for them."

"I'll take the sound of a screeching subway any day," she says.

"Spoken like a true New Yorker." Another wave rolls in, folding in on itself before splashing down on the sand.

Bobbing on the surface of the ocean are thousands of flowers in full bloom. The stems have been trimmed and weighted down so the head of the flowers face up toward the sky, where Arlo will be ready with his camera to get the perfect shots during golden hour. The flowers are guided to shore on the bubbling waves and quickly pulled back out to sea when the water retreats. A rope floats fifty feet from shore so they don't float out too far.

Apparently, Arlo purposely chose this beach and time because of its incredible sunsets. Minus the traffic, the West Coast may be starting to grow on me, especially when there are pastel blues and oranges coloring the sky like an oil painting. Or a nebula.

As soon as I make this interstellar connection, my phone dings with a text message from Jack. Attached to it is a photo of a thin, wispy cloud that looks like string. I respond with my own photo of the nebula-esque sunset. I go back to my photo gallery and sneak a look at the photo of Jack at the butterfly exhibit. He's relaxed, caught in the moment in his navy shirt with an orange butterfly on the neckline. Catching him mid-laugh was like photographing an erratic butterfly, rare and magical. I keep my phone in my hand, as though Jack were here with me. He's just a text away.

I startle at the crowd's "oohs" and "ahs" as the door to the helicopter slides open. Everyone angles their head up to catch a glimpse of the artist at work.

Arlo's show begins with him taking photos of the flowers from the sky while nature creates its arrangement. As he does this, his voice booms out of speakers strategically placed around the beach. It sounds prerecorded, the sounds of the helicopter absent.

"Every year, an estimated eight million metric tons of plastic are dumped into the ocean," Arlo's voice says. "There are three thousand six hundred and twenty-nine flowers in front of you. Each flower represents two thousand two hundred and five pounds. Now take a look at the flowers on the table."

Set up in the sand is a folding table with vases containing the same flowers from the water. I lift one from a large round bowl and hold its weight in my hands, only to learn that they're not actually flowers. This one's a sunflower made of plastic. Its petals are shiny from what must have been chip bags, the center a navy blue spiky rubber ball cut through the middle.

Arlo's voice continues, "What you see in front of you doesn't even begin to scratch the surface of what's out there right now, floating around sea creatures who also call this planet home. Every flower you see was made from plastic found this past year alone. If we don't take action today, right now, this number will increase. These flowers are for you to take home with you as a reminder."

"Well, this is depressing," Mom says, picking up a bundle of purple Mardi Gras beads shaped to look like a lilac.

"I think it's compelling," I say. "Without seeing this physical representation, big numbers like that are hard to visualize. People will remember seeing this."

Mom snorts. "They'll remember, but it won't stop them from using a straw with their iced pumpkin spice oat milk lattes."

I sigh. "You're still going to buy a photo, aren't you?"

"He's my friend's son. Of course I am," Mom says with a shrug.

I lift a rose made of the remains of red plastic cups and have an idea for Fate Test 6. I ask the volunteer for a permanent marker and write my phone number on one of the petals.

For proof, I snap a picture and send it to Jack with the message, If I put it up to my ear will I hear the sound of ping pong balls splashing into ale?

Jack responds within seconds. A rose by any other name would smell just like beer.

I mix the plastic rose back into the flowers and leave it for someone to grab. Fate can take it from here. I've officially completed Red String Theory. The moment doesn't feel as grand as I had hoped. No epiphanies come to me. Maybe my muse is stuck in traffic.

I feel no different until Mom asks how the fundraising is going. Now I feel anxious again.

"My pieces are hardly selling," I admit. "I had higher expectations."

Mom knowingly raises her eyebrows. "The higher the expectation, the lower you feel when reality doesn't align."

I kick at the sand with my sandal. "With half of the NASA payment, a few recently sold commissions, and what little savings I have, I'm sitting at, like, sixteen thousand dollars. That's not even half of what I'll probably need for the auction."

"Have galleries or museums been in touch? Having the NASA name behind you should help. I can make some calls."

"No, thank you," I say a little too quickly. "I appreciate your offer, but I want to do this on my own."

"Roo, there's nothing wrong with asking for help."

I reach for a daisy made of pull tabs and beverage caps to keep my hands busy. "I don't want a handout or someone to pretend to like my work because you called in a favor. If—when—I can make money as a working artist, I want to know it was because of my talent and not because people agreed since you're my mom. Because of who you are, if I accept even just one phone call, that will stay with me for my entire career." I pull at the plastic flower petals one by one until the whole thing falls apart in my hands. "You have confidence because you know your success is because of you."

"It's because I went big. I took risks. Sometimes it worked, other times it didn't," Mom says, adjusting part of my bangs that are sticking straight up from the wind. "You can play it safe or go after what you want. These days it's harder to stand out. You have to get yourself noticed."

I make a face. "That's what I'm trying to do with my large installations."

"Even if you do everything completely on your own, there will be people who think you got to where you are because of your name," Mom says. "They might even think that's how you got your current gig, even though we know that's not true."

I move the deconstructed daisy parts from one hand to the other. "But to be fair, I wouldn't have ever been in the position to do *Entangled* without my previous experiences, going to art school, or being exposed to art and traveling with you. I had time to create, to even think that I could do art as a career. I am privileged. I'll never deny that."

"That's important to recognize. I worked hard and made connections for myself, but also for you. If you won't accept that, then I hope you'll hear my advice," Mom says as she looks out in the distance. "I don't regret my work. Everything I've done had its time and place."

"It paid off for you."

"It doesn't for everyone." Mom turns back to me. "You know, when you pulled that paintbrush as a baby, the first emotion I felt wasn't excitement or pride. I felt dread," she divulges. "Not because I didn't want you to be an artist or that I didn't think you would be one of a kind, but because this industry can be unrelenting, especially for women. Ageism is real. Sexism is real. Our work is still valued less than men's, touring is stimulating but exhausting, and it can be hard to be away from home for long periods of time."

I let her words wash over me as I process them. "Really? Do you still feel dread?"

She frowns. "Mostly no. Slowly, over time, I saw how interested you actually were in art. How hard you worked to be good. It was then I felt hope, like you were really going to make a difference and do things your way. Part of me worried you were only ever interested in art because of me."

"Maybe it was a combination of fate, you, and me. Fate was the seed, you helped me grow, and now I'm keeping that interest alive," I say.

"You're much more self-aware than I was at your age," she reveals. "You sure you still don't want to go half and half on the auction?"

I shake my head. "If you give me money to take care of my problems, that defeats the entire point of me being in control of my own career. Besides, the last thing you should be doing is spending money on something you don't even want."

Mom twirls the fake lilac in her palm. "It's a waste for either of us to spend money on *Baby Being Born*. The video has literally been out there for as long as you've been alive."

"For a long time, *Baby Being Born* defined me, and I would love for it not to also define my future. And right now it's in private hands, but who knows who will buy it. And you know what that means."

"That my work will increase in value," Mom says bluntly. "Maybe I should come out of retirement."

I let out a humorless laugh. "Let's be honest. You never retired."

Mom shrugs. "Inspiration did strike recently. I'll probably never be able to stop."

"I know," I say, nudging her. "And thanks, but taking your money doesn't feel right."

"I'm not going to press it. I can't force you to do anything," Mom finally says.

The helicopter flies lower to the water, the waves below rippling outward. An extra-long rope is thrown from the side as Arlo leans out of the helicopter, a shadowy silhouette against the setting sun. The audience gasps as Arlo dives headfirst into the ocean. He grabs the end of the rope floating on the surface and ties it to something clipped to one of the yellow buoys dotting the surface of the water. He effortlessly swims the thirty feet or so back to shore and emerges from the waves.

"The ocean renews us, and we have a responsibility to renew it *from* us," Arlo says, ending the show with a parting statement. He signals something in the air, and the rope tightens, moving back up toward the helicopter. As the rotorcraft flies higher, the plastic flowers are pulled from the ocean, lifting higher and higher in the sky until every last one dangles in an upside-down bouquet held together by string. "Leave no trace. The fate of the ocean is in your hands. And yours. And yes, yours," he continues, going one by one through the crowd until he reaches me and Mom.

"Is it in ours, too?" Mom asks, looking at her hands.

Arlo laughs and runs his hands back through his wet hair. "You both made it."

"Congratulations on a thought-provoking show," Mom says. "The photos came out nicely?"

Arlo breathes in. "Oh, yes. Mother Nature was good to me today. The moon created just enough pull," he says, closing his palms together and shaking them toward the purple sky in gratitude.

"You put on quite the show," I say as he rings out ocean water from his T-shirt.

He extends both of his arms out. "Art is entertainment," he says.

"There's no doubt you made an impression," I say, nodding

toward a group waiting to talk to him and take photos. "Was that wax rope?"

Arlo nods, and water drips from his hair down his face. "Exactly. Gathering up all of the plastic like that is what helped convince the city to even let me do the show here. It took so long to get permits and approvals."

I swallow down this information. If I want to do something public, it will take months to do it. I don't have that kind of time. I unknowingly ball my hands into fists, the aluminum "petals" digging into my palms.

Arlo clasps his hands together. "I have to meet and greet, but it means a lot that you two are here." He makes his first stop at the group, who immediately turn their phones around for selfies.

Mom and I walk down the beach, away from the crowd. "Is that type of show what you mean when you say *go big*?" I ask.

"It makes a statement, and it's memorable," she says.

And Arlo doesn't have to be anonymous to do it. He's out there with his first and last name, taking photos with people, talking to them about the bigger themes of his work. My types of conversations with people are one-sided. I release an artist statement and tell them what the inspiration was. There's never a dialogue.

"How has working with Jack been?" Mom asks.

"He's been a great partner throughout all of this," I say. "Very inspirational."

"You two are getting along?" Mom says with a hint of reserve in her voice.

I smile at the thought of Jack. "I'd say so."

Mom looks preoccupied with a thought. "I'll say this once, then I'll leave it alone, but be careful, Roo," she says. "Don't let him cloud your judgment."

"What do you mean? My judgment isn't clouded," I tell her. "We're getting to know each other."

"You have a trip together next week, right?" Mom says skeptically.

"We do," I say slowly, wondering where she's going with this. "More suit-ups."

"Roo, when you're there, do one thing for me? Remember that you work with the man. You're a professional. So is he. You live three thousand miles away from each other. At the end of the day, it comes down to one thing: don't sleep with people you work with."

I give her a look. "Are you saying this because of what happened with you and JR?"

"That is exactly why I'm saying this," she says. "When it comes to people you work with, don't have relationships with them, don't marry them, and definitely don't sleep with them."

"What else? Don't have kids with them?" I joke.

"Certainly don't have kids with them. But you're a treasure," Mom says with a smirk before she pats me on the back.

"Gee, thanks," I say with a roll of my eyes. I wrap my arm around her shoulders and pull her in against me, knowing she despises affection.

"I mean it though, Roo, protect your heart," Mom says, her face growing serious.

"You're always telling me to stop being so careful in work. Why doesn't that apply to love? Wasn't it you who said that I have to test the strength of my string? Why the change of heart?"

When I look into her dark brown eyes, I can tell there's more to the story of her and JR. My eyebrows lift in surprise.

"You—you loved him," I say, stunned by this realization. "I can't believe it."

"Ah, love. I was forty-one. I was young," she says.

"Wait. Did you think he was the man on the other end of your red string?" I ask.

Mom starts to say something but then stops herself. "I misread the signs. Our professional proximity confused me. I was wrong. I know you don't want what JR and I had. I don't want that for you, either. You're looking for real love, for your stringmate, but don't let proximity confuse you, too."

So she had loved him. All this time I thought their relationship had been platonic until the night they got together, but it wasn't like that for her. She thought JR was The One.

"Let's say when you one day do have feelings for someone and you see the signs, then what?" Mom asks.

Exactly. Then what? It's the question I've wondered for a long time.

Then she speaks my feelings out loud. "Do you think you'll scare the person away?"

I look at her surprised. "Yes. How did you—oh."

She returns my expression. "Oh what?"

"I'll be careful," I tell her. "When you start to be less careful."

The wind whips our hair around our faces. "What's that supposed to mean?" she asks.

I cross my arms around my body as the temperature drops with the sun. The pink sky plays off the teal water, a giant mirror reflecting the particles in the atmosphere.

"I just mean, it's never too late for love."

For a moment, I think I glimpse disappointment in her expression, but she quickly brushes it off. Even in a moment that allows for vulnerability, Mom's attitude remains unchanged, her beliefs an armor from more heartbreak.

"Wǒ ài nǐ. I've been practicing my rarely used language," she says, thinking for a moment. "Maybe too rare."

"The tones sound good. And I love you, too. Maybe you also need to go big," I continue before hearing what I've said out loud. I groan. "I did not mean it like that!"

Mom waves me off. "I think I've reached the end of my string."

I dig my heels deeper into the sand, thinking of all the supernovas required to create this beach. "Do you think you'll scare someone off because of the Red Thread of Fate or because of, well, you?"

Mom grunts. "Both."

A wave rushes higher up the beach, cutting off our path. We take it as a sign that we've gone far enough and make a U-turn back to where we started.

"The thread will never break," I remind her. "Maybe yours has just been tangled for a while. Likely used for inappropriate things and stretched out a bit. Maybe it will be for a little longer, but it's still there."

She sighs. "If you say so."

I reach around Mom's shoulders to hug her. "It's not up to me."

Chapter 21

ROONEY

That was so trippy," I say, my head still spinning from the micro-gravity and full-motion Mars rover simulators. "It feels like I was spun around in a rolling chair a thousand times. Maybe I could re-create that and make a string maze for people to get disoriented in. Then they'd know what that was like."

"I'd go to that!" Jack says, zigzagging his way behind me. "I feel like a shaken can of soda. This is what being drunk must feel like." He falls behind, disappearing behind a corner.

I stumble out the entrance doors of the Kennedy Space Center on Merritt Island, Florida, as the sun lingers inches above the horizon. It's the beginning of November so there isn't much humidity, but the air is still thick.

Seconds later, Jack bursts through the doors, waving his arm in the air. "I got us a little treat! Astronaut ice cream bars."

"You stole those?" I ask.

"They were in front of the kids' exhibit. I only grabbed two. You're a big kid, aren't you?" Jack says, laughing and wiggling the bars in front of me.

"Jackson No-Middle-Name Liu, you stole ice cream bars from children?"

Jack smiles slyly and hands me one. "I left twenty dollars on the table."

I clutch the ice cream bar. "This is officially the most expensive ice cream I've ever eaten."

The clouds are heavy and hazy, the threat of a thunderstorm looming. In the distance, the sunset is as vibrant and textured as a Van Gogh oil painting. Jack guides us toward the Rocket Garden, which we passed earlier but didn't have time to explore. Now, it seems, we're about to.

"Should we be here?" I ask, eyeing a security guard walking the perimeter of the Space Center. He turns the corner to do a loop.

"I just took ice cream from kids. You think I care about being in here after hours?" Jack asks. "Okay, fine. I spoke to the guard earlier. We're good. I work at NASA, remember?"

The Rocket Garden is empty, even though earlier it was jam-packed with tourists taking photos. Some of the rockets must be over a hundred feet tall, their noses sticking straight up in the air.

We cross over the grass to one of the curved pathways. The garden contains a bouquet of nine rockets of varying sizes, each of them with their own history. Who needs roses when you can have rockets? They're mounted in their stands as if they could blast off at any moment. The lights at the base of each rocket illuminate the steel in a soft glow, accentuating their length.

I rip the pouch open across the top to discover a cookies-and-cream freeze-dried ice cream bar. I tentatively bite into it, the dessert crumbling between my teeth.

"I've gotta be honest, I don't love it," I admit. "I prefer the kind that melts."

"Wait until you try the ice cream I make. Gōng Gong is hoping to have a sundae party at his house next month. A belated welcome for you. I thought it could be nice to invite the team," Jack says.

"That's a great idea," I say, taking another small bite of the dry dessert. "You should definitely invite everyone."

Jack lifts his arms up slowly. "Oh no. Space ice cream side effects."

I laugh and reach for his arms to lower them. He levitates them back up. Once again, I push his arms down gently and slowly, holding them firmly at his side. As if he'd really float away. After a few seconds too long, I let his arms go.

"Whew, thanks," he says, his cheeks rosy.

I try to remind myself that Jack and I are on a work trip. Someone could see us, and we both have our careers on the line. I glance around and confirm that there's no one nearby. I loosen up more, letting myself enjoy the full effects of the simulation from earlier.

"This would be a cool installation spot," I say, looking from rocket to rocket, trying to conjure string in my mind to see how it might take shape. If I try hard enough, I might even be able to feel the string between my fingertips. Nope. I only see lines dangling from rockets with no meaning behind them. Even my imaginary thread is a mess.

"It'd be exposed to the elements," he says, following my gaze. "But I can see it."

"That makes one of us," I admit.

Jack's eyes flick back to me. "Still no ideas?"

"Red String Theory is done, but it clearly didn't work. I've got nothing!" I say.

"That's not necessarily true," he says, frowning. "The tests have made you experience things you normally wouldn't have, like butterflies. Now you know cloud names."

"And that the Hollywood Sign looks like a constellation of letters from a distance," I contribute.

Jack lifts his half-eaten ice cream bar like he's toasting. "See? That's not nothing. Tests can take time to reveal results. The effects aren't always immediately obvious. You'll think of something."

I lean against the railing circling the Mercury-Redstone rocket. "Honestly, I don't know if I'll even remember how to tie off a knot."

Instead of trying to convince me otherwise or keep up a can-do attitude, Jack says, "That must be tough. It seems like being creative is such a big part of your identity."

"It is, and I love what I do." I break off a piece of the ice cream bar and drop it into my mouth.

Jack stuffs his empty wrapper in his pocket and offers to take mine, too. I hand him the remains of my ice cream. During this exchange, he doesn't say a word or try to problem-solve. He gives me time to think.

"I feel like I don't know how to create anything while also feeling assured that, once I actually get started, I'll somehow know what to do. Does that sound weird?" I ask, playing with the button on my red knitted cardigan. I'll be wearing this for the next few days until the airport delivers my lost luggage. The one time I go against Mom's golden rule of only carrying on.

"Of all the things you've ever said, Rooney, that is the least weird," Jack says. His tone is gentle, and I can tell he's trying to make me laugh. A small one comes out. It feels so good to laugh in this moment, my tightly packed emotions shaking loose.

"A lot of this is probably in my head," I say. "I want to believe I can do this, but what if it's not good enough and people think my work is awful?" I let out another laugh, but this one's humorless. Jack's expression doesn't change. Steady, as always. "I want this to be successful."

"And what does that mean?" Jack asks. "What does success look like to you?"

"Positive reviews of my installation," I say right away. "Lots of people coming to see it. NASA being happy with choosing me."

Jack nods. "So you need a thousand good reviews and a million people who want to come see your art?"

I'm caught off guard by his response. "I mean...no."

"How many positive reviews do you need to feel successful? How many people need to show up?" He doesn't ask these questions in a mean or judgmental way. In his voice is curiosity and thoughtfulness.

I don't have an immediate answer. I run my hand along a railing guarding a silver rocket, taking the time to think. Overhead, gray clouds roll in slowly.

"I've always wanted my art to mean something. To have a positive impact on even one person's life," I admit quietly.

"So, one. If one person understands what you're trying to do with your art and feels something from it, then you'll feel successful," he hypothesizes.

It clicks into place, what he's trying to do. "Are you going to try to turn this into another test?" I groan playfully.

"Not a test. But let's keep going through this. If one person is positively impacted, then it's also likely they'll have good things to say about your work. Do you think that's true?"

I nod, a small grin forming on my face.

"And let's say the average museum has roughly three thousand visitors in a day. Your installation will be up for about three months until the next one. Minus a couple of holidays. That's, what, two hundred and seventy thousand visitors who will see your work in person? And then there's social media. I think it would be safe to assume that one—no, more than one—person will be positively impacted by your work."

I'm stunned not only by Jack's mental math but by the way he broke down my anxieties and made them tangible.

"Okay, fine. So maybe one person is inspired. I also want to be a financially independent, working artist," I tell him. "I know that this will take time. My mom wasn't an overnight success until she did *Baby Being Born*. That exposure changed the game for her."

"It does take time," Jack says. "I know this from missions I've worked on. It takes literal years before there's even the chance to see if we're successful. For you, your work will compound. One person will see something you do, and over time, your audience will grow. It's hard to do one thing and expect everyone to know your name."

I sigh. "It's just that, between my birth and everything in between that led me to art, I really do believe this is what I was meant to do. I literally picked a paintbrush as a baby."

Jack must be able to sense my hesitation. "But?"

"But if everything is fated, what was earned? Is what I do actually good or is it only successful because it was meant to be? What if I'm really not that good and people are going to find out that I'm a fraud?" I ask. "It's like everything I've done in my career is built on top of unsecured string and it can all unravel at any second."

Around us, bushes rustle as the wind picks up. I'm in nature's version of an air shower with my hair flying across my face. When the gust temporarily dies down, I flip my bangs back into place and meet Jack's gaze.

"You aren't a fraud, Rooney," he says kindly, slowly reaching toward me to tuck a loose strand of hair behind my ear. "You made choices about what installations you were going to design. The way I see it, you chose to be an artist. You make that choice every day when you wake up and create."

"I construct installations about the Red Thread of Fate and love and bringing people together... when I haven't ever been in a serious relationship before. Who am I to have anything to say about that?"

"You can have an opinion on love, even if you've never been in a relationship worthy of it," Jack says. "Don't discount your achievements. Have you ever considered working under your own name now that you've established yourself? I know there are people who love your work. I've seen the reviews."

I shake my head firmly. "I can't risk outing my identity. People will think I'm successful because of my mom. I don't want them to think differently about my work."

"It's up to you and what you're comfortable with," Jack says. "But what you've accomplished is because of you. You're NASA's artist-in-residence. These things don't just happen."

I give him a weary smile. "Of course these things just happen. You literally called out of the blue."

"Let me put it this way. If you were fated to be a success as Red String Girl, who's to say you weren't fated to also be successful as Rooney Something Gao?" Jack asks. "No one is going to make the switch for you. You have to be the one to choose it." He takes my hand in his. "When you let fate take credit, you discount your hard work. You've had the ideas. You've executed them. Have you ever considered that maybe you are good enough, and it's because of you?"

A somber laugh spills out of me and into the wind. "I don't know how to answer that." With my free hand, I squeeze the guard rail tighter. "I've been working at this for years, and I want to make the most of this moment, this second chance. I don't want another *Entangled* on my hands. I don't just want to shine. I want to sparkle, Jack. Like the stars."

"*Entangled* led you here," Jack says with a soft expression. "To me."

It takes my breath away, the way he phrases this. It's like our minds are following a similar thread.

He clears his throat. "But I think this is the start for you. I'm excited to be around to witness it."

We continue to stroll, not feeling the need to fill the air with words. We can just be.

The more time I spend with Jack, the more I feel myself pulled toward him. A tug on my heartstrings in his direction. What is Jack to me? What are we to each other? Trying to understand the signs feels like stargazing on a cloudy night.

Beyond the nose of a turquoise rocket called Delta II, storm clouds that I forget the official name for take on a plum hue. In the distance, there's a muffled roll of thunder. Not wanting our night to get cut short, I will the storm to blow in a different direction.

Our pinkies touch as we drift toward each other walking along the path, the point of contact sending chills up my arm. The proximity to each other puts every nerve in my body on high alert in both a good and an alarming way. In the back of my mind, I can hear Mom's advice.

Jack slows to read the sign in front of one of the rockets. "These remind me of the intricate experiments I used to do as a kid. But these are way cooler than a paper towel roll and baking soda."

I lean closer to get a better look at his face. "How intricate are we talking? Erupting volcano? Tornado in a water bottle?"

"Please. My experiments were next level. My most intense experiment was what I called The Exploding Star," he says proudly. "It involved balloons, baking soda, ice cubes, vinegar, and too much glitter. It's how I got this." He sticks his lip out. "An experiment gone awry."

I tilt my head. "It's your Supernova Scar. You wouldn't be you without it."

Jack smiles. "Supernova Scar. I like that. I was self-conscious about it for a lot of my life."

I tentatively reach out and brush my thumb over his bottom lip. He lets me. "It reminds me of a crescent moon. But it also looks like a parenthesis, as though everything you say is just extra information."

Our bodies gravitate closer together. We're completely lost in the moment until Jack gasps, his gaze directed behind me.

"It must be Kenneth," he says, watching a man round the corner back toward the Rocket Garden. "He mentioned something about being in town at the same time as us." We're too far away to confirm that it's him, even when the person turns and calls out to us. It almost sounds like he's saying Jack's name. Jack pulls me around to the back of the rocket and not a split-second later he whispers, "Run."

I'm frozen in place. "Wait, what? You said—"

Jack wraps his arm around my waist and gives me the forward momentum I need to move my feet. We sprint behind the base of another rocket and out of view.

"Think he saw us?" Jack pants.

"Maybe. He was too far away to know for sure," I shout-whisper. "Could've been a guard? You did confirm we could be in here, right?"

Jack makes a face. "Well, no. We're not supposed to be here. We're breaking every rule there is. If they catch us, deny everything."

Adrenaline pumps through my veins. Jack reaches for my hand, gripping his fingers around mine.

"When I count to three, we head to that space capsule, okay?" Jack says, nodding toward a black horizontal pod with steps leading up into it.

I agree and grip his hand tighter.

"Three!"

We run for our lives toward the capsule, trying not to make too much noise clambering up the metal stairs.

We squeeze inside the pod, and I practically fall into Jack's lap. We're holding our breath, careful not to let our panting give us away.

"That was close," Jack whispers, his chest rising and falling.

"I can't believe you," I say quietly, still unsure who might be around. I push Jack gently against his shoulder.

Jack catches my hand in his, holding it against him. Our faces are a foot apart, given that we're crammed into a space capsule the size of a bathtub. I can practically hear our pounding hearts echoing off the walls surrounding us.

My mind swirls with colors from moments of our time together. A red scarf in the print shop. Cream lanterns. The orange hue of Jack's jazz show. Golden table dumplings. Bright yellow cabs. The blinking green neon light. White bunny suits. Fuchsia sunsets. Jack's brown eyes. And now, the charcoal interior of this capsule. It's a rainbow palette in shades of Jack, and it's all I want to paint with.

My heart flutters as erratically as butterfly wings in topsy-turvy flight. Up, down, side to side.

Our eyes find each other, my thoughts trailing off. The moment feels like a loose tangle, the space within it still flexible.

Jack traces his fingers up the length of my arm, over my shoulder, and along my neck until the side of my face rests against his palm. I tilt my head into his warm hand. Gently, he sweeps his thumb over my cheek.

It's delicate, his touch. I want him to grab me tighter, hold me close. There's no choice in this, no decision making. It's what's meant to happen. It must be.

"Have you ever wanted to do something that you know you shouldn't do, but can't help it?" Jack asks.

"Just kiss me already," I say, leaning into him.

As if defying some sort of physics and logic, our bodies somehow move even closer than they already were. We don't break eye contact until we close our eyelids at the moment our lips touch.

And just like that, the string pulls tight, collapsing into a smooth line.

I'm kissing Jack. Jack is kissing me.

We shouldn't be doing this.

We're doing this.

My tangled-up thoughts last until Jack runs his hands through my hair. His kiss is slow, unplanned, explorative. His teeth gently brush against my upper lip as I press into him. My head is spinning faster than it was in the simulator. My lips graze over his Supernova Scar, and I can feel the small crescent mark on my tongue.

We softly breathe in rhythm as we break for air. He holds my face in his hands. It's a gesture that's tender and protective and purposeful. His eyes search mine. I'm lost in his gaze, weightless against him, spacewalking without a tether.

We're apart too long. He pulls me back to his parted mouth, and I twist his hair between my fingers to secure myself to him.

Then, a bright flash of lightning illuminates the capsule, shortly followed by a crack of thunder filling the silent air. We both startle.

"We're in a garden full of metal," Jack says. "We have to go."

I scramble off his lap, out of the capsule, and down the stairs. Above us, the sky has split open, the downpour of rain soaking us. Another rumble of thunder overhead speeds us both up, and we sprint to shelter, exiting the Rocket Garden hand in hand.

Chapter 22

JACK

The rain does its job and soaks us completely through. The air-conditioning of the hotel makes everything feel colder. Rooney's hand is still in mine. I keep a lookout for Kenneth just in case it was him. From what it looked like, though, he was going into the Space Center.

Rooney's cardigan and pants are drenched, and she has no luggage.

"You can borrow some clothes," I offer. When she nods, I lead us to my room, which isn't fancy by any stretch of the imagination. There's a bed, a dresser, a nightstand, and a chair in the corner. It's small, but it's not as cramped as the rocket. I'm both relieved and disappointed by this.

"I feel like my bones are wet," Rooney says as she peels away her cardigan and kicks off her shoes at the door.

"Let me get you something to change into," I say, leaving my jacket and shoes next to hers. I present Rooney with a choice of a blue button-down or a white T-shirt.

"Do you have anything red?" she jokes, taking the blue button-down. "I'll go with this. Less, uh, see-through."

It's an image I know I won't be able to get out of my head any-time soon. An internal burst of heat pushes back against the room's chill.

While Rooney changes in the bathroom, I put on a dry white T-shirt and gym shorts. My skin is still damp but at least my clothes aren't. Rooney comes out wearing my shirt, the length of it hanging down to the middle of her thigh. I keep my eyes trained on her face.

"Blue's not my color, but at least it's dry," she says. Her hair is still wet, her bangs plastered across her forehead. She sits on the side of the bed, watching me. Without her signature color, a new shade of Rooney emerges. She seems more vulnerable with her shield of red yarn gone.

I lower myself onto the other side of the bed across from her. It makes a creaking noise that breaks the tension between us. Rooney's the first to laugh. I follow her lead and turn to face her.

"So…" I start.

"Yeah," she says, nodding like there's an unspoken agreement between us.

"That can't happen again," I say.

"Completely agree," she says, tucking her legs under herself. "We got caught up in the moment."

"It was a really tight space."

Rooney sits up on her knees, gesturing with her arms. "It's like the thing we do. We walk, talk, kiss at the end. Totally normal."

I move toward the center of the bed and cross my legs. "Right. It wasn't the first time, but it has to be the last."

We fall quiet, staring at each other. My eyes drop to her lips. She's not wearing lipstick today, but they're still a little red from earlier in the space capsule.

Somehow, we're closer to each other, gravity pulling us together without much resistance. Our faces are inches apart.

A knock at the door ends the moment before it can begin. We jump back from each other. Rooney slides off her side of the bed and takes an entire three steps to hide in the bathroom.

On the other side of the door is Kenneth. Did he see us in the Rocket Garden? Is this why he's here? I pull the heavy door open and force a smile onto my face.

"Jackson!" Kenneth says before I can say hello. "Sorry to surprise you like this. Was that you I saw in the Rocket Garden?"

"In this weather? That would be reckless." I inhale sharply. "I was there earlier, though," I say, not being able to commit to the lie. "What brings you to town?"

Kenneth laughs and lifts his arms. Drops of water roll off his sleeves. "Good point. I had a meeting with the Center Director. They had shirts for the team," he says, handing me a Kennedy Space Center T-shirt. "There's one for Rooney, too."

I take it from him before he offers to bring it to her. "I'd be happy to give it to her tomorrow. I think she's...busy," I interject.

"Great. Thanks. Oh, hey! Congrats on being put up for a promotion. Your manager reached out for a recommendation," he shares.

"I didn't know...That's great," I say. Did I miss an email about this? I make a mental note to check.

Kenneth smiles reassuringly. "Don't worry. Only good things to say here. You're doing fantastic work. Keep it up. My fingers are crossed for you."

"Thanks," I mumble.

"I won't keep you. See you back in LA!" Kenneth says as he turns toward the elevator.

I return with a half wave and close the door.

Rooney peers out from behind the door. "Can I come out?"

I nod, handing her the T-shirt. "My manager put my name in for a promotion."

"I heard," she says. "That's really great news."

"Yeah."

"Are you okay?"

"That was dangerously close, Rooney," I whisper.

"Completely agree," she says in a hushed tone. "I don't want to compromise anything for you."

"And this program is too important for you," I say. We stare deeply into each other's eyes. It feels like saying good-bye in New York City all over again.

Rooney nods quickly. "Yes. These opportunities mean too much. We can't risk anything." She pulls at a wet strand of hair. "Friends, then?"

Before any semblance of hesitation takes over, I agree. "Friends."

"Great," she says, her voice wavering. "I should probably go."

I peer through the peephole in the door. "Maybe wait a few minutes to make sure he's gone."

Rooney holds her hands up in the air. "I'm getting under the blankets then," she says quietly. "We can talk in a normal volume. The walls can't be that thin."

"I'm going to...sit in that chair," I say, pointing across the room. At this moment, thankfully, notifications light up my phone. "It's Sprinkles."

Rooney pulls the comforter up to her chin so that only her head pokes out. "She learned to text? They grow up so fast."

I chuckle, and the worry melts out of me. Everything will be okay if Rooney and I never do what we did in the Rocket Garden ever again. We got the residual tension from New York out of our systems.

"They're camera notifications. I set them up so I could keep an eye on Sprinkles and see what she's up to."

"Ohhh," Rooney says playfully. "That makes a lot more sense. What's she doing?"

I analyze the video, zooming in. "She's curious to know about everything. Every time she walks or jumps in front of the camera, I get an alert."

"I bet she misses you," she says, lowering the blanket a few inches to free her arms.

"Gōng Gong comes by twice a day to check in on her. Sometimes three," I say, placing my phone on the table. "I hope Sprinkles isn't mad that I'm gone for so long."

"She's probably excited to have all that space to herself. I bet she thinks she now owns your apartment," Rooney says. Her eyes linger on mine. Typically it's her eyes that draw me in and undo me. Now, though, with her in my shirt and in my bed, I try to focus on her eyes and nothing else.

"Let's talk about something, just for a few minutes until the coast is clear," I say quickly. "Have you enjoyed your time at NASA so far?"

Of course, work was the first thing I bring up. A metaphorical bucket of ice water. Actually, that's perfect.

"Jack, we don't have to make small talk, but work is a great topic," Rooney says while fiddling with the shirt collar.

I will myself to concentrate on the words Rooney is saying. I'm certainly not going to think about her in my button down that I'll be wearing tomorrow.

"Okay. So. Work," I mutter, hoping my overheated face isn't completely giving me away.

If Rooney's aware of my bumbling, she doesn't let on. "You asked me how I view success. Now I want to know how you define it," she says.

I lean forward to ground myself, resting my elbows on my thighs. "Moving up in my career. Being excellent at what I do. Proving that what I chose as my career was worthwhile."

"And is what you do worthwhile?" she asks, watching me.

"I think so," I admit. "It satisfies me to make scientific advancements. To help push the limits of our universe's boundaries."

"To run experiments that involve more than balloons and glitter?" she asks.

"Honestly, NASA's lack of glitter usage in experiments is a missed opportunity," I say in a mock-serious tone.

"Especially when it comes to running tests in the clean room," Rooney says with a laugh. She drags the pillow higher behind her, propping herself up. The movement causes the edge of the comforter to flip over itself, revealing more of her. This alone sends my imagination to off-limits places, even though she's still mostly covered.

"From where I lie, then," she continues, "it looks like you've already proved whatever it is you needed to. And it sounds like you're going to be moving on up pretty soon."

I bounce my knee, my arms bobbing with it. "We'll see."

The heat finally kicks on, the vent rattling as it dispenses hot air. The noise drowns out our conversation, and we fall into an easy silence. I look out the dirty hotel window. The moon is a thin sliver against the charcoal night sky.

"Hey, can I ask you a serious question?" Rooney asks, resting her cheek in her palm. "Every time you look up at the moon, does it make you think of work? Because that sounds exhausting."

What's exhausting is refraining from kissing Rooney. From telling her how I feel about her. I better get used to being fatigued.

I smile in response as I convince myself that keeping our distance is for the best. If the past two months were hard, the next ten will be even harder.

Chapter 23

ROONEY

It's not every day that people get to be strapped into a device attached to a crane that lowers them into a pool holding 6.2 million gallons of water. Unless those people are astronauts, of course. And yet, here I am. Wèishéme shì wǒ?

Today I get to do an underwater moonwalk at NASA's Neutral Buoyancy Laboratory at the Sonny Carter Training Facility in Houston, Texas, in a real flight suit that the astronauts wear. It took an hour and a team of people to help me get into the suit, which was an endeavor that deserves an entire installation dedicated to it. I never thought I'd wear liquid-cooled underwear to prevent me from overheating, though honestly they're not the most uncomfortable thing I've ever worn.

I want to be fully present for today, but I woke up to a text from Talia this morning with news that's hard not to spiral over. I'm in my underwater suit feeling cocooned and a little bit stuck.

"I can't believe a place like this exists," I say, trying to focus on the once-in-a-lifetime opportunity ahead of me. I'm speaking into a headset directly connected to Jack's, who's been helped into a suit of his own. The communications is set to always being on, resulting in me being able to hear him breathe, a level of intimacy I haven't experienced before. We're back-to-back on the platform that will lower us into the pool.

"What we're about to do is pretty incredible," Jack says, his voice directly in my earpiece. "The average backyard pool can hold about twenty thousand gallons, so this is significantly more. They don't let just anyone in here. Or wear these suits. I still can't believe they're letting me join."

"I'm glad you're coming," I manage to say on an exhale. I smile to myself, the feeling of weightlessness taking over even though I'm not yet in the water.

Another team of people hooks me up with more cords, video cables, and wires. "This suit has been in space, Jack."

"Made specifically for it, too. Though ours are modified for underwater use. They're three hundred pounds," he says.

My eyes pop at this number. "It can withstand the pressure, right? How far down is it? Will we be able to get back up?"

"Forty feet deep," he informs me. I glance over the edge of the pool.

"I don't have a fear of heights, but to be determined about a fear of depths," I wonder out loud.

The water is so still, it looks like glass, the mock-up International Space Station and lunar surface trapped underneath. Three divers in gray wetsuits file out from one of the side doors.

"We're going to guide you around underwater and keep you safe," one of them explains. "This is a weightless training environment and the closest we can get to microgravity, but the water drag in the pool is the opposite of what would happen in space."

"Should anything go wrong, we'll get you to the surface in seconds," another adds.

Sandra Wilson, the test director who's in charge of the day's operations, joins our huddle. Earlier she introduced me to everyone, explained what happens at the Neutral Buoyancy Laboratory, walked me through what to expect, and gave me a crash course on everything that goes into the usual six-hour dives for the astronauts. Magic happens here. That, I'm sure of.

"The moon has about one-sixth the gravity than we do here on Earth," Sandra tells me. "This is good training for our astronauts to practice gathering samples, test new tools and suits, and execute the movements and motions they'll do on the moon and in space. Hopefully this firsthand experience will be helpful as you learn more about how everything works together here at NASA."

"I'll be taking copious mental notes," I say.

Jack agrees, sounding so excited that he's practically vibrating through the headset.

The helmet is placed over my head, making me feel like a goldfish. The men who helped suit me up lower me to the bottom of the pool. Through the clear bubble, I watch as air turns to water, everything submerging with me.

"Tell me this pool wouldn't be the most unique installation space ever," I say to Jack.

"I'd agree with you there," he says.

Under the surface, it's a completely new world. I almost expect fish to swim by, but none do. I'm in awe. It's the closest and, at forty feet belowground, the farthest away from space I'll ever be.

Near the bottom, dry land is a concept, a glimmer of light from above. Upon touchdown, I clumsily take my first step into the lunar area intended for moonwalk training. My boots have weights attached to them to keep me grounded, but still I stumble through sand and chunks of rock.

I can now see Jack, his face peering through the window of his own helmet. He gives me two thumbs-up and nods frequently to remind me I'm doing great, his simple gestures calming me.

The umbilical that provides oxygen to my suit tugs at me from behind. I take a moment to look up and around. There's such clear visibility, I almost forget I'm surrounded by water. The underwater training facilities in the far end of the pool loom over us.

I want to sketch it all. In front of me, imaginary red strings cross the pool from one end to the other, stretching diamond formations. I watch as these nonexistent threads float in spirals, twisting and turning around the divers, above the American flag planted firmly into the sand pit.

I feel another pull at my back and look behind me. The imaginary string that wraps around Jack isn't a fabrication of this underwater daydream. He's actually tangled up in my umbilical with a small loop tied loosely around his ankle.

The moment lasts just long enough to sear itself into my memory. It's an unusual visualization that I didn't anticipate seeing at the bottom of a pool the size of a small building in a space suit on a mock moon. My heart pounds underneath the thickness of the suit.

Jack pulls his boot through the loop and is free within seconds. He's graceful in the water, even in a 300-pound suit. I refocus on the replica of the planetary surface beneath me. The sound of Jack's breathing inside the suit relaxes me.

In the past few days since the hotel room incident, we've kept our promise by maintaining a distance. Being suspended underwater in suits, behind the clear plastic of helmets, reflects the new normal of our relationship. I wish we could keep them afterward. It would be a much easier way to prevent us from touching.

Light from the surface trickles down to the bottom of the pool in fragments. Jack is a watercolor painting of navy blues, gray, and the brown of his eyes. Even with every color on my palette, I wouldn't be able to capture the exact shade of him in this moment.

I push forward through the water, bouncing with each step. All divers' eyes are on me, watching my every move. Meanwhile, I'm watching every one of Jack's.

We're given a task to pick up rock samples in the lunar area so we can experience what the astronauts do. There are a variety of tools at our disposal, and this generation of suits apparently have greater mobility. My heart nearly stops pounding when Jack kneels in front of me and lifts a rock up in front of him. He looks at me and grins. I laugh to myself. That is a very different type of rock than what his stance typically calls for. Our gazes catch as we both take deep breaths in. It's too intimate hearing someone breathe like this.

I attempt to lift a mock space rock of my own with one of the tools. I'm able to pick up a few but the water slows down my movements and I can't get a grip on my fifth rock. I sigh with frustration and have some choice words for this task.

"How's it going over there?" Jack's voice crackles into my ear.

For a second, I forgot that Jack can also hear me.

"I'm not as nimble down here," I say, trying to wiggle my fingers.

"You're doing great. Is that all, though?" Jack asks. "You've been quieter than usual today."

Am I that obvious? "Oh. I'm fine."

Jack's back on his feet and testing out a new tool. "Rooney, the clean room strips us down. The pool washes us clean. Tell me what's going on."

I look back up at the surface. It's not like I can swim away from this conversation.

"There are rumors that a museum in Europe wants to buy the video," I share. "Apparently, they may be trying to put together a permanent exhibit that showcases nostalgia. They want pieces that are conversation starters. *Baby Being Born* checks off both of those boxes. The range is officially twenty-five to thirty-five thousand dollars. That's slightly higher than I anticipated, which was already too high for what I can afford."

"Wow," Jack says, walking in slow motion toward me. "That blows my mind, and I'm in fake space."

I huff out a laugh. "I don't have museum competition money!"

"Hmm. The museum may want it, but it doesn't mean they'll get it." He points toward the handle of my tool. "Angle it like this, and you might have an easier time using it with your gloves."

I adjust my hand positioning as Jack instructed. "That's easier. Thanks. But yeah, this adds more pressure to the showcase."

"It certainly does. But having an installation will help," Jack says as he bends down again to touch the sand. "There will be a lot of press on opening day. That'll be good exposure. Exposure will drive sales. It has to. And don't worry. An idea will come. Give it time."

For a brief moment, Jack's words comfort me. Sure, we're underwater, but talking to him in a mock lunar area is as easy as it was at the hotel. Not just in the hotel. In his room. Me in Jack's shirt, in Jack's bed, after having kissed him in the Rocket Garden. I can totally survive off two, almost three, Jack kisses in my lifetime. That should be plenty. It has to be.

Stay present, Rooney.

I place my tool back on the metal table connected to the bottom of the pool. "Will it be enough sales? is the question. I'm in way over my head."

Jack slowly stands and turns to face me. It takes him a moment to turn all the way around. "Would you say you're feeling underwater?"

He says the unexpected comment with such a serious face that I burst out laughing. "Even after I save up just to spend it all on this piece, how will I stay afloat?" I counter.

Jack raises an eyebrow. "You'd think that down here, the weight of the world would be off your shoulders."

I attempt to throw up my hands, but it's more of a slow raise because of the water drag. Still, it captures the dramatic effect I was aiming for. "It was poolish of me to think this would be possible."

It must be because I'm smiling that Jack takes it as a sign that he can laugh because it's exactly what he does. Behind the plastic of his helmet, he's amused, but the sound of chuckling only comes through in my earpiece after a short lag. It's like watching a movie when the sound doesn't match the actors' mouth movements.

I exhale slowly and take in my surroundings of the pool, of the divers, of Jack. Of everything I'll see and experience today, the one thing I'd want to bottle up is this moment right here, the feeling of weightlessness that takes over when I'm around Jack, and maybe most of all, the sound of his laughter.

Chapter 24

JACK

Gōng Gong's house smells like waffles. When Rooney and my team arrive for our Sunday Sundaes party, it's the first thing they all notice. That, and Sprinkles, who I always bring with me to Gōng Gong's. She's scooping rainbow sprinkles out of a bowl with her paw like it's a fun game. Her tail narrowly misses the stack of waffles on the counter. Next to those are tubs of homemade ice cream and smaller bowls with all the toppings you could want: sprinkles, cherries, chocolate chips, chocolate sauce, caramel sauce, marshmallows, mixed nuts, whipped cream, and cut fruit.

Once a month, it's just me and Gōng Gong who do this. Today, Gōng Gong is excited for new people to try out our ice cream flavors. We made matcha, blueberry muffin, and red bean, since he wanted to include "a little something red for Rooney." I purposely don't read into the fact that red bean ice cream is what we ate together in New York.

Nell, Maria, and Brian have come, as well as Toby and Mac, FATE's operations systems engineer. The people I work with most but who I don't know very well. I introduce the team to Gōng Gong, and he tells them that formalities aren't needed with him and that they can call him Bohai. At this, Rooney makes an unreadable expression.

While Gōng Gong pours batter into the waffle maker, I make

sure everyone has what they need. Bowls, spoons, napkins. We move through the line, piling ice cream on top of waffles, and gather around the kitchen table. Earlier, I pulled chairs from around the house to accommodate the eight of us. It's a tight squeeze or, as Rooney's calling it, "cozy."

"This was so nice of you to invite us into your home, Bohai," Maria says.

"Yeah, thanks for setting this up, Jackson," Brian says. "I was certain this would be a freeze-dried ice cream party with waffles, but admittedly I'm glad it's not."

As Rooney passes me, she lowers her voice and says, "It's nice to see your Spot." She settles into a chair a couple of seats away from me. Great. Distance is good.

"It's best when the ice cream soaks into the waffle," Gōng Gong says, getting everyone's attention. "But you've reminded me that freeze-dried ice cream makes for excellent toppings. I'll crumble some."

I observe the situation, suddenly hyperaware. I see Gōng Gong and his house through my team's eyes. In his late eighties, Gōng Gong looks like a shorter James Hong. He's smiley and cheerful, which didn't always come easily to him. Grandma died in her late fifties shortly after I was born, something Gōng Gong didn't see coming. He thought they'd have not just years together, but decades. He hasn't remarried since, and every day he wakes up choosing to be optimistic. If he can't control anything else, he says that he can at least have a say over how he reacts to what else life throws at him.

Another thing he chooses to control: his nautical-themed house decor. Now that Gōng Gong can't spend as much time out at sea as he used to, he brings the ocean to him. Assembled wooden sailboats and ships are positioned in front of the windows throughout the house, buoys and life preserver rings tucked into corners and hanging on walls. Even the round wooden kitchen table we're all crammed around has a compass image engraved into the top. Why is it that the people I surround myself with love a good theme?

I'm pulled out of my thoughts by Rooney, who's saying my name.

"Did you hear that? Toby and Mac have a band. You'll never guess what they're called," she says, her fork mid-lift with a piece of waffle on it.

It could be anything. I shake my head, not even trying to speculate.

"Red String Theorists," she says slowly, her eyes widening. Sprinkles has taken a liking to her. She's purring in her lap and kneading her fuzzy sweater.

"Red for Mars?" I ask, venturing a guess.

"That's right. Rooney says you play bass, Jackson," Mac says, gathering ice cream on his spoon. "If you ever want to jam sometime, let us know. We play local shows every now and then for fun."

"Oh, maybe. That could be cool. And you can all actually call me Jack," I tell them. "Let me know when you practice, and I'll see if I can come." The jazz club in New York was the one and only time I've played bass in public outside of high school. I didn't have plans to increase that number.

Rooney openly smiles about this.

Mac and Toby look slightly stunned that I've agreed. "Yeah. Okay. Yeah," they say over one another. "We have a show at the beginning of December. We'll...text you?"

I grin. "That would be great."

Suddenly, Gōng Gong speaks up. "Oh, Rooney! I can't believe I didn't think of this earlier. Jack, would you please grab Skipper?"

Rooney glances between the two of us.

I don't know how I've forgotten this or failed to mention it to her. I close my eyes and do as Gōng Gong says. In his study is the

string art seahorse that I ordered back in July. When I walk into
the kitchen with it, everyone's silent in anticipation. Or confusion.
Probably both.

When Rooney sees it, her eyes go even wider. "Wait, you're Bohai
from Alhambra! Your name sounded familiar, but I couldn't quite
place it. You ordered this months ago. Before I got the NASA call,
I think."

Gōng Gong smiles. "Actually, it was a gift from Jack."

"I placed the order before I knew…before you were officially
chosen," I tell her. My tone comes off unexpectedly defensive.
Maybe she's thinking that this is a sign. But it was a choice I made,
and I needed to get Gōng Gong a gift anyway.

"The shading on that is incredible, Rooney," Nell says as she sets
her spoon on her plate. "You take commissions? I'd love to have something made. Unless you're too busy, of course, with the program."

Rooney finally tears her eyes from Skipper. "No! I'm not too
busy. I'd love to make anything you want."

Nell looks pleased.

"Those are pretty good. So you do animal portraits in addition
to installations?" Toby asks. He wipes his mustache with a dolphin-
patterned cloth napkin.

Rooney shifts on her stool. "I appreciate that. For now, yes, I do
both. My ultimate dream is to do large-scale installations in public
spaces exclusively. I love that element of surprise and showing people
something new somewhere they don't expect. It'd just be out there
for everyone, not limited to a ticketed museum or gallery."

"It's so important for more people to be exposed to art without
barriers," Nell adds.

"How wonderful," Gōng Gong says. "Your themes are thought-
provoking. With your art, you can share bigger ideas with people
about the world beyond us, the world we live in, and how we can

engage with both as humans." He drizzles chocolate syrup around his scoop of matcha ice cream, the chocolate lines hardening as they freeze.

"Yes, Bohai! You get me. That's why I love working with string. It's tangible, and I enjoy taking something ordinary and turning it into something grander. As long as it doesn't get littered in," Rooney says with a laugh.

The joke doesn't sound like one that Rooney sometimes uses to mask her pain. Instead, she sounds like someone who has had time to process it. She's not letting it define her anymore.

Rooney watches Gōng Gong's spiral motion carefully. His ice cream is almost entirely covered at this point. When Gōng Gong is finished with his masterpiece, she smiles. "That's a solid technique, Bohai. Do you always wrap your ice cream?" she asks.

"That was a little too much chocolate string, wasn't it?" he says with a chuckle.

Rooney adds chocolate to her own ice cream. "Never too much string."

"Can I just say that I love seeing someone who looks like me doing cool stuff in the world?" Maria jumps in. "It was so meaningful that the first artist for this program was a mixed-race Asian American woman. I mean, I only know that because I know who you are, but still."

"That means a lot," Rooney says. She falls quiet, looking like she's working through something in her mind.

As we talk, Gōng Gong flips through a copy of the *Los Angeles Times*. After a few more page turns, Rooney gasps and points to a photograph of a guy surrounded by flowers in the Arts section.

"Who's that?" Maria asks.

"That's Arlo Hart," she says, her brows furrowed. "I went to his show. What does it say?"

Gōng Gong lifts the paper and adjusts his glasses, squinting at the small print. "Arlo Hart...twenty years old...son of a famous photographer...ah, here we go. It was a sold-out show in Santa Monica. It was so popular, they ended up selling not only the photographs but the flowers from the net. It's followed by an interview with him."

This artist sold all of his photographs and then some. I can practically hear Rooney counting numbers in her head across the table.

Rooney sits up straighter and pets Sprinkles so she doesn't jump off her lap. "Good for him."

"That could be you, Rooney," Nell says. "Well, not a photo of you, obviously. But maybe your installation. Your first showcase is coming up."

"Yeah. It's a couple of months away," Rooney says. She has a smile on her face but there's worry in her eyes. "I hope there's coverage at this level. My mom warned me that it can be hard for women in art."

Maria waves Rooney off. "Nah! One day that'll be you on the front page."

"It can't be if I'm always hiding," Rooney says, pushing leftover waffle around on her plate. "I used to think that my anonymity would let my work stand out. Now I wonder if my hidden identity might overshadow the bigger messages of my art. People have been even more curious about who Red String Girl is."

"You can do work outside of NASA, right?" Brian asks.

Rooney shifts in her seat. "Honestly, that's where I'm a little stuck."

The team encourages Rooney to tell them what's on her mind.

"I feel like I'm on the verge of inspiration," she tells them, looking at me when she says this. "My mom is an artist, too. A bold one.

Sometimes I think I play it a little too safe because she's so fearless. I used to want to take more risk like she did. But now I just...hide."

"You know, we take a lot of risks at NASA," Maria says. "We're doing things that haven't been done before. If we want to make change, we have to push boundaries."

"And we have haters. There are people who think we shouldn't be trying to go to Mars, or even back to the moon," Toby adds. "Some people only want to look. Others believe we should be spending resources to make this planet better first before trying to go to others."

"Everyone's going to think what they think," Mac says. "No matter what you do, even if what you think you're doing is right, you'll have people rooting against you. I'm sure you can relate, being an artist."

Rooney laughs. "Like you wouldn't believe. Going to another planet is the epitome of going big. To be totally honest with you all, doing something very public is a way for me to get my art and the themes behind it seen, but right now I also need the money. Which means I need the exposure. I'm not in trouble or anything," she adds quickly.

"Specifics aren't necessary. You need to make money to survive like the rest of us," Maria says supportively. "I've lived in LA for a while so I take it all for granted, but I'm sure there's something that would be exciting."

"Like the Hollywood Sign," I mumble.

A surprised expression washes over Rooney's face. She looks at her plate of scattered waffles like she's reading tea leaves. As if the bites hold all the answers. And then she smiles.

"Jackson No-Middle-Name Liu, you're a genius!" Rooney says with excitement. "I want to wrap more than dessert." She taps the chocolate shell encasing her red bean ice cream. "The Hollywood Sign. That's what I want to wrap. It's something that hides in plain sight, and I want to make it be seen again."

My jaw drops but no one else even blinks. There's risk, and then there's risky. Risk with the law and risk being on the mountainside. But I don't say any of this because everyone is nodding and smiling. They're saying supportive words, even.

"There's no way you could wrap that all by yourself," Toby says, offering up a hopeful deterrent.

"True. I guess I won't be doing that anytime soon," Rooney says. "It would take me days."

Gōng Gong's face lights up. "I love a little bending of the rules every now and then. I would help you if I could. I once took a moon jelly home from an expedition."

I make a face and ask a clarifying question. "You stole a jellyfish?"

"He was alone, and I wanted to give him a home," he says. "I called him Jelly Belly. Eventually someone found out, and I had to return him. Sometimes bending the rules isn't so bad. Giving him back was a sad day, but Jelly Belly kept me company through some hard times. I'll always be grateful to him for that."

My eyebrows pinch together as I process this. Rooney is feeling a different kind of inspiration. The last thing I want to do is take that away. Maybe this is where I can even be the ultimate team player. Show my support for her not just through tests but through action. If this is what Rooney wants, this is what I want. It hits me that I would scale a mountain for this woman. I would even risk getting in trouble with the law for her. Why would that be? Unless...

Unless it's because I love Rooney. I am not allowed to love Rooney. A light sweat breaks out all over my body. I press my clammy hands together. I overthink everything. But I don't have to overthink this. I love Rooney.

"I'm in," I say, the words leaving my mouth before I have chance to stop them.

Now the group looks surprised. They also look impressed.

Rooney looks at me with exploring eyes. "You want to help me wrap the Hollywood Sign?"

"You could use the extra hands, right?" I say.

Rooney's face softens.

Next to her, Gōng Gong smiles. Something behind his eyes tells me that he's happy to see this side of me. This is a side of me I didn't even know existed.

"If Jack's going to help, I also want to," Maria says. "I want to be part of Red String Girl history."

"Isn't it illegal, though? Can't you go to jail?" Toby asks, looking slightly pale.

"It's trespassing. You'll be in more trouble if you damage the sign," Gōng Gong says.

He says this like it's nothing. Why is he saying this like it's nothing?

"So whatever you do, don't damage the sign," Mac echoes.

"I'm in, too," Brian says. "I never thought you'd do this, Jack. So cool. My uncle went to Caltech in the late eighties when a group of students pulled a prank and changed the Hollywood Sign to read 'CALTECH.' He still wishes he were a part of it. The police were there and everything, but they still completed it. Apparently, the police sergeant even said that they did a good job. Can you believe that?"

"That was the eighties," Toby says. "I can't imagine we'd get a pat on the back for doing something like that now."

"If you get caught, Rooney, you're going to be exposed," Nell says with concern. "That's the opposite of hiding."

Rooney shakes her head. "I don't want to hide anymore." As she says this, she slams her spoon against the chocolate shell. It cracks open, the ice cream underneath revealed.

Rooney is willing to shed her hidden identity for this art piece. There has to be more behind it than just not wanting people to see her being born. She was known for it once, and she shares her mom's last name so it's not like people don't know she's Wren's daughter. What else is in that video?

She looks around at all of us, locking eyes with me. "I am so appreciative of the support, but no one should feel like they have to do this with me. NASA will get me to the edge of space, but I need something else to catapult me into the exosphere. It's time that I take a risk."

Chapter 25

ROONEY

W e're way past The Dumpling Hours," Jack says as he wraps red fabric cut into two-foot-wide strips around the base of the first "L" of the Hollywood Sign.

It's 3:30 a.m., and we're up in the quiet hills of Griffith Park with Talia, Maria, Nell, Brian, Toby, and Mac.

This past week, Jack and I went to every fabric store around the city and bought red cloth to cut into "string." The actual string I typically use, the kind that's thinner than floss, would've taken literal months to wrap the sign.

As a team, we went over the camera and motion sensor locations, what to wear, and how to wrap the forty-four-foot letters of the sign. Everyone contributed ideas and thought through ways to work more efficiently. We're synced on the exit strategies with A and B alternate routes. The FATE mission team pushes boundaries every day, and their willingness to do this is more proof of that. For this, though, we're Team Hollywood.

Talia and Nell are working on the second "L" while Toby and Mac take care of the "Y." Brian and Maria are wrapping the two "O"s, and whoever is done first will take the "D." The Hollywood Sign letters are relatively climbable from the back with metal beams to stand on.

Down below, the sweeping view of LA is showstopping. The

moon is a crescent but the city sparkles like the ocean in sunlight, even at this hour. I can't believe we're actually doing this.

On handheld radios, I check in with the group. "Two hours down. How's everyone doing? We have three hours until sunrise, but I think we can get out of here sooner. We're making good time."

Jack and I pick up our paces and walk the roll of cloth around the "L" as carefully as we can.

"I'm keeping Sprinkles," he says so casually that it takes me a moment to process it.

The news stops me in my tracks. "Jack, that's wonderful! What changed your mind?"

"We're basically best friends at this point. I can't leave her." Beneath Jack's cautious voice is something heartfelt.

"She's lucky to be on the receiving end of your love," I say, my eyes darting up to him.

Jack's eyes find mine, locking in place. We hold our stares for a stretched moment until someone on the team shouts for more cloth. Jack clears his throat and continues wrapping. "You're going to be leaving a mark. That's exciting to think about."

I smile. "But not a mark on these signs. Remember, no damage."

"Right. No damage," he says very seriously.

We continue our stringing, passing by each other on opposite sides of the sign.

"Do you mind if I ask you something?" Jack says when we meet back on the same side. When I agree, he asks, "Have you ever seen the video?"

I twist the cloth in my hands. "I've seen it once. When it went up for sale in 2010, I went to the auction. They played it to attract interested buyers."

Jack's quietly waiting for more. For the truth. He stops wrapping and looks at me intently.

"He was at the birth," I finally say after tying off cloth on one of the metal bars. "JR."

"JR was there. Why?" Jack asks, stalling with me at the base near the tall side of the "L."

"I wonder the same thing. It's the only time I've ever seen his face. I was born, and he wouldn't even hold me. Not once." I close my eyes. "He walks away as soon as I start crying, and the look on my mom's face, well, I'll never forget it. That was the last time we were in the same room together."

There's compassion behind Jack's eyes, not pity. "Rooney, I'm so sorry. I can see why you wouldn't want that to be out there. You don't want to relive it again. Or for your mom to."

"She doesn't regret the video or me, but people don't need to see that," I say. "If I can buy it, I can move past it. We can be done with him."

Jack nods. "I was looking at how much I have saved up, and if you need more money, please let me know how much. I want to help."

"That's nice of you, but you're already helping," I say, tucking leftover cloth between the folds. "Hopefully after this, money won't be a problem. I made Hollywood-themed string art pieces that will be available to buy tomorrow morning. They're priced pretty high. More than I've ever asked for."

"That's good. Your work is worth it," Jack says.

"A portion of proceeds from those sales will go toward helping fund art programs for kids," I ramble. "The budget cuts have been terrible."

Spikes of nervous energy are starting to poke through, and Jack can probably tell. I clamp my mouth shut. There are so many things not to think about: my feelings of inadequacy, the auction, this big risk not working, kissing Jack. What I do need to focus on instead is wrapping these signs and not falling down the mountain.

"You'll already be using your voice for good," Jack says as excess cloth spills out of his arms. He's quiet for a moment, and when I don't respond, he says, "Did you know, on the morning after a clear night, the temperature continues to drop even after sunrise?"

I frown and shake my head no.

"At night, the earth cools down, releasing energy it received from the sun that day," Jack explains, raising his hands in the air, the cloth dangling below them. "You'd think everything would warm up when the sun shines. But because the sun is still so low, the solar radiation isn't strong enough yet, and the temperature continues to drop. Maybe *Entangled* was your sunrise. Barely peeking over the horizon. And now the sun is higher. Things are starting to warm up."

A real smile takes over my face. "Thank you."

I fill my lungs with cool air and slowly begin to feel hopeful. This just might work.

"Pull that a little tighter and move this corner up," I instruct.

Jack does as I tell him. "Like this?" he asks, rotating his hands and pulling gently.

"Here," I say, tucking my strand of cloth in between secured ones. I sidestep back in front of him, our bodies touching, and reach around his hands with my own to guide them into the places I want the string. Even out here on this breezy night, Jack's hands are warm and steady. I love seeing them intertwined with my string, making loops with his fingers to tie knots, like he's now a part of my work.

"Are you okay? Where'd you go just now?" Jack asks when I've gone quiet and don't respond to whatever it is he's asked.

I redirect my stare up to his face and look into his darkened eyes. "I was definitely not thinking about you tied up in string."

Jack coughs out a laugh and looks around to see if anyone heard. He pulls the cloth tightly. "I don't think this would be strong enough."

I gasp.

"Looking good," Talia says over the radio. Jack steps back from me as I let go of his hands and collect my cloth. "On our letter, I mean." She clears her throat, and Jack and I laugh quietly together.

We stand behind the sign, out of sight from the team, and tie off the cloth to complete our "L." The entire time we've been here, I've been oddly calm. Now, though, being this close to Jack, with everyone around the corner, my heart races. The riskiest thing about this night is us right here, right now, not keeping our distance.

Jack's foot slips and sends a rock tumbling down the mountain and into the darkness. Our faces are inches away, and if his foot slipped again, we'd be kissing. Which is all I can think about as everything else fades away. The city lights, the fabric in our hands, the rest of the team wrapping the letters, any sounds from the handheld radio. They're nothing but blurs. What is clear to me is the person standing less than a foot away, his face illuminated by my headlamp.

Jack has been right here with me through all of it, from the moments that were hard, uninspired, and precarious. I've gotten through them with him. Because of him. And then because of me. He helped me find myself again.

I was always hiding in plain sight. While that won't be true after today, my feelings will be in hiding if I don't share with Jack what he means to me. And what I feel is love, pure and true, like the feeling was always meant to happen. I think he might be my stringmate. After everything, how could he not be?

"Jack," I start. "I—"

And that's when the floodlights from a helicopter pour down on us. Everyone springs into executing the exit strategy when I notice that the lower half of the "D" sign is halfway done.

"You all go!" I shout. "Exit Route A, like we planned."

Team Hollywood gathers up the supplies, encouraging me to come with them.

"We're not leaving you, Rooney!" Talia screams. "Let's go!"

"I'm staying. I got this," I shout back. "Let me do this."

Talia holds her gaze for another second before nodding knowingly.

Jack grabs my arm. "Rooney, come with us."

I'm breathless. "Jack, we're so close. This is my responsibility, my risk. It was only a matter of time before they got here. You can't get caught. Please. Go," I urge, pushing him to follow the others. "Don't let them see your faces."

Before he and the team can try to stop me, I jog to the "D" to finish the work. The police won't come up here yet. When I'm done, I'll go down to them.

The exit plan works, and Team Hollywood leaves no trace behind. I savor the last moments of anonymity, bracing myself for whatever comes next. It's time to be me.

Chapter 26

ROONEY

Outside the Hollywood police station, the sun casts a burning orange glow in the hazy morning. As soon as I finished wrapping the "D," I walked down the trail and surrendered. A few hours later, I'm free to go with a fine since no damage was done to the sign. Bohai will be proud. So will Mom.

I find Talia waiting for me on the sidewalk.

"You're a bad girl, RSG," Talia says with a smirk.

"Thank you for not staying behind with me. Had it been me, I never would've left your side but..." I say playfully, giving her a hug. "You all made it out? No one saw?"

"We all made it back to Jack's Gōng Gong's house safely," Talia updates. "Everyone's sleeping. Jack wanted to come, but I told him we needed our time."

We walk ten minutes to the Hollywood Forever Cemetery, a place where, because it's so early in the morning and because of its occupants, there's no risk that someone will recognize us. We need to process this in peace.

Apparently, the Hollywood Forever Cemetery is an active cemetery, but it's also a landmark and cultural events center where they host movie and literary events. In the grass are a couple of blankets and candy wrappers. There must've been an outdoor film screening last night. It's also the final resting place of icons like Judy Garland, Cecil B. DeMille, and Douglas Fairbanks Sr.

Having just opened for the day, it's quiet. I enjoy my final moments of feeling at ease before the art world gets wind of this. Even if they don't care who I am, I know there will be interest because of who Mom is.

Talia and I finally check our phones to see what's waiting for us. I have dozens of missed calls and text messages, mostly from Mom and Jack. In one of Mom's texts, she's sent me a link to an article. Her words underneath read, This is BIG. Proud of you.

On my website, I scheduled a post to go live with my artist statement for online art publications and news outlets to use. I even included a photo of myself so they'd use that over a fuzzy photo a bystander may have taken once the police arrived. And it worked. Journalists have included their own context with my statement, along with photos of the red-wrapped Hollywood Sign.

I tap into an article from *Art in the World* magazine.

Red String Girl Asks Hollywood "HOW?"

It's a Red-Out! Red String Girl blasts off in Los Angeles, California, with an art takeover of the Hollywood Sign. Known for her red string work and as NASA's first artist in the newly reinstated Artist-in-Residency program, Red String Girl creates large-scale exhibits that touch on themes of fate, love, and the interconnectedness of the universe. Last night, out of the prying eyes of paparazzi and strangers' camera phones, Red String Girl managed to cover select letters on LA's most iconic and beloved sign, leaving the letters H-O-W left unwrapped. How what, we wonder?

According to Red String Girl's artist statement, "In all the themes I cover and have a personal investment and interest in, I always wonder "How"? How did we get here? How can we take care of each other, our world, and the worlds that exist beyond our own? How do we make ourselves known? How do we make our dreams come true? How do we find our way to each other? How do we fall in love? So much of life is unexplainable, but maybe the answers are in the signs. And when it comes to signs, what bigger than Hollywood's?"

What else does H-O-W spell? WHO. A question we've wondered ever since we reported on *Entangled* last February. Who is Red String Girl? Turns out, according to the police reports, she's none other than Rooney Something Gao, daughter of artist Wren Gao. Yes, she was *that* baby, from Wren Gao's infamous video art piece *Baby Being Born.*

Of course, after everything, it came down to Mom and the video. I will never escape my past.

I click my phone off and set it facedown on the grass.

"What did I do?" I ask Talia, my heart pounding so hard, it hurts.

Talia hugs me. "That information is just a small piece of who you are. What you've done and what you continue to do will eventually overshadow your past. And, Roo, no matter what happens, we'll have this story to tell for the rest of our lives."

I take a breath. "I want to believe you."

"The auction hasn't happened yet. You can still win it," she tells me calmly. "Your spark of inspiration became a full-on bonfire. Fate Tests really did the trick. Going big worked. Your name is blowing up on my alerts. You're even trending on social media as #RSGHollywoodSign."

"It feels amazing to create again." I trace the fronds of a palm tree with my eyes as I reflect on last night. "Do you think I made the right choice exposing myself?" I ask her.

Talia didn't even blink when I told her my plans last week. She was excited that I was getting my edge back. She, too, believes that making art means breaking the rules sometimes.

She thinks for a moment. "There's no right or wrong here," Talia says. "But I will say that, for your entire life, you've felt like you were always the daughter of Wren Gao and known for something you didn't get to choose for yourself. You didn't let that stop you from making art, but you did let it stop you from making art as yourself."

"Red String Girl is me, though," I say.

Talia kicks her feet out in front of her. "But you couldn't tell anyone. You've lived so much of your life keeping yourself a secret. I think you wearing red clothing made out of string was your quiet way of wanting to be seen."

I pull at a loose thread in my sweater until the entire row unravels.

Talia grabs my hand. "You can be you now. No more hiding."

I feel an ache in my chest. "Red String Girl was my shield for so long. Ever since we came up with the name in art school."

"I remember," Talia says, smiling. "You had told me about your childhood and how people only cared about knowing how it felt having your birth filmed live in front of people. I could hardly believe it."

I scoff. "Until that kid, the one who told everyone to call him Maverick because he made art with scrap metal from old planes, brought up my situation in class."

Talia cringes. "You looked horrified."

"It was then that I realized I couldn't escape my past," I say.

Talia nods. "You shouldn't have to hide yourself doing what you love. Just look at where we are. Yes, in this cemetery, but also Hollywood. People want so badly to be seen. It's a completely fair thing to want. Maybe it's time to lay Red String Girl to rest," Talia says, glancing between the headstones dotting the green grass.

"May she rest in red." I hold my hand over my heart.

"Are you going to enter your blue era now?" Talia jokes.

"With the NASA installation coming up and having just revealed my identity, I do have a chance to reinvent myself," I tease.

Talia smiles. "I'm here with you every step of the way. And Jack will be, too. I still can't get over that I was right about your trip. One bed. I knew it!"

I groan. "Like I said, we didn't even spend the night together. I stayed in my own room. All night, every night."

Talia throws her hand over her chest. "Did you hear that? It was the sound of my heart breaking. I'm here for Jooney. At least tell me that the kissing was everything you remembered it would be?"

I pull at dry blades of grass in silence.

"Wait, was it worse? Because when I look at Jack, I don't think bad kisser," Talia says.

"I almost told him I loved him last night," I blurt out. "After we almost kissed…again."

Talia's eyes pop. "You love him? I thought we were processing Red String Girl. Let me take a minute to process this now, too." She presses her fingers to her temples. "You've never loved anyone. Except me of course. You'll always love me."

I laugh. "Always."

"Do you think he's your…stringmate?" she asks in a whisper, as though we might be overheard in a cemetery.

"I want to believe that he is." In the daylight, after the rush of love and the adrenaline high, things look a little bit clearer. "It's weird, though. We kissed in the Rocket Garden, but since then, anytime we're about to kiss, we've been interrupted. Kenneth in the hotel room. The police last night. I can't help but wonder what it means."

Talia scrunches her eyebrows. "I don't know. Bad timing? Pick better places to make out?"

"Maybe what we're running into are knots," I say. "Because we're not supposed to kiss or be more than friends. Who knows where I'll be when the residency is over. I can't make promises to Jack if I don't know where I'll be, and it's not like he can just come with me. His mission is very specific, and it's based here."

"Do you have to go into it thinking it's forever? What if it was another chapter? Like Red String Girl was," Talia says.

I can't stand the thought of Jack only being a chapter in my life. I could barely accept it after one night with him, but if I leave, aren't I doing what his parents did? I just claimed my name. If I'm lucky, my work will take me all over the world.

Talia wraps her arm around my shoulders. "If anything, your beliefs have led you this far in love and work," she says. "Why lose sight of them now?"

Chapter 27

JACK

It's her smile that catches my attention first. Sticking halfway out of my mailbox is today's issue of the *Los Angeles Times*. I pull the paper out so fast that it drags the rest of the mail in my box with it and onto the ground.

There it is. Rooney isn't featured in the Arts section. She's on the front page of the entire thing. A photo of her in a circle next to a larger photo of the sign. Rooney's name is in the headline.

Moments from that night come back to me. Particularly the one of us almost kissing again. And the way she sacrificed herself for the team.

I grab my mail off the ground, momentarily distracted by purple telescope stamps in the corner of a small envelope. I have a hunch about who sent this. The return address confirms that it's from my parents, who have been in northern Chile for two months for work.

I'm meeting Rooney at Talia's gallery in twenty minutes so that we can finally have a conversation about us. There's no time right now for what the contents of this envelope might hold. I stuff it into my back pocket.

The drive to the gallery is surprisingly quick, I find parking one block away, and there was still an hour left on the meter from the previous car. The streak of good luck makes me, for a second, start thinking Rooney-like thoughts.

I haven't seen Rooney since the wrapping last Friday. She's been inundated with interview and commission requests. I also haven't spoken to my parents. I wonder if they've heard about the Hollywood Sign yet. Or if they remember that this artist is who I'm working with. Rooney taking sole responsibility helped Team Hollywood. No one has suspected us. At least not to our faces.

As for Rooney and NASA, something she has going for her is that tickets for her first showcase have already sold out. People went wild for her art on social media, gaining exposure for several of NASA's missions. Some people were torn between preferring the mystery and loving that Rooney is trying to make a name for herself. Many fans vocalized how meaningful it is to see people like themselves represented in the art world.

I reach the gallery and look through the large windows. Lining the walls of the place are dozens of string art pieces of cacti, astronaut suits, butterflies, Mars, a rocket, and clouds. They're moments that Rooney and I spent together, inspired by Red String Theory. Each one a moment derived from a Fate Test. They're intricate, practically looking like photographs from where I stand.

I lean closer to the glass. Every piece has a red dot next to it. If I remember what Rooney told me correctly, that means they've all sold. Excitement courses through me. Maybe she'll have enough money to buy the video. Wrapping the Hollywood Sign unwrapped whatever was blocking her lack of inspiration.

My phone lights up with a text message from Rooney.

Where are you? I have amazing news! It rhymes with SchMoMA.

SchMoMA as in MoMA? Did she get an offer to do something with the Museum of Modern Art? It really is incredible news.

I peer back in through the window. Rooney and Talia are

laughing as they walk out from the back room with cups and a bottle of champagne. Rooney sits down on a couch that looks like a... dumpling?

It's another tally in the streak of happy things. Maybe the contents of my parents' letter won't be so bad. Maybe they're on their way back as we speak so they can be here for Rooney's showcase. I reach for the envelope in my back pocket and rip it open. Inside is a letter on a single sheet of paper.

Dear Jackson,

Hope you are well. We write with satisfying news. The view of the galaxy we came down here to observe wasn't destroyed on the webcam by satellites this time. What a success. By the time you get this letter, Thanksgiving will likely have passed. Given delays, maybe even Christmas, too. As we look into the new year, we're making note of our achievements. We hope you do the same. What you have been able to accomplish with your mission at NASA is nothing short of impressive. You have always been practical and responsible. We are looking forward to seeing what comes next for you. You have worked hard to get to where you are today. Keep up the good work. We are extending our trip to the end of March. The sky is clear, the stars are bright, and we are on to something.

Say hello to Gōng Gong for us.

Mom and Dad

I flip the page over, but it's just the one side. My parents have noticed my hard work. These words send a small jolt of affirmation through me. They must've forgotten the showcase in January because they don't mention it here. I sent a calendar invite but they haven't accepted it yet. Maybe I should've sent a formal paper invite.

And so the good luck streak ends.

I look at the letter and then back up at Rooney. Another text appears.

> Okay, fine! It's MoMA! They want me to come back to New York to do an installation for them in the new year. Ahhhhhh! Get here so we can celebrate!!

I glance back down at the letter and once more at Rooney. The parallel hits me. I lived my childhood like this. I don't know if I can live my adulthood this way, too.

I take a deep breath and tuck the letter into my back pocket.

My chest tightens as I look once more at Rooney smiling in the gallery. I can't resist her.

Last minute work thing came up, I text back. Congrats! You deserve it. Can we celebrate this weekend at the show?

One of us is going to have to make a decision. We can't risk leaving this up to fate.

Chapter 28

ROONEY

R ows of long red and silver tinsel are strung across the room, dangling over the bar and tables at Hugh's, the local bar and grill where Jack will be playing his first show with Toby and Mac. The band's equipment is set up on a stage across the room. On the left is an upright piano for Toby, in the middle a violin for Mac, and to the far right is Jack's bass.

"So this is Christmas in Los Angeles," I mumble, giving the room one more look-over. A cardboard fireplace is positioned under the bar counter, complete with ribboned garland and stockings. Ornaments are individually strung from the ceiling like decorative raindrops.

I stir the peppermint stick into my hot chocolate, a light dusting of the crushed red-and-white candy lining the rim. The air smells of cinnamon but this time there's a hint of evergreen from the Christmas tree in the corner.

"It's fake," Jack says, catching me admiring it. "Hugh lights evergreen candles to make the tree feel real." Jack is sitting across from me at a table for eight, waiting for the rest of the team to join us for the show. We're both early again.

I can hardly take him seriously in his white bunny suit with the hood pulled over his head, blue latex gloves with the fingertips cut off, and booties covering his shoes. It's the uniform of the Red String Theorists, and Jack, after all, is a team player.

"Speaking of fake. This interaction," I say. "You've been avoiding me. Why?"

Jack looks at me, his eyebrows pinched. "I don't want to be," he says finally.

I lean back against the chair and cross my arms. I came here tonight to tell Jack how I feel about him—that all the signs add up—but I don't want to do it before understanding why he's been distant. "We have so much to catch up on. I've been wanting to celebrate the MoMA news with you."

He offers a small smile. "It's wonderful, Rooney. You'll do it in the new year?"

"After the first showcase here, so I'll go back in February. I'll get paid half up front when I sign the contract, but between that and selling all of my string art pieces and having a waitlist, I should have enough for *Baby Being Born*," I explain.

"That's incredible," he says, his encouraging tone not matching his expression. "Honestly, I'm so happy for you. You're going to win it. I'm glad it all worked out as you wanted it to. You took a big risk."

The peppermint stick is thinner now, half of it dissolving into the chocolate liquid. Kenneth and the team were not thrilled, but there's been a huge spike in public interest, and contractually, I don't represent NASA. For this entire artist-in-residence, I am able to work on outside projects, some riskier than others.

Hugh, the owner of the bar, brings over two Holidae Sundaes to our table. Under the cloud of whipped cream are two scoops of ice cream, one peppermint and another I can't quite place. Eggnog, maybe? Hot fudge drips down the scoops onto sliced bananas and gingerbread crumble.

"I think you'll appreciate those flavors," I say as the bite melts against my tongue. "I don't know what it is about this coast, but I eat way more ice cream here."

Jack takes a bite, taking some fudge with it. "California is actually considering making it its official state food."

"Then it's settled. I'm moving here," I joke, scooping up another bite.

It feels like the first time I met Jack in New York when I tried to get him to crack a single smile. He finally lets one through. This is the version of Jack I can't get enough of. He's a star that's light-years away, his light now finally reaching me. In the silence, I study Jack's face, the multicolored string lights casting a rainbow over it.

His grin emboldens me to tell him how I feel and that I want us to be together. I take a deep breath in to steady myself. As I do, Jack's eyes drop to his bowl, and I can tell he's wrestling with a thought by the way his eyebrows twitch.

"What is it?" I ask instead, breaking the quiet lull. I poke the whipped cream waiting for his answer.

Jack lets his spoon hover mid-lift. "I think we need to create some distance between us," he finally says after what feels like an eternity. He looks at me with sad, apologetic eyes.

I open my mouth and then close it. *Distance?*

"You don't want to spend time with me anymore?" I ask.

Jack shakes his head. "That's the problem. I want to spend every second with you. But if we want to achieve our goals, I think we see each other only when we need to and in group settings. Red String Theory is complete now. You've been reinspired."

My chest deflates, as though all of the air is being sucked from my lungs. "Where is this coming from?" I ask meekly.

In this moment, Toby and Mac arrive and go to the stage. They're about to start warming up. Jack notices that he's needed.

"Can we talk about this after the show? Sundaes are on me," he says, pulling out his wallet.

"Wait, we need to finish this conversation," I say.

He lifts a twenty-dollar bill from his wallet. The top of something familiar sticks out, thick and crinkled. I make out the word "lophole."

"What's that?" I ask, pointing at the paper.

Jack removes it and slowly turns it over.

In curvy red words is my handwriting—"This is how it works." These are the words I wrote that day *Entangled* closed.

Why would Jack have it?

Unless...

My breath catches in my chest. I blink slowly and try to keep my face neutral. My heartbeat quickens, like its running on a treadmill set to a speed I'll never be able to keep up with.

Jack grabbed *my* note from my installation.

Blood drains from his face when he grasps what I've realized. "Is this...yours?" he asks on an exhale.

"You're my stringmate." The words come out on their own, taking shape without me being able to swallow them down. I've never said these words out loud before to anyone. I'm frozen in place, my outburst, my feelings, all of it echoing in the chambers of my mind. I can actually feel time slow down as I sit here and wait for Jack to do something with those three words. They hang there as thick as the hot fudge dripping onto the table.

Across the room, someone brushes against the tinsel lining the bar. I swear I can hear the planets spinning from here.

"You literally just discovered that I pulled your note, and now you think I'm your stringmate? Because of this?" He waves the Fate Note in the air.

"Not only because of that. I wanted to tell you at the Hollywood Sign, and I came here tonight to tell you that I want to be together. I thought about all of the signs that brought us together. Even during our Fate Tests, everything kept us together. And now this. Is this not the biggest sign?" I say, feeling myself start to slowly thaw.

"Rooney, I want to be with you more than you can imagine. But it's like you said in New York, timing is everything. And right now, the timing couldn't be worse. You literally just told the world who you are. You have MoMA lined up. I need to focus on getting this promotion. I've worked too hard and am so close now. To give us a fair shot, we should wait until the circumstances are right," he says. "Momentum is building in both of our careers. Let's follow that thread before we follow ours."

"Why can't we have both?" I push back, heat creeping into my cheeks.

"I can't date you while I'm your liaison. The optics don't look good, and I'm too close to a promotion to quit."

I process his words. "You're probably right," I finally admit.

"You'll be in New York for a couple of months in the new year. Where will you be after that?" he asks.

"Back here for the second showcase," I answer.

"What about after that?"

I set my spoon down against the glass dish. "I don't know."

"What about next year, after the program ends?"

"I don't know yet."

"Exactly. There are so many unknowns. What I do know is that my job is here. Your job is... everywhere. Your career flight path is as unpredictable as a butterfly's," he says, his voice thick with emotion.

"Why are you trying to control it?" I ask.

"So I don't get slapped in the face by your wings," he says, referencing my own fear. "When things settle with our careers, we can see where we are and if a relationship makes sense for us. But love doesn't exist from a distance. It's too hard. It doesn't work."

Jack clenches his jaw, his lips set in a firm line. One word in particular stands out among the others, suspended in its own anti-gravity chamber.

"Love?" I whisper. Tears prick the backs of my eyes.

He sets his gloved palms on the table like he's grounding himself. "Rooney, of course I love you. Resisting you has been the biggest test of all. But everything has become intense being together. I literally trespassed for you. Twice. We've kissed," he says, lowering his voice and leaning forward. "I fear how far I'll go if we don't cool our jets and take time to widen our orbits."

I want to focus on the first thing he said. "I love you, too, Jack. I think ever since that night in New York, I've loved you."

Jack's jaw tightens, the scar on his bottom lip more pronounced in the changing light.

"But fate…" he says, his words trailing.

My peppermint stick has completely dissolved, pink and white slowly spinning on the surface of the beverage like a lunar swirl. Bing Crosby croons lightly over the speakers, the jingling background noise at odds with the pounding in my ears.

"I know you have an issue with fate, Jack. How is that possible when you believe there's dark matter, an invisible substance that makes up, what, twenty percent of our universe?" I ask.

"Twenty-seven," he mumbles.

"Thank you for helping me make my point," I say. "You believe that dark matter is real, even though you can't see it or feel it. It's literally a mystery. And yet fate is too difficult to fathom. The signs are more obvious to me now than they've ever been. You can't honestly tell me you don't see any."

"We have different interpretations of what signs are," he says as he rubs his thumb along the back of his spoon.

"You study the universe. You explore it, try to build machines that will get us there in person. Yet when the universe tries to tell you something, you actively ignore it. The signs are there. Sometimes they're big, like *this note*! Or they're us meeting over and over again. Being paired together to release a lantern on the night of the Lantern Festival, you choosing me as the artist-in-residence."

Jack shakes his head vigorously, a strand of hair pushing past his hood and flopping down over his forehead. "Everything you described are coincidences," he says desperately, almost as if he's trying to convince himself. He shifts in his seat. "From space, astronauts see Earth, and it's beautiful. But when they get closer and come back to Earth, they see all of its flaws again."

"Are you saying I'm Earth?" I ask, making a face.

"I'm saying *we* are," he says, biting his bottom lip. "From above, it's easy to romanticize us being together. But the closer we get, the more I start to see our failure points. When you really break down how we'd be together, the messiness shows. We'll rarely be in the same city. The closer we get to launch, the less time there will be for each other."

"What you're saying actually sounds longer than just waiting a few months to figure things out," I say. "You're afraid to believe in fate and admit that you can't control everything. The thing about control, Jack, is that you never really have it. Control is an illusion to help you feel a little bit better about the chaos that is life."

Jack grimaces. "What I'm scared of, Rooney, is that I will love you so much that, if we go any further just to not end up together, I'd never recover."

"I'd never recover if we didn't try at all."

Jack rips a receipt from his wallet into little shreds. They fall like snow from his fingers.

"We're bound. I know you can feel it, too," I add. I'm trying so hard to hang on, but the thread between us is pulled so tight, it might snap.

Jack sighs sadly. "I would choose you every single day of the week for the rest of my life. You should want to be with me because it's something you choose for yourself. Not fate. Not some thread. You're looking for something bigger, more meaningful. And I don't think a simple choice is enough for you."

I stare at the mound of paper in front of Jack. "I'm scared that love isn't enough. Just like making the choice to be with somebody, you can make the choice not to be with somebody. What's the difference?" My tears catch in my throat. "I know choices may give you the comfort of a plan, but even plans aren't always dependable. We're being pulled together by something stronger than a choice you or I could ever make, don't you see? We're meant to be together. It was never a choice."

"But you can't prove that. And neither can I," Jack says. "Sure, dark matter can't be detected, but it also doesn't directly affect my heart. You, Rooney, you do."

I shake my head in protest and pull my sleeves over my hands. "You can't stand that testing fate worked."

"Those were choices that we made," he says. "A literal test."

"They were choices guided by fate."

The sundaes between us are now warm, melted sugar and dairy soups. Overhead, Mariah Carey's "All I Want for Christmas Is You" blares. A new wave of cinnamon drifts our way as cocktail shakers continue to rattle. Somehow, the world around us still spins.

"If you're such a nonbeliever, I'll prove that you're my string-mate," I say with conviction. "I'll show you the Fate Note I pulled. I know the note I grabbed is yours."

Jack frowns. "What? How do you even know I put one in?"

"Because I know you. You wouldn't have taken one without giving one. You think you got one on me, Jack," I say, digging into my pouch for the Fate Note that I pulled. I slap the note onto the table and slide it over to him.

Jack unfolds the note and reads it. He blinks rapidly, his eyes glossy under his lashes.

I knew it.

"I told you, Jack," I say.

He reads the note out loud. "One day we'll be surfing on Mars."

I point to it. "There you have it. Mars. It's right there."

Jack runs his hand down his face and shakes his head.

I gesture to the note in his hands. "You don't need to draw this out for dramatic effect. It's yours. Tell me that it's yours."

His eyes flit from the note up to me.

"Just admit that it's yours, Jack," I press on.

A single tear rolls down his cheek.

Jack slides the note back to me and shakes his head once more. "I guess fate had other plans."

We sit there quietly, the void between us continuing to expand. And there's nothing either of us can do about it.

Chapter 29

JACK

Rooney's first showcase is happening in the Rotunda at the Natural History Museum of Los Angeles. As I step through the museum doors, memories of butterflies flutter to the front of my mind, uncontrolled.

Rooney's greeting people at the entrance to her showcase. This face-to-face time with viewers is new and she seems to be appreciating every second of it.

"Jack! Hi," Rooney calls out when she sees me. She's as beautiful as ever, in a red knit sweater and long blue skirt. Rooney as herself, not Red String Girl. She's fully in her element. Whether she was hidden or not, and with or without me, she was always going to accomplish big, great things.

"Hey. Happy New Year," I say as an icebreaker. Without thinking, I add, "You're like a seahorse. You blend right into your environment, give or take a few more colors. I like the new hue."

Rooney's face relaxes slightly. "I've been seeing a few more colors lately," she says. "How have you been?"

Awful. Missing you. Trying and failing to focus on work. Wishing that keeping my distance from you wasn't an effort every single day. It's been a month and a half since Hugh's. With the holidays, no suit-ups or team visits were scheduled. Rooney disappeared into her work while I refocused on mission-related tasks.

"Fine. Busy." I slide my hands into my pockets. "You?"

"Oh, yeah. I've been busy, too," she says with a small smile. Rooney appears calm, despite today being her first showcase and the day of the auction.

"Right. No, of course," I say, gesturing toward the door. "I can't wait to see it."

"Are you ready?" she asks.

"More than you know."

When we step into the Rotunda, it's as though I've been transported into the cosmos. If *Entangled* was Mercury, the smallest planet, then Rooney's first showcase is Jupiter, a behemoth of an installation. It must've taken Rooney and her team hundreds of hours to put this together. I expected to see her signature color everywhere. But there's not just red. There's also blue and purple and green strung throughout the room.

The string has been strategically looped around the tall marble columns lining the perimeter of the room. It stretches up past the second-level balcony to the ceiling, giving viewers a look from different heights. The string is manipulated to take the shape of a carefully crafted sphere. In the center, the *Three Graces* bronze sculpture stands, with each Grace representing science, art, or history. Together, they hold a globe skyward toward the beautiful stained-glass dome illuminated by sunshine. Strands of colorful thread branch out at different lengths from the raised globe. It's an optical illusion that allows the imagination to take over.

There's something familiar about this installation. My imagination runs wild, wondering if this could possibly be a—

"Looks like I was successfully inspired," Rooney says, breaking my spell. Her eyes drop to my lip for the briefest second.

"It's..." I touch my finger to my lip, and Rooney smiles. It's meant to look like an exploding star. A supernova. My Supernova Scar. My heart twists inside my rib cage. She was inspired by *me*.

This rattles me, and it probably shows. Rooney has taken bits and pieces of our time together and materialized them into this unbelievable creation. I'd need days, weeks, a lifetime, to fully process how much this means to me.

"I'm...stunned," I finally say. "I don't believe there are words that exist that properly capture how entrancing this is. It rivals discoveries we've made in space."

Rooney laughs. "That's nice of you to say, Jack. I couldn't have done it without you. Your inspiration."

We let a heavy silence fall between us, weighted by the limited time we have left together. As Rooney quietly watches people interacting with her creation, I observe her. Red lips. Shining brown eyes. Sideswept bangs. Relaxed shoulders that no longer carry the weight of being uninspired. She took her artist's block and blew it up into this.

"I have something for you," I say, tearing my gaze from her.

I set a keychain of a sports jersey into her palm. She flips it over. On the back of the shirt are the letters R-O-O-N-E-Y.

"I don't get it," she says.

"I just couldn't believe that there weren't any keychains with your name on it," I explain. "And then I found this. It's the soccer jersey for Wayne Rooney, but still. There's your name."

She laughs. My favorite sound. It's been a while.

"I guess I owe you that million dollars back," she says with a smirk.

"Eh, keep the money," I tell her playfully, waving her off. "No matter how the public perceives you and whatever name you go by, whether it's Red String Girl or RSG, I wanted to remind you that, to me, you're just Wayne Rooney. I mean Rooney."

She laughs again. "I won't let you down, Coach. Thank you."

I smile back at her. "Just remember, it's everything about you that makes you so good at what you do."

Her eyes are transfixed on mine. For a beat too long, we stand there, like we're playing a game of chicken of who will look away first. But here neither of us wins.

I'm the first to redirect my stare. Remembering I have one more gift, I reveal a bottle of peanuts. "For good luck. For the auction, now the showcase. Not that you need it, but—"

"It's tradition. Thank you," she says. We take a step back from each other before we're too close to pull apart. "I was able to raise thirty-five thousand dollars, the high end of the range. Talia will be bidding for me while I'm up there." Rooney rolls her eyes while shrugging. "I need all the luck I can get." She twists the lid and pours a handful of peanuts into her palm. She offers me a handful in return. Rooney looks around at the guests trickling into the space.

"Rumor has it, they had to release more tickets. The turnout is incredible. What you created...it's a stellar follow-up to *Entangled*. Pun intended," I say. I look from one corner of the installation down to the center and then back up to the opposite corner. There's string everywhere, making it impossible to follow a single thread. I lean in closer and add, "I'm incredibly moved by it. Now you know for certain that one person feels something."

A grateful expression passes over Rooney's face as she exhales. "Thanks, Jack," she whispers.

For a moment, everything between us feels like it might be okay. Like we could still really be friends after everything. But I don't know how we can get back to where we were. That place is now as distant as Mars itself.

Dusty spots us and makes his way over to congratulate Rooney.

She glows with every kind word tossed her way. Like she's loving the live feedback.

"Rooney, there you are," a voice says behind us.

"Mom, hi. This is Jack and Dusty," Rooney says, sidling up next to her mom.

"Jack. We've met," Wren says, her face unreadable. "And Dusty, I hope your name has an interesting backstory."

"He runs the clean room at NASA and apparently has an extensive cacti collection," Rooney jumps in. "Dusty, this is my mom, Wren. She's actually been working on a plant art collection."

Dusty turns directly toward Wren, his face softening. "It's a pleasure, Wren. What plants are inspiring you these days?" he asks.

"I've been particularly moved by the Hairy Balls Milkweed," Wren says without missing a beat.

"Mom!" Rooney shout-whispers.

Dusty's eyes light up. "Ah, the ol' *Gomphocarpus physocarpus*. Highly toxic."

"That's what draws me to them," Wren says.

"You and the butterflies," Dusty says. His eyes don't leave Wren's once.

Rooney looks amused as she watches what's unfolding in front of us.

Wren crosses her arms, but in her cheeks, I think I actually see... pink. Is Wren blushing? I run a hand over my face. Surely I'm seeing things. Rooney looks up at me, biting down a laugh.

"Oookay... before this gets weirder, how about you two go find seats?" Rooney says, directing her mom toward the seating area in front of a podium. Wren and Dusty aren't paying any attention to us. "We should go, too. The show and auction are about to start." She mumbles something about the timing of life. "How are you feeling, Jack?"

Me? Oh. She must be talking about when I have to introduce her in a few minutes. "I think I'm okay."

Rooney mirrors my earlier movement by leaning in and saying, "Just remember that you're speaking to people made of stardust. If you look closely enough, maybe they'll even shimmer."

It's such a Rooney thing to say that it sets me instantly at ease. She gives me more peanuts for extra good luck. "Congratulations, Jackson No-Middle-Name Liu."

This time together hardly makes up for the time apart, but it's something. The last time we saw each other, it ended with me playing onstage with Toby and Mac to a somber-looking Rooney. She left before the set was over.

"Congratulations, Rooney Something Gao," I whisper.

Overhead, there are a few taps into a microphone, my cue to get ready for opening remarks. We walk over to the podium together. Up front, I scan the audience to find Gōng Gong and my team. They've saved me a seat a few rows back from Wren and Dusty, who's miming what I hope is the shape of a cactus.

Once the audience is quiet, I jump right in, sharing an overview of the Artist-in-Residence program, my role as mission liaison, the FATE Mission, and Mars. I add context about how interest has grown about our work at NASA ever since reinstating the program. Before introducing Rooney, I give a shout-out to my team.

"Our team is like ice cream," I say. My team smiles in the audience. "Each one of us is a base ingredient. Eggs, heavy cream, milk, salt, sugar, and vanilla extract. Add a little science into the mix, and we form something that sticks together. Without even one of these ingredients, the recipe changes. But all ice cream needs a flavor. Something that brings it to life. For our team, that's Rooney."

I look over at her, and we exchange smiles. I become tongue-tied knowing words can't convey how remarkable this woman is. But somehow I mash enough coherent ones together for a decent introduction. Rooney walks out, and the cameras of NASA's professional photographers and the press start flashing while a low murmur hums through the crowd. I take my seat, eager to watch her sparkle.

"Hi, everyone. I'm Rooney Something Gao," she starts, glancing over at Talia, who's positioned behind the audience in the back of the room. Talia's in Rooney's direct line of sight, probably so she can keep Rooney informed about the auction.

Kenneth, Margie, and Nick are positioned to the far right of the podium. NASA stood by their chosen artist. When the press asked for comments, they stated that this is another example of how discoveries really are made all the time here.

"In the past couple of years, my string has guided me to unexpected places...and people," Rooney starts. "Now I get to be here with you all as the real me. I may not be the mystery you thought you were getting, but I assure you, I'm still very much a mystery to myself." This elicits laughs from the crowd. "We are so much more than we, and others, think we are. I am particles from supernova explosions, and I believe in myths."

I watch Rooney watch Talia, who has her phone pressed against her ear, her hand covering the other.

"For my first installation, I was inspired by the idea that when we look at planets and stars, we're looking back in time," she shares. "Moonlight takes less than two minutes to reach us. When you look at the sun, which I'm hoping isn't too often for the sake of your retinas, you're seeing the sun as it was eight minutes ago."

There are more chuckles from the group. Everyone seems to be enthralled by Rooney and her art. As they should be.

"In a way, delayed light from space objects is like mythology. I view myths and the light as the equivalent of learning from the past and letting it influence the present and future. Myths explain natural phenomena and why things exist. Aren't theories like the Big Bang and the multiverse essentially doing the same thing? Aren't myth and theories both interpretations?" she asks the crowd.

To my right, Gōng Gong watches with his hands clasped across his lap. Ahead of me, Wren is taking photos of Rooney with her phone and texting them to someone. Dusty records Rooney's speech and scans his camera across the room, the entire installation hardly fitting in the frame.

Rooney directs her glance at me. "I know what some of you are thinking: But, Rooney, theories are based on the examination of evidence. Myths aren't based on fact."

I smile to myself. She just read my thoughts.

"Here's what I'll say to that: Why does fact have to win out over belief?" Rooney asks. "There are enough coincidences in the world that should make you wonder. They might even make you believe. Myth or science, we're all assigning meaning to our existence in our own ways. Everyone has different interpretations of life and events that occur based on what we're taught growing up, where we live, and what we're exposed to."

It really is subtle when Rooney looks at Talia. I almost miss it. I realize I'm holding my breath, nervous to know the outcome of the auction. Will Rooney get *Baby Being Born* back?

Rooney's voice softens, her cadence slowing. It pulls my attention back to her. "It's all nebulous—vague, uncertain—which is why I present to you, *Nebulous*, my aurora borealis supernova installation."

The sounds of cameras clicking fill the air.

"With the northern lights, more oxygen gives us red and green colors, more nitrogen gives us blue," she explains. "For us to witness aurora borealis at all, and to see certain colors, depends on where we are in the world. The timing has to be right. There are so many variables at play. So many environmental factors that need to align." A weak smile crosses her face. "Just like fate."

It wouldn't be Rooney's installation without her belief of fate mixed in. The belief that has derailed my life since that night in the bar and grill. Ever since then—no, ever since New York, really—Rooney has infiltrated my mind and heart, weaving a labyrinth of a web. I'm still trying to figure out how to escape.

I feel a nudge at my arm. Gōng Gong leans over and whispers, "How beautiful that the northern lights can spark both scientific and mystical perspectives."

"Mystical," I repeat with a small smile. "When you know the science behind something and how something is built or works, you don't think it becomes less mysterious?"

"It's all about perspective," Rooney says, as though she's directly answering my question. "Back when we didn't know the science behind aurora borealis, people had theories about what caused this natural phenomena. At the time, they'd be living their lives when, all of a sudden, a mysterious green light would start flickering across the skies. In China, this event was so rare that, when it did happen, the belief was that it was a battle between good and evil dragons breathing out fire. In Finland, it was believed that fox tails caused sparks that created the colors in the night sky. I could go on."

Gōng Gong motions toward Rooney and raises his shoulders in agreement. I laugh quietly and observe the crowd. Together, we're all seeing the installation with fresh eyes. They take photos of Rooney, of the art. Wren continues tapping into her phone while Dusty watches her with a smile.

Suddenly, Rooney's voice wobbles. It wavers for a moment, but I catch it. She grabs the microphone, shaking her head. There's a shift in the mood, but no one else seems to notice. Rooney's wide eyes betray her exterior confident stance. Something has happened.

I sneak a look back at Talia. She's not where she was standing. To the unsuspecting eye, Rooney looks confident and poised. But I just have to look at her eyes to know she didn't win. If my heart was cracked before, it's now in pieces.

"But maybe, just maybe, there's more to it than you think," Rooney says, pushing on. "There's more happening in the universe than we'll ever see. Some things in the past take time to reach us in the present. In the meantime, we wait."

At this, she looks at me like an unspoken agreement is made. I find myself nodding involuntarily, my heart taking over my head.

For now, we wait.

"Thank you to JPL and NASA for this incredible opportunity," she says, her voice filled with emotion. "Thanks to the art students who helped string this. Art takes a crew, just like any mission. And thanks to the FATE mission team, but mostly thanks to Jackson Liu, who inspired me and helped me find my creative edge again. No matter what happens, we will always be connected."

With these final words, she gestures toward her installation. The room echoes with claps and cheers. Rooney has come out of her chrysalis. And she's a stunning, beautiful, vibrant butterfly.

I catch up to Rooney before anyone else can get to her first. "I'm sorry, Rooney," I say. They're not the words I wish I were saying. "Maybe there's another way."

She shakes her head. "That was my chance. It was a once-in-a-blue-moon opportunity. Now the museum has it, and I'll get interview requests for that instead of this."

My manager, Annika, and a few director-level managers approach us and congratulate Rooney on her show. She wipes her cheeks, her sad tears transforming into what, to everyone else, probably look like tears of joy.

"Jackson, when you have a moment, let's chat," Annika says,

nodding toward the higher-ups. I nod, straightening my posture. My mouth becomes a firm line. For the first time in a long time, I have no idea what happens from here, no plan on what's next.

"I'll be fine. Don't worry about me," Rooney says. "I'm headed back to New York in a few days for the MoMA installation and the Lantern Festival with Mom, but thanks for everything, Jack. I'll see you in a couple of months for the next showcase."

She almost reaches for my hand but instead puts her reflexes to good use again and straightens it out for a shake. I grip it firmly in mine, lingering for longer than I should.

I could walk away right now, tell the higher-ups to wait. But this is my chance. Rooney tilts her head toward them.

"Go," she says.

It's time for me to pursue my promotion and for Rooney to follow her thread. I watch her go with an ache in my chest.

"Bye, Lobster Girl," I whisper.

Chapter 30

JACK

I find myself standing in front of a tank full of sea jellies at the Aquarium of the Pacific with Gōng Gong. "Happy New Year" event posters are still hanging around the aquarium from four weeks ago. We watch as the glowing marine animals propel themselves around one another.

"You know they're older than dinosaurs?" Gōng Gong says, his face illuminated by the neon blue glow of the translucent moon jellies. "By three times!"

"I actually didn't," I say, surprised. "They look like they're in zero gravity."

In front of me, the jellies billow like little clouds in a glass-contained sky. The peacefulness of their movements soothes me. A sharp pang shoots through the center of my chest when I realize it reminds me of being underwater with Rooney.

"Is Rooney back in New York?" Gōng Gong asks, as though he had just felt my pain. It's also possible he sees how miserable I must look.

"I think she went out there for the Lantern Festival. And to meet with the MoMA team," I mumble. "We haven't talked since the showcase earlier this week."

Gōng Gong clasps his hands over his belly. "That show was spectacular. Sounds like this residency is a success."

We linger in front of the tank, mesmerized. The jellies look like translucent portobello mushrooms with their curved umbrella-like bodies. Their short tentacles are thin, practically invisible strings. The aquarium would be an incredible space for Rooney to create an installation.

"No matter what happens with your job or promotion, you should be proud of yourself," he adds.

"The showcase went well, the mission is moving along," I say. "Other than the art program. Everything is going according to plan."

"I meant proud of yourself. Not your work." Gōng Gong leans closer to watch as the moon jellies fold into themselves before expanding again. "Change isn't always the most apparent to spot in ourselves, but you're a different man today than you were this time last year."

"How so?" I ask.

"Look where we are. I felt a need to come here on a Sunday evening, and you agreed to take me. On a whim! We hadn't planned it out, didn't know what traffic was going to be like. The Jack of last year would have required a two weeks' advance notice of any plans, period."

"I wasn't really like that, though. Was I?"

Gōng Gong chuckles. "My boy, you were that and then some."

When I'm quiet, he continues, "It's an endearing trait of yours."

I cough out a laugh. "That's one word for it."

"Nothing to be ashamed of. You seem more flexible. You have for a while now. Heck, you even trespassed to wrap the Hollywood Sign. You're evolving. Maybe you just needed some art in your life. And a little red," he says with a tilt of his head.

More mentions of Rooney, as though she doesn't already fill every crevice of my mind. In my head, I hear her commentary on what I'm doing, what's around us. I glance around for something else to distract me. The jellies are annoyingly peaceful, given how I feel. The placard next to the tank explains how sea jellies don't have hearts, brains, or respiratory systems. That would make life so much easier, not to have to feel or experience or think about love or emotions. For a second, I envy them.

I watch the light filtering through the tanks, twisting and turning over the concrete floors. We pass through to another area of the aquarium. Children have their hands and noses pressed up against the glass. When they run to the next tank, dirty streaks are all that's left behind. Proof that they were here.

We stroll to the next tank, filled with sea dragons and seahorses, Gōng Gong's favorite.

"Jack, look at this one," Gōng Gong says, pointing out a leafy sea dragon, its yellow-striped body covered in long, seaweed-looking camouflage. It reminds me of Rooney hiding in plain sight in her red knitwear.

"You ready for your fun fact?" he asks. "You're not too old for this, are you?"

When Gōng Gong took me to the aquarium when I was a kid, we'd spend the majority of time in front of the seahorses. He'd always have a new fun fact for me. Seahorses are like underwater butterflies as they, too, figure out ways to blend in with their surroundings. They're terrible swimmers, but what they lack in speed they make up for in dexterity. It's the males that give birth to thousands of baby seahorses.

"If you're not too old, I'm not," I say, crossing my arms in anticipation. "I'm impressed that you still have any fun facts left. I didn't think that was possible. Let's hear it."

"You know why I love seahorses so much?" he starts.

"This sounds like the start of a bad joke. You love that they're constantly eating?" I guess, not remembering this specific fun fact.

"Oh. Yes. But that's not it. You must not remember. Ah, well, you were young," Gōng Gong says. "They remind me of your grandma."

"Those," I say, nodding toward a two-inch-long seahorse, "remind you of Grandma?"

Gōng Gong holds his arms up as he wiggles his body. "Every morning, seahorses greet their partner with a little dance."

"You're not serious," I say.

"It's true. Their morning waltz reinforces their bond." Gōng Gong bends down to smile at the seahorses. "So every morning, she and I danced. Just a little cheek to cheek. She insisted on dancing every morning," he says. "When I got too busy or too serious, she'd still make me do it. I'm glad she did."

"Grandma didn't let you get away with anything."

"No, she didn't. You know, you're like her in many ways. You're both ambitious. She'd decide what she wanted to do, then follow through with it until she got it. She made literal plans, wrote them out in her planners, and referenced them every day. She loved to work, loved getting ahead. She'd test different schedules until she found the most efficient one."

I inhale sharply. Will the word "test" make me think of Rooney every time I hear it? "I wish I had the chance to know Grandma," I say.

"She loved you very much," he says, his eyes glistening. "Did you know that seahorses mate for life?"

"Probably for survival reasons," I guess.

"I like to think there's something bigger at play," Gōng Gong says. "Little seahorse soulmates. It makes me happy to think about."

"As scientists, we want clear, definitive answers. The question of whether fate is real or not doesn't fit into that category." He's studying my face when I look up at him. "Rooney believes in fate.

I don't." I debate whether to tell him this last part. "She thinks I'm on the other end of her red string. Does that sound strange to you?"

Gōng Gong inhales slowly through his nose as he thinks. "I think we believe what we need to believe to give our lives meaning," he says. "Or we genuinely believe in something because that's what we've been taught, and that shapes how we view and live our lives. Like with me and your grandma, in my bones, I know we were soulmates. It wasn't love at first sight for her. But when we got to know each other, it felt... big. So, no. Rooney's red string is not so strange to me."

"She puts so much emphasis on signs. It's an unrealistic expectation I don't know how to live up to."

"And you've seen no signs? No clues at all?" Gōng Gong asks, gently prodding.

"Clues from the universe?" I ask. "I guess there have been a couple of odd coincidences." I think of having picked Rooney's Fate Note. "Well, maybe there have been a few."

I think back to all the instances Rooney listed off at Hugh's. My breath becomes shallower as it dawns on me that those might be what she meant by signs. They're personal. Meaningful. And my intuition feels like it's trying to say something. Maybe there have been signs all along. I just ignored them or dismissed them as something else. Maybe I didn't want to see them.

"The only difference between fate and free will is perspective," Gōng Gong says. "To some, like you, life is the sequence of choices you make when you decide how to live it. Small decisions add up. For others, it's the individual moments that have meaning. Both are right."

"You can't believe in one thing sometimes and another thing at other times only when it's convenient for you," I say.

Gōng Gong lifts his shoulders. "Why not? Are we not compli-cated, contradictory beings? I want to be at the aquarium with you. I also want to be home making ice cream. Just because something is the way it is doesn't mean it can't ever become anything different. For her, and for you. Our main goal, when you really boil it down, is to get through the day and live to see another one."

I frown. "You're oversimplifying it."

"And you're trying to troubleshoot too much," Gōng Gong coun-ters. "It's not one or the other, and a relationship isn't a mission. Unlike a spacecraft, you can launch a relationship and see what it does when it's in a completely new environment. If something fails, it isn't a crisis. You can learn what the problem is, adjust, and try again. The stakes aren't quite as high as they are in space."

"It's not only the fate thing. This thing between us is so strong. Too powerful, almost. Rooney will live a lot of her life on the road for her art, which is incredible. But I wouldn't be able to go with her, and Mom and Dad always have 'one more expedition' left in them."

"When your parents traveled, they didn't do a very good job of keeping in touch," Gōng Gong says. "I should've done more about that."

"It's not your fault," I tell him, placing my hand on his shoulder. "When they left, we talked to them, what, once a week? If that. They were busy."

"Something gives me the sense that Rooney would never be too busy for you," he says. "Didn't you tell me that she tried to find you, too, after New York?"

"She called every hotel in the Financial District," I say with a small laugh.

Gōng Gong tilts his head. "Sounds like she really wanted to talk to you. I don't think fate made those calls."

No. Fate did not make those calls. Fate also did not go back to the print shop looking for Dave. Rooney did all of those things. Even as she made all of her string art pieces for the auction and created her installations, I never once felt like she didn't have time for me. I feel like a complete ass. I am literally a Jackass.

Gōng Gong walks next to me with his hands behind his back. "I know what it's like to want to impress parents," he says softly. "Making choices that will yield the best results so one day you have a piece of good news to share. But there's so much pressure in that good news. It has to be the best news. And maybe, just maybe, that will earn you praise. Or a 'good job.' I know you felt your parents weren't emotionally there for you when you needed them. You became self-sufficient, matured young. Became set in your ways on how things should be, how you wanted them to be. There wasn't room to consider anything else."

I let these words live in my head for a moment before I respond. "I don't know why it still affects me so much. I'm an adult. Logically, I know I don't need their approval anymore."

"That feeling might never go away. They're your parents. You have needs and expectations from them but feel let down when you're not fulfilled in the way you need. That takes some adapting, too. But this is your life, and you're the one living it. Not them. They've made their choices, got to do things the way they wanted. So should you."

I grunt audibly. "I told her I wasn't her stringmate. That we weren't meant to be."

"That's not what you feel, is it?"

"I don't know if that's the term I'd use. All I know is I want to be with her. But I don't know how to be. It...scares me," I admit. "She brought out parts of me that I'm not used to feeling."

"In this life, we get to decide who we want to be, for the most part. And other things that happen are us reacting to the circumstances.

You can control yourself, the way you act. Trying to control everything else around you is a losing battle." Gōng Gong pats my back. "Perhaps running into Rooney in New York was supposed to happen, for whatever reason. What is really so bad about that if you want to be with her?"

I shake my head. "I want her to want to be with me, not to think I'm The One because signs told her so. I want her to...to choose me."

Gōng Gong nods. "In the way that your parents didn't."

This was a sore spot months ago when Rooney and I talked about my parents. The pain is still there. It probably always will be. But because of Rooney, for the first time in my life the ache is dulled. There's room for more than just hurt. I want to let those other feelings in and not be ruled by my past.

"Does Rooney jump from person to person or something? Does she read into every little thing?" Gōng Gong asks, turning to face me in front of a tank filled with fuchsia-colored fish. Must everything serve as a reminder?

"She reads into the big things. She's never been in a serious relationship before," I say. Remembering this slows my racing mind.

"Sounds like she's been careful and wanted to make sure the signs weren't false leads. Perhaps she did that because she knows how important stability and commitment are to you?" Gōng Gong says.

"It does kind of sound that way," I say, in disbelief of how foolish I've been.

"Do you know what I'd give for even just one more day with your grandma? She was gone too soon. I'd give everything I own for just one minute. Heck, just long enough to tell her I love her. It wouldn't be enough, but it would be something."

"And something is better than nothing," I say, more to myself than to him.

Gōng Gong points at me, his curled finger directing me to pay attention. "You will always be busy chasing the next promotion, the next achievement. Rooney will, too, with her art shows. But you're never going to get back the time you can spend together. When you find someone you want to dance with every morning, put on your dancing shoes and get stepping."

His words resonate deeply. I thought I lost Rooney once. I don't want to lose her again. I don't want to waste any more time.

"And, Jack, my boy, if it can offer any comfort at all, I choose you every day. Remember that," Gōng Gong adds, clasping my hands in his. We hug, like we always have and always will.

I walk Gōng Gong out to the car to take him home. The sky is inky black, the moon half-illuminated. As always, it's right where it should be. Stars are speckled across our celestial dome, nothing obstructing their view. A few shine brighter than the others.

In the distance, right above the horizon, eight stars in particular grab my attention. I draw an imaginary line through them, connecting the dots until they look like pinned-up string against a blackboard.

It's then that I see it. There, purposely winking at me and quite literally written in the stars, is the Big Dipper.

It's the second-closest thing to a sign, next to a crumpled piece of white paper with words written in red ink. It's as though the universe had been listening.

But just as Rooney was careful, I need to be, too. An idea forms, the beginning of a hypothesis. A new theory on how to test the Red Thread of Fate and to clearly see the signs Rooney has been talking about all this time. I know what I need to do.

Rooney's smile burns brightly in my mind. My heart skips a beat at the image, and suddenly it's as clear as the stars in the sky.

It's 7:50 p.m. Not even close to midnight, and we've already eaten dinner. But dumplings would really hit the spot.

"Gōng Gong, have you ever heard of The Dumpling Hours?"

Chapter 31

ROONEY

I see a woman with blue hair lost in the waves," Mom says. My back faces the artwork, my arms crossed and eyes closed. "There's an essence of Hokusai's *The Great Wave off Kanagawa* in this."

We stand in a large white room with paintings dotting the walls of the Museum of Modern Art doing a Walk and Talk. Ever since I could talk, when we went to any museum around the world, Mom and I would play this game where one person turns around while the other describes the piece of art for the other person to guess. In the early days, I didn't know artist names or titles of artwork, so it was a huge learning curve. Now, with a broader knowledge of art under my belt, the competition has become more intense.

I thought this would cheer me up. I'm in one of my favorite museums where I'll get to create an installation. Despite losing the auction, I should be on Cloud 9. Instead I feel hopeless because I'm 2,700 miles from Jack.

I furrow my eyebrows in thought. "*Drowning Girl*. Lichtenstein?"

"Yes, but you don't have to sound so gloomy about it," Mom says.

I turn around to see the painting she picked. "Really? You had to pick this one?"

"She reminds me of you," Mom says with a shrug.

"I don't look as glamorous when I cry," I joke.

"Eh, well at least you're real. How does it feel no longer being Red String Girl?" Mom asks.

I shrug. "In my heart, I'll always be Red String Girl, but it does feel freeing not to have to hide."

The nearest window overlooks the street. It's a bright, overcast February day. People in puffy jackets point up at skyscrapers, seemingly in awe of this city and all that it has to offer. It reminds me of Jack on that first night. I haven't talked to him in over two weeks since we said good-bye at the showcase. It's still morning on the West Coast, and it's Sunday, so he's probably eating sundaes with his Gōng Gong.

Mom links her arm through mine. "I didn't know how to step aside to let you burn bright on your own, huh? I took up too much oxygen."

"The last thing I would've wanted was for you to stifle your own light for mine to grow stronger. I lived under a shadow that I created in my mind," I admit. "We'll never know what might've happened if I had started out as Rooney Gao instead of Red String Girl. Maybe people would've seen you...or maybe they would've seen me."

We round the corner to another room, the organized maze of art a comfort.

"You really came into your own out West," Mom says, turning more pensive. "I—I'm proud of you."

I stop in my tracks, pulling her to a stop with me. "Thank you."

"I mean it, Roo."

"Something I learned recently is that not all missions are successful. Sometimes things go wrong and what you planned for doesn't work out, but you don't quit. You persevere. That's what I'm going to do. One day, I'll get that video back. So I'm proud of myself, too," I finally say. "For not giving up."

Mom smiles. "Good, that's the only opinion you should let

influence you." She reaches into her pocket. "And now I have something for you."

Before I have even a second to guess what she might have enclosed in her fist, she turns her hand upside down, palm facing up. In it is a CompactFlash camera memory card.

My jaw drops. *Baby Being Born* is written in small letters on tape across the top.

"It's yours," she says. "I waited to tell you until I had the thing in my hands. They took their sweet time verifying it and getting it shipped out."

"You won? I thought it went to a museum," I say, shocked.

"Once it went past your range, I started bidding," Mom admits. "I saw the look on your face and knew you weren't able to go more than thirty-five thousand. There was some back-and-forth for a while, which leads me to believe I was up against a museum, but we'll never know."

"You let me say all that when you had this in your pocket the entire time?" I ask, covering my mouth in disbelief. My body is buzzing as I try to accept our new reality. The video is back in our hands.

Mom extends her hand closer to me, as though willing me to take the memory card. Like if I don't, it'll burn an imprint into her skin. "Are you mad that I stepped in?" she asks.

"Am I mad? I'm grateful," I say, elation filling me up. I take *Baby Being Born* from her, examining the piece of plastic. It's amazing how something so little can hold so much. "I tried. That's the important part. I didn't want it to be handed to me, but the last thing I wanted was for this to be public. I'm going to work to pay you back. I mean it."

"Sure, whenever you can," she tells me.

"Why would you do this for me, though? You don't have regrets about this," I ask.

"The price of my work just went up. I'll need to finish that new collection now," Mom says, looking pleased. Her expression levels out as she adds, "I know you think I became famous on my own, but success didn't come until I gave birth to you. You were right there with me. I know there were ugly moments captured on that video. There were also beautiful ones that I'm forever grateful live on, because that was the moment that brought me you. I may not regret my own choices in life, but I do regret anything that caused you pain."

Tears fill my eyes, the heavy drops not wasting any time before rolling down my face in long streaks. "Thank you. So much. This means more than you'll ever know."

I wrap my arms around her in a tight, forward-facing hug. It's unusual for both of us, and somehow that's okay. We're getting used to new things. "I know you don't like getting gifts, but I figured this might be an exception," I say.

Mom looks at me suspiciously.

"Turn around," I say, rotating Mom in the opposite direction as she huffs in protest. "There are letters. Giant ones. The subject is iconic, but also easily forgotten. A big risk that the artist wouldn't have been able to take without her mother."

"Roo—" Mom says before I cut her off.

"The beginning of something great, even though it doesn't exist anymore," I continue.

"Oh, I've heard of this one," Mom says, spinning to face me. "The artist had it in her all along. I can't wait to see what she does next."

I hand her a snow globe with the Hollywood Sign inside.

She smiles as she shakes it. "Snow in Los Angeles. Now that would be something to see. I'm glad I had *Baby Being Born*. That would've been awkward to not have had anything for you. I've missed you, kid," Mom says, her voice taking on its usual edge.

"I've missed you. And I've missed these Walk and Talks." Ahead of us is a new painting that I don't remember seeing before. "Okay, turn around again. One last piece of art to guess."

Mom does as she's told, covering her eyes with both hands.

"I'm a flower bud or a womb, split in half because no sides of me are the same," I say, first describing the mood of the piece.

"Go on," Mom murmurs.

I take a moment with the painting. "I'm not what I appear. I look like watercolor, easily altered, but I'm oil, once hardened, unchangeable."

"Oh, *Abstraction Blue*. Georgia O'Keeffe. You know she's one of my favorites," Mom says.

"You're a little too good at this," I say.

"What do you know about this piece?" Mom asks.

"Not much," I say, looking at it again.

Mom smiles. "This one in particular is pretty powerful. It represents a time when Georgia rejected the traditional way of painting that she had been taught. She transitioned to abstraction, developing her own form of expression. She tore herself from how she had been influenced to accept her own way of thinking."

"Did you read the card?" I ask, covering it with my hands.

"I happen to love this one. There's room for growth in all of us." She gazes at the blues and pinks of the painting. "It was strange not having you around," Mom says, her tone softening. "It's always been you and me."

"I'll always be your person."

"Yes, you're stuck with me, I'm afraid." She wraps her arm over my shoulders.

"This is a different side to you. I don't know how to handle it," I joke, side hugging her back.

"The other day I woke up with a smile on my face. Isn't that sickening?"

"Is that because you finally created the best Chinese tea egg recipe or because Dusty was cuddled up next to you?" I clarify.

Mom thinks on this. "A little of both, I think," she says, nudging me. "And you'll be happy to know I've made use of our time apart by perfecting milk bread. It's very fluffy."

"Just like you deep down," I tease as Mom groans and waves off my accusations. "Do you think Dusty's your...you know."

"The man on the end of my string?" Mom asks. "Who's to say, but I know I've been waiting for perfect circumstances, and those don't exist. It could be that he's my stringmate for right now. And maybe that will turn into forever. We'll see."

"It probably helps that you didn't work with him," I say. "You were right about Jack, but I wasn't careful. I told him what he meant to me, and he made his choice clear. You know I met him a year ago today, on the night of the Lantern Festival?"

Mom nods. "Tonight's full moon is supposed to be spectacular."

"It feels like a different lifetime. We haven't spoken since the show."

Through the window, we watch dry brown leaves swirl around the sculpture garden after a strong gust of wind blows through.

"There were no signs in my life that told me I'd have you," Mom says. "Or maybe I missed them, ignored them. I really thought children weren't in the cards for me. Sometimes I think maybe the signs weren't even there, and that I just made every other sign up. But then you happened. Obviously."

I pat myself down. "Yep. Still here."

"I taught you about the Red Thread of Fate not to keep you from living and loving but to remember that there are bigger things happening in the world beyond ourselves. That we can influence the world, but that the world can also influence us. Damn, put that on a poster," she says. "This is all coming out because you're back and need guidance."

A laugh escapes. "Uh-huh, it's not because you're in love," I say.

"Nope. Dusty's just a body to keep me warm at night," Mom says, suppressing a smile. "I get not wanting a plan to guide your life, trust me. I went as far as the creative winds took me and never looked back. Even when you have a plan, though, unexpected events will still present themselves and surprise you."

"Like me."

"Like you. Like Dusty. Like your newfound appreciation for Los Angeles."

"It's still no New York City, but it grew on me," I admit.

Mom tilts her head toward me. "And yet this city was your forever home."

"As far as I know, it still is."

"You can continue reading into signs and letting fate decide your life for you, or you can own up and show up for the decisions that you can make yourself," Mom says.

I exhale as I think, my thoughts wrestling one another. "It's not like I'm completely dependent on signs and fate to function."

"For the big things, though, like work and love, what you decide matters," Mom says. "What you choose for yourself matters. When you make the choice to do something because you want to, not because something greater does, it feels rewarding. Like how you felt when you owned up to the world about who you are. Whether something is a success or a failure or is just in progress, there's satisfaction in knowing *you* made whatever it is happen. I've experienced both, and only one of those things makes me feel invincible."

"I don't think I could ever not believe in the Red Thread. It's deeply engrained in who I am. It's a big part of my work. I'm in too deep."

Mom raises her eyebrows in thought. "Look, the Red Thread of

Fate is not meant to control you but to add a little magic to a world that can often seem bleak."

I tug at the ends of the scarf draped around my neck. "I always thought it was romantic to be tied to someone, that your lives could be on different trajectories but you could still end up at the same place. I guess that's not enough. Jack wanted to be a choice."

"And what's so wrong with wanting to be chosen?" Mom poses. "Maybe true love has no strings attached. That one's more of a bumper sticker than a poster."

I swallow any form of defense I can think of because, deep down, perhaps I know she's right. My pulse quickens at the thought of having tangled everything up to the point of no untangling.

"Tell me the truth," Mom says. "If your stringmate walked up right now with a glowing red string on his ankle that was attached to yours, would you forget everything, everyone, and be with him?"

I imagine the scenario: the shortening of the string between me and a stranger, the thread bouncing up and down as it untangles and straightens out after decades of journeying, the man clasping his hand in mine telling me how happy he is to have finally found me.

It's admittedly an exciting thought. A romantic one, in a way. Truth is, I don't know that man kneeling in front of me. I don't know if he likes Times Square or making freeze-dried ice cream or if he'd know that butterflies run cold. He wouldn't have the sliver of a moon on his bottom lip and probably wouldn't know why the northern lights shine like they do. He'd probably not call me a lobster and let me touch anything I wanted in the clean room. And what good is that?

The fact of the matter is, the hypothetical man whose string leads to me, well, he wouldn't be Jack.

And if he's not Jack, I don't want him.

"No," I say firmly.

"No what?" Mom asks.

"I wouldn't. I would want Jack. I would choose Jack over him," I say, fully feeling the meaning behind the words that escape my mouth. It dawns on me how delicate the distinction is between fate and having a choice, how lucky we are to be able to have both in our lives. To let greater forces play a role while still guiding our own path. Maybe it's time that my belief in the Red Thread of Fate gives way to something like...Red String Theory.

Mom wraps her arms around me. "Don't wait around forever being an observer in your own life."

I lean into her rare embrace. "I need to tell him that I choose him," I say, a desperate urgency taking over. It's not a solution to the work problem, and it might complicate us keeping our distance, but at the very least I have to tell him that he's the one I choose.

I find his name in my phone and tap it.

He doesn't answer. What if he's moved on?

"I have to get back to LA. I need to do something. I don't know what yet exactly. It's not like I have a plan here!" I say to Mom, a laugh fueled by adrenaline escaping. "All I know is that I need to find Jack before it's too late."

Chapter 32

ROONEY

As soon as I step outside of the museum, the chill of the wind cuts through every layer of clothing on my body. The overcast sky mostly blends together in grays and whites, but there's one cloud in particular that looks like a butterfly. It's the closest the city will get to having butterflies in the winter. I wrap my scarf once more around my neck, pulling my coat tighter around my body.

Outside the entrance, I catch my breath and let my heart rate come down a notch.

All this time, I've been so obsessed with signs that I let myself think that I didn't have any choice. I grit my teeth in the cold, even though I'm overheating at the thought that this realization has come too late. That I've irreparably scared Jack away from any kind of future with me, that he might not believe he's the one I choose.

I fight back premature tears. I should go back to my apartment to pack. Or I could go straight to the airport and board a flight to LAX. I'd go to My Spot to think but there's no time for that now. I turn away from MoMA and start walking uptown when my phone rings with a number I don't recognize. I answer, thinking maybe it's another installation opportunity.

"Hi, I saw your number on the petal of a plastic rose," the voice on the other end says.

Someone found the flower and actually called me. But why now, after three months? And why does the voice sound like Jack's? I'm done for. He's really in my head now.

"I've reworked some variables and think we should start over with Red String Theory 2.0," the man says. "Fate Test 6: Write your number on something that can be found. Check."

These words stop me in my tracks. It *is* Jack.

I spin around and look up, expecting to see him. Instead, there's a row of giant white signs duct-taped to traffic light poles, bike racks, trees, and garbage cans. It looks as though the cue cards from *Saturday Night Live* have escaped and are making their way uptown. They flap noisily as another gust blows through the streets. I rule out that *Love Actually 2* is filming for real this time when I see "Red String Theory 2.0" written on the first poster. There's an arrow pointing to the next sign, which reads "Fate Test 5: Go the wrong direction on purpose."

I take ten steps in the opposite direction of the arrow on the sign until I reach the next sign secured to a bike rack. "Fate Test 4: Interact with someone online. (Look at your phone.)"

On my screen, there's a notification about a direct chat on my Cloud Lovers League app. I tap into it, and a photo of an overcast sky appears. In the upper portion of the picture is a cloud with puffs that form wings. It's the butterfly! I look back up to the clouds, but it's gone now. Are Jack and I sharing the same sky? My heart pounds harder against my rib cage. I "like" the photo to complete the interaction.

I keep walking down the avenue to the last poster that's taped to a traffic pole. The words "Fate Test 3: Return a lost object. Take me to X marks the spot" are written in the center of the board with a red pen taped into the upper corner. My Discipline Pen. The one I gave Jack one year ago. I shouldn't be surprised to learn that he kept it all this time. I peel back the tape, grab the pen, and practically run to My Spot.

I move quickly down the alleyway until I reach the fence, where there's another sign: "Our definitions of signs may be different... but what if they still lead us to the same place? Fate Test 2: Show up early or late to somewhere you're supposed to be. Wait 10 seconds."

A bright red string is taped to the board. I take it between my fingers and tug. There's slight resistance. Something—or someone—is at the end of this string. I start the countdown in my head and slide sideways through the fence door, following the string to My Spot. A tingling sensation pulses through my body so strongly that it nearly makes me breathless.

The string shortens, the resistance when I pull becoming stronger. Inch by inch, I let the string guide me to my safe place. I follow it all the way up to the opening of my hideaway, where Jack stands with his back to me facing the "X" sculpture. His brown hair is wild from the wind. I give the string one last tug and trace its path down to his ankle, where it's tied off.

I go numb at the sight of him. Jack's here, in New York City, at My Spot. It's just the two of us in this little world of our own, the city rushing around us.

"Jack. How are you—why are you..." I start, speechless.

"Rooney," he says, taking a step closer to me. He burrows his chin into the Red Thread of Fate scarf I gave him when we first met.

Silence hangs between us, both of us searching each other's eyes as if everything can be communicated like this. In a way, it can. In his eyes, I see his apology, a glimmer of belief, and a look of what, I hope, might still be love. I know because I'm looking at him in the exact same way.

"I believe this is yours," I say, handing Jack the red pen.

He takes it, our gaze never breaking once. "I was wrong. I don't want distance. I don't want another day to go by where we're apart."

"Me neither, but what about your job?" I ask. "I don't want to compromise any—"

"I'm not your liaison anymore."

I blink. "You left the program?"

Jack nods firmly. "Before you say anything, I don't regret it. My reason for joining it was to get ahead at work. But it ended up being the best thing I've ever done for other reasons. Personal reasons."

Heat rushes to my face. "Won't that affect your promotion, though?"

"I'll find another opportunity. Brian sent me a couple of groups that he's been a part of and enjoyed. One day a promotion will happen. But every day we're not together feels like a waste," Jack says. His expression is loose, as though the weight of the world has been lifted off his shoulders.

"You've been busy these past two weeks," I say, still trying to process everything I've just heard. "You didn't have to but thank you for doing that. For us."

"I'm just sorry I didn't do it sooner," he says. "I had it in my head that I wanted you to choose me in the way that I viewed being chosen. The way I thought I wanted to be chosen."

"You were fair to feel that. I know it can be hard to be away from those you love. I don't want my childhood, either. Traveling for my art will be a thing, and I hope that we can do it together, but it won't be constant. You'll never be left behind. I want to be selective with what I take on."

"We'll go wherever we need to, together, for the world to see your creations," he says. "I'm tired of being scared."

I nod, quietly listening as he continues.

"In your own way, you were choosing me," Jack says. "We were chosen for each other, maybe. And I don't want to let you down. What we felt for each other, what I think we still feel, doesn't require choice or fate. What we have is bigger than those things combined. I want to follow our lantern and see where it takes us."

His words tug at my heartstrings, pulling them tighter and tighter until I'm breathless.

"Jack, I want that journey, too," I say.

Jack's eyes glisten. "We make new discoveries all the time," he says. "And we're capable of change. Right, Lobster Girl?"

I smile. "Whether we were brought together by the pull of a red string, the whisper of a love spell, the concoction of a love potion, or a series of decisions, I don't care. It doesn't matter anymore. What matters is that we found each other, and that we choose each other," I say, my words rushing out in excitement.

"You're everything I didn't know I wanted," Jack tells me. "You weren't part of any plan I ever thought up for myself. The moment I met you, all the plans I made failed on impact. In science, we search for the truth. Hope for it. But in this search, I was one discovery away from something that changed every truth I've ever known. One discovery, one person, one change of heart away from my soulmate."

"Something I once learned over table dumplings is that it's what you do after that makes all the difference," I say. "Fate could bring you to me a million times, but if I don't choose you, if you don't choose me, then what's the point?"

"An excellent hypothesis," he says. Jack's serious expression dissolves into something lighter, happier. "It's my new life's mission to show you how much you mean to me." He clears his throat, pausing for a moment. "How much I love you."

"You love me," I repeat. "And not just in theory?"

Jack pulls me in closer. "All evidence points to yes. I love how clever and creative you are. You inspire me endlessly. You show up for yourself and your work, even when you're unsure of both. You keep pushing through. I love your irrational fear of butterflies. That you wear heavy knit sweaters in the summertime."

"I can't help myself," I say.

He glides his thumb over my cheek, gazing into my eyes. "I love how every time you smile, this constellation on your beautiful face reminds me that there are worlds beyond what we can measure or see. One that requires believing."

"Jack, I love you, too," I say, wrapping my arms around his waist. "In fact, my love for you is a universe that's expanding faster than I could've anticipated." Jack smiles at this as I add, "I admire that you take what you care about seriously. I also love that you'll follow me around a city to chase a lantern."

"I'd follow you anywhere," he says in a low, soft voice.

I pull Jack tighter against me. "You're curious about the cosmos, even when you're just as mysterious. I want to get to know every part of you. I'll create my own Deep Jack Network and send out missions to uncover those unknowns." This last bit makes him laugh out loud, a noise that will never get old. "I even love that you're bad at figures of speech but are weirdly good at puns."

"Anything for my solar-mate," he says, playing up the sincerity. Jack gives my arms a light squeeze. "So I can still be your stringmate?"

"There could never be another," I say as I hold my hands against his face and stare into his eyes. Whatever it is between us is now untangled, free of knots, and as clear as the moon on a cloudless night.

"It's like your Fate Note says, 'This is how it works.'" Jack speaks quietly. "There's no science to it. But it's so obvious to me now. There was something bigger at play. I may not know what, exactly, but I can't ignore it any longer. Rooney, you make my world turn. Now you've seen the signs. There's one last test to complete Red String Theory 2.0." He turns the final sign around.

"'Fate Test 1,'" I whisper, reading the sign out loud. "'Say yes to something you normally wouldn't.'"

"Will you give me a second chance? Will you still say yes?" he asks.

"Jack, if saying *yes* means being together, then yes a million times."

His grin is like sunshine on this cold day. I'm immediately thawed, practically melting. The crinkles around his eyes deepen. How I've missed those eyes.

"I'm choosing to kiss you now," he says. "Is that all right?"

I rest my forehead against his. "Now *that* is meant to happen."

Jack eliminates any remaining distance between us. He hungrily presses his lips on mine, the tips of our cold noses smushed up against one another. This kiss unravels me, the thread unspooling wildly through me. Jack trails his mouth down my cheek and neck, his hot breath warming the spot his lips hover over. Every touch warms my insides.

I find his mouth and tease it open again with mine. Between soft breaths, I tug his bottom lip between my teeth gently. He tastes like coffee and cinnamon and every cozy flavor that accompanies winter.

Snowflakes leisurely drift down from above, a real-life snow globe forming around us. It's like life is handing me a metaphorical memento for somewhere I've never been before. It's a place Jack and I will go together.

We're two bodies made of stardust colliding, burning brighter and hotter than anything else in the universe. Two people on opposite ends of a string coming together after years of tangling and stretching, but never breaking.

One Year Later

ROONEY

What New York City lacks in stars, it makes up for in twinkling skyscrapers. Jack and I draw imaginary lines with our fingers from building to building, creating constellations in the air.

"What's that one?" I ask, testing Jack to see if he can guess the constellation.

He puffs out his cheeks as he thinks. "One more time."

I form the shape with my pointer finger a second time, dragging my arm from an apartment across the street down to a lit-up office, over to the penthouse with Hudson River views, and back down to a twenty-four-hour gym.

"Pretty sure you just made that one up," he says skeptically.

"And here I thought you were good at this," I say with as serious a tone as I can muster. I did, in fact, make it up.

Jack wraps his arms around me as we watch the last bit of sunlight fade away, letting the darkness in. He kisses my cheek as I lean against him, pulling him closer to me.

This year, we're on the rooftop of Mom's apartment building for tonight's Lantern Festival party, where everyone actually knows one another. Cream-colored lanterns are set up on tables, a déjà vu moment from two years ago. The only difference is that, tonight, Jack is no stranger.

In the absence of light, the illumination of the full moon grows, the night ticking forward. Yuè Lǎo will make his matches, tie imaginary strings to destined lovers. Watching people below us on the streets cross paths with one another, I smile at the thought. Any one of them could find their person tonight.

"Think we'll see a comet?" I ask, looking out over the river, dusk settling in. It's my favorite time of night, especially during the winter. Everything's purple and hazy, like a soft filter has been added over the world. I'm wearing a new knit coat I made specifically for this trip. In my move to Los Angeles almost a year ago, I have become a little too accustomed to the warm weather.

Jack grunts. "Comets are extremely rare."

I point to a blinking light in the distance. "Then what's that?"

"Probably a satellite," Jack answers.

"Oh. What about a shooting star? Let's find one of those."

"Maybe if we look closely. Or if we're lucky enough to catch it streaking by. The odds aren't good," he says tentatively. "You know, you were a meteor in my life."

"We didn't physically collide, but I like to think our souls did. I didn't cause too much damage, I hope," I say.

"I came out unscathed, for the most part," he says with a grin. "You came out of nowhere. Took me by surprise. When you entered my atmosphere, I didn't know what the impact would be. But I'm very glad you didn't just pass by."

"I would've circled back around until you noticed me," I say. "Even if that's not how meteors work."

Jack laughs. "You were a fated meteor. The ones you only see when you're in the right place at the right time."

"Wouldn't that be a coincidence meteor?" I joke.

"That doesn't have the same ring to it," he says. His phone vibrates against his chest pocket. He taps on an app, revealing a camera that lets us keep an eye on Sprinkles back home in Pasadena. I peek over the side of his arm.

"Sprinkles had a big day. Gōng Gong went by earlier to feed her and watch a movie together. And now she's currently lying on my slipper," he says with a laugh.

"It's either that or all my string," I say, hugging Jack tighter. Nothing falling out of the sky could distract me from the man in front of me. All the shooting stars in the world could appear at this moment, and I wouldn't even know. That's how—

"Roo!" a voice calls out behind us, startling me.

Except for Mom.

I break from Jack's gaze to see Mom and Dusty approaching us with their arms interlocked. As sweet as it is, the sight still takes some getting used to.

"Shit, it's cold!" Mom says, rubbing her gloved hands together.

"California's sounding better, right?" Jack asks.

Mom makes a horrified face. "Not even close, but if I can't complain about the weather, what do I have in life?"

Dusty unbuttons his coat and wraps the enormity of it around Mom, sharing his body heat with her. She practically disappears under the cloth.

"Better, my love?" Dusty asks in his gruff voice. "You'd think I'd be the one suffering since I'm new to town."

"All the armor that kept her warm has been removed. Now she's vulnerable, exposed," I say dramatically.

Beneath the fabric of Dusty's coat, I can hear her laugh.

"NASA won't be the same, or as clean, without you. Who's going to keep that room in working order?" Jack asks Dusty.

Dusty chuckles. "It'll be in good hands. I trained the guy but left him a little speck of a surprise as his final test. See if he can find it." He adjusts his footing, rocking side to side and taking Mom with him. "Now I'll be helping with preventing contamination in archives and museums at the Met," he says proudly.

"That's fantastic!" I say. "You could create a brand around yourself. Dust-Free with Dusty."

"I like that. I might take it," he says. "When the job opened up in the city where Wren lives, well, I knew it was meant to be. I've been lucky to have two dream jobs and now the dream woman. Nobody pinch me!"

Mom leans her head back against his chest to try to see his face. He hunches over to kiss her forehead. I've never seen her like this, but love looks good on her.

"What about yourself, Jack?" Dusty asks. "Is FATE still on track?"

Jack slides his hands into his coat pockets. "It had a few bumps, but it's in a good place. We're getting closer to launch. It's exciting."

After Jack transitioned out of being the liaison, he started mentoring junior engineers at the company. Within a couple of months, he was promoted to senior engineer on the team. It took time, but it's like he said. What's the rush? We'll get where we're going.

"What have you been working on lately, Wren?" Jack asks.

"I've been inspired lately by black holes and dying stars." She peers up at me when she says this.

"There's enough room in space for the two of us," I say. "Whatever you're up to, I'm sure it'll be great. Your cacti collection was your most popular yet."

"Big homes means big walls, and some people like to see inside their home what they can see outside their window," Mom says with a shrug.

"Says the woman with a photograph of the city skyline in her living room," I say.

"Hey, even those views are above my pay grade," Mom says. "Besides, I'm happy to take your scraps while you think of the fresh ideas. When do you start installing your next work?"

"Next week," I reply. "Once that's set up, it'll be on display through the spring and summer."

I'm giddy at the thought of even having a next installation. After MoMA, more opportunities came along. Some I said *no* to. Most I said *yes* to. I am still at the beginning of my career. I finished out the rest of the NASA Artist-in-Residence program, which ended up getting more funding for the second year. I worked with Nick for the remaining months until they could find a new mission liaison.

Jack has joined me on multiple work trips, and when he doesn't, we still talk every day. I'm never gone for long. I'm working on taking my art back to the streets and am working with cities so my installations can be public and free for anyone and everyone. I'm also reaching for the stars in places I wouldn't have been able to get permission for pre-NASA, like the Leaning Tower of Pisa, the Great Wall of China, and the Statue of Liberty.

Anyone would be hard-pressed to say that FATE didn't change my life.

"I'm excited to come along for this one. I have a couple more weeks of PTO," Jack tells everyone. "I haven't been abroad in years."

"I'm happy to hear that." Mom smiles. "Rooney, your next installation may be a little harder to mess with. Take that, litterers."

"Why? Where is it?" Dusty asks.

"Paris." I wave my hands up in the air, inviting them to envision what I'm about to say. "*Feux D'Artifice* will be strung up at the Eiffel Tower with silver string as an homage to the nightly sparkle."

"It'll be the most awe-inspiring fireworks Paris has ever seen," Jack says proudly. "RSG's latest creation."

As soon as I outed myself, fans started calling me RSG as a nod to my real name and my former one. After all this time, it's stuck, and I've never felt more like myself.

Jack embraces me. He and I, we see each other. We've always seen each other, just from our own perspectives. It wasn't about trying to change each other but to be seen in ways we each needed. The reality is that we'll continue to grow and change, but together. Our beliefs will evolve over time, but our values will strengthen in the places that matter.

Is Jack the man at the other end of my red string? I like to think so. It's a romantic notion that ultimately led me to him. If I hadn't believed in the myth, believed in the man on the moon tying strings to ankles, I never would have found Jack. But even still, I choose him every single day. And he chooses me.

Talia joins us, bearing large bowls filled with tāngyuán. We each scoop up a peanut-butter-filled rice ball with a porcelain soup spoon.

Talia, whose gallery has been thriving, may not have found her stringmate yet, but she fell in love with weekend hikes, driving, and the sun. She, too, traded her city boots for flip-flops. It's incredible having my best friend out West with me. I miss Mom and New York, particularly in the winter, and the city will always be home. Who knows? Maybe something will bring us back here one day.

After a few more bites of tāngyuán, Jack and I lift our reasonably sized cream paper lantern.

"These are much smaller," I say, lifting the lantern up and down to estimate its weight.

Jack rubs the material between his fingers. "I put in a request to your mom for a material that disintegrates faster and is made of completely natural ingredients. This way it's better for the planet."

Mom, Dusty, and Talia each huddle over their own earth-friendly lanterns.

I place ours on one of the community rooftop tables. This time, Jack and I can see each other over the top. He removes the Discipline Pen from his pocket. "What should this year's wishes be?" he asks.

I take the pen from him. "Here. How about this?"

I write against the thin paper, careful not to puncture it.

"That's perfect," he says.

"There's no wind tonight," I say, holding up my scarf to see if it'll move.

"We should launch it from that side," Jack says, scanning the rooftop. "A corner led to good things last time."

We place the candle in the base of the lantern and carefully light it. The light from the flame bounces off the walls of the lantern, casting a glow on the lower halves of our faces as we wait for it to fill with heat. We know it's ready to go when the lantern tugs our hands up, trying to break free from our grip.

Jack counts down slowly and seriously, like this is the mission of a lifetime. On the count of three, we let go.

We angle our heads back, watching as our lantern floats higher and higher into the night. It floats up smoothly on its own pathway to the universe.

I won't know where it'll go or land or who might see it, but that's okay. Tonight, I don't need to know any of it. All I need to know is that I have Jack by my side. It's better than any wish I could've written over the years.

The words on the side of our lantern decrease in size, our wish being sent out into the world, wherever it may end up. I whisper the words out loud: "May fate bring us close enough to choose."

I rest my head against Jack's chest, feeling the beat of his heart through the unzipped part of his coat.

"What is it?" Jack asks, his voice booming inside my ear. "I can hear you thinking."

"You're not the tiniest bit curious where it's going?" I ask. I can't help it.

Jack laughs. "Okay. You know what? Let's follow it," he says, angling his body to face me.

"Seriously?" I don't even try to sound calm about the prospect of chasing another lantern through the streets.

He runs his hands down my arms and finds my hands, tangling his fingers with mine. "Why not? Let's see where it leads us tonight."

"You're the best choice I've ever made," I whisper.

Jack's eyes burn into mine. "It was hardly a choice."

Then, by string or gravitational force or choice, I'm pulled into him, my lips on his. The planets have aligned, our orbits following the same path. There's nowhere else in this entire universe that I'd rather be. In a galaxy filled with planets and stars and endless unknowns, sometimes when we're really lucky, we end up getting the best of two worlds.

"You ready to go find that lantern?" Jack asks.

I give his hands a light squeeze. "Let's go."

ACKNOWLEDGMENTS

Like Rooney, I understand the desire to want to do things on my own. But the reality is, while writing can be a mostly solitary act, publishing a book is far from it. Launching books is like a mission in its own way, and every mission has its smart, talented, and hard-working team. On my own pathway to publication and beyond, I have been so lucky and grateful to work with incredible people, meet generous readers and book communities and book clubs, and learn from people in industries other than my own. So while I'm by myself writing the words on the page, I am not alone.

I am grateful to the artists and scientists who push the boundaries of our imaginations and realities every day. In addition to reading science and space books in my research for this book, as well as listening to podcasts and watching videos, I also had the pleasure of talking to people who actually know what they're doing when it comes to our planet and the worlds beyond. Thank you to Ralph Basilio and Eleanor Basilio for answering my endless questions, both big and small. Any mistakes are my own.

I'll never forget Christo and Jeanne-Claude's *The Gates* installation in New York City's Central Park in 2005. Set against the brown and gray winter landscape, those 7,503 bright orange "gates" clearly impacted me more than I could've anticipated back then. In 2021, when I was drafting this book, the Arc de Triomphe was wrapped in silvery blue fabric and 3,000 meters of red rope, per the designs of the late Christo and Jeanne-Claude. This felt very fate-itious and full circle. I'm appreciative of the art and artists whose work leaves long-lasting impacts on us.

Thank you to my agent, Ann Leslie Tuttle, for your always-gentle advice and direction. It has been wonderful getting to know you more over the years over iced matcha—rain or shine! To my film agent, Mary Pender, and your team at UTA, thank you for your persistence and guidance. I'm so appreciative to be on this journey with you both.

Thank you to my editor, Alex Logan, for the care you give my stories and characters. I am endlessly grateful for your editorial guidance and support, and for you being open-minded when the story direction changes in slightly unexpected ways.

To Estelle Hallick, thank you for your empathy and creativity and for all you do to help share my books with readers. Sometimes this journey warrants excited screaming, and I love that you're right there screaming with me.

Thank you to Team Forever for being part of my book mission crew—Beth de Guzman, Leah Hultenschmidt, Amy Pierpont, Dana Cuadrado, Carolina Martin, Caroline Green, Daniela Medina, Grace Fischetti, Jeff Holt, Xian Lee, Sara Schaller and the production team, the sales reps, Mary Urban and the digital sales team, Michelle Figueroa and the audiobook team, and Francesca Begos and the subrights team. It has been a joy working with you.

Again, I find myself emotional seeing a mixed-race illustrated character on a book cover. Sandra Chiu, you did it again! Thank you for creating the stunning and enchanting cover of my red string dreams. Raechel Wong, you brought *Lunar Love* to life with your voice in such a beautiful way. I didn't get to formally thank you then, but I get to now, so thank you.

Readers, it has been one of the greatest joys of this journey getting to know you. Meeting you over social media and in person has been incredibly emotional and exciting. Your response to my debut novel, *Lunar Love*, blew me away—I'm forever grateful for your warm welcome, excitement, and generosity. Your support has meant the world. With every stardust particle of my being, thank you.

To the booksellers, librarians, Bookstagrammers, BookTokers, book bloggers, reviewers, journalists, book clubs, festival and event organizers, and podcasters, thank you for all that you do. Special thanks to Brianna Goodman, Jerrod MacFarlane, and the entire Book of the Month team. I'm also very grateful for my local independent bookstores, Parnassus Books and The Bookshop, who have created such welcoming and supportive communities and do so much to connect authors and readers. When readers are matched with stories that end up being exactly what they need, well, that's magic. The conversations you create around books create communities, and I know from personal experience that these communities have made me feel less alone. Thank you.

To the authors who have become friends, who have blurbed, and who continue to respond to my cold emails and direct messages, it has been such a joy getting to meet many of you online and in person over the past year. Your kindness has meant so much to me.

Putting mixed-race characters front and center in stories will always be important to me. When it feels like you're not enough, or when you have racial imposter syndrome, it can be life-changing to know that there are people in the world who are just like you or who are experiencing something similar. I cannot emphasize enough how important it is to feel seen and to be represented. What an honor it is to be able to continue telling stories with mixed-race representation. I will never take it for granted.

Thank you to my parents, sister, and aunties for your support and enthusiasm on this wild journey. My path has been tangled and winding over the years, but you've stood by my side through all of it. And to my sweet nieces for demanding that my sister read you my books from cover to cover before bed, promise you'll get to read them when you're a little bit older.

To my best friend and husband, Patrick, who graciously and fearlessly reads every draft I write, thank you for your blunt honesty, your shared excitement, and for making all of our meals when I'm on tight deadlines. The algorithms of fate brought us together, but every day we choose each other.

ABOUT THE AUTHOR

Lauren Kung Jessen is a mixed-race Chinese American writer with a fondness for witty, flirtatious dialogue and making meals with too many steps but lots of flavor. She is fascinated by myths and superstitions and how ideas, beliefs, traditions, and stories evolve over time. From attending culinary school to working in the world of Big Tech to writing love stories, Lauren cares about creating experiences that make people feel something. She also has a food and film blog, *A Dash of Cinema*, where she makes food inspired by movies and TV shows. She lives in Nashville with her husband (whom she met thanks to fate—read: the algorithms of online dating), two cats, and dog.

You can learn more at:
Website: LaurenKungJessen.com
Twitter @LaurenKJessen
Instagram @LaurenKJessen

RED STRING THEORY
READING GROUP GUIDE

Dear Reader:

Thank you for choosing to read *Red String Theory*. Or maybe you reading this book was always meant to happen...? For a long time, I have been mystified and intrigued by fate, the idea of soulmates, and by the events that occur in our lives that we call "signs." I have had enough "coincidences" and weirdly timed moments in my life that I can't *not* be a believer that there's something bigger at play in the universe. And while I can't confirm that it's fate, red string, lucky timing, or me reading too much into something, I do know that there's something beautiful in believing.

I find it remarkable that fate can be perceived to have an impact on who we're meant to be with, as in the case of the Red Thread of Fate, or on what we're meant to do with our lives. In *Red String Theory*, Rooney and Jack attend a zhuā zhōu ceremony. Zhuā zhōu is a Chinese ritual that takes place at a child's first birthday party where a variety of objects are placed in front of the child. The idea is that the object the baby picks indicates what their future career will be. A calculator might mean working in finance or the sciences. A stethoscope or thermometer symbolizes the medical field. An instrument represents that a life in music is what the child has to look forward to. Pick up a book or a pen? Hello, career in the literary arts.

I find this custom to be especially thought-provoking and fateitious. Are we truly destined to become what we grab from an assortment of objects? Or is it because we're told what we selected and therefore our lives are guided in that direction along the way? I contemplate this often because I had a zhuā zhōu ceremony as a baby. My parents set out a coin, a pill bottle, candy, a pencil, and Legos. Can you guess what I picked? It's going to sound made up, but I grabbed...a pencil *and* the piece of candy. These selections make a lot of sense given I'm a writer and have a culinary background, but my mom reminded me of my zhuā zhōu picks only recently. Did fate have a hand in how I ended up where I am? Or has this knowledge been lingering in my subconscious all along, influencing my choices at various decision points? What if it was a little bit of both?

I think the sweet spot exists in the balance between fate and choice. There's something romantic about the idea of fate, but there's also beauty and power in being able to make choices about your career path, who you love, and who you want to be. Maybe it's a blend of choice and fate that allows us to feel in control while also being open to what life has in store. However you view it, I hope fate brings you close enough to choose.

With love,

Discussion Questions

1. A lantern chase keeps Rooney and Jack together on their New York City night. Would you ever follow a lantern or wander around a city with someone you just met?

2. Rooney believes that a red thread connects her to her destined partner. Do you believe in fate and soulmates?

3. Why do you think Rooney is so adamant about achieving success on her own?

4. The definition of success varies for Rooney and Jack, and it can look different for everyone. What is your definition of success?

5. In a world where there are cameras everywhere and we are all highly visible through social media, do you think you can truly be anonymous?

6. Jack helps Rooney get reinspired by setting up Red String Theory, a series of fate tests. Do you think you can test fate? What tests would you add?

7. Art itself can be abstract. What purpose does art serve at NASA and how can art help convey vast and complex ideas?

8. How much of themselves do you think artists should put on display? Should your work speak for itself?

9. Wren lives without regrets or looking backward. What do you think is gained—or lost—with this mentality?

10. At the zhuā zhōu ceremony, June picks a tomato cushion and the keys to Lunar Love. If you had a zhuā zhōu ceremony as a one-year-old, what do you think you would have picked? What would you like to have picked?

11. Jack and his Gōng Gong make ice cream together—both frozen and freeze-dried. What is your favorite ice cream flavor and why? What foods do you make together as a family?

12. Rooney and her mom bring each other snow globes from places they visit around the world. What kinds of travel souvenirs do you collect, if any? What is their significance?

13. Now that Jack and Rooney are based in Los Angeles but will be traveling around occasionally together for installations, what do you think the future holds for their relationship? Do you believe that long-distance relationships can work?

Wren Gao's Smoky Chinese Tea Eggs

Chinese tea eggs are hard-boiled eggs soaked in a spice-filled soy sauce marinade that are typically eaten as a savory snack. They have a beautiful marbled surface as a result of letting the marinade soak into the gently cracked boiled eggs. The smokiness from the Lapsang Souchong tea leaves make these eggs extra earthy, but you can also use black tea or jasmine tea. Like Wren, Lapsang Souchong is a unique and robust flavor bursting with personality. Chinese tea eggs are flavorful, delicious, and can be eaten with a variety of meals. The patience involved is worth it!

Ingredients

- 1 cinnamon stick
- 3 star anises
- 7 whole cloves
- 3 bay leaves
- 1 teaspoon whole black peppercorns
- 1 teaspoon Sichuan peppercorns
- ½ teaspoon fennel seed

- 3 tablespoons loose Lapsang Souchong tea leaves
- 3 tablespoons dark soy sauce
- 3 tablespoons light soy sauce
- 3 one-inch slices of fresh ginger
- 2 tablespoons honey
- 2 cups of water
- 8 eggs

Method

Prepare the marinade by toasting the cinnamon stick, star anise, cloves, bay leaves, black peppercorns, Sichuan peppercorns, fennel seed, and tea leaves in a medium saucepot over low heat until aromatic, stirring constantly for about 2–3 minutes.

Add dark and light soy sauces, fresh ginger, honey, and water to the saucepot and turn the heat up to medium.

Once the marinade boils, cover the pot and turn down the heat to let the mixture simmer for 10–15 minutes.

After the mixture has simmered, remove the marinade from the stove and strain it. Let the mixture cool completely.

While the marinade cools, cook the eggs by gently placing them in a medium pot filled with cold water (about 1 inch over the eggs) and set over high heat. Starting the eggs in cold water should help prevent cracking and result in even cooking. Bring the water to a boil.

Once the water is boiling, turn the heat off and allow the eggs to cook in the water for 8–10 minutes. While the eggs are cooking, prepare an ice bath (a large bowl filled with ice and water).

Remove the eggs from the water and gently place them in the ice bath. This prevents the eggs from cooking more.

Once the eggs have completely cooled, crack the shells very lightly. We want the shells to be cracked just enough to allow the liquid to seep through and flavor the eggs. Use a spoon to lightly tap the shells to crack them or delicately roll the eggs against the counter with your palm.

Add the cracked eggs to a plastic container or plastic bag. Pour the marinade over the eggs so that they are fully submerged. We want that flavor to soak in! If the tops of the eggs are slightly above the surface, rotate the eggs every 3–4 hours.

Marinate the eggs for 12–24 hours in the refrigerator to really let the flavors absorb.

After 12–24 hours of marination, peel the shells off the eggs. Enjoy Chinese tea eggs cold or at room temperature.

Jack's Red Bean Ice Cream

Red bean is a popular flavor in many Chinese desserts and baked goods such as tāngyuán, steamed buns, and post-meal sweet soups. It is also excellent in ice cream. Red beans are more formally known as adzuki beans and are small and nutty in flavor. They taste delicious when sweetened.

Jack and Rooney eat red bean ice cream at the jazz club. Jack and his Gōng Gong also make red bean ice cream for their team Sunday Sundaes event. And, of course, you can't have a book called *Red String Theory* without red ice cream.

Red Bean Paste

Note: Make the red bean paste ahead of time. Remember that the beans need to soak overnight before you can make the paste.

Ingredients

1 cup adzuki red beans   ⅓ cup granulated sugar

Method

Soak the beans in water in a container overnight. Fill the water to the top of the container, making sure the beans are covered. The beans will absorb the water.

Wash and strain the beans.

In a large pot, add the soaked beans and enough water to cover them.

Cover and simmer over medium low heat for about 1–1½ hours until the beans are soft. Check the water level as it cooks. Add more water if the beans are drying out too quickly.

Remove the beans from the heat and let them cool while covered for 25–30 minutes.

Drain the remaining liquid, if any, keeping the beans in the pot. Crush the beans to keep the paste chunky. You can use a potato masher or a hand blender. A spatula should also work since the beans will be soft.

Add sugar and stir.

Turn the heat back on to medium low. Stir the mixture constantly until the paste darkens and starts to take shape. Make sure that the heat isn't too high—you don't want to burn the paste or dry it out too much.

Remove from the heat and allow the red bean paste to cool completely before storing it in an airtight container. You can keep the paste in the fridge for 3–4 days. Or you can freeze it (I recommend freezing in small batches, so you don't have to thaw the entire batch next time you want to use it) for 1–2 months.

Red Bean Ice Cream

Note: To make this ice cream, you'll need three bowls (1 large metal, 1 medium metal, and 1 plastic), a medium saucepan, a whisk, a spatula, a sieve, an ice cream maker, and an airtight container.

Ingredients

2 cups heavy cream

1 cup whole milk

¼ teaspoon salt

3 egg yolks

⅓ cup granulated sugar

¼ cup honey

½ cup + ⅓ cup red bean paste [Note: these will be used at two separate times during the recipe.]

¾ teaspoon vanilla extract

Method

Combine the heavy cream, whole milk, and salt in a saucepan, and heat on low until the mixture starts to simmer. Remove from heat.

In the plastic bowl, whisk together the egg yolks, sugar, and honey until combined.

Very slowly, ladle or pour the milk mixture into the egg yolks, a small amount at a time, whisking the egg yolk mixture quickly so that it doesn't heat too much to the point where the egg cooks and becomes scrambled. Do this until the egg yolk mixture is warm to the touch and enough milk has been added.

Pour the combined mixture back into the saucepan over low heat. Stir slowly and constantly until the ice cream base is thick enough to coat the back of a spoon or spatula. (This is called nappe. When you lift the spoon out of the mixture, run your finger across it. If there is a streak and it holds its shape, you're good to go.) Remove from heat.

Let the mixture fully cool. If you want to make ice cream immediately, cool the liquid down in an ice bath by filling up a bigger bowl with ice cubes and water. Place the metal bowl with the ice cream base in it and whisk the mixture until it is cold to the touch. You can also cover the mixture and refrigerate for 4–5 hours or overnight.

In a food processor, blend ½ cup of the ice cream base and ½ cup of red bean paste together until smooth. Add this mixture back into the remaining ice cream base and stir until combined. Add vanilla extract.

Process the ice cream base in an ice cream maker following the manufacturer's instructions. Once the ice cream has slightly thickened (or during the last 5–10 minutes of churning), add the remaining ⅓ cup of red bean paste.

Once the mixture is churned to the point of thick ice cream, use a spatula to scoop the ice cream into an airtight container. Put in the freezer to harden.

Enjoy the ice cream with any remaining red bean paste that you have left over.

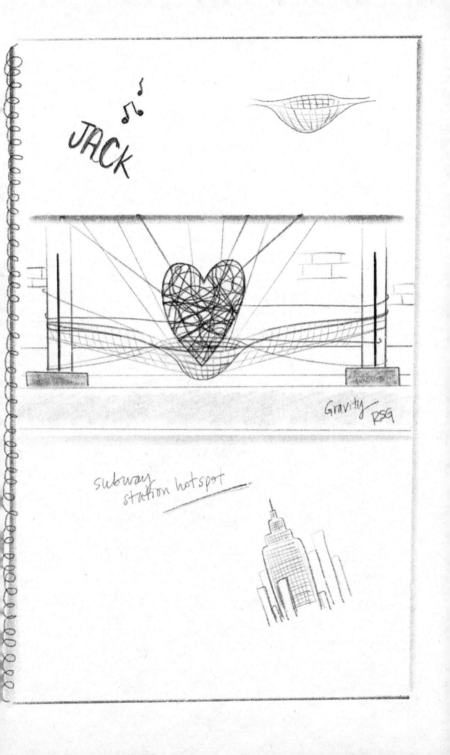

JACK

Gravity RSG

subway
station hotspot